EDGE OF ASCENSION

The Resonance Tetralogy
Book Four

Hugo Jackson

Published by Inspired Quill: October 2025

First Edition

Content Warning: This work contains mentions of Assault, Death (of family members), Hospitalisation, Kidnapping, Attempted Murder, Sexism and War.

Chief Editor: Sara-Jayne Slack
Cover Design: Katie Hofgard
Additional thanks to: ChocolateRaisinFury
Typeset in Garamond

Paperback ISBN: 978-1-913117-33-7
eBook ISBN: 978-1-913117-34-4
Print Edition

Printed in the United Kingdom
1 2 3 4 5 6 7 8 9 10

Inspired Quill Publishing, UK
Business Reg. No. 7592847
www.inspired-quill.com

Praise for Hugo Jackson

"[Legacy] is very satisfying. Jackson brings a complex and colorful anthro world to life. His descriptions are full of lush detail."

—Fred Patten, *Dogpatch Press*

"I can't say enough good things about this book. The writing is great. The world is fascinating. The heroes are intriguing and lovable. The villains are terrifying, and the fight scenes are written as if by a fight choreographer. I loved it. A perfect book for adults, teens, and children alike."

—M. Shaw, *Amazon Reviewer*

"I loved it! This book honestly gave me a huge nostalgia rush — a lot happens once things start rolling. [...] A fun fantasy romp with a great cast of heroes."

—David Popovich, *Bookworm Reviews (Youtube)*

"Overall, a very well written story that kept me entertained from start to finish. Every once in a while, you stumble across an amazing gem, and this is one of those."

—J. Poole, bestselling author of *The Bakkian Chronicles*

"An epic anthro-fantasy [...where] Jackson tenders relatable albeit convoluted motivations, heart-rending tragedy and an all-too-familiar feeling of unease in this dismal chapter of our heroes' history, closing as friends old and new commit themselves to a brighter future for all Eeres. Eagerly anticipating the next in this series!"

—Mark J. Engels, author of *Always Gray in Winter*

"Thoroughly enjoyed reading it. Such a rich, detailed world, a compelling cast of characters, and thrills aplenty."

—Mark Cantrell, author of *Citizen Zero*

For those who fight for their love
knowing that the future may not be kind;
For those who do not obey the laws of cruelty
handed to them by spiteful tradition;
For those who believe that a better world not only *can* exist
but is already here. Under the ashes of greed and hate,
is the means to save it, and us, and love, forever.

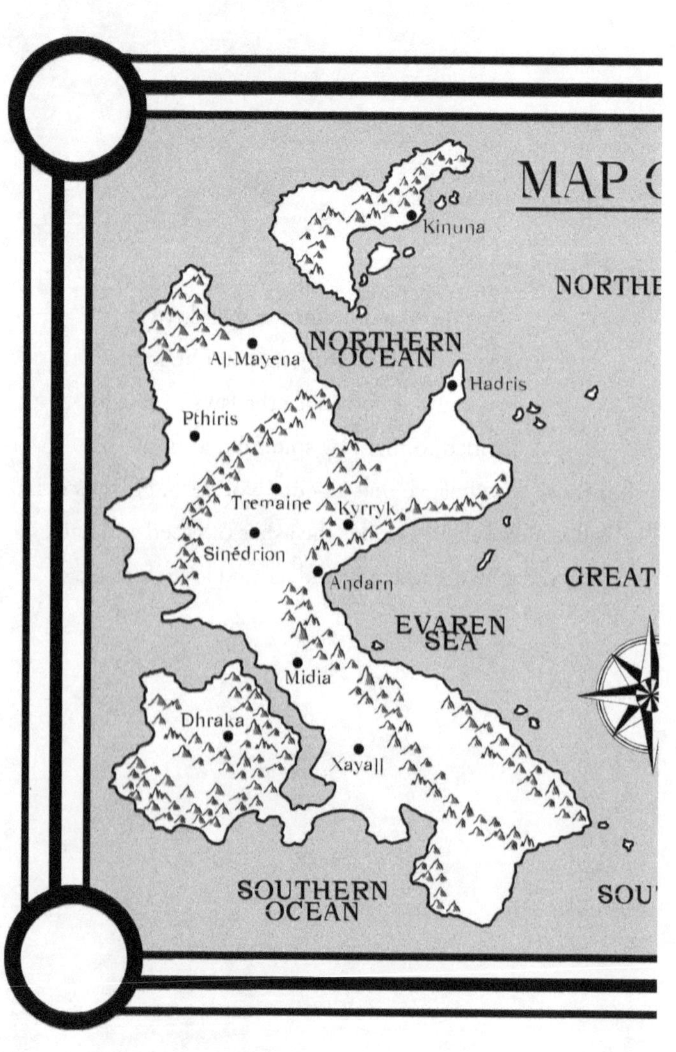

MAP O
NORTHE
Kinuna
NORTHERN
OCEAN
Al-Mayena
Hadris
Pthiris
Tremaine
Kyrryk
GREAT
Sinédrion
Andarn
EVAREN
SEA
Midia
Dhraka
Xayall
SOUTHERN
OCEAN
SOU

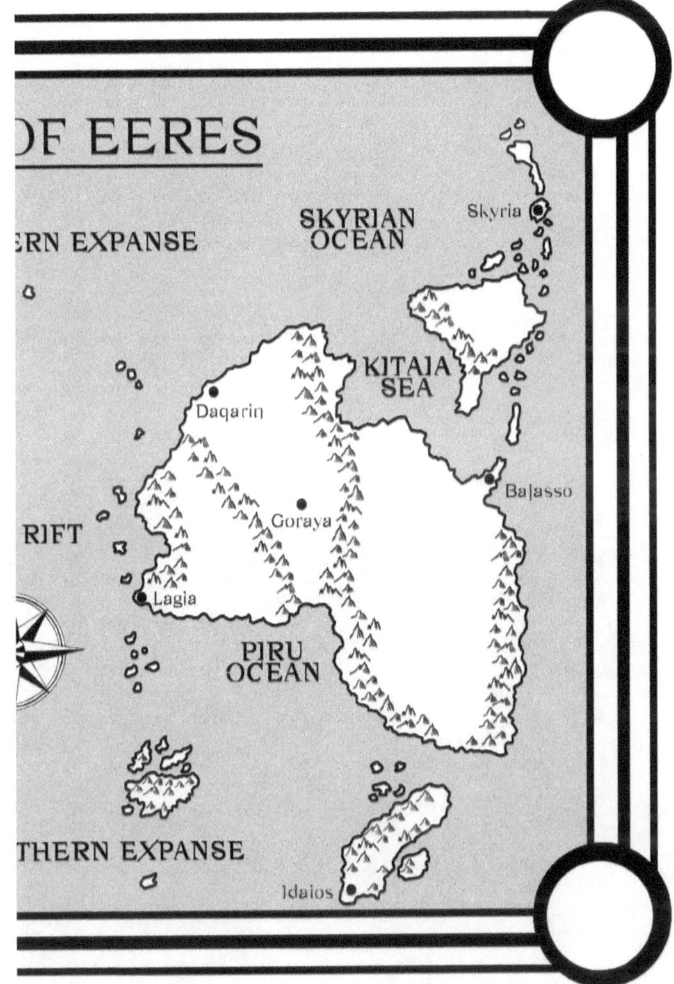

OF EERES
ERN EXPANSE
SKYRIAN OCEAN
Skyria
KITAIA SEA
Daqarin
Balasso
RIFT
Goraya
Lagia
PIRU OCEAN
THERN EXPANSE
Idaios

Table of Contents

Chapter One

Faria hated it here.

The Senate's grand halls, austere and foreboding, softly echoed her padded footfalls. She quickened her stride, her tailored blue-green robes and black shoulder capes billowing behind her. Her ears flicked as she passed Junior Representatives and entourages with their attendants, catching occasional flickers of words, most of which she assumed were at her expense. The indignity of her first Senate meeting hadn't even begun yet, and she already wished it to be over.

She had not been late upon her arrival to the city. The Coriolis was berthed outside Sinédrion to be discreet. She did not want her first meeting to be overshadowed by a controversial display of Nazreal's promise, or an unfair display of power. She had done everything to leave on time; for months she had undergone diligent rehabilitation to make sure she could walk unaided (when not fatigued anyway – she still relied on her staff in the evenings). If her current storming around the continent's political capital with a thundercloud around her ears wasn't proof of her dedication, she wasn't sure what was.

Everything was supposed to have been in place.

First had been the crowds. Angry, vehement, demanding reparations or action for lives disrupted or lost by the recent wars. They had forced her to take another entrance, and be thoroughly screened by security.

Somehow, though, her name was refused upon arriving at the Senate chambers. Administrators had to be sent for, documents retrieved, and signatures compared to affirm that she was the Xayall's Representative and that she had authority to act as envoy despite having acceded to the position immediately after her father's death two years ago. Kier helped her navigate the vortex of bureaucracy, but had been as bewildered and rueful at the Senate's omissions as she was, maybe moreso as it was mostly his administrative work that had been disrupted.

It hadn't been an easy journey either. The Coriolis had to sail rather than fly for fear of losing fuel for the journey ahead to Skyria, with an infinitely precious cargo that had to be safeguarded until its arrival home. Choppy seas and an extra night's berth at a cape south of Andarn added to the anxiety plaguing Faria at the role she had to fulfil.

A role already being undermined. She had yet to decide if it was deliberate, or just her indignation speaking for her.

The meeting had started without her. For all the jokes she'd heard (and often made) about political movement being self-indulgently slow, today was apparently the day they decided to pick their tails up and get moving.

She put the escalating apprehension away as best she could and continued up the illustrious curved stairs to the Senate's upper level, where Xayall's seat lay in the gallery ring. Large wooden doors, newly carved after the Senate chamber's near-destruction over a year ago, stood before her. She threw a quick wave to the attendants operating them, and they duly – albeit slowly – opened them for her, leading the way to the domed hall within. Muttered voices reverberated against the polished marble walls and shining pillars of black and grey. The stained glass ceiling cast its subtle shades of gold, red, and green over the theatre's upper walls, hues which swelled and ebbed as the clouds passed under the bright morning sun.

Heads turned and ears flicked at the sound of the door; there was a brief, murmuring ripple which quickly wavered, giving way to the clearer, more distinct sounds of a presentation from somewhere on the gallery.

Nothing like interrupting a bunch of dignitaries to make a first impression, she thought.

The closing of the grandiose doors was muted by thick felt on their lowest side, but the soft, deep impact of their seams coming together still boomed quietly behind her. She kept focus on her section, which Kier had directed her to verbally, and swept to her seat. There was a small wooden counter in front of her, atop of which, to her right, was a painted wooden relief of Xayall's sigil facing the room, and a goblet of water to the left. She took another set of breaths and gauged the space around her. Some of the already-seated delegation looked away as she caught sight of them. Skyria's Representative Irien, a red panda whom she had met only once before, gave her a supportive nod. The rest of the room she largely tried to blur out of her conscious – she didn't need a reminder of how many delegates she had been forced to disrupt, although she had no doubt the 'important' ones were already regarding her in distaste, if the predominant sovereigns in her gallery were anything to take assumptions from. These were the enclosed, border-defined, established nation states with decrees and contributions to Senate upkeep. Below were free townships and community groups that had petitioned representation, or independent speakers granted permission to attend, and a volley of scribes.

Sovereigns who were under territorial dispute or who had status revoked (such as Kyrryk, and now Dhraka) were forbidden from representing themselves unless under a special resolution session granted and supervised by all of the Senate's senior members, which would aim to solve their quarrels. When Faria had urged Bayer, her former bodyguard, to attend so he could appeal for help towards his war-torn homeland of Kyrryk, both he and Kier informed her that for decades everything had been more or less dictated by rich powerhouse cities like Andarn and Pthiris. Skyria and Xayall were two of the only ones who advocated for any kind of representative equality. It was yet another covert battle that she'd had to inherit from her parents, Aidan and Kaya, although many in the Senate were well aware of the loopholes they used and did their best to resist attempts to close them. No political opponent had been as strong as Dhraka, but with them now divided and warring, and the seal on their hidden dealings now broken, that might mean more freedom for those they formerly intimidated, and leverage against their obstructive tyranny.

At least, that's what Faria hoped. She just didn't want to do it by herself.

Her seat was uncomfortably new. Ornate, gilded in places, and over-cushioned – it felt very much like the kind of chair given to older Representatives who had problems sitting. She would rather have stood, despite her fatigue.

She looked over to her right as she tried to wrest her body into a comfortable position. The current speaker, an older fox with long robes of deep red, black, and gold, and a tall, mitred hat, shot her a sideways glare under his glasses before continuing. The Representative from Pthiris, if she'd identified his immaculately polished crest correctly.

She cursed under her breath. If this Representative was speaking, she had already missed the speech she was here to advocate for – presented by the breakaway region from Dhraka, known as Draik, who had been allies to Xayall even in prior dealings with her mother.

The wizened fox continued from his pulpit.

"…unseemly protestors outside our very walls are indicative of such a problem. These civil wars and pithy border spats are disgraceful to our image and our routine; we must enforce order if we are not to descend into chaos."

"Nothing about those you allow to die," Faria muttered, flicking her cape out from under her elbow.

"Did you have a comment, Delegate?" he sniffed harshly. His greying, angular features felt like an arrow pointing at her. She stared at him for a long second, as she hadn't realised she'd said it that loudly, but maybe her fidgeting had grunted it from her more forcefully. She turned her head sharply down, feeling once more that she would have been targeted for *any* kind of response she'd decide to make.

Best make it a good one, then.

He seemed satisfied with her initial silence and was about to turn away when she stood.

"Actually, I do."

She ran a paw over her ears and looked down at the far side of the circular room, where the stage of the Senate Council lay. At its centre sat the eminent stag she knew as Jed Othera, who cast a discerning eye at her. She felt the size of the room, and the sudden adrenaline rush of dozens of faces turning towards her. She gripped the rail tightly. This was what she was here for.

Her father did this so many times. She could too. She *had* to.

"These battles aren't just 'disgraceful' for us as leaders," she began, "they are ravaging the folk whose lands they take place in. There are thousands living outside city walls who are in constant danger, and no amount of 'order' will stop anything." She looked at the other fox resolutely. "If we're to end the conflict, we need to fix the desperation and greed for which people drive their nations to war."

The fox huffed and turned his head away. "Of course, one could excuse the Junior Delegate for being so naive—" he started.

Her face flushed and she felt the fur rise on her cheeks at his spurious demotion. Junior Delegate? Such a pithy nerve. How could anyone object to… kindness? She remained standing as she watched the Pthirisian fox continue his address, often unconsciously shaking her head. He bloated on about resolutions, assessments and votes; all things she was already familiar with. His lecture felt orchestrated to make her appear ignorant, but any opportunity to protest would likely be seen as further impertinence. The longer it went the less she focused, but the embarrassment of being singled out still burnt in her ears, and escalated into hot ire.

She waited, impatiently, for him to conclude.

"…an impractical idealism sadly not rooted in reality." He half-turned to her, seeing that she was still standing. "Did you have more youthful grandstanding to grace us with?"

Faria pulled the closure of her jacket sharply, banishing some wayward creases. "You are correct – insofar this is my first time addressing the Senate. I believe I owe you all an apology for my unintended lateness, and an introduction: I am the Representative of Xayall, Faria Phiraco," she said, firmly. "Emperor Phiraco, the former Representative, was my father, and Kaya Phiraco, from whom he inherited the title, was my mother. They had both long been supporters of meaningful peace and growth for the citizens of the world." She paused, long enough to take a deep, pensive breath before continuing. "I want to extend my gratitude to all who knew and supported them, and helped Xayall to navigate the ideals they pursued to benefit the world. My father showed me that a better world was within our power, and I firmly stand behind those dreams, idealistic or not."

A quiet, rippling applause spread around the room, led by Irien and a few listeners on the floor below. She bowed her head thankfully, and after allowing the polite response to echo into silence she lifted it back up with a resolute expression. "There are many things I have to learn, but I've already had experiences beyond my wildest expectations, and I will use those to empower whoever I can to help us *all* move forward. I have a responsibility to my sovereign, and to the safety of everyone in this world." She cast the fox a warning look. "Even if some may find my story incredulous."

A smile split his face like the cut of a blade. "Such vocality shows an admirable enthusiasm for one's first time within the Senate. But as many here would advise: be cautious with your accusations."

Her tail flicked. "Would you kindly explain that, Representative?" she replied, doing her best not to respond with bile, but not altogether succeeding.

The fox from Pthiris gave a withering gesture with his paw. "Representative, this reconstructed hall itself is a testament to the struggles we've endured against resonators and their volatile ilk, who, even *before* laying siege to Sinédrion, have perpetuated wars, if rumour is accurate, from time immemorial." He turned to her. "If you will excuse my bluntness, your family's reputation is a complicated one, further entangled in reports about your sovereign amidst this tumult. If you *are* carrying on your parents' legacy, will that include the continual supply of resources to Draik insurgents within the Dhrakan lands, or is your idea of peace to sabotage a long-standing member of this Senate to replace with those indebted to your violent allyship?"

Faria balled her paws. Jed watched the two intently, but his inscrutability left her adrift in need of any kind of support. She knew he didn't support underhanded tactics, but he was obsequious towards the procedure of the reformed Senate, and his public impartiality. That meant no matter the claim, as long as it was said by a member, it had to be played out before it could be rebutted.

That meant the burden of proof was on her.

"I'm aware my father was deeply concerned for Dhraka's situation, given that we share a border. The siege we suffered at the hand of their last commander was devastating and we are still recovering from it. However, the Draik, long persecuted citizens who have as much right to survive in their own land as the late Fulkore Crawn's soldiers, are also being torn apart by battle. We received appeals for aid, and we honoured them." She glared at him fiercely. "I guarantee we've provided nothing more threatening than food and clothing. Unless you believe upholding survival of the endangered to be an act of militancy, I would beg your recharacterisation."

He gave a dismissive snort, and a sneer on the side of his face turned away from the Senate Council. "It isn't out of character to view the sovereign of Xayall as a disruption. Whims of fancy, circuitous debate, unruly accusations of corruption, and much more were common delays foisted on us by both your parents. Many of the Representatives here had hoped to see you taking a more domiciliary approach now that leadership has changed, but…" he flicked his claws absentmindedly. "…it appears that will not be the case."

Domiciliary? You want me to be the Senate's housewife?

She took in another slow breath, although her ability to keep it stable was quickly waning. "I've no intention of unseating anyone honest. But I will not compromise on the safety of myself, my city, nor the world. I've already faced down threats to each, and my experience is not up for debate."

"Ah yes," he responded, with a sickeningly overperformed nod. "These tremors that shook us, the fabled Nazreal unearthed, your vehement request for emergency military aid. Quite an imaginative time. Are these now resolved, or will we yet again see them play into the public eye of the Senate with embarrassing theatrics?"

She opened her mouth to speak; he interjected. "The battles you insist on fighting are of your parent's making. You would do well to put them behind you and approach the Senate with more dignity, to allow us to treat you in kind. Maybe then we can forge a greater tolerance for your requests."

She could barely speak, but swallowed her disbelief quickly enough to raise her voice in reply. "We were laid siege to, three times within a year! Twice by Fulkore Crawn of Dhraka, and the next by Shadow's Claw! We were even granted aid by Andarn—"

"Unauthorised."

"—and we sent countless pieces of evidence of espionage to the Senate!"

He spread his arms in a demonstrative shrug. "And what do they prove?" His robes glinted with shining metallic embroidery, and around his neck hung a long pendant of plated metal linked together like maille. "That your beloved sovereign, allegedly a burning example of peace and humility, has been embroiled in conspiracy since before your life began."

He leant forwards. "It would behove you to lay out an honest statement of your city before anyone may consider you trustworthy, and this includes what you uncovered in Nazreal, which is inexplicably automatically under your guardianship."

She felt her fur stand on end and an electric burn behind her ears. She was glad she didn't have her staff with her.

Perhaps.

He continued, a growing gleam in his eyes. "There should be no secrets with such gravity, no discovery left unshared. Your father sought to enforce that with the Ancient Histories Decree, and it shall be adhered to under supervision of the Senate."

She wavered, claws raking against the wooden frame she leant on. She glared at him, and felt the acid rise in her chest. "Nazreal is not yet stable. It must be assessed and studied in strict caution," she rumbled. "It's still a danger and must be protected with utmost urgency. Currently I, and Xayall, are its best guardians."

The older fox pulled irritably at his large, starched sleeves. "Your sovereign's history speaks otherwise."

"And *your* infiltration by Shadow's Claw proves you better, does it?" she spat, viciously. "*We* had no agents revealed within the lists of saboteurs. Something I cannot say for Pthiris."

He remained impassive, but flexed his claws as she continued.

"What you lack in integrity, my city bears in the ruins of its walls. We survived, and despite everything we are stable and resolute." She straightened again, finding renewed confidence. "I object to being singled out for our conflict at the hands of others when every other sovereign here has suffered in this same battle." She pointed at Andarn and Tremaine. "Two sovereigns, set to war against each other by hidden agents, stand here unscrutinised, while Kyrryk and Dhraka are working to expel those same forces from within their own lands, for *your* sake as much as theirs, and get no recognition, or scorned for their support." She turned back to the Senate. "These battles have waged for too long, seeded from the same greed and darkness."

Pthiris leant towards her. "By whom, pray tell? If you have answers to all this, please provide them directly. Unless you'd like to accuse everyone in this chamber of contributing to your strife?"

"That's not what I'm saying."

"Would you explain, then, how Xayall is always at the centre of this mire, yet you still claim to be somehow innocent of any transgression or escalation of said conflicts?"

"They tried to murder me in my sleep! Senate Council, this is—"

"The Council will not be addressed directly in floor disagreements," came a harsh voice from a puma at the end of the bench, glaring over her glasses. "This is very unbecoming of our meetings and frankly discourse like this should be left to private channels."

Jed, in one of his first displays of reaction, gave her a quiet, if pointed, sideways glance, then looked back to Faria with a stern face.

"There is much we are still in the midst of recovering," his voice boomed. "I will vouch for Xayall's experience and warn against further argument over these circular accusations."

The Pthiris fox gave a bow of his head. "Senate Council, my apologies." He then turned to Faria with a sickening smugness that she wanted to tear at with her claws till she scraped clean the skull beneath it. "My remarks shall be found rescinded."

Although you made sure everyone heard them first, didn't you? Grizzled lump of mange, Faria fulminated internally.

He and Faria gave each other lingering rueful looks before sitting back down. She took her goblet, and within seconds an attendant with a water jug sauntered over to fill it. She thanked them silently, then listened to the next speaker on the rotation.

It would be a long day.

Chapter Two

It was late afternoon by the time the meeting finished. Representatives delivered their scheduled propositions, aired grievances, and gave one or two accolades to themselves or others. Faria had been relieved that the spat between her and Pthiris wasn't the only one to get heated, with some fire coming from the lower floors directed at Tremaine and Andarn for encroaching on free lands, then again at Andarn for the amount of naval traffic they created in smaller ports above and below their lands through their prohibitively steep docking fees, alongside some other pithy back-and-forth between delegates and chiding by the Council. Arguing seemed to be an inherent means of getting things done, providing you could win over the right people with your honesty, lies, or overall theatre.

She still left before she could encounter the Pthirisian fox again, though she thought she caught him glancing her way as she turned to leave. She had no care to learn his name or engage in awkward, condescending asides, so once the final bows and formalities had been performed she left, while others went to their 'private channels' to network with each other directly. Within her was a growing sense that many of them were too long and too far removed from any kind of conversation that didn't involve gold, wine, or political comfort.

She just wanted safety.

The doors had already been opened; she thanked the attendants as she breezed past, lamenting for them the interminable period they would have to wait for the remaining delegates to leave their chamber of public martyrdom. She descended the stairs, swiftly turning left to head towards her next meeting. The wide, curved corridors were already dense with traffic and the hum of conversation drifting into the high ceilings and wooden reliefs above. A trio of polar bears marched by in meticulous filigree armour of blue and grey, extremely elegant and powerful, and honestly she would much rather have stared at them in silence for six hours instead. She bowed as they passed. She wasn't sure if they acknowledged her, but she wanted to do them the courtesy nonetheless.

Not far behind them were two familiar, comforting faces. One was a soldier in blue armour with a slim-yet-flowing white sleeveless jacket, her caracal ears flicking intently with the noise and bustle of the crowd, and the other was an ocelot, whose right sleeve was tied at the elbow with trailing ribbons of red, signifying his lost arm. She rushed towards them; the ocelot flinched briefly before realising who it was, and he reflexively shot out his left paw for her to shake. Instead she embraced him with a hug.

"You probably shouldn't be doing that," he said warmly, although he hugged her back.

She pulled away and scoffed. "I don't care, Bayer. This place is too stuffy, and they do it upstairs all the time. It's only who they deem 'inappropriate' to touch that makes it taboo. I'm not playing that game."

Raede gave Faria an affirmative nod, and shook her paw

with all the strength one would expect from a deadly, but friendly, mercenary.

"I'm really glad you could make it," Faria sighed. "It's good to see friends."

Bayer tilted his head quizzically. "Kier isn't with you?"

She rubbed her paws over her ears and gave an embattled groan. "It's a long story." She looked around. "Although I'd hoped he'd be finished by now. He may already be there."

Bayer glanced round as more folks filed through the hallway and their conversations became louder. His tail stiffened and flicked sharply from one side to another. Raede looked equally uncomfortable.

Faria gestured ahead. "Let's get moving. I'm not one for crowds right now."

They meandered along the tide of pedestrians, skirting by the massive stone pillars that surrounded the exterior corridor of the Senate dome. On the outer circle were smaller meeting rooms, while the larger room, kitchens, and a gallery of artwork and discoveries lay towards the centre, with the address hall at the heart of it all. The clerk offices and private quarters for certain Council members and permanent building staff were on the upper floors, and a new archive had been established under the ground floor with only one, guarded, entrance. This was probably where Kier had needed to go, Faria surmised.

Eventually they came to a meeting room along the outer rim, above which was a classical-style, tasteful oil painting of a snow leopard washing themselves with an ewer of water. The plaque on the door read 'Ewer Chamber'.

Bayer flicked the latch with a deft claw and gestured for her to enter. "After 'ewer', Your Majesty."

"If I weren't so tired I'd throw another ice ball at you," she muttered affectionately, to which he smiled in reply.

Two figures within the room stood to attention as the door clicked open. The first was Kier, who looked about as surprised to see Faria as she was to see him; the second was a slender dragon of pearly-white scales and purple horns, with a long neck and a small fur collar. She wore a series of chains sewn into a dyed-purple leather vest, held at her waist with a maille belt. Hexagonal-maille bracers hugged her arms, and a bandolier, missing its knives, hung from one of her shoulders. Her dark blue eyes glinted in the lanternlight and seemed to flash with warning for a moment as they entered, as if expecting trouble.

After a moment of recognition, the dragon stepped towards Faria. She moved with fluidity like water over stones, graceful and powerful, and reached out a claw. Faria responded in kind, taking it in a firm and friendly shake. The dragon was about as tall as Osiris – once more the fox became aware that she was the smallest creature in the room.

At least those gathered here were friendly.

"I'm so sorry I missed your speech," Faria said, bowing deeply. "I had some… complications."

"As have we all, I imagine," the dragon sighed. "I'm Riemu. My partner would have been here also but she had to take command at home."

"I understand," Faria responded politely, looking up at scales that gleamed more finely than polished Senate marble. "It's an honour to finally meet you." She turned and gestured between her and Bayer, who bowed and offered his paw.

"Bayer Kanjita, of Kyrryk," he said softly, but formally. "We're in somewhat the same situation as you, so you have our solidarity and support."

Riemu nodded back. "An honour to me for both of your company," she replied, shaking his paw. "I appreciate you finding time for us."

Faria let out a nervous laugh. "Believe me, it's necessary. I'd be meeting with you before any others if I could help it." She looked sideways, the fur on her neck bristling at the lingering ire of Pthiris' needling words. "Or instead of."

Raede let the door drift shut behind them. She gave it an inward tug to make sure it was firmly sealed, then leant against it, instinctively moving her paw to the knife she kept hidden under her breastplate.

The dragon took her seat back at the table, and Faria pulled out a chair opposite her while Bayer sat at the remaining free side between them both. Kier sat alongside Faria, with all of the notes and papers diligently (if somewhat hurriedly) sprawled out on the table between them. He suddenly stood back up again and rearranged them, so some were facing Riemu, some Bayer, and the rest were facing Faria.

"Sorry, I didn't have time to get this more organised for you all. I only arrived just before you did."

Faria raised a gentle paw. "Don't rush, we aren't officiants. At least, not in the same way the over-starched old brats upstairs are."

Faria paused and panicked for a second, realising it might be unprofessional to reveal herself as such a disaffected new world leader so quickly to a potential ally.

"I mean, um…"

The dragon shook her head and waved a claw in reassurance. Her eyes, although shining deeply with an almost ethereal reflection of the light around them, bore a look of shared disapproval. "I appreciate the candour, honestly. It's very like your mother. Most folk don't even want to talk with us."

Faria smiled, feeling bolstered by the comparison to Kaya.

"That's certainly something I've encountered. Today was…" she rubbed a paw over her muzzle to massage some of the tension from it. "…somewhat belittling. It feels like they're out to get you before you even arrive."

The dragon seemed to empathise, and thumbed a claw at a small metal funnel located by the fireplace, which had a tube that led into the ceiling – a service call apparatus. The aperture of the brass cone had been stuffed with a cloak.

"I'm used to taking precautions for similar reasons," she replied. "If attendants can be called, we can be heard. It's conspicuous enough walking in as a dragon given folks' vehemence towards Dhraka." She flicked her claws with a palpable air of disgust. "When those who don't know anything you've been through blame you for the malice of a dictator, or view you as another henchman to do their bidding, you find yourself with very few friends."

Faria nodded, a chill running down her tail as she realised the danger Riemu was in from all sides, much like she herself had been when Shadow's Claw had infiltrated Xayall. "I can feel myself being painted in similar colours," she muttered.

Bayer traced his claws over the texture of the leather upholstery on the edges of the table. "To most of the Senate, progress can only be tied to money or power, by threat or by promise. Even at war, most of them won't see a blade except at the side of their personal guards."

Kier glanced at each of them, and to Raede, who stood diligently by the door but listened to every word. "I daresay we've seen more battles than any of them put together," he said bitterly. "Aside from Jed."

"Small recompense." Raede scoffed.

Faria's head swam with thoughts of what they'd each survived, and how tiring everything was. She looked back to

Riemu and opened her paws over the table. "I'm trying to be diplomatic," she said, with plaintive ire. Her voice took on a rueful tone. "But it seems many are using me as the gap in the armour to stick their knives into Xayall."

Riemu gathered her claws in front of her. "We've faced similar things. It wasn't until Crawn's control slipped and their command structure broke down that we were able to make substantial gains on our own land. I'm sorry that it had to be at the expense of your city, and family."

"They've been at your throats for far longer," Faria replied, with a sombre reverence. "It's only fair we fight together so neither of us have that fate in future."

Riemu laughed, a lyrical sound laced with age and memories of narrow escapes. "Sometimes I miss the simplicity of burying an axe in something to get people's attention."

"I could think of a target or two..." Faria returned with a wry grumble.

The dragon's frills perked. "Oh?"

There was a brief pause as Faria tried to ascertain how serious Riemu was. Given the scars she could see on her neck and jawline, she didn't want to make a prophetic joke. "I mean—"

The dragon watched her for a second, and then laughed. "We're trying to break free of our reputation, I'm not serious." Then her face immediately darkened and she leant in with a shadowy voice. "Unless you are."

Faria's eyes widened and her ears flicked straight back. Once more Riemu leant back with an even heartier laugh, and Bayer allowed himself a chuckle at her expense also. Faria's cheek fur bristled; she pulled at her collar as she felt her face grow hot. She looked briefly to Raede, who shrugged as if to offer her own services in taking the joke to more significant levels of action.

"You're too easy, Empress." Riemu's voice had a playful lilt when she was amused, that was both striking and somewhat intimidating.

Faria rubbed the back of her head with a nervous grimace of a grin, and gestured to the papers beside her. "Erm, maybe let's do some official things before joking about unofficial things."

Riemu gave a reluctant sigh. "Sure, give us some kind of progress in this disgusting world of bureaucracy."

Kier laid out a roll of parchment for her and Bayer, all of them daubed with the formal scrawl of Senate intent declarations, border confirmations, and letters of support. Riemu scanned a claw down them and nodded, signed each one in turn, then slid them back to Kier, who passed them to Bayer for the same process. The ocelot had practised a signature with his remaining paw, but it was still slow and shaky. His countenance of equal frustration and concentration threatened to make his furrowed brow deep enough to plant seeds in, but all were patient, and within time the scrolls were dutifully signed, rolled, and sealed with Xayall's wax stamp. It was a quietly tedious display of reluctant decorum, and none of them seemed to relax until all had been placed into the crisp document basket that Kier kept by his seat. After placing her quill back into its stand, Faria took in a halting breath, and then rested her paws on the table, letting her thoughts gather.

"How bad is it in Draik right now?" she asked eventually.

Riemu shrugged, and drew up a sleeve to show off a slowly-healing cut across her forearm. "Plenty of battles, but we're holding out. With more resources or a sanction against Dhraka, we could do more, but we know they're getting supplies from drops off the coast by unmarked ships. They're very well equipped, whoever they are, and Dhraka's artillery keeps growing to make aerial scouting almost impossible."

Faria looked to Bayer, who didn't appear optimistic, tapping a thoughtful claw at his chin. "There aren't any remaining caches that we know of in Kyrryk, and haven't had any signs of movement through our borders."

Faria groaned and leant back in her chair. "I thought we could be done with this by now."

Riemu gave her a blank stare. "These conflicts have been waged for millennia," she said bluntly. "They aren't going to be extinguished in a single battle."

Faria rubbed her head with a sigh. "You're right, I'm sorry. I don't know how you've fought for so long."

"Necessity," Riemu replied flatly. In the light of the lanterns, Faria could see the contours of scars in her scales, chips in her horns, and a tired determination in her eyes. "We both know what it is like to lose something. Our determination to prevent recurrence is what sees this through, till *it* ends or *we* do."

Faria placed her paws together and rested her hands on them, agreeing quietly. "Ideally, nothing would 'end' except the fight itself. But there are those who would gladly work with Dhraka again given the chance, and that's a constant danger."

"The end of Crawn has left his Senate network in disarray, but they're just as eager to take up his reputation," Riemu followed. "They only lack his influence. Lately Dhraka has galvanised under someone they call The Molten King, and it worries me that they've found their old fire again."

Kier was holding a paw over one of his eyes, gently massaging the fur around it. "Sounds like a nasty creature. Any idea who they are?"

Riemu took in a long breath, but largely shrugged. "A

zealot, maybe someone hibernating within their volcano that reawoke, or returned from a campaign elsewhere, or perhaps just an upstart looking to further deepen the fanatical devotion to violence. Regardless, they're competent. Crawn's despots are devoted to power, so the right commander could prove a capable asset to an army as malicious as his. Meanwhile, the rest of us have been working hard to deradicalise them, with… mixed results."

"How mixed?" Bayer asked.

"Well, some survived," Riemu said bluntly, picking her claws. They stared blankly back at her, prompting a shrug. "Listen, we can't compromise our safety. If they lash out in our spaces, there's no mercy. Ignoring that would be a grave danger."

Raede repositioned herself against the door. "I can warn you now: not everyone is salvageable. They must at least know where they're not welcome anymore. Would be *nice*," she said, in barbed tones, "if other sovereigns recognised what we go through for them."

Faria sighed, stabbing the table's leatherwork with her claw. "I know. It's… tough. I'm on my way to Skyria after this, for personal reasons, but also to negotiate what more they can do."

Riemu stood with a resolute grunt. "To get others to fight alongside you, you must be a fighter first. You must vouch for us, and yourselves, loudly, continually. *That* is how you force change in the face of those who resist it." She fixed Faria in a firm glare. "You will be exhausted, at times hateful, but this is what you have to understand, Empress Faria."

She flicked the tails of her tabard back to where they should rest either side of her tail, and whirled her cloak out of the communication horn. "We will maintain our positions and try to warn you of anything that may spill over to your lands, but otherwise will assume to remain on our own."

Faria wrung her paws, her ears flattening slightly with guilt. Riemu dipped her head a little to try and catch her eye, the fire of her years of furious resistance softening a little as she addressed the fox. "Physical battles are more straightforward than political ones. But they both require strength. We know that you have it. Don't give up."

She moved to the door and took a deep breath.

"Are you alright?" Faria asked.

A cynical smile split her face. "I wasn't granted access to the guarded entrance you use. I have to use the main doors. It's… crowded there."

"Can't I take you with me through the back?" she asked.

Riemu sucked through her teeth, but Kier answered before she could respond.

"No. They won't let them through. They're being intensely stringent this time."

Faria growled. Raede offered her paw. "Do you need an escort?"

The dragon let out a sharp sigh as she rolled her eyes to the ceiling. "The proud part of me wants to say no, but my partner was specific about making sure I was safe, and our allegiances explicit. I'm no good to you if the crowd that wants me dead succeeds."

Faria stood immediately. "I'll go that way too. I won't have you walk alone."

She looked to Kier, who had just finished packing the scrolls. He acknowledged her with a brief nod and retrieved a long leather bundle from behind a curtain. She worked her paw between the layers and loosened both ends. A faint flick of blue crystal caught the lanternlight at its tips.

Raede gave a cautioning smile. "Pushing the boundaries already, Faria," she said softly.

Faria returned her a defiant sniff. "It's a *walking aid*. They didn't give me time to prepare anything else, and I need it."

She marched to the door and gave Riemu an affirmative nod.

"Let's go."

Chapter Three

The Senate had largely dispersed, but conversations were still flowing around the chamber perimeters, quietened voices and hushed dealings drifting like an acoustic fog that vanished in the embellished void of the high, arched ceilings.

Kier split away to submit the freshly signed scrolls to the appropriate clerk upstairs, while the others marched purposefully to the entrance. He darted as quickly as he could without raising protest from the stuffed collars of the Senate members or the stern guards who patrolled key points around the area, although his primary focus was a swift return to the group.

For Faria, and probably moreso for Riemu, the intense guard presence made her feel far less at ease. Every encounter she'd previously had with soldiers was in combat; either in pursuit of her, or at her expense, save for the defenders of Xayall. Riemu was representing herself at great personal risk; her self-defense was a crime in her homeland and her presence a crime outside of it. She was a target for any side to boast over taking down.

The Senate could be capable of so much benefit. Faria knew this.

She also knew that they had not been so for a long time.

She caught some of the guards eyeing them as they walked. Between Bayer, her staff, and Riemu, it was a lottery to guess what they were casting suspicion over. Some engaged in quiet asides or barely-hidden snarls and smirks. What concerned her more than the soldiers, though, were the gilded Representatives and their Juniors, some of whom slunk away upon their proximity, casting spurious glances over their shoulders. They could do more lasting harm with written decrees than a single blade.

"I don't like that," she muttered.

Bayer sympathised with a low growl; Raede simply continued, already on alert as a soldier and Bayer's adjunct guard.

"Most of their noise is petty derision," Raede scoffed. "When you make your actions count, you'll shine a light on their ineptitude."

Riemu frowned. "Derision and ineptitude are their lifelines."

She glanced sideways and stopped, then gestured to the window; Faria stepped closer to see.

They were reaching the front of the building, where the grand staircase into the Senate dome rose from the paved plaza that surrounded it. At the base of the stairs, just outside the staunch stone walls that bordered it, was the same crowd that had delayed Faria's entry, and had lit Pthiris' scorn. Most Representatives and Senate folk were descending without issue, but the gathered conglomeration appeared to be taking one or two aside, or at least trying to argue or question them about something.

"I heard a little about them earlier; do you know more?" Faria asked, pressing her pawpad to the window.

Riemu took in a guarded breath. "I was warned that some of the denizens had been told of my plan to attend. I'm both Dhraka, and an enemy to Dhraka, in a confusing mess that makes me disliked for both."

Faria shot her a look of disbelief. "They're here for you? Not anyone else?"

She shook her head. "Yes and no. They're angry at everyone, but I'm a figurehead. In my experience, displays like this can be choreographed to invoke the tides of chaos and convince the other Representatives that more 'order' is required," she said, in a chilling echo of Pthiris' words earlier. "I've been called a kidnapper of children and devastator of homes. Dhraka did that. We tried to stop it all."

Faria turned back to the window. "I'm glad we came with you," she said distantly, with a wary glare at the crowd. She may have been with them at one point, if all she had were her experiences being chased from Xayall.

When she'd found out more about her mother's allegiance with Draik, and especially when they'd contacted her after the dissolution of Shadow's Claw, she'd suffered a sobering view of what Dhraka, and Crawn specifically, had done to its own people in the name of supremacy after Nazreal's fall. Osiris had been slower to convince, despite working alongside them – with her mother – a few times in the past. His resentment was too deep, perhaps, and maybe too much an insecurity for him to relinquish yet.

They continued out. At the Senate's entrance a collection of Representatives were looking down on the crowds, mostly complaining about how disruptive it was, none of them trying to actually address the crowd's grievances. Several appeared to have tried, albeit vaguely, to placate them or get them to move, but the thin line of guards at the gathering's edge appeared to be doing most of the work in that regard.

When Riemu appeared at the stairs' apex, the various onlookers went quiet and split, leaving their group of four isolated in the centre of the entranceway. The stairs yawed below them, and a flaring roar of inflamed anger rose from the crowd as someone signalled her presence. She stood tall regardless, and began her walk down. Faria and Raede flanked her, while Bayer stepped behind.

Claws and accusative paws thrust from the crowd. Clamouring voices rang to a peak, with some folk trying to push through the guards. Accusations of 'Murderer', 'Kidnapper', and various other epithets shot through Faria's ears. Riemu kept her focus ahead, weathering them with a steely expression.

"Do you have a transport?" Bayer asked.

She shook her head. "Not within the city."

"You can ride with us; we'll take you where you need to go."

"Thank you," she said flatly, still focusing on the archway ahead that would lead them to the streets. The early evening sky cast her scales in light like fire.

Faria gripped her staff tightly. The crowd was getting louder, angrier, and pushing harder the closer to the street they came. Some of the guards looked back at Riemu, as if blaming her and considering whether to break rank. Many bore scars, some looked exhausted in their fury. She could only guess whether they had been involved in raids or defence of one side or another, either in the Claw's alliance or the earnest defence of Sinédrion, Andarn, or others that came under siege.

The energy was terrifying, and heightening.

As they crossed the plaza to the street, a swelling cry came from the crowd. They turned, and saw an otter with a large dagger, rushing straight for Riemu.

Bayer twisted, ready to catch him with his left arm. Raede drew her sword.

NO. No deaths, Faria swore.

The blue crystals on the ends of her staff shone; she slammed its butt on the ground and a wave of stone swept underneath them, forming around the attacker's limbs like shackles, then lifted him into the air. He screamed and dropped his dagger, which Bayer snatched from the air by the handle.

The leather wrapping around Faria's staff fell away, revealing its new form: a long half-staff, with a crystal prism mounted at the centre of a spiralling nest of wings at its tip.

Her eyes glinted with the energies of her resonance as she glared at the otter.

He spat vengefully, struggling against the stone that trapped him, raging at each of them.

"You court murderers! Filthy, evil, deceitful monsters that destroyed our homes! I'll kill you! I'll kill all of you who stand with Dhraka! The world won't stand for you any longer!"

More guards were running from the Senate to quell the crowd, some of whom had tried to split after the otter but halted at the display of Faria's power. She looked around at them, and the strung, taut tension, like an animal's tether about to be severed.

Standing tall, she twisted her paw around the staff. The crystal flashed; in reciprocity the stone slowly sank, delivering the restrained otter into the hands of the approaching guards, who wrested him from the receding rock. He struggled and gnashed his teeth but eventually, grudgingly relented as they took him back to the guardhouse adjacent to the Senate building. Faria kept watch at everyone around them. Raede's paw still hovered over the hilt of her sword, and Bayer handed the dagger to another guard, who left in pursuit of the ones detaining the otter. Riemu seemed largely unfazed, although Faria caught sight of her dropping something sharp back inside her jacket.

Faria stepped between Riemu and the crowd as best she could, since they remained flanked on two sides.

"I'm sorry," she said loudly, in address to them. "I'm sorry you've faced so much at the hands of malicious despots and militant tyrants. I promise we're not your enemy. We will do all we can to keep you safe, and make reparations." She looked to Riemu, who nodded thankfully, before continuing.

"Please, keep your anger at the injustices done to you, and turn it towards those who prevent you from making change. I hear you, but many in the Senate do not. Keep them honest. Because without you, they will not be, and this will happen all over again."

She gave the gathered citizens a bow, and then turned to leave. Bayer and Raede quickly flanked Riemu and the three followed on before waiting for the crowd's voice to rise in response. Faria tried not to listen to their jeers, but hoped some might have heard her words above their anger.

As they crossed into the street, there was a distortion of light by Faria's side and Kier shimmered into view, sheathing his sword.

"Well done," he said earnestly, with a sigh of relief.

"Shouldn't have had to," she growled, her expression turning to bitter resentment. It was dangerous for her to use her resonance for a number of reasons, not least was her relative lack of experience with her new staff, and her burgeoning reacquaintance with her abilities after Nazreal had burnt them away and rendered her all but completely expended for over a year. She had designed the staff to be powerful, but the line between retraining and crushing someone was very fine. She had been lucky today, but she wanted more time to practise, and heal.

"I just want us to leave, safely."

Raede took the lead, directing them towards their lodgings in Sinédrion's middle sprawl; a small, modest inn of brick and thick wooden beams, with bronze-painted metal edging and window trim: Dawn's Break. A golden lion, with rays of sunlight as their mane, was embossed in bronze on its hanging sign. Raede opened the door and the rest filed in quickly; Kier last, as he watched for potential stalkers.

She closed it after her. For a second they paused at the inn's fireside, unlit but rich with the scent of burnt wood and coal dust. Riemu stared blankly, distant—not scared, but processing the attempted assassination. Raede kept guard by the window, occasionally glancing out, while Bayer and Kier stood near Faria, who sat in one of the aged, upholstered chairs. Her paw was shaking a little, but she clenched it shut to force the tremors away.

Riemu let out a long exhalation. "It's not my first. Conjuring hate to stoke division was a tactic of Crawn's. It makes you an enemy of the people you're trying to protect."

The fury in the otter's eyes still pierced Faria's memory. "He wasn't an assassin. Just enraged."

"Emboldened," Kier said gravely.

Bayer flicked a piece of grit from his robes. "It happened in Kyrryk too. Old allegiances looking for new blood, or hoping to spill yours by proxy."

Faria shook her head. "It's monstrous."

Riemu took in another breath and sighed, turning back to them. "It'll pass. If we succeed, they'll know the truth eventually."

"If they want to hear it," Raede said in a low voice, flicking the curtain to check further along the street.

Faria shook her shoulders. Her tail flicked with agitation through the gap in the back of the chair. Bayer laid a gentle paw on her shoulder.

"We can see this through," he said, with gentle reassurance. "We've survived more than this already."

Her legs jostled with anxiety. "So far."

She rubbed the back of her neck and looked at the ceiling. Staring back at her were gilded filigree carvings and faces of tigers, leopards, and reliefs of rushing water.

Bayer circled around to Raede, who hadn't looked away from the window. "You have already protected much, Faria, and continue to do so."

Faria played idly with a loose thread on the chair's outer edge, fraying its fabric a little further, while flicking her eyes towards him in an almost stern reproach of certainty. "I've been lucky more than dedicated, and mostly absent recently. You've saved my life at least twice that I know of. I've yet to repay that."

"You saved us all, Faria. Let's hope there isn't need for it again by either of us." His snout scrunched in disapproval as a patrol of eight guards, spear-headed by a black-furred jackal Captain in a gold and white sash, marched to the inn door. Raede, Bayer, Riemu and Kier banded together, and Faria stood as they entered. The Captain saw them immediately, and walked straight across the room.

"You're the group that was attacked in the square?"

It was barely a question, more like an accusation. Faria nodded, giving them a cautious look.

The jackal clicked their claws as the rest of the soldiers entered. "We need statements from each of you."

"The guards' reports aren't enough?" Kier protested cynically.

They gave him a dull look. "The Senate takes assaults on their grounds very seriously, so we take all information we can as to their cause, and eliminate the chances of it happening in future."

Faria stepped forwards. "No problem, Captain. We're here for your questions."

Riemu and Bayer exchanged dubious glances.

The jackal's stony expression inferred cooperation was neither an option nor welcome, but a necessary frustration. Faria took the impression that resistance might almost have been preferred.

With a gesture to the guards, a pair each took Riemu, Bayer, Raede and Kier separately to other corners of the tavern, while the Captain stayed with Faria. She watched with apprehension as Riemu was taken out of sight around a corner, but hoped from where Raede was standing that she could intervene if anything violent were to happen.

The Captain began their questioning, piercing dark eyes boring into Faria and flaring at the slightest hesitancy or perceived discrepancy in her recounting of the story. Short as the event itself was, the interrogation lasted for long enough that it was further approaching dark by the time the jackal had finally exhausted their dialogue. Once they gave their signal that all questioning had been completed, the guards filtered out, allowing the group to reconvene near the doorway. They were all in varying states of frustration, and Riemu looked particularly nauseated.

None were talkative after that. Raede stepped outside to signal for their carriage, while the dragon flexed her wings in a release of tension that wasn't quite what it needed to be, and gave a sharp grunt of irritation.

"Never gets old."

Faria sympathised with an understanding frown, while Bayer seemed to be envisioning his own distant thoughts as he gazed out of the window. It was a look she recognised a lot from his time in Xayall.

A short while later Raede clicked open the door. "We're ready."

Faria offered her paw to Riemu, which she took firmly once more.

"Thank you, for your allyship and protection," the dragon said softly. "It won't be easy."

Faria felt a sigh welling, and decided to kill it before it erupted, not wishing to push fatigue or pre-emptive defeat any further into the conversation. "No. But it's right. You worked with my mother to protect me before I even knew you, so it's my honour to do the same."

Riemu bowed. "You carry their spirit well, and do them a great honour. Take care, Faria."

"You too."

She stepped outside. Raede gave Faria a bow and a polite salute, before following behind her.

Kier moved to Bayer's side to walk him to the door with an arm tightly around his shoulder. The two hugged just before reaching the threshold, and heard the carriage moving around outside with the restlessness of the Elasmotherian, a tall and stocky four-legged reptile with muscular legs and snub-tail, eager to do its burden duty.

"Travel safely," Kier murmured wistfully, letting his paw drag slowly away from Bayer's sleeve.

The ocelot pulled Kier into another hug. "Tear them to shreds," he replied.

A second later Raede opened the door and the two departed through it, leaving Kier and Faria in the small ambience of the tavern.

"It's weird, isn't it?" she said quietly. "Being so far apart, yet still somehow fighting the same battle."

Kier looked at his paw, tracing a claw over the centre. "Yeah." He walked to the door and just before turning the handle, made sure his angled sword with its blade-breaker hilt was set in its sheath. His ears tilted back slightly as he remembered the training he and Bayer had had with it.

He clicked open the latch. "Will you be alright here if I call a carriage?"

She nodded. "Just be safe."

The silver-eyed fox wrested open the door with his elbow, then whirled out, letting the door latch closed. Faria looked distantly into the empty fireplace as the inn's near-silence pressed into her, many of its guests having already departed, and the staff being absent after the arrival of the guards. She wondered how many would blame her for the actions of a vengeful assailant, and tried to calculate whether the otter could even be blamed, considering what most in this world had gone through. Except the Representatives; removed, callous, privileged. Jed and Irien were the only ones she trusted, and even then she had little faith either could act with the same imperative as Jed had when fending off Shadow's Claw. Irien was not a military commander, and Skyria required delicate balance of trade negotiations to remain stable. There was only so much she could ask of him.

She wasn't sure how long she'd been staring into the hearth before Kier rattled open the latch to collect her. She stepped from the doorway and into the carriage as quickly as possible, eager not to be seen, and Kier followed immediately behind. The neatly-dressed quokka in the driver's box snapped the reins and the Elasmotherians lashed to the coach's pole rumbled into motion, pulling into Sinédrion's finely cobbled streets.

"Everything's different, yet some things stay the same," Kier said quietly.

She started a little, his voice rousing her from thoughts well beyond the vehicle's journey. "Sorry, Kier?"

"The last time I left here in a carriage was with Aidan, and it was... the last time I ever saw him. It's just... strange parallels."

A wistful smile warmed her face. "Here's hoping we don't have any more of those."

He gave a soft, whispered laugh in agreement. "How is your new staff, by the way?"

She eyed it with cautious optimism. "I'm pleased with it," she replied, almost more of a question than a statement. "It doesn't feel the same as my father's did, but... I can't risk using such old crystals as they might shatter again, or explode. And I... want to preserve it for as long as I can. For him."

Kier wrung his hands in quiet, tacit agreement.

The coach rattled out of Sinédrion, under the fortified gates and past the guards stationed at it. The attack, the meeting, and Pthiris' condescending hostility set her on edge, and she desperately wanted to reach the Coriolis, and a sense of home, as soon as possible. Even being away from Xayall was an emotional highwire at the moment; the first time she had left it voluntarily since the night of her escape.

The paving abruptly ended and the road rumbled more loudly, transitioning to dusty, flattened ground as the road stretched to the inland dock where the Coriolis lay berthed. Both Osiris and Faria had intended to remain low-key. The accusations of superiority and demands for access to Nazreal were already looming, but to have them all explode in a frenzy over the sight of a metal, flying warship would have been a floodgate too difficult to blockade.

They travelled for some time. The sun sank further under the darkening twilight. The carriage's steady rumble and the tread of the Elasmotherians bore a constant, almost somnolent rhythm, disturbed only by the carriage slowing to navigate strange cambers, bends, or bumps in the path.

The treeline became familiar; they started passing torches and wooden sentry posts that signalled the small dock village they'd berthed at. Faria felt equal parts relief and heightened anticipation sweep over her.

So when the carriage ground to a halt before the village itself was in sight, she and Kier paused to exchange dubious glances. Traffic, maybe?

She chanced a look out of the window.

Scores of soldiers, mounted and on foot, surrounded the quayside.

She heard shouting. She burst out of the coach like a storm gust and marched to the line of guards. Standing in the wide arc of spear-brandishing troops was the familiar, imposing silhouette of a gryphon, one whose crimson armour seemed to burn in sync with the light of the soldiers' torches, golden rapier handles glinting brightly, their blades thankfully still sheathed. Osiris' fierce eyes trained on her from over the top of the figure he was confronting.

The one accosting him was a sable with tan facial fur and dark markings from the corners of her eyes down her cheeks. She wore a shining, pristine armour set of blue and gold, with a long white sash over her left shoulder, tied at her hip to a sword belt. She looked round at Osiris' change of focus.

"Is this your delegate?" she barked officiously, giving Faria a dismissive jerk of her head.

Osiris' wings flexed in discontent. "She is the commander of Xayall. And not to be scorned."

The sable spun on her paw. "We'll see about that."

Faria's muzzle tensed and her ears flattened back with caution. "What's going on?"

The sable flexed her arms, rattling the joints of her armour, and produced a scroll from her sash. She unfurled it and read from it with loud, harsh authority.

"Empress Phiraco, in the interests of security to Pthiris for the ongoing investigations of activities related to the assault on the Senate and subjugation of Senate officials across the Cadon continent, and for withholding information vital to these processes by harbouring a material witness and possible collaborator of sieges and subversive activities, you are under formal investigation. This is an official request to relinquish the witness unto the authority of the investigating parties. Failure to comply with any requests may result in indefinite detention of complicit persons and assets until matters relating to the investigation have been completed."

Faria's eyes narrowed with disbelief and fiery scorn, but the sable remained stoic, regarding the Empress in the same way a parent may consider a petulant child.

"You're interrogating me over attacks made against myself?"

She looked to Osiris, whose face mirrored untold stories of rage and fire. Beyond him, guarding the gangway, were Kyru and Aeryn, staring down the soldiers. The wolves saw her, but kept their positions.

"As such, Empress Phiraco," the sable continued, her voice rising further, as she turned the scroll towards her, "you and your ship are being detained."

Chapter Four

"That's absurd!" Faria snarled. Osiris swept past the sable to stand beside the Empress, wings flexing. The gryphon looked murderous, and Faria was well on her way to joining him.

The sable flicked the scroll in front of her with patronising demonstration. "You're harbouring a material witness to espionage, kidnapping, subversion, and insurrection; a participant in several sieges and infiltrations, *and* you're withholding information vital to an ongoing investigation into the sedition of the Senate and Pthiris' own Council. This is the order that has been given, signed and sealed by decree of the Council."

Osiris instinctively stepped forward to guard Faria, but she brushed under his wing and ripped the scroll from the sable's claws, reading it over. She sent a soft light ringing through her staff to help illuminate the parchment.

"You have no authority to do this," Osiris boomed, once more confronting the sable. Faria paced around as she scanned the calligraphic scrawl.

"The signatures are right there," the officer retorted, with a stern, satisfied glare.

Faria glanced to the bottom of the scroll, where with a rush of alarm she saw the scrawl of the five Council members she had seen barely half a day earlier, including Jed. She dragged her gaze back upwards to finish reading the calligraphic order, but her racing mind made it hard to focus.

"They're talking about Tierenan," she said gravely. "They want to take him."

She rounded on the sable as the realisation took hold. "He isn't conscious! We don't even know if he'll recover, and you want to take him away to interrogate him?"

She gave a dismissive sniff. "We cannot reveal the means of our investigation to a party connected to a suspect. Given that your retinue refused to comply, we were forced to create an embargo."

Osiris bristled. "Your ships were already on the water," he rumbled. "You prepared for this explicitly. Nobody dispatches a flotilla for a single child."

The sable pierced Faria with a look. "That depends on the child."

Faria scowled. "If you mean to arrest me then do it. Otherwise this is shameful 'bravery' to bring the might of a navy down on a diplomatic mission to return an injured, unconscious raccoon back to his parents. He wasn't even involved in Shadow's Claw."

"That will be for the investigators to decide," the sable replied. She held out her hand expectantly, looking down her muzzle at the scroll. Faria clutched it.

"We're not that far from the Senate that I can't bring this to Jed and have him burn it in front of you," she warned. "He would not have agreed to this if he knew the implications."

The sable gave her a patronising raise of her eyebrow. "Do you want to test that? Jed knows the procedure. You're not immune to responsibility."

Faria stared back at her in defiant silence for a few seconds. "Who are you, anyway? What authority do you have to serve this?"

The sable straightened. "I am Commander Dyate Valdona, Constable of Pthiris and Chief Investigator of the Archives."

"Does Pthiris' jurisdiction cover outlying territory as well?" Faria snipped.

Commander Dyate sucked through her teeth. "Ignorance is unbecoming of a sovereign leader. Threats to our safety do not end at our city walls. I would have thought, with what I've heard of your own trials and escapades, that you'd know this already. This isn't something to be taken lightly."

"As you have made clear," Osiris muttered. "Deploying an entire fleet for a single helpless individual. Must be exhausting to live in such fear."

A flicker of consternation danced across her face at Osiris' derision, quickly repressed by austere contempt. "I don't fear miscreants, I dispel them. Perhaps an aggressive audit is required if your knowledge of sovereign boundaries is in such disarray."

Faria's tail flicked. "Being hunted through war, having my body set aflame and almost becoming the victim of an assassination will affect my connection to the world of politics. You're welcome to try it sometime, see how you fare."

Dyate's face fell into a grim severity and her tail flicked stiffly from side to side. "Be careful where you pull rank. I've seen conflict just as closely, without the privilege of mystical nonsense to add histrionics to my scars."

Faria glared at her.

"You may think you can exploit privileges of the Senate and turn misfortune to your advantage, but I promise that you can't." Dyate nodded at the scroll. "My final warning to you is thus: if you do not comply, you will be detained, Xayall will be sanctioned, and every single one of your friends will be arrested for conspiracy, leaving you all at my mercy."

The blue crystals ebbed and coursed with Faria's increasing ire. "Sounds like you want me to resist," she gnarled.

Dyate dipped her head, but kept her eyes focused on Faria. The pommel of her longsword glinted in the torchlight, and its hilt in the luminescence of the resonance crystals. "Whatever your choice, the outcome will only matter to you."

She flicked her wrist and snapped the parchment from Faria's claw. Immediately Osiris lunged forwards, aiming for her with his claws. The soldiers around began an inward charge, and Faria slammed her staff on the ground.

A ripple of stone rumbled outwards from her, creating a waist-high plinth that pushed Dyate away from Osiris' lethal grasp, while the warning noise and trembling ground halted the approaching soldiers. Dyate gripped the plinth in shock, dropping the scroll which tumbled across the floor. Before her, Faria's eyes shone with brilliant blue.

"This is what I am capable of when I'm protecting you," she boomed. She closed her eyes for a moment; the rumbling and glow subsided. "Now imagine what I can do if I wanted to destroy you."

Dyate wrested herself away from the stone pillar and bent down to pick up the scroll, a rueful scowl on her face.

Faria gently put her paw on Osiris' clenched claw. "We can't afford another war," she muttered. "We'll weather it for now, and work out an escape later."

"I have been in enough situations to know the severity of underestimation," he replied in a voice loud enough for the Commander to hear. "Do not sabotage yourself."

She looked to Aeryn and Kyru, still guarding the gangway. "For Tierenan's sake we have to comply. Better for us to be with him than risk them blockading Skyria after we leave. It'd do too much damage to fight our way out now."

The gryphon withdrew his fist with great and furious reluctance and placed it on the hilts of his rapier. He flexed his wings, and marched back to the Coriolis.

Faria squared up to Dyate. "Lead the blockade. We'll acquiesce to your escort."

The sable said nothing, but whirled away and flicked her claw towards the dock, commanding the soldiers back to their boats.

Faria and Kier quickly followed Osiris onto his ship as it gleamed in the light of the soldiers' torches and sparse dockside lanterns. The gryphon strode past Aeryn and Kyru, who had to duck under his wings as he breezed indignantly through them all as if they were merely tall grass. As soon as Faria was aboard they retracted the gangplank, then flanked her as she marched to the sterncastle. Kyru opened the door for them, and gave one last look across the deck as the Pthiris ships began drifting back into the bay. He swept in behind the others and closed the door firmly. Faria made straight for the table at the stern's cabin, making a direct line to Osiris' large, gilded chair to sit heavily in it, and letting the back of her head hit against its padded backrest.

Aeryn perched on the table, using the opportunity to unstring her bow. "I'd ask how the meeting went, but I think I already get the gist."

Faria grunted at length, rubbing her forehead so hard she pulled out a few strands of fur.

"It was just supposed to be presentations, and off to Skyria. Everything got in the way, and now they're hijacking

Tierenan."

"And us," Kyru muttered.

"I'm less worried about us," Faria replied, letting herself slump in the chair. "If I wasn't concerned about his safety or our future prospects in the Senate, I would have given Osiris the okay to fire a warning volley and take off."

The wolves looked at each other dubiously, Aeryn with a sardonic, grim smile. They all swayed slightly as the ship began to move. "If we had more fuel it could have been different."

"Always amazing how much control officials have with nothing but paper and promises. They don't hold any weight with me." Kyru responded, then pointed to Faria. "You're the only one of them I've met who I trust." Aeryn and Kier looked to her supportively, but the fox visibly baulked and shifted in her chair. The ship shuddered while making a reversing turn to the port side, and the dulcet voice of Osiris came echoing down the communication funnels, relaying their departure.

"I'm not one of them," she bit back.

Kier frowned, and hesitated, twisting one of his crystal earrings in his claws. "This will sound harsh, Faria, and I'm sorry: you are."

Her eyes flared. He held up a swift, interrupting paw.

"You don't act like them, but you're of their station and influence. They will betray you, exploit you, destroy you if they can, but you're still in their circle. They'll take credit for your successes and blame you for their failures, as they do with each other." He shuffled forwards in his chair, and spoke with soft resolution. "You can't escape them, but you can resist falling into their traps. That means rejecting their games and parasitic ways of living. Like Riemu said, you can begin to break the system for those who can't, and lift up those who would do better in their places. If you deny your station you give up the power they don't want to share with you, and they win by default."

She shook her head. "I'm tired of this already. I've been tired of it since having to watch Xayall's recovery from a hospital bed. It hasn't stopped, and we're barely better off. But nobody else is changing." She gave a spiteful sigh and leant back in her chair. "So I guess we have to."

Aeryn nodded. "Thinking power was honest is what had me thrown in jail. But I suppose some good came from it," she said with a sly look towards Kyru, who grinned.

"Yeah, we turned you into a mercenary."

Her playful smile burned at the edges with suspicion. "Not a merc. A freelancer."

Kyru shrugged, with a soft laugh. "Point to where the difference is."

She cast a claw in his direction. "*You*, you're the merc. Seedy and brooding and indiscriminate."

"I fail to see the issue," he said nonchalantly, "Captain Abandons-My-Estate-To-Run-With-The-Fugitives."

"*Freelance*," she emphasised.

The two continued to jostle each other for a while, and Faria just listened, letting the sound of her friends become a balm to the stressful drone of officious Senate voices and the derision of that Pthirisian fox and Dyate. After a while she stood, taking a swell of air into her chest, and letting it out with a long, calming sigh of release. The wolves looked at her expectantly; she paused for a second, forgetting she was giving the impression of an announcement where there was none to make, then gave an enervated, awkward smile.

"I'm, er, going to check on Tierenan."

She ducked out of the room.

Faria's stride rose and fell with the rhythm of the ship; the seas were choppy around the North of Sinédrion, and they had not intended to travel via this route, time or altitude. Tierenan was being kept in Maaka's surgery where he could be monitored and kept secure in the event of any storms or other emergencies. The falcon doctor had been as diligent a presence as he ever was, and took as much care with Tierenan as could be afforded. Faria was grateful for his dedication and skill, even though he'd also been at a loss for any means to rouse the raccoon from his torpor.

She gently tapped on the surgery door. After a few seconds it cracked open, and a discerning eye peered back at her over a sharp, hooked beak. It only took Maaka a second to identify her; he pulled the door all the way open with his elbow. "I heard we were embargoed," he said in a low breath, his feathers drifting back to a relaxed position at her arrival. "I was worried you were some kind of Pthiris adjutant."

Faria scrunched her muzzle in disgust. "Absolutely not. I'd rather collect manure for a tanner."

"I daresay that would be the cleaner job," Maaka replied, closing the door behind her. She glanced at him briefly to seek approval to approach her comatose friend; a slight wave of his wing was enough to let her proceed.

"He's much the same, sadly. The sea air hasn't worked the miracles many claim it to."

She walked to the side of Tierenan's gurney, watching his rhythmic, deep breathing. Every now and again his eyelids seemed to twitch, as if a flicker of recognition from a sound or scent had stirred a response, but nothing ever came from it. His catatonia had been immeasurably tough to watch. And now, on the eve of a portended return to his parents, he was being stolen even further away from lands and sights he loved.

She gripped the rail tightly.

"He deserves better, and so much more time awake."

Maaka sighed in agreement. "One beneficial factor of his implants is that they are retaining his stability. Sadly, they are also retaining his catatonia except by particular command, somewhat as their original function intended. But they are at least keeping his muscles invigorated."

Her ears perked. "His muscles?"

He pointed a pinion feather to the raccoon's upper arm, a part not under the blankets nor plated in metal from his augmentations. She tilted her head and moved closer to him. She hadn't seen it before, but just under his fur she could see tiny pulses of movement, like a heartbeat but not in his veins, tiny measured impulses that seemed to travel across every muscle in his body.

"That's part of the synthetic control?"

Maaka shrugged. "My expertise is in biological systems, not mechanics or electronics. But it seems like maintaining a suggestive state such as this requires a kind of bodily hypnosis. There's a chance it's also acted to stimulate repair given his wounds have healed with quite miraculous headway."

"Aside from the care you gave him," she said, with both a smile and emphatic sincerity.

He fluttered his wings a little. "Emergency intervention saved his life; this recovery has mostly been beyond my means of assistance. And I dare not touch the components, as Skyria has far more knowledge of that and I wouldn't risk losing him permanently."

If we haven't already, she thought, digging a fang into her lip. "I'm just glad he's in a state to move."

Maaka flicked his wing over some instruments, sorting them into lines. "We honestly might have been safe to do so earlier. I tend to enjoy an overabundance of caution for folks' well-being."

She smiled softly, her fur almost glowing in the yellow-orange light of the lamps. "Thank you for looking after him."

"I meant you," he said pointedly, looking over the glasses attached to a notch in his beak. Faria made a sort of soft spluttering noise and looked away. He continued, his role as a physician and caretaker coming very much to the fore of his tone. "You may dismiss yourself but I don't. You were *both* incredibly lucky to survive."

She fell into silence again, looking at her paws. The numbness had almost gone before she started using her staff again, and now they pulsed with that familiar, aching burn.

"How are you?" he asked quietly.

She frowned. "It… hurts, again. I had to use my resonance in Sinédrion."

"But you didn't break the crystal?"

"No," she said, with both relief and a hint of reticence. "This crystal isn't as old as Nazreal's – Osiris said it came from Ohé, so its structure is less brittle and volatile."

He raised an eyebrow. "Do they vary that much?"

She answered initially with a yes-no tilt of her head. "The more energy you put through them over time, the more potent any future reaction can become, but also the more likely they are to disintegrate. The crystals in Nazreal, and my father's staff, have a very distinct feel to any you can find in other areas. I needed one with rigidity, instead of power. At least… while I feel like a beginner again."

"A wise choice. At least until you're healthy, perhaps using crystals that could turn you or itself to dust at a key moment aren't in your best interests."

She gripped her paws together. "Yeah. There's a lot I have to protect right now."

He paused, watching her quietly for a few seconds.

"You know you aren't alone, Faria?"

"I do. But… it won't feel right till Tierenan comes back. If… if he can. He saved me."

"As you did us, Faria. Including him." The falcon strode to the porthole at the side of his working area, where his nest lay, and peered out. The rising moon cast a silver-purple light over the sea, and silhouetted against the coursing waves and glimmering stars were some of the Pthiris ships. "And if any of our fears come to pass, you may have to again. You must be well enough to survive that, for all our sakes."

She gently touched a paw to Tierenan's metallic claw.

"I'll do my best."

Chapter Five

Two days of slow, supervised sailing later they had circled around the top half of the Cadon continent to reach Pthiris' port. The city docks were lined with blue-armoured soldiers; their distinctive colour was created by a mixture of regional metallic sands mixed in during the forging process. It was a source of pride, and a great deal of wealth for the ones that controlled the mines from which it was dug. Pthiris was mostly operated by a confederacy of these mining families, some annexed, most with some kind of generational connection to each other in a strange nepotistic web that together held over ninety percent of the city's money. As such, the city's lavish decoration of red and white brickwork, with black lattices and gilded fittings, was more widely pre-eminent than even Andarn's central areas – at least, throughout the parts they wanted to be visible.

From what Osiris said, Pthiris was a sovereign of two halves: extreme wealth on one side; the ones who did the work on the other, and a city for each. The parts used for dignitaries were where the moneyed families lived, their retinues, business chambers, tourist markets, and extended network of influence or personal attendance. That appeared to be the city they were approaching. Further around the peninsula was the *other* city of Pthiris, a perfunctorily-maintained worker town that housed the miners and tradesfolk of less gracious standing. These were the ones on whom Pthiris' back was built. Most of them had accommodations provided for them by the ruling families, but the rest was taken from their wages as 'payment'. There was a common saying about the city state: "You will either make your fortune in Pthiris, or pay for it," and it did not enthuse Faria any further towards Dyate, the Representative, or anyone they may be associated with.

The Coriolis was directed to dock first, while flanked by two Pthiris galleons. Osiris spitefully steered the ship into the quay, watching with discerning glares the soldiers who awaited them.

The ship was tied on, the anchors fell, and the tramping of armoured feet rang along the deck. Faria and Maaka were either side of Tierenen's gurney and were guided into a pathway between the two lines of troops. Not long afterwards, Dyate mounted the deck, having arrived only a few minutes before, marching towards them with the air of a tiger stalking its prey.

"Welcome to Pthiris, Empress. We'll take the suspect with us from here."

Faria held her staff out to block her from touching Tierenan. Dyate halted immediately, but her glare did not relent, nor did she look at all threatened.

"We accompany him. And my bodyguards come too," Faria commanded, indicating Kier, Aeryn and Kyru.

"No weapons," she said immediately.

If fireballs could have shot from the eyes of Aeryn and Kyru, they would, but Faria looked defeatedly round, closing her eyes, nodding with intense reluctance.

Petulantly, Kyru swung off his falchion and shield, and

dropped his volgue to the deck. Aeryn decanted her quiver and bow, and the two daggers she had at her waist.

The sable pointed at Faria's staff. "And that."

"It's a walking aid," Faria and Maaka chorused. Dyate tutted audibly, but not wanting to risk further delay and seeing no threat from three mercenaries, a doctor, and a teenager against her entire army, gave a spiralling wave of her gauntlet, then spun on her paw and began leading the march back to the city. Faria could see Osiris watching from the helm, severe and disapproving. She didn't want to leave one of her strongest allies behind, but Osiris could be a firebrand in diplomatic situations, and would be needed here in case events necessitated a swift exit.

The soldiers folded in line behind them as they travelled; out on the sea the remaining galleons began to pull into their designated moorings.

"Apparently, the threat is contained," Faria muttered.

A sardonic laugh rumbled from Kyru. "In the same way you can hold a fire in your palm, sure."

Faria felt a swell of confidence at Kyru's assertion. As much as she would never want to become the kind of person to abuse them, she knew her capabilities. While this was a grudging, inconvenient diplomacy for now, she would not let them hurt Tierenan, nor impound any of them. If she had to fight all the way back to the shore, so be it.

The sheer number of soldiers they passed was bewildering, however. Each of them stood impassively to attention, staring into the middle distance, spears aligned in rigid unison like armoured fenceposts.

"More guards here than civilians," Kier grimaced.

Aeryn cast disgusted looks at the ceremony of militancy. "That's what happens when all you have is money and a fear of other people getting any."

They were led through streets covered by manicured trees and stringently-aligned paving. The houses and gardens all looked like different annexes of enormous private residences, or sidings for large workshops and extravagant guest lodgings. But the group all spotted the unnatural lack of liveliness within the city. They passed at least one theatre, and an amphitheatre, several botanical gardens, and a strange, almost pyramidal structure with the wrought iron sign above its gateway that read 'Pleasure'.

Aeryn leaned into Faria's shoulder. "I think that's where they store it after they have it surgically removed."

The route, they determined sometime later, was deliberately circuitous, leading around city landmarks in loops where a straight line would have been more efficient. Kyru had nothing but contempt when they made note of it.

"It's an intimidation tactic. Trying to tire you out before you arrive. It's also a means of getting as many people within the city to identify you as possible – not as a guest, but as a prisoner."

He gave Faria a stern look. "They know they can't overpower you, so they're doing their next-best effort to humiliate you."

"Just like in the Senate," she fulminated.

The sun was beginning to redden as they reached the gates of a large, multi-turreted palatial building towards the centre of the city. Hedgerows, inlaid pathways and fountains surrounded it as the centrepiece of ostentatiousness. Its spires and chimneys stretched up like needles as if to pin itself as a flag of ownership against the sky. Coloured banners hung from the walls and blue-tinted metal railings adorned almost every window.

"A very colourful prison," Aeryn murmured. Faria looked about as they trod smooth stone slabs with gold and blue metal filigree along their edges. Twenty-foot high brick walls surrounded the garden in an octagon with guard towers at each corner, and a narrow walkway along the top of each.

Dyate stopped at the entrance, where large metal double-doors yawed open. At their throat was the Representative who had lambasted Faria in the Senate meeting, with some attendants in long brown, double-breasted coats standing either side of him – one a black wolf, the other a light-furred bear. As Faria's train came to a halt, he clicked his claws and the attendants swept to Tierenan's gurney, motioning either side as if to begin wheeling it away. Faria and Maaka went to pursue, but another flick of the Representative's wrist brought the guards' poleaxes pointed towards their chests. She glared vengefully at the return of the oleaginous fox.

"You!" she seethed. "This is disgusting overreach."

"My name is Representative Rynkath, Young Miss Xayall," he said, delivered with all the esteem one might consider for the contents of a recently desecrated chamber pot. He looked down his muzzle at her through his pretentiously-small pince-nez glasses.

"And is it really overreach?" He broadcasted his continuation with a prideful, authoritative tone. "Or is it the same jurisdiction with which you crusaded around the continent, drawing resources and violence from surrounding lands in pursuit of absolution from the conflicts your sovereign caused?"

She clenched her paws so tightly she felt like they'd rupture. "They weren't our fault. They were set against me and my father since long before he came to rule."

A condescending scoff hissed from Rynkath, who kept his

gaze pointed down at her in the way a teacher may belittle an outspoken student. He gestured to Tierenan. "An injured boy. Your relic of a Captain, your father's legacy. All excuses and distractions away from an uncomfortable truth: *you* are the centre of this problem."

"You're levying accusations of conspiracy against my own city, and you dare lecture me on sincerity?" she surged, prompting a sympathetic swell of anger from Aeryn and Kyru.

Rynkath couldn't escape a wry, if slightly strained, smile. "These are confusing times. It's important to be open, and I would hate for those investigating to not consider all possible eventualities. I'm merely broadening their horizons."

Faria's staff flashed briefly with the spike of her anger. Dyate reached for her sword but stopped short of drawing it. Rynkath checked warily at the proximity of the flanking soldiers; the ones who witnessed Faria's brief power display back outside Sinédrion rippled with concern and poised weapons, ready to step forwards.

He pulled sharply at the cuffs of his robe to flatten out a wayward crease that developed in his slight, reflexive retreat.

"We will conduct our initial assessment in private."

"Where will you take him?" Faria demanded, fury rippling through her fur. "He needs an advocate to report to his parents in Skyria."

Kier stepped forwards next.

"Skyria has been notified of our intended passage. Our detainment must be reported or this will be counted as trafficking or unlawful custody."

Dyate stepped in with a warning growl. "Not when under investigation for subterfuge."

Kier locked her in a stare. "He is a *child*," his voice boomed, unnaturally loudly, "Faria is his advocate and is entitled to accompany him and convey all matters pertaining to his guardianship to his parents and sovereign."

Rynkath's ears twitched and he returned to flicking the creases from his large, heavily starched bell sleeves. "You are not in a position to quibble over paperwork," he hissed. "From what our intelligence reads, he wilfully emancipated himself from his sovereign: first to join Dhraka, and then you," he rebuffed. "Those are not judged as the actions of a dependent, but one who is deliberately joining dangerous, subversive groups. Now that you're here," he continued, bile rising in his voice, "any uncooperative actions may be treated with more force than you anticipate."

He stepped down towards Faria, his voice once again low. "Now you see how real power works. A single command in the proper setting, and you are nothing."

Maaka flexed his wings. "I wish to attend merely to present medical history and discuss prognosis. It is my duty of care as a physician. I have no part in anyone's espionage."

Rynkath began a slow, antagonising turn, then Faria spoke up.

"If you don't accept me, at least let Maaka go," she protested. "I'll…" she chewed the words for a second, then presented them like an unwanted fishbone in her food, "I'll stay where you've deemed appropriate while we're detained. As long as Tierenan's safe. If that guarantee isn't kept, you *will* regret it."

Rynkath glanced around for a minute, and then once again waved his paw and the guards withdrew from Maaka. The old fox turned and began his exit alongside the attendants who began to take Tierenan away, satisfied with his authority and the silence it had beaten into Faria. He paused, just as the shadow of the gatehouse passed over him. Eventually he turned back to the castle, and gave a contemptuous command that echoed through the gatehouse chamber: "Take them to their rooms."

As Maaka and Tierenan were separated from the group by Dyate and her soldiers, Faria grabbed the falcon's wing. "Report back to me whenever you can". Maaka could only manage a nod before Dyate wrenched him further forwards, and the other troops stepped in to separate them.

The guards circled them and began a marching escort inside. Faria watched Maaka and the attendants disappear through a door on the courtyard's left side, while the rest were led into a grand hallway opposite them, stationed with more soldiers, this time in blue and gold armour, with long, thin swords and helmets embossed with a mosaic of geometric swirls. Kyru analysed them with a distinct expression of disdain and intrigue, the kind that indicated a fascination aggressively tainted by the poisonous influence behind its subject.

They traipsed along marble floors and up stairs with plush carpet runners, and eventually into a long hallway with windows on one side overlooking the courtyard. Guards each took a door and opened them – four initially, but Aeryn and Kyru took a room together, leaving one guard bereft of a charge.

The rooms were, expectedly, reminiscent of the exterior in their lavishness – marble tile floors with precious stone inlay and a large tapestry-like rug that covered the area under the four-poster bed, the immaculately-veneered furniture, and up to the window. She could just see, in the fading light, the mast tips of the docked ships, including the Coriolis', but the castle's wall prevented her from seeing anything more. She gave a dismissive grunt, and laid her staff by the window alcove so its crystal prism rested against the glass.

Faria had barely been inside her room for a minute when a young hare sprang in, a towel across their forearm. They were in an impeccably-tailored embroidered crimson waistcoat, with a cravat and a small lapel pin of some kind of crenulated tower.

"If there is anything you need, please ring the service bell," they said softly, indicating a long velour cord hanging from a chain that disappeared into the ceiling, with a tassel on the end.

"You can help me now," she said quickly.

The hare straightened their shoulders, attentively awaiting her instruction.

"Can you ensure that my physician, Maaka, reports back to me after his meeting with the medical adjutants? He's a falcon. I don't know where he went, aside from the doorway to the left of us when we came in."

"Of course, I will be happy to guide him," the hare responded, with a polite bow. "Is there anything else?"

She paused for a second, and then shook her head. They bowed again. "Someone will be up shortly to assess your needs for food and refreshment."

Faria nodded as they backed away, then closed the door behind them. She moved back to her staff and touched the prism gently. A soft blue light bloomed from it, bathing the alcove in cerulean luminescence. She hoped it would be a visible enough signal.

Chapter Six

Faria waited, unfortunately. The room's strange, soft silence had the same atmosphere as an oven; an energy made to slowly cook whatever lay within. The creeping anxiety she felt made the walls appear to loom inwards and the floor rise to the ceiling, even though she knew nothing at all was moving. She should not be here. None of them should be. Especially Tierenan, and she already knew he'd be upset if he realised the battles being waged over his safety. He'd probably be the first to chastise her for giving in. The last words he'd spoken to her, even as such gruesome claws pierced his head, were a warning to keep going.

She paced to the wall and ran a paw over its surface. Behind the crisp wallpaper was stone, which at least made it a little easier to meld into shape than old wooden beams. If she was going to be trapped, she would at least not let herself be alone. She grabbed her staff and held the crystal prism to the wall. The wallpaper rolled towards the ceiling like a folding blind, and beneath it the stone folded inwards like unlacing fingers. It wasn't the smoothest finish, but her staff didn't have the balance of her father's and took more adjustment and practise that she'd not yet been able to afford. Her paw buzzed with that familiar resonance paresthesia, which she tried to flick and clench away.

Beyond the wall she saw a rush of movement, as Kyru threw himself into the armchair, and Aeryn rolled onto the near side of the bed, both startled and concerned.

"Faria," she said, a little stilted. "You all right?"

Faria was a little bewildered by their hurry to separate. "I know you're a couple, you don't have to eject yourselves from proximity every time I'm near."

Kyru rubbed his nose. "Yeah, well, it's been a weird day and you could still *knock* before splitting a wall in two," he grunted emphatically. "Lots to be on alert about even before you wander into personal time."

Faria blushed, having not considered that at all. She tapped her staff a little bashfully on the floor. "Yeah, sorry."

Aeryn flicked her paws off the side of the bed and sat up, adjusting the sash at her waist. "Any news?"

A curt, frustrated sigh escaped the fox as she glanced around the room, which had been more or less decorated exactly the same as hers, aside from different paintings on the walls, a different style of rug, and the bed being in a different place. "Nothing yet. I don't even know where they are."

Kyru removed his headband and rubbed the fur that had lain underneath, trying to unflatten it away from his head. "I'm up for an unscheduled expedition if you are."

Faria leant on her staff and looked away, considering the possibilities. "I'm... not against it. Rynkath and Dyate seem to be the kind who'd retaliate, though."

"They've shown us no respect; they don't deserve it in return," Kyru growled. "They won't let us go till they get what they want. And that's Tierenan."

Faria chewed one of her claws. "And he's already alone.

Or, with Maaka at least."

"Maaka's not a combatant," Aeryn warned. "He's got a duty of care to Tierenan and that puts him at even greater risk. They'll interrogate or imprison him first."

"Probably," Kyru said grimly. "Unless they decide Tierenan's parts are more valuable than his body, and get rid of both altogether."

Faria closed her eyes and tried and calm herself. "I don't… I won't let that happen."

Faria thought about the stories Osiris recounted to her about her father, the struggles he went through in building Nazreal and beyond, and the seemingly never-ending cycle of greed and violence that intersected their journey and threatened the world. She hoped she could yet prove Osiris wrong about the world's heart and his defensive cynicism against it. But here they were barely days out from the first Senate meeting and already at the mercy of an officious malefactor holding Tierenan hostage. It was a wonder in itself that the gryphon hadn't laid waste to the castle out of sheer rage. Faria had to fight those temptations too; forming holes in the wall to access her friends and not fester in lonely silence was a temporary catharsis.

"I'm trying to be good about this," she said reluctantly. "Nothing in me believes this bodes well."

Aeryn ran her paw over her dagger's patterned sheath, devoid of its weapon. "It's hard to trust anything anymore." She slipped a claw under her leg bindings and tugged at the hilt of the blade she kept tucked away underneath them. "But I'll be ready to fight against anything that proves that mistrust correct."

Faria gave a tired smile of thankful solidarity, and then moved to the far wall, where Kier's room bordered the wolves' chamber. She formed another doorway with her staff, twisting the stone outwards into columns that flanked the new opening. Kier was immediately attentive and leapt to his feet; Faria held up a paw to stay him.

"Sorry Kier, I didn't mean to alarm you."

"There are only so many ways you can emerge from a stone wall that aren't alarming."

"Right?" Kyru echoed.

She flustered a little, but was also somewhat proud of herself. "I just wanted us to have access to each other, in case anything happens. The guards are watching the corridors, but I don't think Dyate understands that resonance works in three dimensions."

Kier nodded. "Hope they enjoy watching the doors as we slip through the carpet."

Faria smiled, then turned back to Aeryn and Kyru to bring the rooms together as a whole conversation.

"Should we leave now, try to find out where he is?" she asked.

Kyru leant forwards to catch the evening skies. "Maybe when it's darker. A couple of hours, when the guards rotate out."

Kier nodded. "I heard them talking in the corridor – they think resonance is some kind of illusion."

"Guess they weren't the ones trying to stop the Coriolis, then," Faria muttered.

Aeryn let out a bitter scoff. "You can put facts in front of people all you want – doesn't mean they'll accept them." Faria could sense the wolf's own experiences with Andarn's military justice system laced through her voice. A few seconds later there was a sharp rap on Faria's door. She dashed to it, pulling it open fast enough that a draft brushed through the fur of the attendant hare, who blinked in surprise.

"Your physician," they said blankly, gesturing behind them to Maaka, who bowed his head and swept inside. Faria gave a grateful wave to the attendant, who returned to their post on the opposite side of the corridor.

She shut the door firmly, and before she could even speak, Maaka obliged:

"He is in their ward. The facility is… at least on the ground level, seems to be more equipped for small accidents related to sports or sparring than anything substantial. I imagine the barracks surgery is larger and also out of sight. They tend to be functional, rather than ostentatious."

"But he's safe?" she reiterated.

He nodded. "Insofar as they merely recorded his values and my *brief* history of his injuries. Nothing that might… potentially compromise him."

She shook her head ruefully. "I don't trust Rynkath. He seems the kind who would steal your house and then tell you it's your fault for not being rich enough to have paid him off beforehand."

Kyru met her with a blank look from around the corner. "That's a very precise mentality."

She emphatically waved her paws. "He's nasty!"

"He is, yes," Maaka said, resting a wing reassuringly on her shoulder.

Faria stormed around the room, partly wishing she was holding her staff so she could create an actual storm to go with it. She looked over to it, then shook her head with a grunt. "I can't tear the building down."

Aeryn gave a sly look to Kyru; the wolves were leaning against the hole she had made in the wall. "You sound like you're asking for permission."

"Or talking yourself out of it," Kyru added.

The impotent frustration on Faria's face elicited an empathetic frown from the archer wolf.

"If Tierenan's safe, we'll play as Rynkath demands for now," she said, a reluctant, darkening voice of reason. "I'm all for tearing his palace to rubble if he tries anything, but Maaka's already in a precarious position. Rynkath will use everything against you that he can."

Maaka brushed his beak with his wing. "Osiris already put out a message to Skyria while we were sailing. I hope they will be able to attend before long."

Faria shook her head, locking Maaka in a resolute stare. "I am *not* leaving Tierenan."

"Nor I," he replied. "But it will do no good to have him stuck here at the precipice of yet another brimming war."

Faria leant on the window frame. "I think we're already past that."

The wolves looked to each other, and Maaka bowed his head in acknowledgement.

"Can you stay with him?" She asked. "I'm sorry it's not going to be comfortable there."

Maaka nodded. "You underestimate the conditions I've slept in before. I've no interest in seeing him unguarded."

"Thank you," she sighed. "As soon as anything changes, try to send word for me. I'll be ready."

It was a restless night. Faria slept little, and what paltry slumber she did achieve was quickly torn apart by anxieties and nightmares about Tierenan. The sun rose to find her already pacing about the room, drafting out arguments in her head to throw at Rynkath should he insist on backhanded justifications for his intrusion.

There was another perfunctory knock at her door. She only cracked it open this time, and the hare was beyond, with attending staff wheeling a tray of food.

"Good morning," they said politely, bowing only far enough that their ears didn't leave their personal space. "We have some breakfast if you require it."

She glanced between them and the trays of various breads, vegetables and meats grudgingly, not wanting to accept charity but also wondering if being obnoxiously greedy might somehow put Rynkath into destitution. Determining that neither starving herself nor eating so much that she would ruin one of his bedrooms with a gastric explosion was helpful to her cause, she loaded her plate with a moderate selection then returned inside, giving a tired but genuine thank you to the hare and their colleagues.

It didn't matter *why* she was held here; she wasn't going to blame the staff for any of it.

She ate what she'd taken, still pacing around the room, knowing, and also dreading, that it wouldn't be long before she'd have to address Rynkath.

She heard Kyru picking food next door while Aeryn grumbled about it being 'too early', still muffled by a layer of blankets. Before long they too had eaten, and were making active conversation about how to patrol the building for escape routes. Before Faria had much time to interject, another summoning knock came from the door.

She opened it, once again less brashly. Dyate stood before her.

"Your attendance is necessary," she said bluntly.

Faria paused for a few seconds, then went to reach for her

staff. A halting cough from Dyate stopped her, and she produced a gilded cane instead. It would have been beautiful if not stained with the patina of contempt.

"If you wouldn't mind, the investigators would prefer you to be unarmed."

The fox Empress gave a firm, yet grudging nod, and took the cane in a tense curling of her paw. "Very well."

Dyate led her through a maze of illustrious hallways, past giant arched windows framing marble statues and giant paintings of dignitaries in ostentatious regalia. There were a few cultural artefacts that Faria immediately knew did not belong here.

Through painted doorways they entered a large room, its checkerboard flooring almost as disorientating as its awful gold ceiling and mirrored wall.

At the end of a long table stood the slender, greying fox figure of Rynkath. His piercing yellow-green eyes flashed with glee upon seeing Faria. He remained at one corner, while Dyate led Faria to the corner adjacent to him. A tanuki scribe sat at a separate desk slightly away from them, and flanking him was a set of two bobcat guards.

"Miss Xayall. A pleasure," Rynkath oozed.

He paused, somewhat expectantly, and the two exchanged a steady glare.

"It would be more comfortable to sit," he said, indicating the chair set out for her.

"I can stand," she rebuffed.

An edge of frustration cracked his polite, forced smile. "I think you'll find most Senate members prefer to speak comfortably seated. Myself included."

She pushed her shoulders back. "What's your business?"

He stepped back slightly. "Very well." He gave a short,

clipped bow. "I am formally introducing myself, following our spirited conversations thus far. My name is Rynkath Konel, Representative of Pthiris in the Senate."

She extended a paw, curtly, reluctantly. "Faria Phiraco, Empress of Xayall, and Senate Representative." He glanced at her offered limb for a second, then his own emerged from the long, wide sleeve, shook it briefly and weakly, then withdrew back inside its cloth shell.

"So I did hear correctly that you took your mother's name," he sniffed.

Her ears flicked. "As did my father in his time here."

"Indeed. Such an interesting fellow." Rynkath's words had an odd timbre to their pronunciation, as if he had been holding desperately onto information he could use to place someone at an imposition. It was an ominously natural tone for him. "Considering the life he led, one would not be surprised at a need for… a certain degree of anonymity."

Faria could feel her muzzle pulling back to snarl, and she was not inclined to resist it. "I hadn't realised expectations of privacy were ever in doubt."

He brushed his claws on his robe. "I think supernatural abilities and de facto ownership of a lost city fall beyond the safety of a quaint family inheritance," he loomed, prompting a scowl. "But considering his tragic loss is still so recent, shouldn't you still be wearing your mourning veil?"

Faria almost choked. "He was my father, not my husband! And my grief is mine to feel, not others' to police."

Her claw gripped the table's edge and her arm tensed, considering greatly whether she had the strength to slam the hardened oak panel into his face.

He gave a dismissive shrug. "Traditions are fading, it seems. I hope you are still grateful of the lessons he taught you, and the position he gave you."

"I wouldn't be his daughter if I wasn't," she gnarled, chewing in her mouth an indignation that was impossible to swallow. "So, you summoned me? I'm eager for your 'investigation' to conclude."

They stood in silence for a few more tense seconds, and the facade drifted from his face like fog in the wind.

"Your mother was a far more dignified statesperson," he spoke. "You would do well to take after her."

Faria stepped forwards, still keeping a paw on the table. "You don't get to speak for her. She and my father gave their lives to protect this world. That alone speaks to me about what I should do, and how I should present myself to the Senate."

Rynkath stiffened, and looked down his greying muzzle at her. "Fatally idealistic."

"So what do *you* do? Stand among rich tailchasers finding new ways to get richer?"

"A disgusting slander," he spat. "Nobody who makes accusations like that is fit to run a sovereign." He glowered at her over his glasses. "You swim in dangerous water, Miss Faria. You'll find this is not a territory you can just blast away like your father did. You will be alone at the mercy of sharks waiting to pick your body to shreds." He leant in, poison dripping in his tone. "It will be as if you never existed."

She reeled back, baring her teeth at him, fur bristling. "I won't be threatened, and I will not have my family's sacrifice belittled by a power-worshipping hypocrite." She turned away and moved to exit. Dyate stopped her with a paw at her shoulder, a surprising strength behind it.

Rynkath spoke to her back.

"You should respect those in authority. They will come for you if you don't."

"This is not 'authority'," she cursed. "This is subjugation." She turned back around, eyes flashing with resonance energy. "I've faced down enemies that could tear the world in half. People like you are nothing but glass fists: all of your strength is a transparent lie."

The resonance light faded from her eyes but the fire remained. Rynkath licked his teeth, matching her power with the hungry activation of his derision.

"Your bias clouds you. Such is the behaviour of a rebel who shuns investigation," he shot back.

"My 'bias' is experience," she said loudly. "My city besieged, twice. Attempted assassination. Constant attacks against my standing, your seizure of Tierenan, overtures of conquest – you're repeating the Shadow's Claw strategy move by move."

Rynkath leant in, mocking her with a sickening smirk. "I am an arbiter of order and you will be thankful for my intervention."

"While you slithered around Senate chambers I was fighting for my life, even for denizens of Eeres I'd never even known." Her glare was like a storm of arrows aimed at his head. "By saving this world I fought for you too, but you saw none of it, so to you it never existed." Her voice rose, her paws were shaking.

Indignation oozed through his clothes in the stiffness of his shoulders.

His mouth flickered slightly in a subtle show of his gleaming white teeth. "You may have a childish, idealistic flair that amuses a crowd of sideshow idiots, but I wield a command which will dog you at every step. I can turn you into a villain with a single rumour. Every way you resist, I will dig my claws deeper until you have no choice but to submit."

"How noble the ideals that bring peace."

He waved his paw disdainfully. "Do not whimper to me when your plans fall around your tail in destitution," he said, making no effort to look at her as he stood to leave. "I will be nothing but satisfied with your failure. Especially so if it comes by my hand."

He flicked his claws. Dyate marched to Faria's side, gesturing for her to be taken back to her room. He waited for an expectant few seconds.

"It is customary to wish Representatives a good day at the end of a meeting," he said snidely.

She flexed her shoulders, removing herself from the proximity of his guard to stand alone. "I pride myself on my integrity, Pthiris; that would be a lie."

He cracked a wry grin as he turned to leave. "Be careful making a name for yourself, Young Empress. You might get it taken away," he oozed, with a sickeningly rehearsed bow, as she was marched out. He made his own exit through a side door.

A figure stood watching the next room across through the one-sided glass that hung between them. The wolverine's eyesight made any tint or visual obstruction negligible. His claws fidgeted and twitched in his coat pockets, and his eager breath fogged the glass with tiny clouds that evaporated almost as soon as they hit the smooth surface.

Beyond him, tantalisingly close, lay Tierenan, being seen to by the Pthiris attendants, with Maaka closely watching from a chair in the corner.

Talos sucked through his teeth at the stalling progress of retrieving his experiment. He had long since thrown off the shackles of propriety, and felt Rynkath's insistence on entrapping political focus around the group was unnecessary ego-dressing. A simple kidnapping would have done.

His right ear swivelled as a door clicked open. He didn't even turn to look as the intruder into his silence approached and peered through the glass next to him.

Rynkath stood with his hands folded inside his cuffs.

"Hard to believe a key pawn in all this is such an unassuming young figure," he said, somewhat indifferently as he watched Tierenan's examination.

Talos shifted, a low mechanical clicking and whirring coming from his half-mechanical claws. He leered hungrily at the unconscious raccoon.

"It's less about him, more about the information he holds and the work behind him. The work *I* put into him," Talos glowered. "It could have been any child – he was just the perfectly-timed opportunity and a fitting candidate for my control implants." He tensed his arm, as if fighting a destructive impulse from his claw. "I can replicate his limbs, but not what he knows or the way it's mapped his brain. I need his mind to do any further work on the others. If he were to wake up and reveal it all to that wayward Empress, I'd lose all of my work."

"Another inexplicably prominent upstart," Rynkath derided.

Talos gave him a sideways glance. "She's strong. A fascinating power with incredible potential, wasted on bleeding compassion. We had another, with even more intricate augmentations than the raccoon there. A beautiful melding of the natural, supernatural, and artificial."

"Ah, Raikali, was it? I only heard by proxy, never managed to gain an audience with her."

Talos spoke with a rueful bitterness. "My greatest achievement was piecing her back together, turning her into a fantastic, elegant war machine." He gave a short, sharp scoff. "The Empress you scorn was strong enough to destroy her shell and overpower her."

The fox stiffened, his yellow eyes narrowing to a frown. "A disappointing anticlimax. One that has been impossible to fix thus far."

"Not if you keep avoiding the obvious choices," Talos remarked, watching the doctors converse in the medical suite.

Rynkath scoffed. "Overt barbarism only works when you are in the correct position. It's clear the forces we're working against have too wide a support network. They must be strangled before their neck can be snapped and this is what we have been working towards. Isn't that why you're here too?"

The wolverine turned to the dim room, to face a desk lit by a single candle, on which was a journal full of mechanical sketches and notes. It looked to be ancient. Next to the desk, standing in silence, was a slender, wan-looking ferret, her mask of cream fur weathered with dirt and grease. On her shoulder was a small metallic red bird, sitting silently.

He didn't acknowledge her as he lifted a pulsing paw over the journal's pages, delicately flicking a claw under a leaf of parchment and rolling it onto its reverse. Inside, in someone else's signature writing, lay a diagram of some kind of resonance battery, being loaded into a synthetic limb.

"Somewhat. It just happens that the people willing to give me freedom to further my research align with your goals. I have no ideations of war. Only of experimentation."

"You seem to have involved yourself in a war very readily for one not taking sides," Rynkath chided with a sly grin.

"Are you complaining?"

"Absolutely not. Your lack of scruples is an asset."

Talos grimaced slightly. "You infer that I'm immoral?"

A wider smile revealed Rynkath's gleaming teeth. "The company you keep is not what most would consider virtuous. First Dhraka, then that despot bear Kura. And now with your shadowy benefactors in the land that remains. You have run to the violence on all fronts so far."

Talos snapped the journal shut. "So what does that portend for you, after your allies fell to these creatures you're currently detaining?"

Rynkath glanced over his shoulder, not dignifying the wolverine with a full confrontation. "You'll notice I'm still here where they aren't. I've remained so because I did not fly into the face of unknown danger without a plan. I took this position from under my predecessor's paws the moment the opportunity was given to me. I had the knowledge and the will to do what he refused to believe in. That is why the splintered Claw rallied under me, and I have been careful and thorough in collecting resources."

"Fulkore thought his brute force unstoppable. Kura thought his meticulous war victory was inevitable, and Raikali believed she was invincible," Talos warned, moving back to the window next to Rynkath. "Dhraka collapsed, leaving Claw in shambles when he and Kura were defeated. Dhraka only just managed to keep hold of its own research compound by the skin of its teeth." His voice rattled with frustration. "If I had been caught, your precious stolen children would have been taken away, and they may yet if Tierenan wakes – the Senate will descend on you like flies on a fresh corpse, and *she* will be its spearhead. Gold won't fight your war for you. You may consider yourself above all this, but it will drag you down just as unceremoniously." His face lowered into another demonstrative scowl. "They are feverishly dedicated to seeing you fail, and are powerful enough to do it."

"Their impetuousness has already cost them, and I'll see to it they can advance no further. Better to be above them, than below," the fox scoffed, before turning away and sweeping towards the door. "Begin with the child whenever you like," he called back. "We are already losing ground without Dhraka in the Senate and even with the Molten King on our side he seems more interested in his own battles than ascending to anything more grandiose. The Senate is my goal. He can have the rest. I have waited too long for you to deliver my promised network of spies that will show me where I can twist the knives into our neighbours."

Talos waited in the darkness for the door to shut, then turned to the ferret still standing silently to one side of the dim room.

"That impatient idiot is going to lure us into the same traps. The sooner we return to Dhraka and The Molten King, the better. I have far bigger things to build than Rynkath's ambitions."

He tore open a leather satchel and began inspecting the implements, arranging them in a small wooden tray that folded out of the top of the bag. The movements of his metallic, augmented claws were sharp, quick, and precisely erratic with his growing frustration. "*I* was the one who had a plan. I was the one who repaired their machines, constructed that creature's body, made weaponry that they used to exploit weaknesses and break down walls. None of them, not a single one would have had anything other than fruitless, impotent rage until I gave them the tools they needed to rise to action."

He threw the satchel onto a wheeled trolley made of bronze and wood; it rattled away from him and towards Feith, who watched it grind to a halt a few feet from her as Talos' shoulders heaved with his heavy breaths.

"They are all so close, and so reckless," he growled.

He spun on his paw and stalked towards the door. "Gather the tools and start taking them down to the armoury. I'll get rid of the doctor."

She clutched her arm tightly, looking away. He marched forwards, taking her muzzle in his claw and turning her to face him, inches from his muzzle.

"I don't care about your nostalgia. Tierenan doesn't belong with them. Neither do you. Now go."

Chapter Seven

Faria once again paced her room as the evening fell, like a starry kettle lid being lowered over the horizon. She had imbued her stave with enough energy to keep it glowing softly at the window as the light faded, and although she needed it to be a signal to Osiris, the worry of it drawing more hostile attention jabbed at her thoughts. She had been brought a plate of food, which she barely touched, the crawling disquiet of their confinement overriding the pit of hunger in her stomach. Kyru, Aeryn and Kier were playing cards in the other room, yet she couldn't focus despite their welcome companionship.

A knock at the door startled her. She leapt to it and cracked it open – the dutiful hare attendant who had seen to her meal was waiting, with a polite, necessary smile. "Is everything to your accord?" they asked brightly.

Faria glanced at the food. "It's very nice; I just don't have an appetite right now. Have you heard anything from my physician?"

The hare frowned. "I have not, I'm afraid. I sent for him but apparently he is still indisposed," they replied. "I will be taking my leave to sleep soon but will still be available by call if you ring the bell."

She gave a sympathetic, slightly frustrated smile. "Thank you, I should be fine. Maaka is my priority."

They nodded. "As you wish. But please, should you require it."

Faria bowed and closed the door again, and kept waiting till the day's expended energy finally called in its due.

One by one she snuffed out the wall lantern flames with a swirl of air from her staff, then laid it against the window once more. Her gaze snagged on the moon, which tonight wore a soft halo of cold reflected light through the upper clouds. It still unnerved her, though ultimately she couldn't assess why. Perhaps knowing where the crystals came from, it felt almost like a yawning well, threatening to envelop and consume her if she were to somehow fall into it. Or perhaps it was more like a distant watcher, a sentinel to the power it had involuntarily bestowed upon the creatures who lived here.

She felt almost as if it might take the resonance away one day, or come down to retrieve it. Faria wondered in part if there was a faint resonance within the moon itself, and that that may have been the cause of her chronic insomnia, and that of other resonators she knew.

Despite its haunting presence, there was a strangely disparate comfort in the luminance now. Some kind of anchor, perhaps, or a warning to use her powers responsibly under its gaze. Not that she needed telling.

She and the moon; bodies torn by the same power. She finally pulled herself away as the light made her eyes tired. She lay back on the bed to stare at the ceiling, with its rings of golden leaves surrounding an ornate candle fitting hung from a chain at its centre. The outer sheets of her bed were stiff, like a tightly-woven rug, while the mattress was plump, full of down and wool in separated layers. It was uncomfortably over-comfortable. She threw the outer sheets off (they almost stood upright on the floor by themselves, they were so firm), and tried to wrap herself in the less extravagant lower sheets, about the only thing of relative normality. Her mind raced with the delayed travel to Skyria, the isolation of Tierenan, and the lack of Maaka. Eventually she realised she had drifted to sleep at some point, waking briefly to turn over, then closed her eyes once more.

Faria awoke to movement in the corridor. She scrunched her eyes to try and rid them of their dryness as her ears pricked and her brain engaged her senses to work out the source of the noise.

Footsteps. The hefty rattle of an armoured cuirass and chainmail. She sat bolt upright, swaying a little with dizziness, and scrambled to the edge of the bed. She kicked the sheets away and stumbled towards the door, while the room around her spun and lolled from side to side as her equilibrium failed to catch up with her. She pressed her ear to it, trying to breathe softly.

Her instinct was to reach for the handle to peek out, but a sudden paw on her shoulder stopped her. She jumped silently and froze, then looked round quickly to see Kyru's silhouetted form holding a finger to his lips. Behind him, she could see another figure: Kier.

"Guards," Kyru whispered. "Don't know what they want, but it won't be good for us."

She nodded; the two of them listened at the door; outside they could hear rough, stumbling footfalls, grunts of resistance, and the hushed insistence of terse voices. She looked to Kyru in alarm.

From the room next to Kier's, came the structural sound of a mass hitting the floor, and a door being shut and locked. Immediately Faria grabbed her staff and strode through the bedrooms, past the quickly-preparing Aeryn, and planted her staff in the wall once more. Inside was dark, but the lights from the city and the glow of her resonance cast enough to see the form of her falcon doctor picking himself from the floor, still looking down for his glasses.

"Maaka!" she cried. "What happened?"

He grunted, stretching a wing stiffly. He had a strap around his beak, which Aeryn deftly sliced with her hidden dagger to allow him freedom to speak. "They threw me out of Tierenan's surgery. Said I was 'no longer necessary'," he added, with a severe look.

Faria's staff flashed with dangerous energy, as did her expression. "Did they take him?"

He shook his head. "Not before I left, but I imagine that's their next course."

"Right," she growled, beginning a march back to her window. The others were already prepared, in as much of their gear as they had brought in with them. Once she reached the window she sent a flash of red light through her staff – a long, glowing pulse that radiated on repeat five times, till she withdrew it.

"Hopefully, that'll be enough."

In little time afterwards, a shadow swept over the city. A strange, fluttering darkness covered the creature's wingspan as it rose high beyond the reach of torchlight's revealing flare, arched forwards, then dived sharply down to the city's heart, and the fortified tower in the central gardens.

Faria stood by the window, foot tapping in agitation. She'd taken the time to get dressed, but every second spent waiting was one that added to Tierenan's peril.

She looked back at the window.

It had gone dark. She frowned for a second, trying to squint through the obscurity, then a rapping at the glass made her jump. The shape drew back slightly, and pulled the dark cloth from its face to reveal itself.

Osiris clung to the building, wreathed in darkness to obscure his golden wings from being spotted over the city.

Even in the timid light of the staff through the glass, she could see his burning ferocity. She melted the wall open once more, allowing him to drop inside with a heavy, but controlled, step.

"What is the alarm?"

"They threw Maaka back. We don't know what they've done with Tierenan."

Osiris rumbled, a noise of intense and rather violent disgust. "We trusted so little, and should have done so even less."

Faria shook her head in vexation. "We knew they'd do this. They cornered us specifically to pry him away." Her voice was laced with fury and frustration. She bashed her staff on the floor, burning a small hole in the carpet in the impact's wake. "I shouldn't have agreed," she muttered.

"You were held hostage," Osiris replied, angry at the circumstance but not her decision. "As fiery as we are together, I do not believe you made the wrong decision. What they have proven is their bloodthirst, and you have every right to defend against it."

She clenched her staff tightly, feeling the tension build.

"We have to find him. I don't… I don't care what it takes."

Kyru spoke from his position near the door. "Time for a diplomatic incident?" Aeryn shot him a glare at his phrasing but didn't disagree. "We're more or less unarmed, Faria. We'll need to—"

From across his back under the veil, Osiris slung a bundle in front of him and cast it onto the bed. A muffled clink of blades wrapped within revealed its cargo.

"I would not leave you so unprepared," he said, with a slight bushing of his feathers.

They quickly retrieved their weapons; Aeryn ran her pawpads along her bowstring, checking its tightness. "Thank you, Osiris."

"It would be my pleasure were it not such a dire circumstance."

Faria turned to Osiris. "Can you get the Coriolis running? We'll need an escape as soon as we find him."

"I was not built to stand by," he rumbled irritably. "You may encounter much resistance."

She locked him in a stern gaze. "Nobody else can be our pilot under these circumstances at night."

"Can you sabotage the other ships?" Kier suggested.

At that addition, he seemed much more confident. "*That* will be a pleasure." He dug under his veil, and laid his claw on a clay canister with a fuse at one end.

"Your distraction will be imminent. Get ready."

Maaka swept his wings out. "I'll take you to his surgery."

Faria nodded, and gave the gryphon one last acknowledgement. "We'll be safe, I promise." He saluted sharply back. "You will hear my distraction in a moment. Wait till then, but take the opportunity immediately." He took to the sky with a heavy bluster of his wings, and vanished directly upwards, skirting the manor's wall to its roof.

Faria pressed her staff to the floor in readiness. Maaka was just in front of her, wings tense, while Kyru, Aeryn and Kier stood behind her, weapons drawn.

They waited intently, then:

The building jolted, and a sound like thunder cracked the air. Faria jumped briefly, but quickly took the noise of falling tiles and clamouring of guards to mask her power as she pressed her staff into the floor. It bowed downwards and out, forming into a platform that swept them into the room below. Maaka took to his legs, beginning a dash towards the surgery, and the rest followed swiftly behind.

Alarm bells rang, soldiers shouted, and heavy, armoured pawsteps began to ring through the corridors. A group of five, one with large wings, was hard to hide. Above they heard soldiers bashing at the bedroom door, then split the wooden barrier. Quickly Faria reversed her distorted platform to seal them away, before letting Maaka take the lead. Each swell of armoured steps had them pause, or break into a nearby room until they passed and their sound faded. Faria was not keen to cause any unnecessary bloodshed, despite the desperation in their flight to their companion.

Soon enough, but still under the furious impatience of concern, Maaka drew them to the surgery. He pushed open the wooden doorway with haste, and froze as he entered.

Nothing.

No bed, no gurney, no Tierenan. They fanned out and checked everywhere inside the long, rectangular room, but a catatonic raccoon atop a metal rolling bed was not a subtle obstacle to miss.

"They've taken him already," Faria growled shakily.

Kier ran a paw over the walls, trying to find gaps that

indicated a passageway or hidden entrance, but couldn't sense anything. His ears pricked and his eyes flashed with resonance-enhanced discernment for any kind of clue. A small trail of scratches along the varnished floor led back outside, but as he turned to touch the door, a loud, low horn rang out, and warning bells pealed throughout the towers, again splitting the night's quiet air.

Kyru cursed, taking his voulge into his grasp, ready to fight their way back out.

"We have to find him," Faria hissed. "We can't just leave!"

"We may not have a choice," Aeryn responded, counting the arrows Osiris had deposited for her. "If we don't get out, we may lose all chances of rescuing him."

Kier knelt and stroked his pawpads over the scratches. They looked new, and occasionally a slight smudge in the shape of a pawprint lay next to them. They led into the back wall, the one covered in mirrors painted at its edges.

He skirted his claws over the perimeter of the glass, trying to find a gap he could pry into.

Kyru watched him for a moment, and frowned.

As the fox passed a paw over the next panel, the shattering of glass rang through the room, followed quickly by the scattered rainfall of mirrored shards cascading over the floor. They all looked round in alarm, as the wolf withdrew his shield from the one-way mirror.

"We're past being subtle," he grunted, scraping the shards lodged in the frame away with his shield-edge, then hauling himself over the wall. On the other side, he could see where the skirting board could slide away to hide the door's seams. He gave it a kick, but there was a lock somewhere he couldn't budge, nor did he have time to investigate.

Kier blinked, and gestured to the broken shards. "Found it."

Faria spun to face Maaka. "We'll take it from here. Get back to the ship with Osiris."

"As you wish," he replied, with a reverent dip of his head. "Be safe, Faria."

"You be safer than us," she warned, taking him in a quick one-armed hug.

The falcon swept from the room and disappeared along the corridor. Aeryn had already climbed through, and Kier was on hand to help Faria over. She took his paw, and used her staff in the other to half-vault over. She swayed a little as she landed, and was caught by Aeryn.

Kier leapt nimbly over, just as Faria swept her staff across the gap, stretching the other panes of glass to cover the hole they'd previously made and hopefully make their entry less obvious. She pulsed her paw tightly after the energy's burst, as her joints threatened to tense angrily at her exertion.

She turned to face the room, choosing to deny the pain any more of her time. "Where to now?"

Kier studied the floor – the tracks were easier to follow in a room much less maintained than any of the Representative building's 'public' spaces. A simple but wide wooden doorway stood before them – as they opened it they saw, stretching beyond, the long, dark arch of the sloping corridor ahead, like the throat of some large monster. Kier kept a paw over his sword as his eyes scanned the ramp that he could see till it descended around a corner. "Nothing ahead," he assessed.

Aeryn gave a dry laugh, stepping in front of him to the tunnel's mouth. "I'm sure there's plenty. We just haven't met it yet."

Fast footsteps rang in the corridor, swelled, then mercifully turned in another direction and receded into the distant hallways.

Faria let out the breath she'd been holding onto as a terse sigh. "Let's go."

After the other three stepped through, she closed the door and arced her stave against the ceiling. Her staff's nest of wings reflected the blue light against the painted stone, and within seconds the rocky ceiling had melded downwards, sealing off their previous entrance. Anyone who opened that door would now have a wall to contend with.

She rubbed the numbness out of her wrist, and followed the others.

Chapter Eight

They began their descent, keeping a quick pace through the sloping corridor but wary at each bend in case of guards. The floor was plain slab and the walls undecorated, lit with much smaller, sparser lights than in the main building. It looked like old servants' tunnels or defensive burrows to protect the fort from a siege, but evidently something else now lay shrouded beneath the hewn, thickly-painted rock if the tracks led here. Somewhere above, the muted bumps and clashes of frantic searches and probable raids on empty rooms disappeared into the swollen, near-silent ambience of their new path.

It was cold. The stone paving had a radiating, sting-like quality as their paws touched it, but their goal was far too important for it to be a hindrance.

It was eerily empty, too. Faria hoped Osiris' distraction was doing the trick at drawing soldiers out from the mansion and likely to the docks, to leave them mostly unhindered, but the atmosphere pressed into them all the same.

After the corridor took a wide bend to the left and continued its decline, they passed several double-doored rooms with bulky iron chains lashing them closed. Quick glances through those that had large enough gaps, or a swift slashing of the metal links from Faria, opened them up to reveal stores of grain, food and building supplies, one housing a well, and others with weapons and armour.

"Enough to defend a siege," Kier muttered.

"Or mount one," Aeryn retorted, somewhat darkly.

Faria grunted in even further disgust. "Only one?"

Towards the bottom of the corridor's path, as it began to narrow, came a larger door. When Faria struck open the lock, letting it fall to the floor with a resonant crash, she and Kier opened it up to find armour in other sovereigns' colours strewn on benches; banners from everywhere including the Senate, all alongside ceremonial weapons and liveries in various regional specialties. It looked more weathered than for mere collection purposes, and too hidden to be for visiting dignitary use. Beyond the initial benches and racks, deeper into the chamber, were long wooden rails covered in white suits of armour of varying sizes, made for many different body types, and helmets to match.

"Pithy liar," she hissed.

"Did you expect anything different?" Kyru responded, giving a nearby breastplate a nudge with his sword. It had a slash across one of its facets, and he couldn't tell if there was dried blood or rust around the collar.

Aeryn glared at the Andarn armour particularly, the sheen of white glinting in the darkness as a bitter reminder of her own exposure to the corruption at the heart of their aggressors' schemes. "They're all as bad as each other; it's almost boring that they'd be working together."

"Fulkore had a long time to build a network," Faria growled.

"An army doesn't die just because you kill its commander,"

Kyru replied, keeping his head in the corridor. "All those minions who insist they know their leader's mistakes vie for command as the new executioner."

Faria spat a disdainful scowl into the room. "Now we have the Molten King to deal with, whoever that is. I'm sure he'll bring himself to just as deserving a fate."

Kier's cautious look gave her pause. She stopped, tilting her head in brief, impatient query.

"What?"

"You… sounded just like Osiris then," he murmured. "I'm not sure it fits."

She scrunched her muzzle, a little dismayed. "I won't become him, but a certain degree of cynicism is…" she sliced her hesitancy with an exasperated huff, looking at the sharp prismatic crystal at the end of her staff. "We've been chased into corners so many times; something has to break. They want it to be me. I can't just… ignore that."

Kier nodded, looking away, and she surmised that he was probably disappointed in her. She clutched her staff tightly as she left the chamber. Aeryn and Kyru looked more understanding, having seen more of her fights directly they knew more intimately what she had suffered and how she'd fought. But Faria was disappointed too – partly in herself, and partly that any of it had to happen in the first place.

"I'm not giving up on having a world where optimism can survive. Just… we have to fight. Now, and probably for a long while yet."

"It's okay, Faria. I'm just… sorry it's come to this, when we wanted better."

She turned to the end of the corridor, where the path split into opposite directions on either side.

"I promise, I still do."

After edging up to the corner and carefully glancing round, they took the left path. More storerooms lay around them, then eventually one wall opened up into a series of arched pillars over a larger, darker space. The four of them ducked behind the pillars and listened.

The sounds of metal tools being laid out rang quietly. Faria glanced at the ceiling and saw chained lights hanging just above the arches, with candles flickering in glass orbs, hanging too low for this to be the ground floor. Briefly craning her neck forwards confirmed there was a lower level, where someone was muttering quietly to themself as they worked. She jolted softly as they gave a loud, impolite dismissal of another who had just arrived with something large and wooden that was placed loudly onto the ground. Faria covertly peered around the edge into the circular chamber, its lower level daubed in torchlight, rough stones casting a network of shadows that rippled in the light's undulating flames.

On their far side was a long stone concourse that adjoined a long antechamber, perhaps another tunnel. Taking up most of its space though, was a long carriage of black metal, very similar in its dark lustre to the Dhrakan pyramid that had once loomed from the ocean and swallowed the Coriolis.

Attendants in the same uniforms as the hare by Faria's bedroom were loading machinery onto the carriage. Wooden crates fortified by strong steel banding were lifted, gently, and placed with extreme care. A strange iron engine sat at one end, its pistons hissing and rumbling with a steady, idling rhythm, smoke and steam softly pluming from exhaust tubes that sprouted from its main body.

At the centre of the chamber was a rolling bed of silver and gold – the stolen gurney, on which Tierenan still lay, unmoving. Faria felt a massive wave of relief wash through her as she got to see him, though her tail bristled and curled as she thought about what they might have planned for him if her party didn't intervene. Next to him stood a table covered in tools Faria couldn't discern but didn't trust regardless. The muttering figure below – a wolverine –moved between the tools at his trolley, the devices, and the helpless subject on the platform with angry, skulking movements.

Tierenan's headplate had been pried open already. The wolverine peered and prodded at what lay below, flicking at things with a needle-like awl to assess, giving more guttural, non-verbal mutters to the darkness.

A door closed; a soft impact of wood on stone, and a clicking latch ringing through the room that made the hidden group's ears shift as one. They gripped their weapons in preparation of the new arrival.

A small bird swept around the arches in circling flight. The group watched it spiral and sweep, then land next to the surgeon by Tierenan's shoulder with an affirmative, metallic cheep. Its delicate metal wings and bright trill was a stark contrast to the darkness the wolverine was wreathed in.

"You took your time," he said, his sharp voice piercing the gloom.

A wan, young ferret appeared from the side door, holding a leather bag that looked like it weighed about as much as she might.

"Sorry, Talos," she said faintly, as she placed it down, half-dropping it with the strain of effort, by the table. His claws clenched at the impact; he moved with the jerky irregularity of someone who looked ready to hit something, and wanted to give the impression he would, but was holding back by the grace of luck or waiting to be given one final reason to do so.

Aeryn stared into the scene with a fierce focus. "Faria," she hissed.

The fox glanced to her in silent acknowledgement.

"That bird," she continued, with a nod of her head, keeping her eyes focused on it hawkishly. "It's like the one that saved us from the Gargantua."

Faria looked between the ferret and Aeryn. "Does she control them?"

The wolf shook her head. "I don't know. She might be our best chance to get him out."

"Can we trust her?" Kier glanced behind them; his ears tilted in the direction of some distant sound.

"They're coming. We don't have long."

Faria's mind rushed as she felt the sand running through the hourglass. She couldn't let Tierenan fall into their hands again.

She gave Aeryn and Kyru a nod. "Get Tierenan. We'll hold off anyone else."

The wolves moved out, skirting quietly around the pillars at the room's edge, while Faria and Kier prepared themselves for any intruding soldiers.

Talos was deep in focus, though his ears flicked with the sounds of the attendants loading the carriage, and the rumblings of movements above.

"Sounds like someone got overconfident," he muttered to himself. Beside him, Feith fished inside the leather bag to produce a glass and metal cylinder, inside which swirled a glistening, vibrant liquid of blue and purple, almost metallic in nature. He took it sharply from her and laid it on his table of tools.

Talos gave her a sideways glare. "Once this is set, we're leaving. Get everything else ready."

She nodded quietly, with a lingering glance to Tierenan as she watched Talos tweak and realign the electrical components of his cranial augmentations.

"Never should have expected this to be done properly by proxy," he muttered, as he turned to the cylinder. He leant down and took two thin needle-tipped hoses from the satchel Feith had left, and twisted them into sockets at one of the canister's metal caps. At the cylinder's other end, he attached a small dark box, which, with a wrenching of a small switch on it, began to whirr. The viscous liquid rippled and began to gently circulate. A whining pulse of air hissed from the needle's tip, till the metallic liquid silenced it and began dripping from the aperture. He leant forwards, and began applying it to Tierenan's head in delicate, precise locations around the circuitry.

Tierenan's body jolted slightly; the liquid stuck in place around the metal connectors for a moment, bubbled, then gradually sunk into panels on his head, running into the grooves and contours of his open plate. The bird whistled in short bursts, its beak almost touching Tierenan's fur, in an odd tone that rippled the fibres of his fur without being high in volume.

Feith trod, obediently and silently, towards the piles of equipment that were near the concourse. She heard the clicking of the latch as the attendants left to ferry more materials from upstairs. Ahead of her was the black metal track-bound vehicle that would travel all the way to Dhraka along the coastline. It was a ride she hated. Dark, with the constant eerie howl of the wheels on the metal, and the wind screeching forlornly over the carriage.

It reminded her of the mines. She hated travelling under rock and stone, but she also hated being so close to the hidden, destitute and broken side of Pthiris that was pitifully referred to as 'home' before Talos took her. He had lied many times about where she was from to cover his tracks, but the stain of her origin couldn't be erased.

Not his first experiment, but the first to survive. From her, the rest came. Picked at first from spaces she knew they wouldn't have been noticed. In truth she hoped their obedience would help them escape, and maybe if he got what he wanted, they'd one day be free, too.

It hadn't happened. Her first taste of a renewed hope was when she met Tierenan.

She had a plan, once, or perhaps more of a forlorn hope, to free them both, though she doubted she would ever find bravery, or even just opportunity, enough for it again. She hadn't even been the one to save him directly back on that monstrous Dhrakan ship – she'd had to save others, and hope *they* could save him instead.

Now, she was trapped. At Talos' mercy once more. Nothing she needed was within her power.

She stared silently as she moved to pick up a bag of tools. Inside was another metal bird, this time made from the plain blue metal dug from the Pthirisian land, undyed. Such a shame that the most beautiful thing about this place was what it plundered from the ground.

She reached into the bag to pick it up. Maybe if she activated it, she—

A blade met her chin. A gasp stuck in her throat and she froze, shaking. The wolf in front of her tilted the point of his falchion gently upwards to bring her eyes to his. He raised a finger to his lips, and shook his head.

Her eyes widened in shock.

Kyru leant forwards in a low growl. "Do you want to save him?"

She nodded desperately.

"Can you bring him back?" he whispered.

Her gaze darted from side to side, then she gave another, tentative nod.

"Good."

Talos grumbled at the table as the needle stopped oozing. He flicked it, shook it, and twisted it in his twitching, rapid claws. A soft jet of the resonance liquid spattered Tierenan's fur – he snarled in ire and jammed the tip back inside.

"Feith!" he called. "Get the suction pump."

He waited a second, using his time to tweak one of the panels.

"Feith!" he yelled, louder, more irascibly.

He whirled from his seat, and was halted in his stride by two wolves – one with a bow, drawn and with its nocked arrow aimed at his head, and the other holding Feith before him, with his blade at her throat.

Aeryn glowered at him. "Step away from Tierenan." Kyru's face was thunderous, teeth bared. He was taller than Talos and already the wolverine could tell he would be outmatched by strength and fury. He held his claws up, alarmed, but rising with anger.

"You don't know what interfering will do," he growled.

"You should take your own advice, coward," Kyru returned. "You expect us to roll over while you steal an unconscious child?"

Talos locked him in a stare. "If I die, so does Tierenan," he warned. "He'll be nothing but a shell without me."

Kyru kept his eyes on him, but addressed the ferret whose paws were trembling. "Is that true, Feith? Seems to me you can do just as well as he can."

She looked fearfully to her master. The iridescent liquid was about two-thirds of the way drained through Tierenan's head.

"Her?" he scoffed. "She's barely an assistant. She knows the importance of this. If it's disturbed, he loses consciousness forever. Is that a risk you're willing to take?"

Beyond them, Kier faced the corridor he and Faria had taken. Voices, and the rattling of armour.

He gripped his sword; Faria's staff began to glow. She slid the point along the ground, forming a ridge of spikes that blocked the hallway.

Talos's head whipped left at the sound of the distortion. Kyru's anger flared. "You can't win. You can live long enough to give him back, or you can die."

"He was a fanciful, idealistic nuisance. I gave him purpose." Talos sneered.

"You stole him from his family!" Aeryn snarled, bowstring pulled tight to her cheek. "Nothing about you was ever his purpose."

The clatter of rushing armour rang through the tunnels, followed by confused shouts at the spikes, along with calls for explosives. Kier's left ear flicked, making his crystal earrings ring slightly, as noises began ringing from the other pathways too.

Talos grinned. "I don't think I'm the one at a disadvantage here."

His claws began to flex backwards.

Kier and Faria ran towards the other corridor, but already the shouts of alarm had run out as the Pthiris guard spilled into the chamber. Kier flashed his sword through the dim space, while Faria swept a small group against the sides of the wall, trapping them in stone.

The sound of conflict drew Kyru's attention for just a second.

It was enough.

Talos leapt forwards, jerking past Aeryn's loosed arrow. Large spikes extended from his wrists, which he thrust towards Kyru's face. The wolf leapt back, releasing Feith. The ferret dived out of the way and immediately ran to Tierenan's gurney.

Kyru sliced and defended against Talos, while Aeryn shifted tried to angle another shot at the wolverine's back. He dodged aside; as she prepared another shot, a crossbow bolt sparked off the stone in front of her. She ran to a pillar and returned a shot back in its sender's direction, finding its mark in the guard's bicep.

Feith scrambled to finish Talos' work on Tierenan while the red bird circled around her head, chirping in shrill panic. The wolverine caught a glance of her as he slashed back across Kyru's middle, and tried to swipe upwards into his snout.

"Activate him, Feith!" he gnarled. "Let him tear them to pieces!" She flinched but kept working at him. The wolverine tore away from Kyru, but the wolf was faster, rounding in front of him with a swipe of his blade that Talos had to block with both of his wrist spikes.

"Don't listen to him, Feith! Bring him back!" Kyru barked.

Talos launched another punch to Kyru's muzzle; he ducked away and slammed his shield against the wolverine's midriff, shoving him aside. Talos glared back to Feith.

She looked between the two in a panic, and after a final application of the leaking resonance needle to Tierenan's control chip, shut his headplate and began screwing it closed.

The raccoon's claws flexed.

More guards sprinted into the hall from behind the first incursion, while others found themselves blocked by Faria's piercing defences. Aeryn spun and loosed two shots into the fray, but couldn't tell whether they hit anything. Beyond the spikes, among the bellowed commands she heard a heavy wooden object get laid down, and saw a flare of orange light burst at the gaps between the spines, followed by the shadows of retreating guards.

She flexed away and surged across the chamber, readying her bow from behind one of the other pillars. A heavy *boom* hit the chamber and flecks of stone spike flew across the space. Kyru broke from Talos as the two dived in opposite directions, and Feith ducked behind the gurney.

Kier, unprepared for such a loud noise, stumbled sideways, losing his equilibrium. The dragon facing him took a swing with his whole arm and caught him on the side of the face with the guard of his sword, knocking him completely to the floor with a pained grunt. Faria wrought a pillar of stone under the dragon, knocking them up against the ceiling. She collected Kier to his feet and ran, facing the cloud of debris billowing from the other side of the chamber.

But something else caught her attention more.

Tierenan was sitting up. The raccoon blinked, and slowly looked down at his claws.

Talos pulled himself upright. "Kill them!"

Tierenan turned his head slowly towards him, then to Faria, his expression unchanging.

Next to him, Feith gently put her paw on his.

"Tierenan…" she whispered. "Do you… remember me?"

He looked to her next.

His other claw clenched.

In a fury, Talos leapt towards the gurney, spikes forward, aiming for the both of them. For a second, Feith caught the flash of the blade against the sputtering light of the candles near-suffocated by dust, and closed her eyes.

There was an arresting thump just in front of her.

Everything went quiet, save her burning heartbeat and the

whine of terror behind her eyes.

Then, carefully, she opened them.

Tierenan stood in front of her. So did Talos.

Except the raccoon's claw was around the wolverine's throat, and Tierenan wore an expression of fiery determination, of awakened anger, and desperate realisation as Talos tried to wrench himself free. A voice rasped with months of involuntary dormancy as he finally spoke.

"Leave… her… alone."

Talos' shocked scowl turned into a fearful, grimacing rage.

Kyru was up and running; before he could reach Talos to pull him away, Tierenan's other fist drew up, snapped round in a twist, and careened into Talos' snout, sending him reeling back across the floor.

The raccoon shook his hand gently.

"Waited… a long time to do that," he croaked.

Faria's heart leapt as she saw him returning to himself, the colourful being she'd met in the forest two years ago, but cries from the hallway beyond took them all from their amazement and relief.

Soldiers poured in, arrows loosed. Aeryn shot back one more, Kyru dodged to help Tierenan down from the gurney and shield Feith, while Talos scrabbled to his feet and bolted across the stones to the carriage. Feith watched him go; for a moment his fangs bared and his eye tracked her with vengeful focus, but he was gone in the darkness and a slam of the tank's metal door before she could react.

Faria raised her staff once more. "Everyone, here!" she bellowed. Kier opened his maw to release a piercing lance of sound that kept the nearest soldiers from reaching them as Aeryn, Tierenan and Feith drew close to her. The wings around the staff's tip flexed outwards, the crystal shone. She brought the haft slamming into the floor.

The room rang like a stone bell, gathering in intensity. The guards paused their advancing strikes, and began instead to back away. In moments Faria had summoned a stone platform that encased over them like a spiralling shell. It rose from the floor, slowly at first, then faster, plunging into the ceiling and drawing a huge column of rock behind it as it punched through the floors above, lifting them all the way to the ground floor of Rynkath's fortress, and taking a portion of the ornate building's outer wall with it.

The rocky shell split as it burst into the blue night air, crumbling into the flowerbeds that surrounded them. Showers of glass and metal filigree dashed the grass. Alarms continued to ring, soldiers shouted from their positions around and above them as they had barely finished dealing with the fire that had erupted on the roof.

Faria glanced around, trying to get her bearings.

"Which way to the ship?" she called.

They looked around quickly. An orange glow illuminated plumes of dark smoke towards the bay, ahead and slightly to their right.

Osiris.

While she fought against the instability of her muscles, with a burst of determination she stumbled, then managed to find her balance again, as she moved towards the wall in the ship's direction. More arrows shot their way, spearing the ground, spitting up gravel. Kyru supported Tierenan and held up his shield, while Aeryn sent back covering shots. Kier jumped an arrow that would have hit his legs, while Faria had to stop dead in her tracks at a shot that impaled the ground in front of her. In angry retribution she cast a shield of wind around her that would deflect any that might aim her way till she reached the wall. Her chest pounded, her ears rang, but even so she unhesitatingly thrust the tip of the resonance crystal against the brick.

The swirling fog of fatigue was trying to drown her senses and made each new moment of battle feel like being jerked awake. Instead of the controlled melding of a door that she'd hoped for, the stalwart, eminent brickwork ballooned outwards and exploded, sending stone shards hurtling into the sky and streets beyond, pebbledashing the city. She felt the burning, sudden burst of painful feedback rock through her arms, and nearly dropped the staff as a result. In defiance she gripped it more tightly and, with a glance over her shoulder to check for the others, continued leading their escape through the streets.

Her beacon between the rooftops was a blue light shimmering at the tip of the mast, as smoked billowed around it from the decks of the surrounding ships. She waved her staff, emitting a reciprocal glow with the Coriolis' signal. After a second, the light flickered and disappeared; Faria knew they'd been seen.

Tierenan pulled away a little from Kyru. "It's okay. Let me run," he said, croakily, voice grinding back into life like air through a dusty organ pipe.

"We've taken you this far, we're not letting you fall now," the wolf growled sternly.

"Just want an excuse to hug me, don't you?"

"Amazing how quickly you change my mind," the wolf bit back, lifting his arm away slightly.

Tierenan grabbed it back. "If I go down I'll take you with me."

"Grumpy in the mornings, aren't we?" Kyru responded. Even in the coursing lanternlight of the Pthiris streets as they hurtled through them, his grin was impossible to hide.

Faria found the walls to the dock. The Coriolis was already rumbling fiercely. Thankfully between the two epicentres of chaos in the city – the alarm ringing at the fortress and at the inferno of surrounding ships – most guards had dispersed elsewhere and the docked ship was no longer a priority; those who remained were mainly sentries and guards, not equipped for an escape as bombastic as Faria's nor sabotage as brutal as Osiris'.

Faria's group thundered up the golden ship's metal walkway; immediately Aeryn and Kier hauled it up behind them all, and the Coriolis began its swift reversing arc back into the ocean, wearing only a soft patina of soot and char from the raging ships either side of them.

Osiris slammed the helm into action the moment they were clear. The blue roar of the engines erupted from beneath the hull, setting the ocean alight with its activation, and with rapid acceleration the Coriolis took to the sky.

The rapid ascent caused many within to grasp at furniture or each other to remain upright – Kier failed at both and tumbled back towards the door. Tierenan had been pushed into an anchored-down chair in the galley, which he still clutched tightly even as the others swayed and skidded by him.

"You were all… more upright… when I saw you last…" he breathed, a smile broaching his muzzle.

As if on cue, the ship levelled out, and everyone was able to stand more regularly.

"Ah, there we go," he followed, sitting back in the chair. He let his eyes close for a moment, although he opened them quickly afterwards, as if he'd already had more than enough in the darkness.

"I, er… guess it's been a while," he said, a little sheepishly. He looked around at them all. "I must have been really… really tired."

Faria leant on her staff and wrapped an arm around him tightly. "You're fine, Tierenan. Thank you… for waking up."

He hugged her back; gently at first, then tighter, burying his face gently against her. He looked around again as he pulled back, and saw Feith, holding her paws together very tightly, looking like she wanted to disappear inside the walls. Gently, he stood, and walked over to her. She shrank back at first, then paused in her movement, and looked up at him the closer he got.

He took her paws in his and squeezed them gently.

"Thank you, Feith," he said, his voice barely a whisper. "You saved me."

She swallowed, and nodded. "I… I had to," she replied quietly. "You… you were the reason I felt I could be anything other than what I'd been told." Her jaw tightened, and she held his paws more tightly. "I'm just sorr—"

He pulled her immediately into a hug against him, almost falling over, but holding onto her tightly.

"No apologies. Not now, not ever," he said, as his claws trembled slightly at her back.

She rested her head against him and hugged, letting out a soft, deep sigh.

Chapter Nine

"Two years?!"

Tierenan's hoarse shriek was in danger of shattering the glassware. The small red bird that followed them to the ship with Feith leapt up and flew circles around the room before fluttering back to the safety of the ferret's shoulder where she stood a step behind Tierenan's chair. Aeryn was applying a salve to where Kier had been smashed in the face; he winced but bore the pain and self-consciousness of being tended to.

Faria held up her paws to try and calm Tierenan down. "Well, no, I mean… yeah, almost. You… were really badly hurt."

The younger raccoon rubbed his head where Raikali's claws had penetrated. It seemed like something still hurt somewhere, or perhaps it was the brief memory of pain from when it happened, and the lingering sensations of ache in his unconsciousness. He stroked his metal claws along the ridges of the plate, then gingerly over his fur, then slowly brought them back to his lap and stared at them for a while in silence. Feith looked at the bird, which chirped softly and fluttered down to the raccoon's paws, and nestled down in them. For a second he flinched, then delicately let his claws relax around it. It trilled affirmatively up at him, tilting its head as if looking for instruction.

"You're very pretty," he murmured to it. "Your friend was too, and I… I had to crush him." He curled a claw under its beak, giving it a solemn stroke. "I'm sorry. That's one of the last things I remember before everything gets… very fuzzy."

The others looked to each other carefully, and Faria tentatively reached out for his shoulder.

"I've… I've missed so many meals," he said quietly.

Faria almost fell over. Aeryn looked away to stifle a snort, and Kyru sighed through a reluctant smile. Feith's shoulders dropped and she scratched her muzzle awkwardly.

"You're not wrong," Faria replied, with a breath of laughter to her sigh. "We can help you make up for that."

He looked up, eyes wide and glistening, the realisation of his absence battling against his attempts at humour. "I'm sorry… that I wasn't here."

She took one of his paws in both of hers. "You saved me. You fought for me. And you survived. What you've done in all those things is more than I could have ever asked for."

He wiped his nose and pushed a wide, slightly tearful smile into the room. "Then, um… I'll keep doing those things." He looked around at them all, then back at the bird in his paw, and once more fell quiet.

Faria wondered if he was truly awake yet. He looked so tired.

"Is there anything we can get you?" Aeryn asked quietly.

He shook his head. "No, you've done enough for me for a while. I want to be doing things for you, now."

Kyru chuckled gently. "You only just woke up, mate. Give yourself some time."

Tierenan shot him a look that was almost a scowl, but perhaps more of scornful determination. "Did you give *your*self time after coming back from your hypno-servitude?"

Kyru's jaw tightened.

Tierenan stuck his tongue out victoriously. "That's what I thought. I'm not as grizzled and fashionably scarred as you, but—"

"Not scarred?!" The wolf spluttered. "You're covered in metal—"

Aeryn slapped a gauntlet into his chest and he grumbled into silence. Feith smirked a little to herself.

Tierenan gave the bird in his paw a little nudge; it flitted back to Feith as he lifted his arms to flex them above his head, which he did successfully for a few seconds before releasing them with a tired sigh.

"As you can see," he breathed, "it's exhausting being as strong as I am."

"I'm sure it is," Aeryn returned, laughing.

"So…" he chewed, taking in a deep, preparatory breath. "What did I miss?"

Faria took in a deep breath.

The story of Xayall after his unconsciousness and the political upheaval throughout the continent of Cadon in his absence went on for some time. Tierenan listened ravenously, often wide-eyed, as the others filled him in on the trials after his injury. From Faria destroying Raikali at the heart of Nazreal to the battle for the Senate, and the slow rebuild after that. She watched him consider the story with a much similar countenance to when she'd first met him in the forests outside of Xayall. It was a quiet, wistful, somewhat anxious processing that was a world apart from the bounce and spirit she had most missed. But they were each made of facets, she told herself, and Tierenan was one of the most receptive and caring of any of them. He took his ability to help and be present very seriously. She hoped this was his way of assessing where he could stand, and immediately know what he was to do next, very akin to when they were lost in the forest together, meeting for the first time. When the storytelling had passed, Tierenan pulsed his claws into his plain, post-surgical clothes, staring towards the floor.

"That's a lot," he huffed.

"Yeah," Faria replied gently. "But we're still here, and so are you. And we're far from finished with anything yet."

He looked up, alight with determination. "Good. 'Cause I'm not sitting out anymore."

He stood, maybe a little quickly for his legs, but caught himself on the chair as his knees wobbled and threatened to tip him onto the plated deck. Almost everyone jumped to try and assist him, but he held up his free paw to stay them. "First, I need a shower."

Faria held his shoulder for a few seconds as he reorientated his balance; Kyru supervised in a tacitly earnest show of care and attention. The raccoon was determined to move under his own steam, however, so by the time he'd reached the cabin door he was free of Faria, though Feith still followed quietly behind him. Kyru still stepped in to open the door for him; Tierenan gave him a courteous bow and pretended to flip him a coin for his service, to which the wolf rolled his eyes.

"You missed me, didn't you?" the raccoon grinned.

Kyru gave him a low, spurious look. "Don't worry; I'm sure it'll pass."

The raccoon blew him a kiss as he breezed through. Kyru gripped the frame in his claws with an irritated growl, but couldn't hide the smile that peeked through his fangs.

Tierenan's gait was uneasy in the ship's buffeting through the air; Faria or Feith, sometimes both, ran to catch him when it looked like a swell of turbulence or change in altitude might knock him over but, much as was expected for his intense resilience and determination, he managed to steady himself every time. Faria watched with protective caution as he teetered and wobbled down the deck to the shower unit near Maaka's surgery, wondering if this was what a parent would feel like watching a toddler take meandering journeys into uncertainty. Aidan had told her a few times of her own escapades, and from Osiris' tales of Aidan's past mischief he sounded like a joyful nightmare. At least Tierenan didn't have resonance abilities to get into further trouble with.

He stopped at Maaka's door and gave it a swift knock. The falcon's head peered out, quickly donning an expression of shock when he saw Tierenan's smiling face on the other side of the gap.

"Well well, the young master arises," Maaka beamed. "This is a sudden turnabout."

Tierenan waved with a half-grimace. "Not as sudden as I'd have preferred, honestly."

Maaka nodded. "I can understand. How are you feeling?"

"Smelly. I would like to wash."

"Ah. Do you need extra care for your augmentations?"

Feith chimed in – she had been so quiet and Faria so focused that the fox forgot she was there for a moment, and jumped slightly. "They should be fine."

Maaka nodded and dipped his head back around the door. After a few seconds of rattling and the shifting of drawers and cabinet doors, he came back with a small bundle of clothes and towelling wedged between the elbows of his wings.

"I should think it fits, I keep some spare crew clothing just in case anything gets too bloodied or charred."

Tierenan nodded thankfully and proceeded to the nearby shower units. They weren't luxurious, but were a necessity for making sure potential patients were clean, and that Osiris had somewhere more discreet to bathe than a public bathhouse, given how often he had to avoid visibility.

Feith's small metal bird had fluttered onto Faria's staff and perched atop the prism. She watched it with guarded caution, not wanting to question that it was friendly, given Feith's presence and heroic saving of Tierenan under the scorn of her abusive master. She felt uneasy though, remembering the fear and heartbreak on Tierenan's face when he'd had to crush his green-feathered companion in the Tor before the battle there. She waved to Tierenan as he slipped inside the shower cubicle, and then turned back to Maaka, who was holding his wing to his upper chest.

"Are you alright?"

He shrugged. "A little roughed up by the guards, nothing substantial."

She winced. "I'm sorry. I should have been more forceful, so you wouldn't have had to offer yourself as a hostage."

Maaka gave a soft whistle of dismissal. "I've taken far worse in mere journeys across the ocean," he replied, adjusting the glasses on his beak, which were slightly askew thanks to a bend at their centre arch.

"You're not a fighter, though. It's unfair of you to be made to battle."

"You don't know that," he said, rather gravely. She stopped in her tracks and gave him a wary look.

"...True. Sorry, I haven't really asked you about your history. But for now..." she gently put a paw on his shoulder.

"I'd rather you be there to repair us, if that's all right to ask."

He let out a light chuckle. "I'm only halfway teasing, Faria. I have fought, but that's not my priority anymore. We're all of us here to move forward in whatever way we can, some more forcefully than others. Thank you for caring."

She smiled in reply, and gently reached up to adjust his glasses so the curve fit the notch in his beak more snugly. He bowed his head in thanks, then looked to Feith.

"I see we have a new passenger," he said, in a soft welcome. Feith immediately drew her paws to her waist again, but Faria placed an arm around her shoulders and held her in reassurance that Maaka wasn't being judgemental.

"We do. This is Feith. She's been... through a lot," she said, giving the ferret a gentle look. Feith glanced shyly back, and nodded with thanks that she didn't have to explain herself any further.

Maaka nodded, already giving her a visual assessment as they stood before him. His discerning eye passed over her rather emaciated state, and brief furrows of his brow punctuated his scan when his gaze caught on slightly worn patches of fur or uneven contours in her musculature that indicated bruises or welts from uncomfortable, unprotected work or sleep. But before too much silence passed, he spoke.

"You've likely gathered, Feith, I'm the ship's physician. Is there anything you feel you'd like addressed in yourself currently?"

Feith looked around briefly, and then gently closed her paw around itself in anxious request.

"Can I... have some water?"

"Alright," Maaka replied softly, with a smile. "Give me a moment."

"Thank you."

He disappeared into his surgery, and only a short moment later returned with a small tankard of water for her. She took it thankfully, before returning to her quiet analysis of the space around her, examining the walls, the panels, and then suddenly remembering something in the pocket of her jacket, which she took to the bench behind them.

Maaka once more returned his attention to Faria. "I'm elated you were able to get him out of there. Nothing short of a miracle, once again. And in restored condition, no less."

She smiled nervously. "He's a constant surprise…" she looked to the shower, where a small cloud of steam rose from the gap above the hinged door.

He nodded. "As I have come to expect on your journeys, or Osiris'."

"You… never had a chance to examine Raikali, did you?" she asked tentatively, her focus on some grave visage in her memory.

He shook his head. "No. I ventured into Nazreal's heart once with Osiris after taking you to Xayall but nothing was left except her armour – not a scrap of flesh, bone or blood. Why do you ask?"

She scrunched her muzzle. "Was kind of hoping to know for sure that she was gone."

He shook his head, somewhat darkly. "Having no body to examine does leave some kind of suspicion, but with powers like yours, and hers… I can only imagine what it would do when combined."

She nodded, feeling her fur bristle up and down her back to think about how her power had been weaponised against her, and even now how the feedback rippled through her body at every attempt to use it. She returned to the bench next to Feith, whose red bird was perched on her shoulder while in her paws she now cradled a blue one. Its shining black eyes looked around with innocent discernment.

Faria smiled. "They're very pretty," she said quietly.

Feith stroked a claw over its crest. "Thank you." Even though they had only known each other for a short time, this seemed to be the most at peace Faria had seen Feith – a physicality reflected in the way the bird relaxed in her paw.

"Did you make these?" the fox asked.

"Yeah. Took spare parts from Talos' work. He…" she paused for a moment, tensing very slightly, then relented with a quiet, timid sigh. "…he wanted me to be a long-distance contact for him." She pointed up at her shoulder, and now Faria noticed the metal cables running up her neck to behind her ears, where curved, mesh-covered plates mirrored their round-tipped shape. "I was the first to be able to speak to others across distance. But he hadn't got to making anyone else I could talk to, or even himself so… I did it myself. The birds can show me what they've seen, emit signals, things like that. But for me… they mostly help make the whine of the signal quiet. It hurts a lot, some days."

She smiled gently again. "They've always been my friends. Something… I could focus on, to remind me of where I wanted to be." Her face darkened a little. "It always hurt me when I had to use them for things Talos had planned. I just wanted to see the things I was being kept from."

Faria nodded, unsure of what to say. She leant down to inspect the blue bird a little more closely. It chirruped and shifted to face her, bringing a smile to Faria.

"They're beautiful."

Feith smiled, and nodded subtly towards Faria's staff. "I think that's beautiful too."

The fox smiled as she watched the low lights of the

Coriolis shimmer in the facets of her crystal staff. Despite how she felt when using her powers, she had always found the crystals themselves to be very pretty. Even with her skilled, instinctive construction, it was impossible to separate the sensation from their lustre, and the darker facets hidden within, refracted through the glimmering outer surface. She couldn't help but be reminded of her parents. In a way these felt like reflections of the bright and complex souls she knew in them both.

A short while later, after Maaka had refilled Feith's tankard before moving to the crew deck to examine Kier, Tierenan's cubicle clicked open, and he emerged with a towel draped over his face. He wore a neat white shirt, which already had a few snags in the sleeve where he'd poked his claws through the fabric when trying to roll it above his mechanical elbows. Over that was a slate blue waistcoat with a high collar. He flexed his tail back and forth to make sure his black trouser robes fit properly. Overall he presented very nicely.

He smiled from under the towel.

"I'm all shiny now. Got rid of two years of bed-fur."

Faria responded with a mildly admonishing expression. "We *did* have people sponge you, you know. We didn't leave you to grow fungus."

He looked a little disappointed. "You mean I could have been a mushroom farm? Maybe they would have tasted like me."

"Nobody wants that," she said quickly.

"You haven't tried it," he sniffed.

"I don't like mushrooms."

He held out his arms and turned away from her dramatically. "Cannot believe the Empress of Xayall has no mycological tolerance, absolutely shameful."

She took the towel from his ears and flapped it over his snout. "Look, if you want to be eaten alive by nasty spongy undead vegetables then fine, but don't stink up my sovereign doing it, all right?" She gave him a menacing glare; he peeked his eyes round to her and stuck out his tongue, with a soft chuckle.

"*Fiiine.*"

She shook her head, and swallowed down a lump in her throat that was half laughter, half welling emotions at his return.

"I missed you," she said softly.

"I missed you too," he replied with a smile as warm as the sun through the leaves. They stood together for a second. He looked aside, trying to pull some thoughts from his chest, tugging at the roll of his right sleeve. "I knew you were there, sometimes. It was like being underwater. Or more like… being in a different room. I knew you were doing things but somehow a voice, the room itself, maybe, was telling me it didn't matter, and I didn't have to move. Until something changed, and all the voices became loud all at once. Then I *had* to move. I couldn't help it."

Feith looked up at them both, then back down. "That was probably the control chip. Wasn't repaired properly."

He gave a distasteful scrunch of his whiskers. "Yech, I'm glad to be free of that," he grimaced. "But I don't remember much overall. I had a… a vague sense of needing to be somewhere, but until you and Feith woke me up again…"

He looked at the ferret, and pulled the towel down from his head.

"Um, Faria – could you give us a minute?"

She nodded. "I'll be on the bridge with Osiris." She let her paw linger for a moment on his arm, then left the two of them together. He sat next to Feith on the bench; she withdrew, but after a few seconds she grew slightly less guilty for her own presence next to him. The timid ferret cupped her hands around the small metal flagon, staring into the water that swayed and flicked reflections of the ship's interior lighting in oblique patterns on its surface.

"How are you doing?" Tierenan asked quietly.

She froze for a second, as if the question itself were some cold application of ice down her back. She nodded, slowly. "I'm… I'm really here, right?"

He smiled. "Yeah, you are. We all are. Finally."

She gripped the flagon tightly. It shook slightly in her grip. "I… I'm s… I tried…"

He rested his claw over the mouth of her cup, breaking her focus. She turned to look at him, with shy and apologetic eyes that brimmed with tears.

"You did nothing wrong. You saved me, *again*."

She shook her head. "I did so much wrong. I watched them, over and over." She gave a wary look around as if she would be overheard, and judged. Her breathing quickened slightly and her ears flattened. "When I heard what happened to you in Xayall, I didn't know what to do. I couldn't fight. I… I thought the best way to keep them safe was to keep *him* occupied, find distractions and research for him. Thankfully… thankfully he found the dragons instead. That war in Kyrryk, and that thing from Nazreal."

She raked her claws into the back of her paw, digging them into her skin. "I didn't have your spirit. And I… wasn't sure if you…"

He gave her a soft, sideways bump with his shoulder. "Well, I didn't. Die, I mean. Unless you were about to say survive, because I did do that. I'm not a ghost, is what I mean."

A hint of laughter breathed from her nose. "I figured that much."

He took his claw from her cup and held it in his other. "You shouldn't say you're not strong, you know. Survival is strength. You put up with a lot that you never deserved. And," he said, with a much deeper level of soft sincerity, "you broke his hold over you for long enough to bring me back. And I'm… really grateful you did."

She nodded. "I had to. Out of everything, you kept me going. From the moment I met you in Skyria, you were just… one of the best things in this world. Even if… I couldn't be part of it. So I… that was my resolve. To save you."

She half-smiled at him. "When I found you in Kinuna, I thought you'd forgotten me."

He shook his head. "I never did. I… got distracted, I guess. And sleepy. I'm sorry it took so long."

She took one paw from the cup and poked him in the thigh, prompting a soft grunt of protest. "Of all people, you have nothing to apologise for."

He drew back, in fake aghast. "You didn't smell me after I got out of the cavern."

"Tierenan, I was *in* the cavern with you."

She paused.

"…you were pretty ripe."

"Thank y—hey!" he protested, immediately breaking into a laugh. He bumped against her again, and she bumped him back, laughing softly.

"Can you take me to Osiris?"

Tierenan glanced around. "He gets kind of grumpy when he's flying, but he likes me, so we're probably okay."

She sliced him a dubious sideways glance.

"He does!" the raccoon insisted. She frowned suspiciously.

"Well, ignoring that… I owe him an apology."

He tilted his head slightly and watched her expression for a few seconds. She stared towards the doorway, somewhat distant, probably trailing off in memory of the things she'd been forced to do, and he could think of which a particularly relevant one may have been. He kicked his legs off of the bench and stood in front of her, holding out his claw. Quickly she finished her water and placed the flagon gently on the bench. She took his paw in hers and he led her towards the sterncastle.

When they reached the ladder-like stair that led to it, he could see the gryphon's wing feathers swaying gently as he operated the helm. He climbed up gingerly and poked his head through. He saw Faria poring over the maps on the navigation table, then turning her attention to the window, trying to ascertain the lie of the land, which was tough in the night air, and required a good deal of her concentration.

"So we're… approaching Andarn?"

"Not for a while."

"Damn," she muttered, going back to the maps.

"Better luck next time?" Tierenan offered. She jumped, her ears and tail snapping to attention.

"Tierenan!" she barked, accidentally. "What—don't do that, for the love of stars."

He grinned, showing his gleaming white fangs. "Wakey wakey!"

She gave him a narrow-eyed glare. "You're the *last* person who should be saying that."

"Then prepare never to hear it again!" he said triumphantly, leaping up through the stairwell, before lending a hand down to Feith, who quietly pulled herself up. She shrank slightly at the sight of Osiris, whose feathers ruffled with surprise at the sight of the awoken raccoon.

"I thought I saw you among them," he said, his voice resonant even when spoken in a kinder timbre, "but I had not expected such recovery." He bowed his head. "It is good to see you awake again. Many were bereft without you."

Tierenan grinned, scratching the back of his neck. "Thanks, Osiris. For looking after Faria, too. She says you pulled her from Nazreal."

He nodded, looking to the sky ahead. "I have pulled many things from Nazreal; she is among the most valuable."

She wasn't sure if that was a compliment or not. He was still learning how to assimilate humour into conversation and it never seemed to come naturally. He was cordial even under his severity, though, and that was often enough.

"To what do I owe your company?" he asked, inviting the raccoon to introduce Feith, who was half-hiding behind him.

Tierenan marched in front of the helm, preening, and pulled Feith alongside him. She gripped her paws in front of her, trying to keep her focus on Osiris even in his imposing eminence.

"Osiris, this is Feith. Feith – Osiris Tallon, Captain of the Coriolis."

He bowed his head again, although more casually this time. "A pleasure, I hope. Tierenan has a habit of making me doubt otherwise."

"Osiris..." she started, quietly. "I... I was the one who sabotaged your ship, before the Gargantua took it away."

He kept his eyes on her but didn't move.

She raised her head, finding her voice a little. "I'm sorry," she said, with growing firmness as she felt Tierenan stand beside her, although she was still trembling. "There are many things I've done, and now I wish to undo the damage caused by them. This ship… is beautiful. And shouldn't have been harmed the way it was."

The gryphon let out a soft breath through his nose. "It is one of my greatest treasures," he said, with a wistful nod of his head. "However, at the time, the mission, and our cargo, were far more imperative. I am glad to see you have turned to a nobler path."

She scrunched her muzzle, in a sign of self-dissatisfaction. "I wasn't always able to help. My… the person who kept me was the only structure I had ever known. A kind of… comfort, I think," she muttered, "even an unwelcome one." Her tail curled around her leg. "I'm… not proud of what I had to do."

The gryphon looked to the horizon again. "You make it sound like resistance is easy." He glanced back down to her with a piercing sincerity. "Believe me, it is not. When you must contend with the safety of yourself, of those around you, most of us at some point will wrestle with decisions that we rue for not having made them more quickly. It is a dreadful hindsight that screams in our ears until the root of it has been thoroughly absolved."

His voice softened. "Some never get that opportunity. But for what you have done," he continued, rolling back his shoulders, "you should be proud. Every step taken against a force far greater than yourself is one taken with our truest heart. A lack of opportunity does not indicate a lack of strength."

She nodded, letting her death grip on her paws release softly.

"Thank you, Osiris."

"I trust these current birds of yours align with your feelings."

She nodded.

"Good. They are masterful in construction, even if I am still wary of what they are capable of."

The ferret let the blue bird land on her claw, while the other perched on the wheel for Osiris to inspect more closely. "They contain sonic amplifiers that can cause microfractures in metallic and resonance structures, affecting the energy flow in very specific ways."

Faria and Osiris looked to each other in shared ignorance, and a rather tired bewilderment. Feith straightened, finding her confidence in her knowledge. "I knew where your ship was vulnerable thanks to an old journal Talos stole from Skyria."

The gryphon grunted ruefully. "Another plundered relic undeserving of their control."

Faria laid her paw gently on the wheel. "Maybe we can convince the Draik to recover it for us?"

Osiris said nothing, staring over the sky beyond.

Before too long, the long night demanded its toll of sleep, so Faria and Tierenan disappeared below deck to heed its demand for time. Osiris wasn't alone, though. He found a strangely willing companion in the ferret, who kept poring over the maps and looking at the dials on the console. Her ability to sleep was greatly hampered by anxiety of the dark. She wasn't used to such a calm ambience of friendliness, and wanted instead to busy herself in study where Osiris would allow. She ran her paws over the panels, analysed joins, kept looking over at the aerofoils in the mast and sails in analytical wonder, all lit by the softly shining moon above them.

He watched her with burgeoning curiosity and regard until, finally, she spoke.

"Where are we heading?" she asked quietly.

"Xayall. It is safest there till we can regroup."

She looked ahead, in silent acknowledgement of her

destination, a new venture away from Talos, and instead alongside Tierenan. As she had wanted a long time ago.

The gryphon took in her quiet timidity and curiosity and, just as she turned back to the table, asked her a question.

"Have you ever piloted a ship?"

She shook her head.

He curled a claw in a gesture for her to come closer, and motioned to the wheel. "You may have read her journal, but nothing will teach you more than taking the helm for yourself."

He kept hold of one of the spokes as she gingerly pressed her paw to another, keeping it steady as she felt the weight of its resistance, and grew accustomed to the vibrations of flight.

"It… feels so powerful…"

He smiled. "It is. She built it that way."

Chapter Ten

Even in the Coriolis' familiarity, Faria found herself wracked with discomforting chills and the creeping doubt that safety or rest would be truly available anytime soon. She couldn't even answer *why* specifically, but the fear, the expectation of being chased, remained like a maw over her shoulder. She tossed and curled in her bed in the cabin, feeling like the dark was reaching out with skeletal fingers to pluck her from the ship and drag her beneath the ground. She sat up a few times to get her bearings, observe the room, and try to comfort herself in a mantra of familiarity. Aeryn and Kyru. Kier. Tierenan. The ship, still stable and in the air.

But it wasn't enough. The haunting spectre of a voice, glowing eyes, and metal claws that already felt like they were clamping around her throat. It wanted her, or her life. It crawled over her skin like a chill shadow, seeping over her fur like spilt blood, leaving her unable to breathe, her fur in electrical pricks of discomfort, and a gaping nausea in her stomach. Worse, to look at the moon felt like staring into the eye of nothingness. She could see the scar of its ancient meteoric impact that brought the resonance crystals to Eeres as if it were a spider web before a silver void, beyond which yawed like a terrifying, blank oblivion.

She threw herself out of the bed, pulled her jacket back on, and traipsed back up to the sterncastle with apprehensive fatigue. The gryphon gave her a respectful bow as she entered. She jolted slightly, realising he was not at the helm.

Feith was.

The ferret gripped the wheel with a look that was all at once fascination, determination, and terror, while Osiris stretched out on the navigation table, flexing his claws free of their tiredness.

"I'm surprised you are not waking up Tierenan," he said to the fox, nonchalant about the ferret having shocked Faria to silence with her new position as pilot.

"He—uh, yeah, no." She shook her head and found her words again as they settled into place. "This is *actual* sleep he's getting now. I won't rob him of that."

She looked to Feith, and smiled. "The helm is a good look on you."

The ferret gave her an energetic look in return, with a shadow of a smile under her inscrutably overstimulated expression.

Osiris chuckled. "You can take a break if you so wish."

She glanced between him and the sky ahead thoughtfully, then nodded, stepping back while still gripping the spokes of the wheel. He stood and took it from her. She rubbed her paws, residual excitement still flowing through her.

"Thank you, Osiris."

"Most welcome," he replied.

She gave Faria a quick, off-guard smile, before disappearing below.

Faria leant on her muzzle on the navigation table, looking at the gryphon with a soft, admiring expression.

"I know that face," he said, a little nonplussed. "Your father wore that face when he was about to say something heart-warming."

"You don't like heart-warming? For shame, Osiris."

He tutted, and allowed himself a roll of his eyes. "I am not made of ice and stone. She has a very acute mind and already rudimentarily understands the ship's systems well. She might do well as a navigator or engineer, in truth."

"She has the freedom to be either or both, now."

"It remains my hope that we should all find such a place in our lives," he murmured wistfully, keeping the ship tight in his claws.

Faria smiled, closing her eyes once more.

When she woke, she had been tucked under the navigation table, and light was streaming in through the sterncastle windows. She winced and grumbled, rolling over to pull her jacket over her head.

"Where?" she drawled, attempting to say more words but ultimately losing them in her transition from one side to the other while wrestling to keep the sun from her face for a few minutes more.

"About to begin our descent to Xayall. I will try to keep it steady, but I regretfully suggest you are awake for the landing."

She groaned and shoved herself gently out from under the table. Her whiskers were a mess and her ears were moved somewhat sporadically as fresh noises of transit, descent, and people moving below deck wormed their way into them before her brain could identify what was going on. She ran her paws over her face and picked herself up, a little unsteadily, and wondered if the crew had put anything together for food in the galley yet.

Her quest for culinary satisfaction would have to wait

though, as only moments after she was standing, the ship began its downward trail towards her city. She watched it get closer and closer, till it disappeared behind treetops and the Coriolis touched down in the long, straight reservoir that had been built alongside the city walls to berth it. It wasn't a rough landing, but her addling lack of awokenness added more disorientation to her motion than normal, and she had to save herself from a rapid reunion with the floor by way of the navigation table again.

Once appropriately manoeuvred into the dock, the crew lowered the gangway to let Faria and her retinue disembark. Her plan was to head to the Tor's kitchens, or maybe find a closer-by tavern to drop into.

The appearance of Henryk, the staunch, scarred wolf who was Captain of the Xayall Guard, at the end of the dock, threw that plan into the fire with rather devastating speed.

He saluted smartly as she approached; she gestured back, evidently giving away her tiredness and hunger a little too succinctly, as he gave her a slightly awkward and apologetic look. Something in his expression worried her though, moreso than the visible discomfort at still sporting his winter fur in full plate armour (she had expected to see him in his sleeker charcoal coat by now). The hollow in her chest deepened. She knew it was her first trip out after being fully recovered, but hadn't expected a significant security briefing on her return.

He bowed his head. "Your Imperial Majesty," he said reverently.

"Captain Henryk," she replied. Behind her Tierenan was marvelling at the walls, while Feith clung to his arm. "Is... everything alright?"

"Largely yes, the city is safe. However..."

Her ears pinned back in concern.

"…your father's tomb was vandalised." He spoke with shame in his voice, very clearly taking personal responsibility for the oversight to security and her respect.

Her paw tightened around her staff. Behind her Osiris was just as livid and she could hear his wings bristling. Before she could even speak, the gryphon pushed forwards.

"I am presuming by your quieted shame," he rumbled, with a storm of anger in his voice, "that you do not know the reason or origin of this disgraceful malice."

Henryk pushed his shoulders back a little. "We don't. It wasn't a place we've had to monitor before. If you—"

Osiris shoved past him immediately. Faria turned back to the rest, already beginning a hurried step to follow him. "Meet me in the Tor, please."

Tierenan moved his paw as if to reach out for her, but let it drop to his side instead.

Faria gave chase to Osiris, whose stride was bigger and more powerful than hers. Henryk accompanied her, whether out of duty or guilt or some mix of both. She was glad for someone a little more removed from her personal feelings than perhaps Tierenan may have been, though she knew Osiris was equally as dedicated to his ire and anguish as she was, if not moreso. The pit in her stomach kept gnawing, eating further as thoughts roiled about what the state of her father's resting place would be. What she might see, what she was already being forced to relive in the memory of his death.

They turned the corner and blustered past the guards of the Tor's southern walls, who barely had time to salute Osiris – not that he paid them any attention anyway – before he disappeared into the gardens where the mausoleum stood.

Faria's blood ran cold. Despite the peace of the gardens the building lay in, it reminded her a little too much of Nazreal in some ways, the deafening silence of expectation and legacy hanging in words left unspoken, and slowly, in time, forgotten.

The building itself was a similar design to the Tor. Sleek, angular, with stonework both carved and formed to accentuate its design. She'd never spent much time looking at it, but now it was an almost willing distraction to what lay within, and she found herself tracing her gaze along its contours, following the story of the reliefs and repeating patterns that lay just underneath the domed and vaulted roof sections.

All too soon, however, she came to the door and the ascending steps to its halls. Looming above her, she caught the tip of Osiris' wings disappearing under its yawning mouth of an archway, and could already see the cold stonework within.

The chamber of the mausoleum opened up before her as she reached the stairs' apex. Rows of Xayall leaders and their families lay in sarcophagi mounted into the walls, carved reliefs of their likeness and achievements on each slab. They lay in relative familial groups, those who had them – though her lineage was not complicated by any means. At the very end, in the larger domed atrium where she had laid Aidan to rest some two years ago, she saw Osiris standing before where his crypt had been. Her footsteps slowed, but she continued on, while the void in her chest grew exponentially. On the ground lay hacked and broken stone, flecks of metal from the inlaid gold and silver that highlighted the faces, achievements, or clothing of those within. For all its forlorn remembrance she had found her father's to be a very touching tribute when she had first seen it. She tried to fix her eyes on the debris and not what the sundered stone revealed beyond. But investigation demanded she know, and had to keep the glances towards her father's interred body brief. The first time she shut her eyes reflexively and flinched. Fighting through her tightened jaw and dizzying chill she forced her eyes to open again.

Clawmarks within the sarcophagus. His body had been moved. The mask and layers of cloth that hid most of his form had been displaced, then hurriedly thrown back across him again. Anger and grief welled up in her throat again that she had to breathe away. Her staff shuddered as she strained to hold herself up on it.

Henryk reached out an arm to support her, but she shook her head and silently bolstered herself.

The gryphon bore a cold, distant stare at the scene before him, analysing it in sharp and hard discernment.

"And you have nothing on who did this?" he muttered to Henryk.

The wolf bowed his head. "Nothing. We know it occurred sometime between yesterday evening and first light today, but nobody was seen entering, leaving, or bearing any signs of desecration."

He rested his paw on the pommel of his sword. "We did, as a matter of urgency, redress His Imperial Majesty as best we could, and have alerted the stoneworkers to repair it as soon as possible. However... I thought it prudent that you might need to see, given your history, and ability."

Osiris flinched, but rescinded his attempt to admonish the Captain. It had been Faria's choice to give the information about her powers, and Nazreal's history, to him upon his return after the siege, and allow someone else a degree of knowledge that could safeguard their intent. Faria nodded thankfully, and looked more closely at the broken tomb. It didn't show signs of being hammered with tools. There was dust, but it looked like it had been cracked in a single blow somehow, but not with something that left a visible impact crater. No chips of metal, burnt sparks, burs, not even a hint of blood or clothing to suggest what it could have been done by. All of the evidence, or the distinct lack of it, painted a deeply disturbing picture. She looked at the rest of the tombs for other signs.

Above Aidan's body was the grave of her mother Kaya, still pristine, and thankfully so. To their left were the graves of two other figures she now knew well. One was a fennec, Elysser, upon whose relief was a golden hand-axe and small shield, as well as a shining city reminiscent of Xayall. The other was a gryphon, and a series of mechanical reliefs in honour of Teratai, even though her body had never been here to inter.

They all seemed untouched.

Henryk glanced between them both. "Have you any thoughts to direct us?"

Osiris scowled, a thunderous expression that spoke of a growing, likely adirectional rage that would find anyone remotely under suspicion to come to the swift point of a blade. Faria felt more concerned by the implications than the desecration itself. She shook her head.

"He had nothing interred with him. I can… only think it was someone raging against me, maybe. If word of the unrest, or my contact with Draik returned to Xayall before I did."

Henryk leant down a little. "Empress Faria, if I might ask… did anyone *know* he wasn't buried with anything of interest?" he asked, looking knowingly to her staff.

She froze. Osiris turned his head towards them, and his body followed after.

"His staff would be a powerful artefact. Especially if it is known that *you* no longer carry it."

She held her arms out. "It's broken! All that's left in it is the mostly-depleted crystal, and that—"

"Might be the prospective thief's only chance to get hold of some," he interjected.

She narrowed her eyes. "You... think it's another resonator?"

His tail flicked stiffly from side to side. "In all my years, I have known *one* conflict that has outlasted all others in both time and in their depths of violence. Dhraka hunted and exploited resonators at every opportunity, even before that mongrel Vionaika and Kura allied with them against you. They may have sought others since then to align with their goals of supremacy. But if their caches are raided or under guard thanks to Kyrryk and Draik, the only other place to find crystal easily would be here."

"Or Nazreal itself."

"Hence why we resealed it once you were back up to strength."

It was not enough to assuage her worries. "It's only stone and sandstorms. A determined group could find a way inside again." Thankfully she had always kept her father's staff within close reach, when she was able. Right now it was on the Coriolis. And she was even more thankful that her ancestor Elysser's resonance weapon was far less known, only to herself and Osiris.

She ran a paw roughly over her head in exasperation. "Thank you Henryk. There's not much we can do except repair this mess. Increase the guards around the Tor, the ship, and here. And um... be vigilant," she added with a sigh.

The wolf bowed his head in solemn reverence. "Of course, Empress Faria."

She gave a lingering look to the crypt of her father, then turned back towards the entrance, and the sun that beamed into it.

"I need some breakfast..."

Chapter Eleven

The kitchen staff in the Tor were given a run for their gold by Tierenan, whose enthusiasm for their ability and ingredients was an energy mostly unparalleled in recent months. Faria returned to find them being grilled by the young raccoon, who seemed immediately eager to catch up with every last mouthful he had missed in his catatonia. She had a feeling he might have ended up balloon-shaped if Aeryn hadn't politely calmed down his ambitions. He opted for a salad of roasted nuts and fish, and had already dipped into the offerings of appetisers that had been brought forward to herald their arrival home. It was a scene that heartened her despite the cloud of uncertainty hanging beyond the dining hall's walls.

Once the food arrived, the words all but ceased, replaced with (mostly) quiet appreciation for well-crafted sustenance, aside from the odd moment or two where Tierenan ate a little too enthusiastically and had to be forcibly reminded about his ability to breathe.

Having survived to eat another meal, he leant back in his chair with his paws behind his head, and let out a long, whistling sigh.

"Never knew I could miss food so much."

"Never knew you could miss your *mouth* so much," Kyru muttered next to him, glancing at the raccoon's radius of crumbs while hooking some meat fibres out from between his fangs with a claw. "Surprised your tongue isn't down there too."

In reply, the raccoon stuck his out as far as he could, making a '*blllllll*' noise, and grinning triumphantly. Kyru eyed him for a moment, then snapped his fingers up, and caught the offending organ between his pawtips. Tierenan laughed awkwardly, his grin turning from one of triumph to a little of bashfulness, and optimism for mercy.

"Point that at me again, and I'll use it to polish my armour."

"I gon'k schink zhack'll ge goog schor your argnour."

Kyru's eyes narrowed. "It's not about the results, it's about the punishment."

"Thair enough."

Kyru released Tierenan's tongue. The raccoon sucked it back in quickly, and licked his lips in a distasteful grimace. "Ugh, your paws are rough."

Kyru smiled, leaning back in his own chair. "Years of practice."

Tierenan's eyes narrowed. "Being prickly, you mean?"

The wolf blinked at him, slowly. "Sword fighting."

"Oh. *Tactically* prickly."

Kyru huffed and rolled his eyes. "Look, my prickliness is to your benefit, you steel nuisance. Helped get you all out of trouble one way or another."

Tierenan preened at his nickname, finding immense pride in it. "Thank you, I'm good now," he said with a grin, patting Kyru's elbow.

Feith looked at Tierenan with entranced caution, knowing

how comfortable he was, and had always been, in more or less any space he occupied. She wondered if she would be able to do that someday, or if she'd remain forever quiet.

Maybe if she asked to—

"Hey," Tierenan said quickly, standing, before pausing and remembering himself a little. "Can… we go for a walk? I kind of… want to see the outside a bit more. I miss trees."

Kier and Osiris both looked at Faria to grant permission. She saw the soft brightness in the raccoon's face and smiled, pushing her resignation away for now.

"Yeah," she said softly. "Let's take in the sun a little."

Osiris stood a little more stiffly. "I need to re-provision the Coriolis and check our battery reserves. We should be fine for a few more trips but this has been the most intensive flight it has seen since the fall of Nazreal," he said, not in admonishment, but it made Faria a little wary nonetheless.

"You don't…" she started, before letting out the rest of her prepared words as a sigh.

He tilted his head.

She lifted her eyes back up to him. "You don't have to go immediately, Osiris. You've been on the ship for days. Come with us."

A gruff noise reverberated in his throat that seemed to infer reproach both for himself and a potential lack of caution for developing situations.

"I… as you like, Faria," he replied quietly.

Tierenan grinned and pushed himself up from the table by his metal claws, rattling them as he stood. Kier also rose, albeit with more reserve.

"I have to do some of the reporting to the clerks, and see if any news of Pthiris has come this way yet. There'll be administrative damage control to do for our escape, I'm sure."

He looked to Osiris. "And I'll see to it that the ship is restocked as well."

Faria's paw clenched with guilt, forgetting the paperwork of political disobedience. "Ah… do you need me to come too?"

A soft laugh bubbled from his lips. "No, and I mean this with the utmost respect, Faria – I don't think it would do the situation any good, you nor the clerks. It's just… preparedness at this point."

Her jaw stiffened a little, but she acquiesced and dismissed him with another nod.

"Alright," she said quietly. "Thank you."

Around the opposite side of the Tor to the mausoleum were the stables, in which were kept the impressive beasts used for transport: the Elasmotherians, four-legged reptilian beasts with squat tails and powerful muscles, and the Theriasaurs, the more slender, bipedal creatures with short, sharp front claws, a whip-like tail, long necks and sharp, discerning eyes. They were immensely different, but docile and enjoying each others' company, with the Elasmotherians' sloping faces making them look placidly up at the Theriasaurs' more alert posture. Occasionally the bulkier beasts would bray with low, rumbling cries, and shake their haunches, with the bony ridge running along their back shaking the thin layer of feather-like fur that covered their bodies. The Theriasaurs also shook in response, their finer, sleek feathers preened back, and small tufts of feathers poking from the crest of their heads.

Faria leant on the fence as she watched them, with Tierenan to one side and Feith standing quietly by him, watching the creatures with great interest. With them, but less focused on the creatures, were Aeryn and Kyru, who talked between each other and kept an eye on anyone passing by.

"I'm kind of jealous," Faria said quietly. "Simple work, free food, constant companionship…"

Tierenan held out his hands demonstratively as he hung onto the rail by his armpits. "I mean, when people aren't trying to kill you, the only thing you *don't* have is the simple work."

She gave him a spurious sideways glance. "Oh yeah, that makes it so much more worth it."

"Sorry Faria, your only choices are labour or murder, that's how it goes."

She scowled, sinking her muzzle to the fence. "I don't want this. There's absolutely a third choice somewhere."

Kyru spread his arms in a wide shrug. "You could abdicate. Give the authority to someone else."

She frowned, looking down. "You've seen the kind of people who take power for themselves though. Nobody who takes it deserves it, and those who deserve it don't deserve what other people do to them for using it responsibly."

Osiris bristled a little beside them.

"The idea was to create a world where stability was accessible to everyone. It might not have erased greed or malice, but it would have removed a deal of its network to propagate. That is what we intended Nazreal to be."

Faria scrunched her muzzle. "I'm sorry it didn't work out that way."

"I cannot change it, nor can it be restored the way it was, but… now, at least, I have a degree of hope for something new. I have spent rather too long in pursuit of the past, though I think as equally it has been pursuing me." His voice held a genuine core of hope to it, though Faria could tell his tiredness was greater than he would ever admit.

She smiled to him; he looked a little surprised at the

expression, and quirked his brow.

"What?"

"Nothing," she replied. "Just... glad to have you here."

A gentle puff of air snorted from his nostrils, paired with a hint of a smile at the edge of his beak. "You are very kind, Faria."

"*I'm* kind? You've been protecting my family for a hundred lifetimes!"

He dipped his head from side to side. "More like eighty."

"That's still a *lot* of lifetimes, Osiris! It's okay to just... want to be somewhere and enjoy the time you have."

Another snort of air. "Maybe someday," he relented eventually, softly, staring into a distance somewhere. His head drifted back round to look at Faria. "I... I will look forward to it."

She replied with a smile of her own, just Aeryn appeared next to her, and drew her focus away. In the wolf's hand was a white canvas sack about the length of her forearm. She shook it lightly; the Elasmotherians lumbered over, their large spade-shaped snouts snuffling closely with deep investigation.

"Where did you get that?!" Tierenan marvelled, eyes wide, watching the creatures eagerly focus on the wolf.

She laughed softly as she held out her paw flat, with a handful of feed crumbs on her palm. "Just talked to the stablehand. Here."

She poured some into his metal claw, which he flattened as carefully as possible. The reptile sniffed and nudged, then curled a thick and sticky tongue over his palm and scooped up the pellets.

"*It's so gross!*" he shrieked quietly, with a wide grin. "I love them..."

He immediately took another handful and placed it on

Feith's palms, pulling her gently to the fence. She froze as the creature looked at her with a head almost as big as her torso.

"Uhh…" she murmured, her knees shaking slightly.

It snuffled over her paws, then gently took the food from her, leaving her palms with a few crumbs and a lot of bovine-reptilian saliva. She looked at her hands in a mix of wonder and disgust.

"That was…"

Tierenan grinned.

"…fun," she finished, with a smile of her own, before shaking her paws and wiping them on the fence.

"You want to do it again?" the raccoon offered brightly.

"No thank you."

Faria rested her head on the fence, listening to them softly. This was what she wanted, what she had to protect. Peace, happiness, innocence. All the things that people like Rynkath, Raikali and Fulkore saw as unnecessary or weak. She had to be ready.

There was no other choice.

Something tugged at her sleeve.

She rolled her head round to be greeted by the shy form of Feith, whose birds were perched on each of her shoulders, looking around with sharp, inquisitive motions.

"Faria?" she asked quietly. "I need your help."

The fox's brow furrowed and she tilted her head. "Of course, Feith. What do you need?"

The ferret bounced softly on her feet for a moment, taking in a big, swelling breath, looking briefly up to the sky as if to mentally confirm whether the question even had the right to be asked, before looking back at Faria.

"I want to save the rest of them. The children Talos stole. The ones I… helped steal," she finished shamefully, looking aside.

Faria laid a paw softly on her shoulder. Feith looked shyly back to her till their eyes met; she saw the fox's gaze held with kind resolve – even in her shyness, it matched her own desire to see her debt redeemed against her inescapable complicity.

"We'll save them, Feith. I promise." She looked up to the Tor. "In fact…"

Chapter Twelve

The dark tunnel roared. Wind, stale and empty, howled around the carriage's body while the rumble and screech of metal rails rang beneath it. Talos' deep scowl had been worn down to a darkened expression of sombre rage, one that faced against the fast-piercing darkness as he drove the machine through the underground passage.

Geological instability around Dhraka alone made the passage that had once supplied Kyrryk with weapons and smuggled resonance artefacts a conduit on borrowed time. It felt even more desolate to the wolverine now, between the pools of orange light created by dim crystalline torches, fuelled by anger at Pthiris' disastrous attempts at political grandstanding, instead of steady, clandestine progress.

This would be his final journey along here. After this trip he would remain in Dhraka and build from there, but first his work had to be moved. All of it. He'd known time was of the essence from the very moment the cards began to fall away from Dhraka's grip. The Molten King was his last bastion of uncompromising brutality: both in the King's own aims and in allowing whatever needed to be done to protect his assets. There had been no qualms whenever more children were rounded up for his trials, even if he dismissed the venture as unnecessary in comparison to his intended assaults.

Finally up ahead he spotted a growing point of light. Forges' roaring flames cast the approaching platform in the strong orange of industrial labour. He wrenched back the lever to his right – in response the carriage shrieked and began a rising shudder as it decelerated, quicker and quicker. He released it gently, then gave shorter, stern punches of it to bring his transport to a hissing, grinding halt at the granite concourse, then wrenched shut all of the valves that fed the engine. Teams of receiving dragons immediately began working on the freight that had been loaded – not nearly as much stacked as there should have been, but Talos was past that point of resentment now.

He stormed through the lower level of the forges: a massive, craterous cavern dug high and deep within the Dhrakan central mountain range. Geothermal rivers of laval flow made heating them easy and the metalwork quicker, which had been a boon for The Molten King's aspirations.

Above Talos were the large metal walkways spanning between smelters that belched heat into the chamber. Their spouts hung over channels to create plates of hardened metal, ferried after their formation through the wide doorway at the cave's edge to supply the efforts of their massive, and somewhat accelerated, renewal of construction. Talos would have been prouder of the work he took from the captured journals were he not currently preoccupied with his own humiliation and the safe harbour of his stolen children.

He had to report to The Molten King. Talos knew him well already, but as important as the pretence of his enigma was, he also knew the fiery lack of mercy was very real. If he did not approach things carefully it could result in him taking the fall for the disaster in Pthiris. The more projects that neared completion, the more Talos' necessity was reaching its expiration. Engineers of war machines were only useful up until the conquest. Spies were only needed to exploit advantages until they were taken. If that didn't happen soon, Talos would once again need to skulk through the darkness to find an outlet for his research.

He swept past guards who recognised his authority, giving him acknowledgement but no obstacle, as he reached the large set of midnight-blue-steel doors through which The Molten King conducted his reign.

"Open!" he called to the teams of guards. The dragons, three per side, grunted into action, winching open the doors enough for the wolverine to slip through, then reversed the process to let the doors boom shut, leaving Talos in a chamber of mostly oppressive, hot darkness.

Ahead stood a large throne. Its contours of hewn and molten metal glinted in the quiet, almost fearfully reverent luminance of the crystal torches. At the heart of the throne was a winged mass, whose neck hung slightly to one side. Above its hanging head was a broken wing with its membrane burnt away, now merely a frozen, skeletal remnant of what once, with its remaining twin, might have carried the creature's body into the sky.

The harsh, rasping breaths of the broken tyrant ripped into the room's deadened ambience. It was like preparing to be devoured.

An eye opened, piercing yellow.

"You're early," came the hoarse rumble, similar to dragging a rusty saw blade across a stone. It was more dismissive than accusational, a clear sign of contempt which Talos had come to accept in his dealings and perception from The Molten King, who saw machines as weapons but the wielders of them to be the true warriors, rather than their architects. The wolverine bowed his head in perfunctory respect, though he held a comparable disdain for the dragon for the opposite reason – that blunt force was often reckless when applied too liberally, and that a machine or augmentation with a speciality could outperform any living thing by itself. The machine made the warrior, not the other way round. That was why he, and his work, were so important. It was their impasse, a mutual disrespect that forged a strangely coherent independence from each other, with an implicit acknowledgement that the other was still reluctantly necessary to complete their aims.

"Yes, Molten King." Even the epithet he was forced to use sounded bilious coming from his muzzle. "There was a disturbance in Pthiris."

The King's eye rolled his way. "She escaped, didn't she?"

Talos' paw clenched, metal claws dug into his palm. "Yes."

Not a sigh, not a growl, more like a shifting of rock rumbled from within the dragon King's chest.

"I warned them it would not be enough to be sly. They need to be *extinguished.*"

Talos tutted under his breath before composing himself to respond. "We were moving as we could under scrutiny of Shadow's Claw being discovered. I had warned you about the lack of resources for those ships and the delays it would cause."

The King's neck shifted, pulling his head lop-sidedly up like a half-broken marionette to loom a little higher in the flickering half-light. Something dripped from his maw. "These have been in construction since before the pyramid tanks. I know the capability of that wretched flying golden atrocity." he growled, with each word like a regurgitation of something abhorrent. "You were the one who set delays in motion by insisting on turning those forsaken starvelings into spies instead. Where has that brought you?"

The dragon's eye cast over Talos once again. "You don't even have your other one, do you?"

Talos gnarled and twisted his head in reluctant, rageful defeat. "The Empress freed them both. It's only a matter of time before they make an advance towards us. If your plan for supremacy is to succeed, you need these to remain in your control so we can work on them. They have to be moved."

The King leant forwards slightly, allowing his head to loll and both his eyes to become visible. Or, the single eye, and the shining, glassy cavity that remained where the other used to glare from. "All this time that you've had, scientist, what did you produce? A soldier who defected after a single battle. A resonance gun given to a vainglorious brat who couldn't fight. A silent waif to serve as your shadow." He drew closer, looming taller in the dark, his voice rumbling louder, spitting, gurgling in its boiling rage. "The only thing you provided of any substance was Raikali's prosthesis. If you are to have any usefulness to me, then you will finish the repairs to my body and throw yourself back into construction of the Skypiercer."

Talos shied down slightly, gritting his teeth. "You... don't understand the importance of—"

"I *do not care* about your whimpering pests!" The King roared, flecking something thick from his maw at the wolverine. "Either you complete your work for me or your corpse will feed the forge and provide the sole utility I will have seen from you in two dark years."

Talos' claws rattled as their metal joints tightened. Rivulets of blood brimmed at the points of his talons as they dug into his paws. "Your body is near complete! My... my research—"

A claw swept from the darkness and took him by his

jacket, pulling him closer. The dragon's maw oozed; the stench of burnt scales and acidic, bloody breath permeated the air between them. "Let me warn you one final time," The King gravelled. "*I* am the reason you are alive. Do as I say and complete me."

Something shifted in the darkness beyond the King's tail.

A small figure, almost skeletal, barely visible except for the glowing lustre of a pair of sickly green eyes and the shimmering threads of the same ichorous green light covering what was left of a body.

"Who is this?"

"You know me very well, Talos," came a voice with a light but silken, gravelly tone, like water rushing over pebbles, and a cadence very familiar. Despite their smaller size, the malice in their tone was almost more piercing than the King's. Surgical. Honed.

Hungry.

He furrowed his brow trying to peer into the darkness at the emaciated, knifelike figure of stretched and bound skin. They looked reconstructed, held together by the seams that the glowing threads travelled along. His eyes narrowed.

"Who…?"

"She's coming for the children?" the voice asked, softly, but with a danger that set the darkness alight with electricity.

"I… believe so," Talos replied, with a pounding in his chest that a wrong answer might be the last he ever gave. "It will… only be a matter of time." A smile flashed with green-hued teeth. "Good. Let her have her perceived victory. It will be the key to her downfall."

Talos' eyes widened.

"*You…*"

He tensed in the dragon's grip. As more of her strange

form became visible he wanted to draw himself away. Even with the bodies he'd sewn together, nothing had matched the strange nature of hers. Between the dark and melted creatures it was like being held halfway into a grave, with inhabitants from somewhere else staring hungrily at the body he wasn't sure he'd get to keep.

"How?" he rasped.

A sharp snort rushed from her nostrils. "I escaped death once at the paws of the Arc'hantaels – the second time was much the same. A folding-in of power as they destroyed the world around me." Her face scrunched, and her voice took on a glassy, growling tone. "This time I was left with far less of myself, and a body I had to scavenge from the dust."

Talos remained tense, trying to reel his body away from them both, but The Molten King was still forbiddingly strong.

"Will you take Nazreal again?"

The strange, familiar newcomer's visage shifted to a grin. "In a way." Her claws flexed, and a thin, skeletal tail rattled behind her with a slight echo of vibrating glass. "It will become a vessel for something greater than the sum of all of us," she oozed. "What I need first is my catalyst."

"Catalyst?" he groaned, jolted by the King's flaring grip as he turned to face her.

The dragon's eye narrowed and a rivulet of that viscous, dark liquid landed on the floor with a disgusting splat. "You didn't find it?"

The creature's look turned resentful. "No. That's why I need her." She reached a claw forward, long, needle-like, and pressed it delicately to the underside of Talos' chin. "Continue your work. She will take me directly to what I need."

She drew back, and looked up at the ceiling, although seemed to be focusing past it. "The Moon sleeps."

Her eyes flared with hunger. "But soon, I will wake it."

Chapter Thirteen

The forests of Draik looked much like any other from across the river. Faria stood at a bridgehead behind the wooden walls that had been erected after the Dhrakan siege, looking out over the land that stretched beyond Xayall's borders and, just beyond that, into the land from which the dragons had invaded.

On the other side of the bridge were Draik soldiers, each carrying long javelins and shields. They weren't threatening Faria's group – far from it. They had been hailed, greeted, and offered rations, which they politely accepted. They had not taken the Coriolis this time: another source of Osiris' consternation. Faria had worried not only that it would be more necessary for an escape, but also that the fuel reserves were not as optimal as Osiris had hoped, allowing for maybe another long flight or two before it would need to recharge, and she would need to spend time studying how to do that. The last such service was done by Kaya within the year that she died, and although the ship had only flown after finding Faria in Andarn, each trip was exhaustive on the ancient vehicle. When the first set of power cores had died on its way to Nazreal, Osiris had been lucky enough to have had a second to replace them with. Faria had yet to recharge either.

As such, the journey had been long, quiet, and rather tense via carriage, with the anxious tension heightened by Osiris' growing misgivings and loud, angry silences between whatever few words he chose to rumble. The vehicles they'd ridden in were drawn to one side of the new 'road', which was more of a rough clearing of foliage allowing enough egress for a beast-drawn vehicle to access. Not much, but it did what it needed.

Osiris flexed his wings behind Faria, ill at ease with the Dhrakan soldiers across the river. He had killed many in his time, before and after Nazreal, and even with open allyship between Draik and Xayall it was a situation he found himself reticent to fully engage in, but compelled to witness. His beak clicked in frustration as he surveyed the forest. "I told you what happened the last time someone close to me insisted on attending Dhrakan lands." He watched as one of the Draik soldiers pointed at something in the forest behind them with a spear, a move that made the gryphon's wings briefly flex. "This time the land is contested. We don't know this Molten King or his methods. There are more unknowns here than in a previous lifetime."

Faria nodded thoughtfully. "Yes. But we have more allies than before, more knowledge of what we need to achieve." She looked up at him. "I don't want to lose this opportunity. *You* might be able to fight and fly your way from one encounter to the next, but I can't." She gripped her staff, in a sort of resentful comfort. "Not anymore, anyway."

Faria knew it was a risk. She knew it well enough that she had shed the formal attire she had been trapped in by the unscheduled diversion to Rynkath's fortress, and instead donned a more practical set of robes – more importantly, accented with armour. A shining silver breastplate and fully-plated legs were an unusual weight for her, but thanks to the skill of Xayall's fine armourers, and some secret refinement with her resonance abilities, it was a similar quality to that which shielded the Coriolis – light, and strong. Gold edging along its contours caught the light like seams of sun.

To spearhead the charge, she would need all the protection she could muster. Despite her abilities, she was still mortal.

"This is a rescue mission, not a negotiation," she said eventually. "I'm trying to break their control." She looked to Feith. "And help a friend. This is the only chance we have to set things right."

After a reluctant sigh, Osiris turned away to lean against one of the carriages, which swayed rather alarmingly with nobody inside to bolster it against his weight.

"I hope they are swift. We have to know our destination as precisely as possible, and each moment drags Pthiris closer to our doors once more."

She didn't disagree, and the rolling grey skies above weren't doing her optimism any favours. Noises in the distance kept tweaking at her ears, pulling her concentration or alarm into images of impending conflict. Even with the presence of Kyru, Aeryn, Tierenan, Kier, and Feith alongside, and the regular station of the Xayall guards on this section of the border, problems had a way of making themselves overflow into any space she happened to be in at any given moment.

She paced between the bridge gate and the carriages, where Tierenan and Feith sat inside with their snouts poking through the open door, while flanked by Aeryn and Kyru. Kier was mostly a silent observer on top of one of the neighbouring transports, casting his gaze out further than any others were able to see thanks to his abilities. The sky rolled along, dimming slightly as the afternoon wore on. Just as Faria was about to suggest making camp, Kier stood to attention. Faria whipped her head round and saw the Draik on the opposite bank drawing to attention as four dragons strode through the trees: one with brown-black scales, horns and spines of gold and a partially-closed eye thanks to a facial scar; two shorter, red dragons who looked a good degree younger and less weathered; and one of purple and white, under whose dark grey armour were layers of hide and fleece. She was the one taking the lead. Osiris strode away from the carriage immediately, and Faria swore she heard a dark, rumbling breath roll from him as he drew behind her, but couldn't be sure it wasn't just the open breeze, or some other distant sound. Eager to put personal complications out of her mind, she met the dragons with a smart, sincere bow.

She had underestimated how difficult a breastplate made that.

The purple dragon bowed her head in subtle, but formal reply to them both. She was similar in build to Riemu, although a little taller, bulkier, had as many scars as she did muscles, and owned eyes of a dark, rich shade of blue that Faria hadn't seen before. They were powerful, and beautiful. She held out her claw.

"My name's Cove; Riemu's partner and counterpart leader of Draik. I knew your mother well, and many of those who came before you both," she said, with a slight flick of her gaze to Osiris, who stiffened very subtly. They stood at roughly the same height, although the gryphon was a little bulkier. She had strength of her own though, although clearly its application was different to Osiris'.

Faria took her claw in a firm shake, wanting to show as much strength and affirmation as she could in the face of such a dauntingly weathered and elegant warrior, with much the same energy as Riemu had held herself when they'd met at the Senate.

"It's an honour to meet you. Thank you for coming on such short notice, and on such indistinct terms."

"The honour is mine," Cove replied. "You carry the image of both your parents with you, and I mean that with the strictest respect." That last line seemed addressed more to the gryphon specifically, but he remained stony faced.

The dragon continued. "So, what can Draik assist with? I assume this is a matter outside of prying Senate eyes."

Faria grimaced. "Yes but likely not for long." She motioned behind her to the carriage. Tierenan immediately swung through the door and landed on the road, gesturing his arm out to the remaining passenger. There was a second before Feith stepped anxiously but directly towards them, keeping her fists tightly at her chest. She straightened as she drew next to Faria, partly because the dragon was so tall that to not look up meant she would only see her knees. But also they had been summoned here at her behest, for something she'd done, and intended to help fix.

Faria rested a paw softly on the ferret's shoulder. "This is Feith. She's… been though a lot."

Cove and looked to her politely, and expectantly.

She took in a deep breath. "I used to work for a wolverine called Talos. He's… an engineer… or a surgeon. Sort of both. He's been working with Dhraka for some time, and—"

"We're familiar," Cove interjected, gently but firmly. "He's been helping Dhraka broker their recent technology. Seems he's had projects and protections in other sovereigns, too, and moves in the dark."

Feith nodded, looking up at them with growing confidence.

Faria looked behind her, and gestured once more to the carriage, whereby Tierenan stepped forwards on cue. His metal augmentations reflected the shades of the muted grey skies. "He has. This is one of his former subjects, Tierenan Cloud."

The raccoon gave them a salute and a bow, and stood next to Feith. Cove craned her neck down to view his metallic parts more closely, with rather serious scrutiny. "Were it not for the grey steel finish, I would have sworn that was Dhrakan machinery."

Tierenan tilted his head from side to side in a yes-no motion. "Kind of, yes. I was first seen by Talos in Skyria after an accident, where he gave me smaller, basic arms – I guess to test his prosthetics, then he took me and a bunch of other youngsters from the hospital to Dhraka for more experimentation."

Feith nodded in confirmation. "I was the first," she said, pointing up to her shoulders, and the curved metal receiver plates behind her ears. "But we were not the last. There are many more, and they're all hidden within Dhraka."

The dragon's lip curled in distaste. "I assume this is where we're due to play our part," she said, turning her attention back to Faria.

"Yes. We need to rescue the kits and bring them back to their sovereigns."

"Do you know where they are?" Cove asked, with a scrutinous voice – not aggressively so, just cautious.

Feith nodded firmly. "I do. I can take you there."

She held up her claw to halt the ferret's next words. "I'm sure you could – but *first* we need to assess where exactly you intend to go and who controls the land. *If* we can find you a path, then we will do our best to support you. But I imagine a resource like that is likely to be deep at the heart of Dhrakan territory and well-guarded." She turned her head over her shoulder, as if to scan the treeline, and the sky beyond it. "Let's convene at our nearest command centre. We can strategise a little more openly there."

She turned, and Faria went to follow, but caught Osiris' claw at her shoulder.

"Do not tread recklessly, Faria," he warned.

She gently put her paw on his claw, and removed it from her shoulder. "I won't, Osiris. We need them, and we need *this*."

Without another question, she continued after Cove and her soldiers. Kier, Kyru, Tierenan, Feith and Aeryn all followed suit, while Osiris rolled his wings in discomfort, and grudgingly took up the rear as they entered Dhraka.

The forest lay surprisingly calm. To look around at its soft verdancy, it was hard to picture the threads of war that had been sewn through its history. Even though this was the region closest to Xayall that Draik had been able to sweep in and quickly defend, there was a serene kind of disharmony to it. The land was merely a passive observer in the conflict waged above it or among its roots, yet still strangely integral to battles of supremacy and tactical strikes. For Faria, the land's historical name had held so much fear and intimidation, and even now struck cold nails down her spine when she thought of Fulkore catching her within the Gargantua, and how close he came to tearing out her throat. She was sure that for Osiris it felt the same, and likely for Feith it held a very different kind of anticipation.

The group talked little as they followed the dragons along their route. The Draik soldiers exchanged little asides and mutterings of duties or prospects in the conflict, but seemed reticent to say anything too loudly in open forest. Tierenan was lost in the wonder of the trees he'd never experienced before, while Aeryn and Kyru were mainly focused on guarding the area around them and watching for potential assaults, something she was sure the Draik were also wary of.

They trailed a long path that meandered far from any kind of road, between trees and across streams, sometimes feeling like it circled back on itself, till further ahead they began to hear a collective group of voices, alongside sounds of wood and stone construction.

Soon they emerged through a line of trees to find a more sparse area of the forest. There was still coverage enough to make it seem like a full canopy from an oblique view, but they had been thinned enough to make room for buildings – quite a large settlement, it looked like, where dragons of all colours and sizes were taking part in putting it together. There were even a few mammalian species too—presumably sympathetic volunteers Cove had rallied from other lands like Kyrryk. A heartened smile grew on her snout as she saw a brass-scaled wingless dragon and a deep orange fox gently brushing paws against each other as they padded leisurely towards the treeline.

Cove turned her head to speak over her shoulder. "This is one of the footholds we've been able to establish recently, as we've gained more ground and security."

Faria's eyes echoed the gleam of her smile as she looked around, giving nods to those she caught the eye of, including the couple passing by the group. "It looks great so far," she said, impressed by the energy and promise of it.

Cove nodded, but coldness coated her sighing response. "We could yet do more, but all things in time. Creatures such as us, as ancient as we are, undergo frequent periods of long hibernation. We try to rotate to make sure there are enough of us awake to protect and build, but after the catastrophe of Nazreal we have all suffered from more intense fatigue." She cast a look to Faria. "I am not sure if your father ever told you that was why Dhraka disappeared for such a long time. When Dhraka was buried in ash and volcanic collapse at Nazreal's fall, though they survived underground it took centuries for their bodies to recover from the radiation and gases, as we did also. We are resilient, but not without cost."

Faria listened quietly, with a brief mental detour into how they might be able to support them through future hibernation cycles, if her mother hadn't already negotiated something.

Cove led them towards a single-storey building that had a low profile, with few windows and a single entryway.

"Down here, if you would."

Inside the stone-floored building, flanked by soldiers, was an immediate slope downwards. Further along Faria could see the orange flicker of torchlight dancing over the slabs. If she hadn't trusted Cove already, she might have considered it sinister.

Immediately down the slope which, each of them noted, had large stone doors that could be rolled into place to close the way off entirely, the passage opened up into a cavernous chamber, where lanterns hung from tree roots poking from the gaps. Tunnels with odd carvings – some kind of directional cipher known only to the residents, maybe – led off in numerous directions. A few dragons bearing weapons or supplies strode by, bearing cautious looks at the non-scaled guests, while regarding the purple dragon with respectful authority – she acknowledged them back with polite but curt nods. Her attention remained on a partitioned section of the chamber, separated by panels of wood that were flush against the ceiling and floor. When they reached it, she spun one panel open, flicking her head as a gesture for them to enter.

Still followed by the red dragons, the group marched inside, Osiris most uncomfortably obliging. Within stood a solid table of red wood and dark iron fittings, strewn with maps and compasses on which were scrawled arrows and designations of territory. Next to it, Faria and Kier recognised Riemu instantly, the dragon from the Senate. She greeted Cove with a firm hug and nuzzle to the cheek. More surprisingly to Kier though, causing him to freeze in his tracks, was a distinctive snow leopard of dark panther-like colouring, his seasonal fur greying under the colour of his markings and with the tip of his right ear sliced off. He wore a steely glare that matched the cold familiarity of his dark indigo armour and short, tattered demicape. Where once he looked like he could slip into midnight, now his age was beginning to frost the edges of his fur.

"Commander Enyart?"

The panther-snow-leopard looked back to the maps on the table, an expert in strategic nonchalance. "Finding new ways to expand your lack of tactical awareness, are we?"

A low rasp rumbled in Kier's throat. The feline cut him a steely look over the maps.

"I see from the bruise on your snout that something cut through your defences."

The fox bristled with tension, his voice tight. "Never got taught to parry an entire dragon, Commander."

A ghost of a snort puffed from the feline's nostrils. "So why are you here, Master Lugos, escorting your Empress to the middle of a dangerous territorial campaign?"

He gave a bow to Faria, which she returned with a slightly confused reverence as his familiarity from her youth began to take hold. Osiris recognised him immediately, and twitched as though his muscles didn't know whether to relax or tense further – sharing some of Kier's unspoken misgivings about why the leopard had left Xayall in the first place.

It took Kier a stern breath not to over-respond, letting out some of his surprise and ire before potentially losing his temper. Thankfully, Faria interjected, not eager to stoke any further discontent between people she intended to all be working on the same side.

"We're conducting a rescue mission," she said firmly. "We need help entering Dhraka's land to recover children abducted from the sovereigns around Eeres."

Enyart's muzzle flinched briefly as if in distaste or questioning, then he shuffled around one of the maps as muffled sounds of artillery fire reverberated through the ground. "If you will forgive my impertinence, Your Imperial Majesty, but why now?"

She sucked in a somewhat exasperated breath. "We just escaped unlawful detention at the hands of Pthiris, and discovered their connection to the kidnappings of children across the continent," she said, gesturing to Feith, who was used to people arguing around her and simply answered Enyart with a nod.

"It's related to Talos," Cove confirmed, which summoned a growl from the wizened commander.

He tapped his claws on the table, his fur bristling ever so slightly as he contemplated the ramifications. "I doubt it will be enough to cause a full sanction against Pthiris, but at the very least, it might increase our favour to become a brazen rescuer."

Kier blinked. "Is this all about tactics for you? Nothing about the safety of these children, the risk of Faria setting foot in their land?"

Enyart kept his paws on the table and his head down, but

raised his eyes to Kier. "Do you believe in sacrificing long-term strategic positions for the spontaneous intrusion of a vigilante?"

"Is this about Aidan, still?" Kier growled, stepping closer to the table. "Where were *you* when Xayall was under siege? What good were you to the city by being underground here?"

Enyart stood, sharply, and rounded the table, quickly grabbing Kier's collar and pulling him close with a snap of his wrist. Others jolted as if to stop him, but Osiris remained still.

"Once again impetuousness outpaces your experience, Lugos. I left Xayall on Aidan's request."

Kier reeled back slightly, still in Enyart's grip. "He… told you to leave?"

"I had been an envoy for Empress Kaya's support of the Draik before you even existed. It was the reason we came to Nazreal and found Aidan in the first place. Kaya's ambition had been to support Dhraka's vulnerable in finding liberation and independence from Crawn's rule. Something that got waylaid considerably with the advent of her mystical pacifist of a partner," he gnarled, releasing his grip and flexing his claw, showing a burgeoning sign of frailty that Kier had never witnessed before. "To his credit, Aidan recognised that Dhraka's increasing militancy meant Xayall would soon have become a target. He directed me to increase procedures for city evacuation and told me to support Draik directly using the networks Kaya had built. I left when I knew the city would be safest and he gave me assurance the plan was set."

His eyes flared with anger, and perhaps a hint of regret. "And yet their might was still overwhelming. I heard of Aidan's loss, which will mean an entire reintroduction of matters to the young Empress." He paused, tapping his claw on the desk before looking to Faria. "We had not yet begun that point of redress due to your recovery."

She took a step forwards, with a soft and respectful look. "I appreciate what you've done for us, Enyart. You saved hundreds who wouldn't have survived if not for your preparations. Thank you."

He paused for a moment, then bowed his head, more sincerely this time. "My duty is set. I'm glad to still be here to carry it out in honour of your family." He straightened, and as he did, seemed to regard her with a look of more gracious authority. "Now, do you know where these children are?"

Faria turned to Feith, who immediately drew a claw over the map while her birds flitted around the table. The ferret trailed her paw from their position, over to the coast, then up to a point further northwest of their current settlement. It was an area designated by peaks drawn in ink, a range that travelled in a curve like a grinning maw towards the sea.

"Here," she said bluntly, tapping it twice for emphasis. Her birds circled back up to her shoulders and chirruped in soft support of her triangulation.

Enyart frowned gazing at her with deliberate gravity.

"Are you sure?"

She nodded.

He let out a descending growl and stiffened. Riemu and Cove peered over, and shared his sentiment, albeit with less outward disdain.

"This," Cove explained, "from what we've learned from captured sentries and defectors, is one of their most fortified compounds. We've intercepted several supply runs of iron and blue metals lately between there and the far coast, which to us suggests arming for war, or something far more ambitious."

Osiris's feathers bushed with anger. Kyru and Aeryn looked to each other urgently, thinking about the skeletal remains of the Gargantua war machine that had been dismantled not too long ago just inside Xayall's walls.

"Is there any indication what it's being used for?" Faria asked gravely.

"Not without breaking in there, which would be a greatly ambitious, and potentially costly, spearhead. As much as I see its benefit, I don't know if we can honour such a request right now."

Faria shook her head. "No. It has to be now," she insisted. "Talos will either take the children or alert the Molten King of his compromising, if he hasn't already. We already have Pthiris on our tail and can't afford to be on the back paw any longer."

Enyart bridled slightly, and seemed about to make a dismissive rebuff when Cove stepped forwards. While not passing directly in front of him as a barrier, she seemed to act as a calming presence for Enyart regardless. She held the same kind of wizened, tacit exhaustion and experience that Osiris wore in his eyes. It was a palpable atmosphere of someone on a very long journey not yet completed.

"I understand too well the necessity for an assertive response to a dangerously fluid situation. Even when a battle's been raging for two thousand years, a moment's turn of the head can quickly liberate it from your body." She turned back to Enyart. "We can help them break in, draw their forces out, and aid in relaying the captured younglings. Better to have a battle front outside than within their defences, but escape will be dangerous with the battle and pursuit so close."

Faria gestured towards Osiris. "That's where the Coriolis will come in. Usually its flight would attract too much attention, but our assault on foot should provide enough distraction for it to approach and offer us a swift and direct escape."

Enyart looked sceptical still, grumbling quietly over the strategic maps he had curated for months.

Faria tried to enter his line of vision from the other side of the table. "We're at the precipice of something massive, and it *has* to fall in our favour."

Cove stood with her; Riemu placed her claw on the map and dragged it away from Enyart's view, giving him a reproachful look.

"We reached out to them for a reason. This battle has been fought for too long in the same circles."

Kier's tone was sharp, and severe. "You don't know Faria, but she embodies every bit of the strength of both Kaya and Aidan."

Enyart's gaze met his; equally as fierce, just as devoted to his loss. But faced with each of them before him, in resolution and solidarity, he closed his eyes, and let out a gruff breath of acquiescence. "Fine. Gather yourselves; attend your ship so that it can be ready for an evacuation. We will assemble for an assault."

Osiris turned to Faria as the dragons left to shore up their soldiers. "I will fly back to the Coriolis and make ready. I…" His feathers pulsed with a deep sigh. "I would not leave you alone by choice. Please, do not think I would not prefer to be fighting alongside you."

She nodded softly. "I know, Osiris. I only ask this of you because I know you'll give it everything you can to get us out safely. I trust that with my life."

He smiled gently as he lifted his head. "Thank you, Faria. I will bring us all home. I promise."

He swept from the bunker. Even among the noises of readying soldiers, she could hear the sweep of his wings as they took to the sky.

Chapter Fourteen

Night had fallen over Dhraka. Around the inner peak of a cone-shaped mountain, like a hollow volcano with a well at its centre, hung a gantry of wood and metal. Its dark frame barely visible against the dancing glow of the torchlight below, its use was to monitor the captives within the cages carved into the walls.

On the gantry stood two dragons. Well, one stood, while the other leant on the wooden railing, looking down at the strange caldera with a somewhat regretful expression. Their bulky form of red-black scales was slightly hunched and their oversized wings were drawn in about their shoulders, a posture their companion and sentry partner Faunt knew rather well. It normally preceded a long conversation of some morality, and much to Faunt's disapproval, provoked a significant amount of thought.

He didn't want to ask. He knew it would bring him grief.

It was only a matter of time though, as he listened to his companion's breath deepen into sighs and mounting grumbles as they stared into the torch lit crater below. His lighter scales of a bloodier red seemed to flare with ire in the firelight at the thought of having to broach a conversation. He ran a claw over his blackened horns, up to their golden tips, and cleared his throat.

"What's that sigh for, Dagre?"

Dagre scrunched their snout, clutching their spear. "War's not a place for young'uns."

The other shrugged. "Everyone's in it one way or another. War's been going on for centuries, really."

Dagre's wings bristled as they rapped their claws on the stone railing. "Not them though, Faunt. They got brought here, kept here. Nothing's even being done to 'em."

Faunt shrugged, with a slightly sardonic sigh. "May be safer down there. Kept out of line of battle, fed and watered. Not that much to complain about, right?"

Dagre shot him a dim look. "Not something I feel a 'righteous' side does if you ask me," they mused, looking down at the circle of cages hewn into the layered cavernous walls.

Faunt rolled his eyes. "This about the new siege orders?"

The taller dragon puffed heat form their nostrils. "Kinda. Why you think they want us to just leave them?"

"Who knows?" Faunt growled. "Probably want us to protect the ship instead."

The answer didn't seem to satisfy Dagre, who jabbed their claw on the railing again. "Seems like either way we're asking for trouble. We've done some brutal stuff to folk, and ourselves. Draik is still dragons too."

A reluctant scowl darkened Faunt's face. "We had it better when we were under one banner."

"Weren't exactly united, though – anyone'll tell you that. Folks pushed aside to make way for conquests. Plenty thrown in prison for objecting. Just… doing what we thought was best because we were told it by the commanders. Don't get me wrong, I believed it, at first. Now… I reckon we damaged ourselves with it from the beginning."

Faunt stared into the darkness alongside them. "Well, wasn't it best? The commanders are gonna know, right? Cause everyone's tried to take us down one way or another. Can't survive unless we stamp that out."

Dagre's wings flexed in time with his wide-armed shrug. "You don't think after enough battles that maybe Draik had a reason for breaking away? Here we are mounting sieges in alleged self-defence, taking part in secret wars, hording a bunch of other sovereign's hatchlings, and nothing in that tells you 'maybe they've got a point'?"

The tension swirled in the darkness around them. Eventually, Dagre's exasperated sigh perforated the gloom. "I dunno. It just... I'm tired of this. I'm beginning to think we should try and work something out with Draik."

Faunt shot them a look of consternation. "You're serious? After all they've done?"

"All I know is, we've allied with folks who ended up becoming enemies of the bigger world and we and our allies fell apart every time our leaders vanished. That's not a sign of a steady environment."

The smaller one gnarled at them resentfully. "So what would you do then, desert to Draik?"

There was a pregnant pause while Faunt finished tying off the leather over their stock.

"Thought so," he muttered.

"Is it desertion though, if you were both on the same side once?" Dagre asked, thumping their spear on the walkway. "Feels more like I'm making the decision I didn't know I could take. We stayed here by default but nobody really told us there was another option. So... maybe we should consider it."

Faunt raked his claws into the railing. Talk of desertion

could get you killed by less scrupulous commanders. Which, granted, wasn't exactly a sign of free choice. "I… It's still too much risk," he muttered.

"Maybe it's worth finding out how much, or if that's a lie too."

Just as Faunt made to reply, a rumble echoed through the chamber. Even under the shelter of the cave, the sound of cannon fire was immediately distinct. They looked around, tightening their grip on their weapons. The fire grew louder, met now with shouts to action, and the pealing of alarm bells through the dark, firelit corridors.

Faunt loaded his crossbow and took aim at the caldera's aperture above them. "Gonna be your chance to find out who wants to keep you alive," he growled.

Dagre gripped their spear, glancing to the huddled forms within the cages. Some began to whimper.

"Ain't right…" they muttered.

Cannonfire bloomed clouds of flame into the night, breaking from the tree line into the mountain slopes. Invisible projectiles whistled for mere moments before crashing into stone battlements with explosions of dust and sparks of fire, illuminating for a split second the point of destruction, before the light faded and the plume of smoke stained the empyrean above. Cries of assault and defence rang beyond the sounds of fire as dragons clashed in the darkness. Faria, Feith and Tierenan crouched at the treeline, guarded by Kyru, Aeryn and Kier. Ahead were the ash-black mountains at the heart of the Dhrakan lands, with one lopsided, decapitated peak standing tall above the others.

Faria wasn't sure if she was in a state to be part of the battle at all, but absence was not an option. Nearby, Cove raised her arm to signal the third wave of cannon fire – the next would be their chance to enter. Faria waved in acknowledgement, somewhat abruptly, and hoped the speed with which her arm dropped to her side didn't give away to anyone how much she was resisting fatigue. A year and several months' recovery still didn't feel enough. And the battle to escape Pthiris had exhausted her more than she wanted to let on. But the fight was now. Rest could come later.

Feith stood watching the slope to the conical mountain they needed to ascend, as her two mechanical birds sat quietly on her shoulders. Her eyes scanned back and forth as if already plotting a route inside for them to follow. "It's a long drop inside," she murmured.

Faria's tail rippled. "I'll get us down.'"

"Will we be enough?" Aeryn cautioned from behind her.

The fox sighed gruffly. "We have to be. If Cove and Riemu can secure the base's entrance and draw everyone away, we can enter through the top and free the cubs."

"And getting out?" Kyru muttered, his eyes locked on the mountain's summit entrance.

"Kits first. I'll blast us out if I can."

"If?" Kyru hissed. "Faria, are you—"

"I'm fine," she cut in, keeping her eyes ahead, softly defiant.

Cove's arm raised once more. The air was alight with the echoing, dead silence between rounds of fire, punctuated by responses from the Dhraka, bellowing orders some distance away.

The dragon's arm dropped. The cannons' boom once more shook the ground.

"Go!" Faria commanded.

They kept as low as they could, dashing up the slope

towards the cresting mountain entrance, whose guards had scattered at the incoming artillery fire. Thunderous explosions of continued cannon fire echoed ahead. Iron missiles flew over them, some crashing into the distance. Eruptions of smoke billowed overhead as the Dhrakan stronghold returned fire and the crack of trees split across the dark behind them. Faria hoped it was not anything more she'd heard breaking.

Metal shadows flashed against the sky. Kyru lifted his voulge in warning, then crashed his shoulder into Tierenan to push him away. The Dhrakan's black-armoured form slammed into the ground with his spear blade just where Tierenan had been standing, and shaft grazing against the wolf's pauldron. The wolf's weight snapped the shaft, and the wide blade of his voulge slammed into the creature's back, pushing him to the ground. More black-armoured soldiers dived from the skies; from behind Kier slammed into a second one that dived for him, while Kyru and Aeryn deflected another each. Tierenan laid out a punch to another, making them double back into the sky to try again, with a bloodied maw and a missing fang. Faria kept her focus ahead, taking hold of Feith.

They were close. So close.

A dark shadow blasted by her, the wing membrane dusting her ears. It crashed into Kier, sending them both rolling down the slope a short way. Immediately Aeryn sprinted after him, while Kyru took over punching out the Dhrakan she had been defending Tierenan, Feith and Faria from. Aeryn skidded to the fallen pair. Before she could haul Kier up, the dragon whirled round on its back and jumped to its claws for another attack, trying to bodyslam her. Her arrow was too quick; she loosed it into his shoulder and he veered away. She quickly threw the bow over her shoulder and took hold of Kier, who growled with discontent and roughly asserted his ability to run free from her, all of them trying to catch up with Faria and Feith.

Faria cast a vortex of wind at a pair of swooping Dhrakan soldiers, spiralling them downwards, then looked once more to the entrance ahead. The end of her staff glowed; with a heavy strike into the ground, a V-shaped wave thrust ahead and forked outwards, dividing the guards away from their running path, and splitting the top of the caldera to make the torchlit walkway within visible.

Faria careened towards it, with Tierenan and Feith at her shoulders. The walkway had been distorted by her rift, no longer flat but twisted and hanging downwards, and its former occupants fled to steady ground. She clambered onto it and looked down into the vast space below, docked with flames whose flickering seemed to cower at the rumbles of battle and barely lit the bars of cages, and the even smaller gleam of fearful eyes watching through them.

Before the group, though, stood the dragons on guard below. A quick sweep of her staff across the rocky wall brought a spiralling path for them to make their way down on. Just as Faria began to descend, Kyru, Aeryn and Kier appeared behind her, keeping close, and behind them were Draik flyers, ready to start retrieving the stolen cubs.

The worried voices and anxious cries of the caged children rang through the cavern, calling to each other in the sudden tumult. Faria raised her staff once again – a light first flickered, then shone brightly, illuminating a large swath of the mostly-circular cavern.

Stood in front of the cages were two dragons. One brandished a spear, while the other stood behind them with a crossbow. Aeryn drew her bow immediately, but Faria held her paw out to stay any untoward bloodshed in front of the children.

She locked them in a fiery glare. "We're freeing them. Stand aside and you can leave."

Dagre kept their spear forwards defiantly. "You're not gonna make them fight, are you?"

"No," she boomed, loudly enough that all of the trapped cubs and kits could hear. "They're going home. To live."

The dragon glanced back to their shorter companion, whose bow rattled a little in his claws. With a bow of their head to Faria, they let their spear fall, and stepped away. Faunt grunted in reticence and laid down his crossbow too, tipping the bolt from its nook and onto the floor. Tierenan and Feith stepped up to take the keys from their belts, and began seeing to the barred doors while the furore of excitement and relief rang through the dark, a strange symphony against the blasts and yells coming from the not-so-distant battle outside. "We're here to get you out!" the raccoon called brightly. "Just give us some time to get to you, and stay calm." He looked to Faria and Kyru, who affirmed his statement with nods of solidarity but kept their guard up, watching the two nearby dragons while Kier and Aeryn kept guard on the other entrance to the cavern, barred by iron gates that would soon be swarming with Dhrakans. The night sky above flashed with blasts and tearing shadows. It might not be long before they had to contend with an attack from above, too.

Each child ran from their cage as their doors were broken open, and gathered around Faria's light as Tierenan marshalled them and comforted them. A few he recognised, and those he did remembered him too. One, a young collie with piercing, bright blue eyes named Seanathan, gripped the bars eagerly as he awaited the door to be wrenched open by Feith, looking fervid enough that he might have pushed it open of his own accord in sheer excitement. He ran straight to Tierenan and wrapped his arms around his waist in a hug.

"You made it!" he said gratefully, pulling back to rest his paws on his hips.

Tierenan scratched the back of his head with a bashful, if slightly harried, smile. "Yeah. Sorry it took so long. Wow, you got big, though."

Seanathan nodded defiantly. "Had to keep the dragons from hurting anyone too badly. Got a couple of scrapes for it, but we survived."

The raccoon looked around at the others. Some had bandages from small experiments, a few had wires and plating attached to their arms, but most appeared to have been left alone, likely rejected as priorities when Dhraka and Talos had to move around. If there was one benefit to their captors' disrupted journey, it was keeping the cubs from further experimentation, even if it did prolong the undeservedly long absence from their homes and families.

Faria looked about as Feith opened the lock of the final cage, swinging the bars free to let out the small quokka contained within. There looked to be about forty children in all. Some looked fearfully, or vengefully, at the two dragons still held at bay by Faria and Kyru. Aeryn and Kier helped rally them together around her staff's light. Mostly they looked to Tierenan or Seanathan, who had a younger olive-furred hyena clutching his paw.

Seanathan strode towards Dagre and held out his paw. "Give it."

They looked confused. "Give what?"

"Your falchion."

The dragon glanced down to the sword that was tucked into the sheath at their belt, and then looked back with disdain. "You don't want that."

"Yes, I do. If we're going to escape I'm gonna protect my siblings. It's the least you can do for us."

Dagre looked suspicious, but gently pulled the blade out, with Kyru supervising from the point of his voulge. Gingerly they turned it around and held the handle towards the collie. He took it with a smile "Thank you. Don't worry, I'm not gonna stab you."

The dragon snorted, a little bitterly. "Wouldn't blame you, but keep that mind about you."

The flyers looked at the group of children with deep frowns of concern. "There are far more than we anticipated…" one admitted to Faria.

She looked a little more urgently between the dragons, the kits, and the entrance they'd wrought in the ceiling.

"Is there a more direct way out?" she asked Feith.

The ferret shook her head. "Not from here. Dragons get to fly out above but they knew the kits couldn't do that, so they'd have to go all the way out through the base to escape." She felt a pang of self-admonishment. "That's why Tierenan was only freed when you broke his control chip."

Faria took in a long breath, looking at the amount of cubs she'd have to guide up the walkway, in poor light and with the thunderous impacts of cannons around them. If they panicked, or too heavy an explosion landed above them, there was a high chance they might lose one.

"How many more flyers can you call?"

The first dragon, with pearlescent blue scales, thumbed a claw over her wing. "There are six of us total. That would still make a lot of trips in active fire. We're being covered, but—"

Dagre pressed their shoulders back. "We'll help."

The dragons, including Faunt, looked to them with surprise. His smaller companion hissed slightly. "We… will?"

Dagre shot him a look. "Yes, we will. And we'll all be better for it."

With a reluctant, rising growl, Faunt folded his arms. "Oh, fine. Guess it's better than dying in a hole."

Faria nodded, and directed her attention to Aeryn and Kier. "Cover them at the caldera's entrance. I want every one of us out of here."

They acknowledged her order and began a run back up the walkway Faria had twisted down. Once they were towards the summit, the dragons began taking cubs in their arms and taking flight into the darkness, disappearing through the opening one by one. Once the four had gone, two more dove inside, took up the next waiting charges, and leapt to the sky. Kyru kept his focus on the prison's entrance, the dark and flickering hallway that led to the rest of the base, so far disquietingly dormant. Two by two the children were rescued into the air, a process that was both electric and tenuous. Occasionally Aeryn would loose an arrow or Kier release a bursting boom above them, shaking free some small stones that clattered to the ground around them.

Kyru flexed his claws around the shaft of his voulge, and growled at the sky. "This is taking too long." He stopped himself from saying anything too severe, even though looking at Seanathan, he knew it had already been thought of, and was being shared in whimpers among all of the kits.

The young collie held his captured falchion ready, though his arm dropped every now and again.

"Too heavy for you?" Kyru asked.

Seanathan nodded with determination. "It's a sword. It should be heavy if it's going to defend anything."

His candid response prompted a rare exhalation of humour from Kyru, normally reserved for a reluctant admission of one of Tierenan's jokes. "I can't disagree," he replied, with a shade of admiration.

A rumble shook the cavern. Aeryn braced herself against the torn entrance above and called down. "They're gathering reinforcements!"

Tierenan looked hurriedly around at the group, and then to Faria. There were about eight children remaining, as well as the two of them, Feith and Kyru. Too many for a single trip, and too long to wait while the conflict escalated. "We're running out of time."

She held her staff aloft, casting her gaze to the tunnel. Nobody had come yet. Were they all running to defend from the outside?

There was another boom, directly above them. The ceiling shook, larger rocks tumbled down from the cave's peak. Aeryn had disappeared from the gap above, and the sounds of fighting had replaced any calls of sentry or conveyance of the cubs.

Faria grit her teeth. The mountain wasn't safe anymore.

"Feith," she asked, firmly. "Can you lead us out that way?"

Kyru shot her a warning look. "You think we can defend everyone at once inside the heart of their fortress?"

Her eyes flared slightly, accentuated by the resonance energy surging through her at the growing severity of their escape. "Yes, I can." She was not in the mood for reluctance or dismissal. They had no choice, and she had to lead it. She looked to Seanathan, Tierenan and Kyru. "If we can escape the Gargantua, we can escape this."

Kyru's fur bristled around his neck. "I didn't escape it, Faria."

"We're not back there," she hissed. "I'm not losing anyone. We are *all* leaving."

If she had to burn herself out to get them to safety, she would. But the sacrifice wouldn't be Kyru's, or Feith or Tierenan's. They'd all lost so much already.

They stared at each other for a couple of seconds as the rumbling grew louder, more frequent. Kyru growled at the tremoring ceiling, and the battle raging above it.

Faria looked urgently to Feith.

"Go. Get us out."

Chapter Fifteen

Faria moved quickly along the tunnels, leading the group alongside Feith. The dark rock of Dhraka's makeshift jail facility was strangely warm, and muffled the sounds from above, leaving them in an eerie echoing ambience of their combined movements. It made it hard to judge what lay ahead, something that Faria became increasingly cautious of, especially with the conflict still raging beyond the stone. Her staff was glowing, albeit softly, as the blue light would be an immediate alarm to anyone against the otherwise dim or torchlit corridors. An odd humidity clung to the walls, smearing dusty water on anything that brushed past it. The group of cubs shied away from it, keeping to the centre as much as possible, with the bold Seanathan holding his sword proudly, vigilantly up in guard. Kyru bore a strange sense of pride to watch him, but his wary glances indicated an air of caution.

"You ever used one of those before?" he whispered.

Seanathan looked back to him with a slightly awkward smile. "Only pretend ones. You were right though, it's pretty heavy."

A soft laugh huffed from Kyru's nose. "Hold it straight if you can, 'til your wrist is used to it – it's big enough that you can use both paws too. Just defend for now if it comes to it. We can teach you more later, if you want."

Seanathan nodded, adjusting his grip to take hold of the leather-and-wire handle with both paws, curling his fingers around to find the most comfortable hold for him. Once there, he gave a satisfied grunt as he squinted into the murky tunnels.

Faria half-turned back to the group. "How often did guards come down here?"

"Aside from the ones in the tower, once a day," the young hyena with olive fur and a red mane spoke up.

Faria paused at a crossroads. In the distance to one side, she saw the shadow of a wing; immediately she closed off that path with a jab of her staff to the ground, sprouting a thick stone wall between them. She morphed another slab of rock behind Kyru, sealing away any potential pursuers, and then had to dig her claws into her pawpads to try and pierce away the creeping numbness of resonance fatigue. Feith pointed them in the opposite direction.

Faria nodded, and kept a brisk but cautious pace along Feith's indicated path, quickly sealing off any branching channels they passed.

A distant bell rang; low, heavy, rhythmic. It sounded like an alarm. She readied her staff, brandishing it forward as it shone with a warning, dangerous glow. The bell grew more resonant with every section of tunnel. Distant voices echoed in further corridors, and the rattling of armour rang among them. There was another set of sounds, something weirdly familiar, but cushioned by the stone and its strange, reverberant matrixing. A drone, perhaps – the whirring of machinery, or an engine – mixed with deep, heavy clashes of large pieces of metal. It sounded like a forge, one either distant or hidden, but unmistakably large. Faria's ears kept twitching as they walked.

She felt the vibrations grow louder, and the heat of the rocks increase.

"What else do they do here?" she asked in a low voice. Feith kept her gaze ahead.

"It's an armoury. Weapons and vehicles." She clenched her paw gently, and the birds on her shoulders ruffled their wings. "Spies."

The ferret halted and tensed slightly, reaching with an elbow for Faria, hitting her in the ribs. She snapped round to see her other outstretched claw pointing down the left tunnel at a large, iron door studded with reinforced plating and bars…

…and three large dragons.

The guards were already running, letting out angry cries that shook along the halls, spurring rattles of armour and more shouts of affirmative support from other directions.

Faria struck the ground with the butt of her staff, forcing rock into the open pathways either side of the dragons to block their support. Kyru took Feith's place; the ferret backed against the kids along with Tierenan and Seanathan, whose sword glinted in the light of the torches.

Faria and Kyru ran forward; the wolf swung the lower end of his voulge upwards into the muzzle of the left dragon, then jabbed it heavily forwards to plunge into its clavicle and tore downward, smacking its head with a pass of the first end again to have it slump to the musty floor. Faria swept her staff along the wall and created a large outcrop that wrapped around the remaining two dragons' waists, and with one forceful jab of her crystal weapon against the stone they were swallowed within it; their confused cries echoed in a distant, adjoining corridor.

Kyru glanced back at the cubs and kits, and to the bleeding dragon on the floor.

A rueful look flicked across Faria's face for a moment,

then carefully she swept the stone over the top of the fallen dragon to hide his body, and jabbed her claw for the group to follow. Seanathan, eyes wide with anticipation, followed Feith's lead in bringing them closer to the door, as Faria gently touched a paw to it.

"Through here?"

Feith nodded. "It's… going to be dangerous once we're past this room."

"I'd expect nothing less," the fox muttered. She could dig through anything with enough time and energy, but the thought of what lay beyond, the rumbling vibrations now sounding much nearer, was the greater worry. Whether a hive of creatures, a resonance engine, or a new war machine, it would be a danger to them all; one she knew she would have to lead the battle against.

She lowered her head, keeping her eyes forward, and with a push of her staff willed the doors to open.

A strange, cold quiet blustered into the corridor. A long room opened before them, flanked by tabletops strewn with armour plating and lengths of wire connecting one piece to another, trailing along the sides of the room on hooks and stands like armoured cobwebs. The plating lay in various stages of assembly and resembled fully mechanical limbs more than augmentations or plating. Hands, legs, and metallic bony segments like vertebrae were strung together, hanging from the wall like some mineralised abattoir.

"Well, this looks familiar," Tierenan said darkly, as they crept through. Faria could only agree, grimly. From one end to another they seemed to progress from simple hinged limbs to constructions with far more articulation and detail. Most of them were similar to Tierenan's, but others, the further they went, bore a sinister sharpness that was more akin to Raikali's angular, jutting metallic form. Coldness emanated far beyond the touch of the metal itself, a piercing chill that she wondered if Tierenan felt even more acutely for having been victim to it directly.

He and Feith seemed more focused on the path ahead, and she didn't blame them. The small birds hopped about unsteadily. Faria wondered if it was in response to the group's growing trepidation or a proximity anxiety to whatever they were about to stumble upon.

Kyru eyed the racks warily, untrusting that the limbs might not move of their own accord as he passed. Among the mess were metallic bones and physical structures for other creatures: birds, hind legs of indeterminate species, teeth, jaws; some beady, leering eyes lined a shelf in deactivated, empty stares.

Towards the end of the dark hallway of cold and sharp body parts, Faria laid eyes on a set of thick leather journals, seemingly ancient for the chipped leaves of paper jutting out from them, and the myriad layers of wear and scratches on their surfaces. She held her paw out to touch the cover of one, hesitated, and withdrew, remembering the charge of escaped children she had to return to the Coriolis. Relic hunting could wait.

Ahead was another doorway, just as large, just as foreboding. Feith stood next to her and gestured for the two birds to fly into the pockets of her jacket. The blue one stuck its beak out, and fluttered its wings in discomfort.

Yeah, me too, Faria thought.

She looked back over her shoulder to Kyru, who gave an affirmative nod as he gripped his voulge more firmly.

She pushed open the door.

The stifling heat hit her in the face, forcing her to blink and fold her ears back. Leading from either side of the doorway spread a walkway that encircled an upper region of a cavernous, almost conical chamber. An orange-red glow lit the space from somewhere below, while wide pipes belched clouds of steam and smoke into the narrowing darkness above. Resonant noises of construction rang from below, while opposite them on the same level were two sets of winches powered by teams of dragons, lifting something into place that was just out of sight beyond the walkway's edge.

Faria extinguished the glow of her staff and ducked. Kyru bade the children crouch with an urgent lowering of his paw, while Faria crept towards the railing's slatted edge to see what lay beneath them.

She craned her head to peer over the edge of the uncomfortably hot plating feeling like it would burn her if she lingered too long.

But even in that heat, the sight of the construction below sent a piercing chill up her spine.

A mass of blackened metal, not as large as the Gargantua, but slender, more like the Coriolis, with a jagged nosecone that looked like a spearhead or harpoon, its serrated edge like a row of teeth hungry in the firelight.

Cannons were lined up on the foundry floor, being loaded into the construction by teams of two. She could just catch the edge of what looked like a nest of massive funnels at the ship's rear, undoubtedly its engines.

Tierenan slid carefully alongside her, and muttered under his breath at it.

"Another machine? How can they keep making these?"

She shook her head. "They never stopped," she growled. "They never stopped because we didn't get a chance to finish them, or help the folks who knew how to."

An insistent hiss and gesture from Kyru caught their

attention. He flicked his head left. They turned, and saw a dragon advancing. It didn't take him long to see them – within seconds he gave a cry of alarm, and ran back for the others around the cranes.

Faria leapt to her feet. Her staff began to glow, and the air around its crystal tip shimmered with more than just humid heat.

The dragons rounded the walkway of the hangar pit. Faria cast her staff forwards, crystal shining. The air around its tip swirled and tightened, sucking inwards in a decreasing, strengthening vortex. With a thrust forwards she released it; the cannonball of wind spiralled through the air and slammed into the advancing soldiers, exploding violently as soon as it made contact. The first Dhrakan it hit was blown back against the others; the impact of the wind missile unleashed gusts that cast them into the wall.

The sounds of work paused from below as the bewildered cries and sound of the aerial explosion rang in the chamber. She could hear confusion, dropped tools, the beating of wings as the workers took flight.

Kyru was already on his feet. He ran forwards and met an ascending Dhrakan as it broached the railing, while Faria focused on the group to the left. A slash of his voulge took the dragon down, dropping them back to the metal ship below.

Faria whirled her staff in her hand and stabbed the tip to the metal plating in front of her while the Dhrakan winch crew belted towards her. A low, shuddering vibration rose around it, angry enough that it began to warp the sounds in her ears. Her eyes flashed with resonance, and in a sweeping movement she slashed her staff in an upwards arc ahead of her. A surging, rolling wave of undulating steel barrelled along the floor, rising higher as it travelled, throwing one dragon into the air, one over the railing, and the other two squashed against the far wall unceremoniously. The one who launched into the air righted themself and began a downwards dive for her. Faria was about to counter when a steel fist cannoned past her ear, cable whipping and rattling, and slammed into its face. The dragon's snout crumpled around it, and their dive ended unceremoniously and unconsciously on the walkway next to Faria. Tierenan wound in his arm with a snap and a flourishing twist, ready for another hit.

There was no time, though. More dragons were taking flight. Ahead was another doorway.

"Come on!" she bellowed, breaking into a run.

The rest followed swiftly, with Seanathan and Feith pushing along the children at the rear as they sprinted to the massive steel doorway. More pipes led into this chamber, and above it had been attached a forged emblem of a dragon's skull, surrounded by fire.

The Molten King.

It was their only escape.

Faria threw her staff against the barriers and blasted them open, hurrying everyone inside. Kyru and Tierenan quickly slammed their weight behind the doors again to close them. Faria shot a wave of air through the gap to assail the approaching Dhrakans, and with another touch of her crystal, sealed the two doors together with a flashing seam of light.

The room was left in ominous quiet, aside from the banging of the attempted invaders from the other side of the door. It quickly began to fade as they regrouped for a different entrance.

They were in another large chamber, with a roof made invisible by creeping, stretching darkness. In the murk of it were more pipes, leading to a central point on the furthest edge of the room. The silence was pressing, a lack of sound that was in itself almost deafening, as if conjured to steal away the senses of those inside. It felt like the room had a pulse, a breath almost, some surging rhythm of pressure that made it swell and ebb like the depth of a disquieted ocean.

Faria's ears flicked uncomfortably. Feith felt the birds burrow deeper into her pockets, and Kyru peered into the darkness with his fangs softly bared. Seanathan was more nervous, twitching slightly from side to side as his eyes caught shadows in his periphery.

"Faria…" Tierenan said, voice almost a whisper.

Faria glanced down, and caught sight of the large sigil on the floor. A dragon, bathed in flames. The Dhrakan symbol.

Crawn's symbol.

A shrill noise pierced the silence; everyone jumped. A spray of sparks shrieked from a set of metallic claws, glinting as they dragged along the stone wall ahead of them.

"As resourceful a nuisance as ever," Talos growled. "You won't make it out of here."

Tierenan strode forwards. "Want a rematch between my fist and your snout? I can take it way better than you can!"

The wolverine glowered at him, eyes reflecting the sparking blue light at his metallic clawtips, and said nothing.

The raccoon stepped forwards again, his own claws gleaming in the glow of Faria's staff, sharp, and flexing with anger. She could feel the uncharacteristic but deeply kindred rage in the pull of his snarl, the flattening of his ears. "You can let us leave, or we'll walk over you to do it."

A strange metallic grinding noise began filling the room from the darkness opposite them. Crystal torches around the edge of the room bloomed dimly into life, the light within appearing fearful of what it was about to reveal. Faria saw the silhouette of the enormous structure leading down from the ceiling, spreading across the floor towards the crest, and her ear caught the origin of the room's pulse.

A breath.

A throne.

A dragon.

Tierenan's tail fur flared and he tensed to leap forwards, but Faria crossed her staff against his chest in stark warning. She glared into the darkness at the thing before them. Something that both glinted and dripped. A hint of crimson scales. A torn wing. A single yellow eye, glazed, unfocused, that rolled open. The scent of blood.

Talos gripped a metallic handle by his side, mounted onto a strange, spiralling column that fed into the throne room floor. The electric sparks danced into it, summoning a soft yellow-green light from small circular crystals mounted around the altar-like structure. In their sickly luminance, they found the broken form of a figure Faria had not seen since Nazreal. Her stomach yawed, her muzzle half-opened with alarm and anger.

"Fulkore."

The dragon's unsteady eye leered at her. Glints of metal and drips of something wet caught the light as he moved, barely. His left wing and arm had been blown away. His chest was a dark cavity of wires and mechanics.

But the voice that met her ears was not the one she recognised.

"No."

It rumbled with disdain before reverberating through the chamber around them. "Unsurprising that Arc'hantael's progeny would refuse to tell the difference between those she seeks to exterminate." A long, breathy rasp cut through the room like a claw of frost.

She glared fiercely, bile in her throat and a warning gleam powering through her staff.

"I have been watching you. Since the moment you were born, I have known your movements, your hopes, your defeats, your recovery. I have watched you grow, like your father, as a blight on my waking memory."

Her paws stung as she gripped the staff even harder. "Who are you?" she demanded.

The dragon shifted in the dark.

"I… am Sarr Crawn."

Her fur buzzed with dread. "You—Fulkore's father? You *died!*" she seethed through gritted teeth.

A disgusting, rasping, gurgling laugh spilt from Sarr's maw. "Many, many times over," came the sardonic, rhythmic reply, punctuated by a hoarse and wet in-breath activated by the artificial bellows behind him. "By your father, by the gryphons, by your ridiculous fennec ancestor. By the crushing weight of Eeres itself. And yet you all failed in your weakness."

Kyru brandished his voulge. "We can fix that!" he barked.

Talos shot them a warning glare, his claws flexing over the handle he grasped. "You're in the den of my creations," he threatened. "You might have poisoned Feith's resolve once, twice even, but here is where you fall."

He plunged the column downwards, and with a whirring of deep machinery the lights flared more brightly, illuminating the room fully. The half-Sarr rolled his shoulders back and let out a spitting, guttural rumble, before rising to a stand.

"How pathetically ironic," he spat, blood dripping from his teeth, "that you would try to murder me in my cave much like Tallon and your father attempted so many years ago." He took a step, gaining strength with each second. "The same tricks. The same traps. The same useless ploy, time and again it repeats. And yet," he glowered, eye flaring. "I *still exist!*"

She slammed her staff on the ground, forcing a ripple of stone towards him. He lumbered aside – with only one wing he wasn't balanced or fast as he had been. Talos lunged in response, swiping for her; Tierenan met the wolverine's claws with his own, stopping him in his path. Kyru kept his guard by the children, growling deeply.

"Time is running out for you, Arc'hantael!" Sarr roared. "The spiral grows ever smaller. Soon you, pathetic scourge of the world, shall be crushed into its surface and from your blood shall arise a new order, blissfully absent of your family's meddling. I now exist to see you die. All of this, my broken empire, brought together to fuel my hunger for your messy, ignominious death."

She glowered at him with fierce defiance. "If my blood is spilt, it won't be without yours hitting the ground first!"

He lowered his head, keeping his eye on her as his maw continued to run with blood. "Oh, but you are so naive, Arc'hantael. I have lived a hundred lifetimes and nothing has yet killed me. You, though," he taunted, flicking his snout in an uneasy, sweeping look of disdain, "you can barely stand your own powers."

He grinned. "This will be the end for you. A final, far-past-deserved end."

Faria chose action over words. She let out a strained, vengeful yell, and flicked her staff forwards again. Another surge of rock threw the metal crest embedded into the floor towards Sarr; he raised his powered, metal arm and caught it dead with a heavy, roaring grunt.

"Sickening whelp," he thundered. "A pale shade of your ancestors' malice."

She raised her staff.

Chapter Sixteen

Aeryn heard the roar of the Coriolis' engines circling over the trees. She, Enyart, Cove and Riemu, along with a company of other dragons, had fallen back from the mountains after ensuring the rescued children had been taken on board the golden ship. She kept her eyes on the peaks ahead. Barely visible against the night sky were soft pillars of steam coming from fissures in the stronghold. More defensive artillery fire from the Dhrakan compound shook the trees, much closer now, and a secondary set of explosions split the air, followed by the sound of echoing, collapsing rock. She could hear harsh voices barking orders, but wasn't able to make out what they were. Beside her, Enyart halted himself against a tree, curling his head round it to view ahead. The dragons who had flown overhead were now alongside them, swords drawn.

"Where's the front entrance?" the snow leopard hissed.

"Top of the slope. Artillery cavern is down at the right to the rear," the grey-blue dragon replied. "Looks like standard dugout guard stations."

"Are they all deployed?"

The dragon shrugs. "No clue."

Enyart looked back to Aeryn. "What's your ship going to

do?" A barrage of cannon fire answered his question. The glint of gold flashed across the cannon's bursting barrels as the Coriolis circled around the Dhrakan positions. The guards from the entrance took to the air. Aeryn pointed to the ship.

"*That's* what it does. Now, we go in for Faria."

She readied her bow, nocked an arrow but left the string loose for now, and bolted for the entrance. Enyart broke into a run behind her, and the rest followed.

As she burst into open ground, a draconic head peered through a slit in the rock. A crossbow bolt sliced through the air beside her. Upon their miss, the dragon rounded the corner with an axe drawn. The wolf stopped, drew her bow, and effortlessly released the arrow into its neck, causing it to keel over and writhe on the floor in desperate agony.

Another dragon emerged, this one with a shield over its upper body, charging towards her. She knocked an arrow, drew her bow again and loosed, sending the projectile deep into the creature's ankle. It tripped and collapsed on its shield; a second later Enyart plunged his sword into its neck. It twitched, and fell still.

He eyed the entrance, seeing Dhrakans begin to retreat from the Coriolis' barrage and sprint towards their former cover, now assailed by Aeryn, Enyart, and the approaching Draik.

Aeryn drew her bow once more.

The light of Faria's staff flickered defiantly as she faced Sarr. Her tail was stiff, fur flared, and her eyes glowed with vehemence. But even in her adrenaline-fuelled anger her temperature flared hot and cold, and her fingers coursed with burning numbness that threatened to make her grip on the staff falter.

"I'm tired of your taunts, Sarr. I'll bring this chamber down on you in a second."

A rasping laugh spat from his throat. "Do it!" he roared. "You'll *never* be enough to destroy me!"

Talos wrenched himself out of Tierenan's grip. The wolverine whirled round and launched a punch to his face; he ducked aside and planted his steel fist deep into his attacker's stomach. Talos spluttered and recoiled, lashing out with his claws at Tierenan's face. He missed, but it was enough to give the wolverine room to break away, and make a sprint towards Feith.

Sarr raised his arms and split the chamber's air with a deep, harsh growl. From the far wall, a shaft of orange appeared as the chamber's second door rumbled open. Dhrakan guards marched in, spears and shields raised. Between their entry and Talos' surge towards her, Feith split away from the children, wanting to keep them out of harm's way.

Kyru gathered the cubs behind him, as Seanathan flanked their other side.

"Hold fast, and get ready."

Faria glowered at Sarr. All they needed was an opening.

The dragon lumbered forwards. She cast her staff upwards and brought columns of stone aiming for his chest. He took a glancing blow his armoured side and tilted away from the others, unable to move completely freely thanks to the cables and conduits still leading to his back. But his furious return swipe still clawed the air a bare inch from her snout. With her resonance she moved the ground beneath her, sweeping her out of danger.

Kyru's ears flicked. An alarm bell rang once more. Some of the dragons turned and bolted out of the chamber as a deep, thunderous impact shook the room.

Sarr snarled at Faria. "Legacy of cowardice. Like your father, you refuse to fight alone."

"That's my strength."

Talos growled as Tierenan caught up with him, trying to land a punch as they fought for proximity to Feith. She spun on her paw and shoved him back, landing him square into the advancing raccoon. As Talos aimed a backwards swipe at him, Tierenan grabbed hold of his forearm, avoiding his lacerating claws, and with his other claw fired his winch directly into the wolverine's elbow. Talos let out an agonised cry; his arm crunched and bent out of place. He swung his other fist round but Tierenan responded with a headbutt to his nose, landing his metal plating perfectly to the wolverine's soft snout. He let out a muffled, gargling cry and stumbled back against the wall, while Tierenan tore Feith away from him and back towards the kits and Kyru. Sarr flinched at the sound of his cry for a split second – just long enough for Faria to draw up a wall of stone from the floor and block him from another charge.

Talos scrabbled to pull himself to his feet with only one functioning arm. "How dare you! I gave you this!" he hissed desperately at the raccoon. "All your strength, your survival, is down to me! I made you who you are!"

"No."

Tierenan advanced on him. As Talos raised his unbroken hand to slash, Tierenan grabbed his wrist in his free claw, holding it firm. Talos began to quiver in his grasp, as Tierenan pulled him closer, growling in his face.

"I would have been me without you. I survived *despite* what you tried to force me into." He tightened his grip; tiny sparks fissured from Talos's mechanical hand. The wolverine let out a pained scream, trying to withdraw. Tierenan relented, dropping him with a dismissive casting aside of Talos' splintered golden paw.

"My strength is mine, and I owe you nothing." He drew back his fist, causing Talos to shrink away. A second passed, then two. Talos blinked a small, cautious glance under his defending paw, and saw Tierenan lowering his attack. "And I'm who I've always been."

Then the young raccoon flipped him an obscene gesture, and returned quickly to Faria with Feith's paw in his. The fox was almost in an encirclement of stone that she kept casting out towards threats from Dhrakans or Sarr himself, trapping him increasingly in the direction of his throne.

Kyru pushed back a dragon that got too close to the children. He still had a path to Sarr, if he dived through two columns of stone.

He could finish it. He could distract the dragon enough to get them out.

Faria saw his stance shift. The large half-despot dragon cast a looming shadow in the steam, and began to lumber forwards.

She'd seen Fulkore fight, but not Sarr. If she knew one, she knew the other would only be more brutal, more relentless. Bravery or not, Kyru wouldn't win.

She would not leave him again.

A sharp whine emitted from the tip of her staff. She grit her fangs, focused on the tunnel the soldiers had advanced from, and pressed her staff to the floor once more.

Just as Kyru began his counter-charge, the tunnel's walls extended over them, cutting them off from the dragons on either side, providing an escape route. Faria collapsed against her staff, struggling to keep her arm from quaking.

Kyru's run had been halted by the wall – initially his expression as he whipped back to look at her was irate, but seeing her straining under the exertion of her powers, and the collection of kits sheltered by Tierenan and Feith, he punched his shield against the wall in self-scorn for being so reckless.

"Let's go," he growled, flicking his head towards the door. He led the way, checking quickly for sparring soldiers, and led them into the side tunnel through which the external cannonfire reverberated more clearly.

Two confused Dhrakans spun round midway up the corridor, jumping in alarm at the sudden advance from within their own base. One roared and was met by a vengeful, cathartic bash from Kyru's shield, and just as the other reared up to attack the wolf, he stumbled and fell forwards.

An arrow lodged in his neck.

The other, staggering back, was met with an arrow to his flank barely a second later. Beyond stood Aeryn, already nocked for the next shot. She held in a swelling breath of relief to see them all again, but immediately turned to let fly her prepared arrow at something charging from the left.

"Hurry up! Here!" she barked.

Faria intended to seal the hall behind them, but with the frantic rush and the growing undercurrent of instability in her body, she dared not risk it. Aeryn led them quickly past Draik soldiers who had created a flanking path through the stronghold's tunnels to the opening outside. Faria could feel the fresher air breathe into the stone hall as they ran, and the sounds of battle outside begin to ring down the walls. They sprinted as fast as they could, as the Draik behind them began a fighting retreat to guard the last of the children.

The group burst into the open. Cannonfire thundered, blades clashed, and dragons swept and careened into each other in vicious aerial fights. Before them, banked against a jagged peak with its gangway lowered, was the Coriolis, shuddering softly as its engines struggled to hold a steady hovering. Its sails were set at acute angles, engines pointed downwards, and its anchor dragged into the stone to try and keep it stable, but every now and again it still lurched a foot or two along the mountain.

The moment they emerged, Kier caught sight of them from his lookout on the deck and launched down the slope to begin ferrying the cubs up the rocks to the ship. More Draik troops swept by and lifted the cubs with striking speed. Faria stayed by the gangway's entrance, watching for aerial attempts to stop them. Her eyes kept darting back to the tunnel they'd broken from, expecting to see the lumbering shell of Sarr charging after them.

How? *How* did he get out of the Leviathan and the cataclysm?

And if *he'd* survived…

A chill swept through her fur, as if something were reaching for her neck. She heard footsteps, a rasping breath, the familiar pull of a shared, twisting, mingling consciousness.

She whirled round as something brushed her fur. With a writhing thrash of her body she threw her staff out to release a defensive burst of wind from its crystal. The last child swept past her in the arms of a dragon, thankfully avoiding the fevered retaliation against her fear. She panted heavily on the slope for a second, as cries of battle and cannonfire split the sky. Aeryn was immediately by her side.

"Faria, are you hurt?"

She shook her head, looking around her in alarmed disorientation. "N-no. It's nothing."

The she-wolf pulled her aboard and immediately Kier and Kyru hoisted up the plank behind them. The ship burst into motion, not even waiting to raise the anchor, tearing it instead through the stone as it winched back in their desperate ascent to freedom.

Faria looked back over the battle, the fires in the night, with shadows of dragons passing over them, beginning to circle back to their respective groups under the boom of retreating cannonfire. Still caught in the fury of her chill, Faria strode to the sterncastle.

The gryphon still gripped the wheel. Some of the windows had been shattered during the fray, and several crossbow bolts were lodged in the metal panels. One had dented the helm. His feathers looked immensely ruffled, but he seemed otherwise unhurt. He gave her a ferocious look – not out of anger, but out of the echoes of desperate evasion and resistance of the assault on his ship.

"Everyone safe?" he snipped.

"Yes. Thank you, Osiris," she panted, with deep sincerity, slumping back against the wall. "I'm glad you are too."

He gave a clipped, sarcastic laugh. "Safety seems to be relative in the company of your family."

She leant her head back against the wall. "That's something I'm very much hoping to fix, some day."

He paused for a moment, his feathers slowly returning to their normal, relaxed flatness.

"You will get there," he said quietly. "We will ensure it."

The ship was quiet in the wake of the battle as it rumbled over the forests below, taking a path high enough to avoid landscape, but low enough for the moonlit clouds to sweep above them.

It would be morning soon; Faria had gotten some accidental sleep after talking with Osiris about what she saw within the mountain, but even through her fatigue the urgency of returning the cubs to safety and trying to both clear her name and pin Pthiris to its own misdeeds was too great.

And beyond that, the creeping anxieties of an adversary still lingered. Watching.

Approaching.

They had set course for Sinédrion, rather than Xayall, as they had a better communication network to all of the sovereigns from which the cubs had been stolen, and it could be made as a more convenient and less conspicuous emergency request than to have everyone converge on her city, which had seen more than enough political strife in recent years.

The rescued young were huddled in the middle deck, mostly being assessed by Maaka as he and the crew tended potential injuries and malnourishment, in-between making sure wounds suffered in the skirmish were treated. Thankfully Osiris' crew was not only acutely drilled for ship defence, but also adept at combat, so the ship had avoided most of the efforts that had targeted it during the rescue, but there was still some physical cost that had to be tended to.

She trod carefully between them as they mostly rested – the crew had given up their beds for the kits, and while the comfort for some was more than enough by comparison to the months of darkness and distressed cave bedrolls they'd been subjected to, others were still yet unable to relax, facing a break from traumas and separation that Faria could only begin to imagine.

She hoped they would be safe. She'd do whatever she could, give whatever aid needed, to ensure it. But they had to get home first.

As she gingerly navigated the resting kits, one of those nearest to her flinched softly. She turned in soft, apologetic alarm and held up a paw.

"I'm sorry, did I bump you?"

The cub, who seemed a little taller in comparison to the others, and was swaddled in a hooded cloak presumably given to them by the crew, shook their head. Faria could see a blocky, feline muzzle of dark, dusty fur poking from just under its edge. They didn't look like many of the others, and Faria wondered if she'd been there closer to Feith and Tierenan's time.

"You doing alright?" the Empress asked gently. The hooded cub looked up slightly, tufted lynx ears perking through the holes in its borrowed hood, which was big enough that the cut-outs didn't quite match and rucked the fabric in odd directions.

They shrugged. "Strange to be free."

Faria frowned softly in sympathy. "Well, we're going to do our best to get you where you need to be. Home again." A sudden pang of realization stabbed through her that 'home' could be a very loaded word to call it, or whether they even had one in the first place. "Do you… know where that is?"

Almost as expected, and with a slight drop of Faria's heart and stomach, the young feline shook their head and looked down. "Think I had one, a long time ago. Gone now though."

Faria tightened a paw around her staff in sympathetic resolve. "If we can't find it, we'll find you a new one. With us, if you want."

Faria couldn't be sure, because their head was still down, but she felt the hint of a smile in their voice.

"Might be nice," the lynx said quietly, before gesturing under the cloak to her staff. "And that helped you save us?"

Faria looked to her stave. "More than this. Everyone came together for the rescue. This was just… a tool, part of it, that helped bring it together."

"Can I touch it? Without it, none of us would be here, isn't that right?"

The question took her off-guard for a moment. She withdrew slightly, but if they weren't a resonator, would it really matter if they touched the resonance device?

She kept hold of it, but brought the staff towards them. "Here. Take hold of the handle."

The lynx's claw paused for a second, then reached out and gently pressed to the haft, before pulling quickly away.

"It's cold," they muttered. With a subtle turning up of their muzzle they seemed to study the haft a little closer. "Does it make you cold?"

Faria sighed silently. "It… sometimes. It depends how much I use it."

The feline's chin gave a little flick upwards. "Ever met others like you?"

Faria nodded. "Yes. My father was one. He had a staff too."

"Like that?"

She shook her head. "A little different. Smaller. He… used it a lot."

"He still have it?"

"N… no," she replied, after a soft intake of breath. "He's gone."

"The staff, though," they insisted. "Not with him?"

Her brow knitted slightly in concern. "No, it's somewhere else. These are dangerous, so they have to be kept safe."

The feline grunted in response. "Bet it's cold where it is."

A short breath of ironic laughter rushed from her nose. "Couldn't tell you," she replied a little absently, with a brief look over her shoulder towards the stern.

Definitely not cold back there.

"Hate the cold," the lynx replied bitterly, quickly. "It

always finds me. Makes me lonely. Angry. Like the moon. Cold, all the way up there." They paused briefly, head lifting very slightly. "You see it too, right? It shares the cold with all of us. And it shouldn't. It wouldn't have to, if it was here instead of up there."

Faria's expression darkened, and she leant to the side a little, trying to see their face a little more clearly. "How… would it get here?"

"I bet you could make it. Or someone like you could," the lynx replied, with a little smile. "Bring it all back down here and make it warmer, so nobody can be alone in the cold again."

"What do you—?"

A soft grasp on her shoulder interrupted her and made her turn her head quickly. Aeryn stood before her.

"We're getting to Sinédrion, Faria."

"Y—Uh, yes, sure," she murmured in reply. She gave a lingering look over her shoulder to the feline, who had tucked themselves back into the cloak. As she left the deck, Faria swore she saw a glint of something under the hood.

Chapter Seventeen

"How do you want to approach?" Osiris' voice rose over the rush of the wind and rumble of the engines.

They had kept their distance from Sinédrion previously out of fear of exposing too many of Faria's advantages, and to refrain from drawing attention to her. Now, though, things felt more urgent and emphatic. Faria wanted to keep everything dear to her close by, safe, within reach, and have their favourite escape ready to go in case dire circumstances were to follow them even here.

She was tired of running. She had been for some time.

"There's a canal for barges and cargo ships on the eastern side. Take us down there."

"Aye, Faria."

The approach would be anything but subtle. But she would be hiding herself no longer. The golden ship swept from the horizon like a splinter of sunlight against the dawn, growing in view of the Senate city guards and citizens. They had to circle about to find the best angle of approach – thankfully with the Senate meeting finished some days ago (though it felt much longer to Faria that this whole ordeal had started), the blockage of trade had been shifted, and the way was mostly clear.

The Coriolis descended smartly, slowly, and touched down with a deep rocking along its keel, making the otherwise still water cast great waves along the canal's length, upsetting the few barges that had docked along its edges.

Sinédrion guards hurried to greet the incredible skyship, as did dozens of astounded onlookers.

The secret was out. But that might now have played into Faria's favour.

The gangplank lowered onto the side of the canal; she descended with a confident stride, flanked by Aeryn and Kyru, supported by Osiris and Kier behind her. The Sinédrion guard stood to attention, drawing up their spears and shields in reception of the young Empress. She kept her staff in front of her, its crystal thrumming with an eminent glow, casting her group in a gentle blue light in the breaking dawn of the Senate city.

Over the soldier's heads, Faria could see a familiar set of horns advancing towards them. The soldiers parted and before her arrived Jed Othera, the towering stag who sat on the Senate's governing Council. His armour gleamed, and his cloak of black and gold was wrapped around his upper half from his right shoulder to his back.

He gave a deep bow, but kept his rather severe stare on her.

"Empress Phiraco," he addressed, in curt formality. "This is a very theatrical disturbance."

A wry smile split her muzzle as she bowed in return. "Council Othera. We are in somewhat of a theatrical situation."

She was met with a disapproving frown. "So I have gathered."

She quirked an eyebrow. "What do you mean?"

A glance over his shoulder indicated another figure on

their way, this one having a harder time breaking through the ranks of soldiers that accompanied the estimable stag. Slipping through to approach them was a familiar figure: the heavily-armoured sable of Commander Dyate. Faria straightened herself as tall as possible, still not enough to match the sable herself, but giving the true impression that she held more stature on this ground than the Commander did. Dyate, her eyes glinting in the light of both the dawn and Faria's blue resonance, approached her severely, but not aggressively. Faria hoped she was wary of her abilities now, and unable to do anything other than posture in front of Jed.

"I wasn't aware we were interrupting a storytelling session," she called. "You should send ahead for us next time so we can provide more fireworks."

"Don't be cute," Dyate barked back. "You assaulted the Representative grounds and carried out massive acts of destruction to the Pthiris central city!"

Faria glowered at the soldier. "Is that what he told you? Perhaps if Rynkath had treated us with dignity, and hadn't been colluding with known agents of the Dhrakan tyrant Crawn beneath his own mansion, we would not have been forced to make such a retreat for our own safety!"

Jed watched with disdain at the escalating argument, a frustrated sigh tensing through his shoulders.

Dyate threw her claw towards the Empress. "You insult my sovereign and demean my authority. None of that is true!"

"Do you really believe that?" Faria retorted, glaring, with a sideways look to Jed to try and invoke his memories and experiences in fighting Shadow's Claw alongside her. "After all this time, all of the parlays and military movements you've had to supervise, you *still* believe this is part of the justified order of the Senate? Does he lie to you too? Do you even know what he does inside his walls?"

Dyate shook her head vengefully. "You're playing with fire here, Xayall."

Faria jabbed her staff on the ground. "I *am* the fire!" she roared back. "I am the one who knows the heart of this world and who tries to take it from us. We are not moving, and will not be taken."

The Commander flexed her shoulders. "No. We came here drafting an emergency resolution to have you stripped from the Senate and put you on trial for your terrifying destruction; all of you involved in the attack on our sovereign, for evading our rightful custody, for stealing a suspect. You're all culpable, and if you refuse to yield, consider this an official declaration of hostility!"

Aeryn stepped forwards. "You don't have that authority!"

Dyate grinned, giving her a vicious narrowing of her eyes. "The Senate does."

Faria took to the front again, this time addressing Jed directly and ignoring Dyate's hostility. "In our ship are dozens of rescued children from sovereigns all around Eeres – many of them from Senate members. They must be given a chance to be returned home first and have the kidnappers be held responsible."

"I don't care what excuses you conjure," the sable growled. "You can prepare for arrest or prepare for defence."

"Enough!" Jed bellowed. "Stow your rage, or you will *all* be held at separation until process is due."

Their outward aggression quelled. Dyate bowed her head slightly. "Apologies, Council Othera. But we—"

"I know what your intention is, I have been listening to the endless posturing of your Representative all morning," he bit.

The glow of Faria's staff intensified with her defiant ire in the face of Dyate's militant prosecution. "I will not risk the lives of these children, nor be held responsible for their injury at Pthiris' hands. Their sovereigns will be contacted before any other discussion."

Dyate leaned in. "No quarter for criminals, no matter their age."

The fox Empress watched her for a moment, and her gaze darted to Jed.

"We're not yielding," she said firmly. "And we *will* protect the children."

Jed watched her for a moment, looked up at the ship, which was being commented on by bystanders around the canal, and raised an arm. "Take in the children to the hospital and begin processing them. Take a statement from each of them as they are willing."

Dyate's face darkened, but she held a gloat to her expression and voice.

"Charity is not a sanctuary for your crimes."

"The law is not always moral," Faria growled back, with a brief glance to Jed. He looked back mostly impassively, but when he turned his eyes away she knew she'd been able to penetrate his conscience a little more.

The crew helped guide the children down the gangway to the waiting Sinédrion guards, and begin leading them towards the hospital. Tierenan brushed his claw over Faria's shoulder as he passed.

"It might be good for Feith and me to go with them," he said, almost asking for permission.

She nodded. "I don't know what happens from here. I'll make sure Kyru and Aeryn can find you."

He wrapped his arms around her in a brief hug, then followed the rest of the children.

She scanned over them for the one in the hood she'd spoken to earlier, but couldn't see them. Maybe they'd returned it to the crewmember who lent it to them.

Kier approached her next, with Osiris right by his shoulder. "If Pthiris has prepared an emergency session, you'll get the chance to speak at it. I'll help you get ready." At this moment she didn't feel like she needed anything other than time and her voice, but she appreciated that Senate dealings were often about worming through a labyrinth of technicalities and historical gotchas than actual earnesty or truth.

Jed accompanied them towards a specific annex of the Senate building, one normally used for higher security matters, and used as a fallback fortress for the Representatives in case of a further siege like the one under the bear Kura and his collected Shadow's Claw forces two years prior. The guards attended their posts one by one, leaving her to be escorted into the meeting chambers with Osiris, Kier, and her two loyal wolven bodyguards. Once Jed had left, she sat in a carved wooden chair and sunk her muzzle into her arms with a long, vocal sigh, then ran her paws over her ears with visible disdain.

"The temptation to just close us permanently off inside a stone bubble is very tempting."

Kyru picked some dirt out from underneath his claws. "Well, you're very good at it."

Her tired but sardonic look prompted a shrug.

"It's not diplomatic, but it's still protection."

She shook her head. "I know, but we're fighting on *their* terms," she grumbled, sticking out her tongue in a grimace of disgust. "Not sensible ones where people fight against things that are wrong."

Osiris swung open cabinet doors and pulled open drawers till he had gathered a stack of parchments and quills, and laid them next to the fox.

"Your armoury, Faria."

She groaned, and took one of the quills; Kyru quickly slid an inkwell towards her, and she began scrawling her decree. It would have been neater if a scribe did it outright, but she didn't have time or energy to dictate, and a number of them were already waiting to reproduce her missive in the halls above. She headed each parchment with an address to each sovereign she thought could reasonably attend, and continued writing her emergency request on a single piece, though finishing with her signature and seal on the base of each. Once finished, Kier slid the papers from her desk and quickly strode to the Scribe's Hall to drop them off.

Faria slumped in her chair. "Fighting for myself in this feels like I'm turning into someone I don't want to be. I thought kindness and dignity would be some kind of standard, seeing as people tout it so often as part of civil diplomatic existence."

Kyru sat in a chair opposite her, leaning on the table with his jaw on his hand. "It's surprising what you see as a merc," he began, with a gruff sigh. "The things people say because they think you don't care or aren't capable of understanding, they'll tell you their contempt outright. 'Civility' is a facade. It's 'obedience' they're after. And they don't care how they get it, as long as they can have their reputation laundered and dress it up in gold and stature."

The gryphon gave a curt nod of agreement. "I saw it in Arete, and Nazreal, and again in the changing of the world through the Senate. The respectability of corruption has risen under the disingenuous creed that all ideas are valid, even when they are not. The righteous angry are painted as radicals, while the polite poisoners are lauded for their appearance. It is a disgusting farce."

Faria stared blankly at the table. "So what do you do?"

"Have integrity. Speak plainly. And learn where your recovery lies so you do not lose yourself to vehemence," he said firmly, pointing at her staff. "It is a delicate balancing act, sadly one that you are forced into by those who control the weights you carry."

She also looked to her staff, leaning in the crook of the chair and the table, as the rising sun cast the room in a fiery glow.

"I worry we're already far too late to ever go back to anything except desperate survival."

Osiris took in a long breath. "It has been far worse, I promise you."

She glanced down at the table, thinking of Sarr's reanimated form lurching towards her, and the odd sensation of creeping shadow that hadn't escaped her since leaving Dhraka.

It may yet be again…

Deep in the mountains of Dhraka, the warped floor of The Molten King's throne room shimmered in the crystal torches' wavering light. It was like a dying fire, surrounding the charred and angular walking corpse that yet loomed within.

Sarr looked round to the creature painfully working at his back. Talos had learnt quickly to mask the agony of his twisted arm, and strapped it into one of the metal support armatures he'd built, but the lack of mobility and inconsistent dexterity in his fingers among the swelling pain meant progress was tenuous. With Sarr's bloodthirst rising every second, he had to work quickly, silently, and through constant shooting pains.

At last, the final panel was shunted into place by a slam of his wrist, and the twisting of a lock. The dragon's wing flexed, and from his maw came a hoarse, deep exhalation of satisfaction. Talos half-dismounted, half stumbled from his position standing on the throne behind the massive bulk of decaying dragon and smooth metal, and made room for the fiery despot to move and flex and acclimatise to the final adjustments to his body.

"It's finished."

The dragon grinned with bloody teeth, as a set of lights danced under his prosthetic seams in synchronicity with the device Talos had just completed.

"Finally…" he growled.

Around the room's edge, Sarr's devoted warriors stood in silent, reverent observation, awaiting their prompt with fiery eyes hungry to exact vengeance on behalf of their fanatical leader and see him achieve glory.

Sarr swept round to view Talos once more. "Do we know where she is?"

The wolverine winced as he reached into the pocket of his long coat and produced a strange kind of circular dial, on which pivoted a needle-like thread of green crystal. It swung and yawed timidly towards a specific direction; where its kindred energy lay, along with its target.

"The compass is working," Talos replied stiffly.

"She had better collect what she needs," he rumbled. "We are ready, and I will not show mercy to those who severed my legacy."

The wolverine grunted as he held his arm, and adjusted the metal brace that kept it supported. With a gentle flex he found the better position, and was able to ease his tension a little.

Enough, at least, to begin asserting his agency again.

"I want the gryphon's ship."

The dragon cast a rueful glare through the darkness. "You may salvage what remains. I make no promises against that contemptible golden wreck."

"You have power already!" Talos snapped back. "That craft is from a pinnacle of invention, a waking dream of power and prosperity. Why are you so adamant to destroy it?"

Sarr lumbered towards him again, and straightened to his full height, mechanical seams bulging slightly to reveal the pulsing light within.

"This world was to be mine. *My* prosperity was torn from my claws, my warrior league crippled, by the architects of that gilded abomination you covet. I watched my war machine disintegrate under my claws and was burned by the lightning of that wretched storm. That I have had to wait this long is yet another grievous insult to my deserved reign."

Talos lanced a derisive, bitter scowl up at him. "And what of you? What could you have built if you weren't so obsessed with vengeance? Barely anything left of your proud Dhrakan lineage, held together by bolts and fear, unable for years to do nothing but bleed into your seat and convince others of your superiority. Fulkore should have let you die. He may have survived if he wasn't obsessed with your destructive vendetta."

Growls of protest rippled around the room, and at least one snap of jaws from the surrounding guards. Sarr leant forwards slightly, his scaled snout still hanging, underlit by the ambience of his throne's mechanisms.

"My plan has never wavered; Fulkore knew its perfect simplicity. My military focus has provided me with a constant, reliable force. From my throne I have spread my influence throughout the world and unseated whole empires. My military focus has provided me with a constant, reliable force. *You,* Talos," he spawled, "have slunk from master to master in a cowardly dance to shelter a bruised ego and a frail body." He straightened. "And yet, here we exist, together. One way or another, this shall be our final cooperation."

"A perfect arrangement," the wolverine gnarled in retort, before turning away and marching towards the steel door that led towards the furnaces. Sarr turned to address the ring of soldiers.

"Advance. We leave," he called to the room. The Dhrakan guards raised their weapons and began a devoted, hungry march behind him towards the finished airship's fiery domain.

Sarr lumbered at first, then, finding his pace, strode and straightened, his metal articulation flexing in sync with his organic, ruptured body. He marched down the walkways, bringing soldiers with him, until the metal form of the ship lay immediately before him.

Dark, blue-black metal glinted like an obsidian blade. The diamond-shaped vessel with its powerful array of engines sat in the cavernous chamber, awaiting its crew. Even in the burning lights of the furnaces, it looked cold as a frosted spear.

Sarr's crimson scales flashed in the torchlight like burning blood, with his metal plates glinting as weaponised darkness.

The day was tense, and passed too slowly. It felt like there was a fire raging in another part of the city, unseen, and the indifference of the Senate officials added to the feeling of being cast out into a storm with no oars. In his flights to and from the Coriolis, Osiris saw that Pthiris had travelled with a considerable force, and now lay parked outside the city to the north east. By sheer luck, bad weather had stalled the journey of their other ships, presumably containing the weapons they intended to use to intimidate Xayall further. Faria had cursory meetings with Dyate to ascertain the charges. The commander was a wall of her own conviction, and refused all advances to negotiation that didn't end with Faria in chains and heading back to Pthiris.

Unfortunately for her, though, both the Coriolis and the advent of the stolen children were causing somewhat of a sensation among both Senate staff and Sinédrion townsfolk. Messengers and scribes entered, took notes and statements, and left, and soldiers from the hospital returned to corroborate comments made by Faria and her guardianship. All too long the day wore on, however, till it turned to night. The new scribe shift rotated in, pulling double duty for the two cases of rising urgency within their walls, and while Faria was eager to tell the truth of her story, the energy which she had to convey it dwindled rapidly when night fell. She stayed awake for as long as she could, but even she had to concede defeat to sleep eventually, and was escorted into the fortress wing to finally take some rest.

The sun was strong through the clouds the next day, on the day of Pthiris' purported emergency summit. Both sun and cloud were intense, trying to outdo each other for control of the sky, culminating in a sheet of softly-rolling, backlit grey. As pleased as Faria was for the opportunity to bring the children here to a semblance of safety, the fight was far from over, and even the return of some lost loved ones may not be enough to halt the tide of militant officiousness and political sabotage. She steeled herself as she paced the room, awaiting her summon to the Council chamber.

"Of all of them," Kier said, with an optimistic sigh, "I had hoped Jed would be a voice on our side."

She met him with a dismissive shrug. "I've learnt not to have expectations from allies who aren't already standing by my shoulder."

She didn't know if Skyria would be attending, as the journey was too long to make in such a short time without using the Coriolis. It meant losing an important mediator, even if they were wary of being explicitly supportive. Andarn and Tremaine could go in either direction, usually swayed by whoever talked loudest or who had the greatest deference to them, being the two biggest sovereigns on the continent. Although Bayer was hopefully due to arrive as well, he was not considered official by any means, and would have little sway politically, serving more as a material witness much like Tierenan would.

The door rapped with a knock. She strode to it, bypassing Aeryn and Kyru to pull it open herself, and was met by a falcon who bowed their head in graceful formality.

"They are waiting for you, Representative Xayall."

"Thank you, Quill."

The falcon nodded, and sharply strode away. Faria took a moment to close her eyes and centre herself.

This was it. A chance to appeal for her space. Directly to them.

She had to hope.

No, not hope.

She had to *fight*.

She opened her eyes, picked up her staff, and led the way.

Chapter Eighteen

I t had barely been a week, and she was back inside the Senate hall.

This time, she stood in the centre of the lower hall, on a sort of auxiliary circular podium that directly faced the Council dais, one used for visiting or non-Representative speakers to address the room. Around her on either side, in an arc, were the regular amphitheatre seats of the Senate gallery, with wooden platforms at set intervals to designate spaces for attending sovereigns. There was a large public viewing as well, something Faria hadn't anticipated. Apparently Pthiris, or Rynkath specifically, wanted to depict her as a danger to as wide an audience as possible.

A comfort in the stall behind her were the forms of Kier, Aeryn, Kyru and Osiris. Kyru and Aeryn had been allowed in with their melee weapons only, and relegated to the line of guards around the exterior of the room. She could feel all of her allies at her back though, and knew among them were Tierenan and Feith, with Seanathan and some of the older children, ready to give statements that would, hopefully, provide a defence for her actions in Pthiris.

She had walked in, as her accusers intended, after they and

the Council had been seated. She had given as resolute looks as she could to those who watched her enter, but couldn't stop her fur from standing on end when she saw the wizened but starched and smug form of Rynkath standing sanctimoniously at one edge of the Council dais. He saw her reaction, and visibly bristled with pride and glee at once again being able to undermine her, by forcing her into a theatrical defence with himself in control of the script.

They didn't have *time* for this. Sarr wouldn't take the theft from his vaults lightly.

Regardless, here she now stood before them all.

Kier would act as her sovereign Representative – it had been made clear that she was being tried as a personal assailant with a political motivation. The ultimate goal was likely to hold Xayall hostage as part of some kind of deal, or to have her removed and someone with their 'approval' instated by forced exchange. He stood next to her, saying nothing, but providing firm companionship and a knowledge of Xayall laws that she could rely on for clarity if needed. The Andarn and Tremain Representatives sat adjacent to each other – a puma and dhole respectively – but looked as if they didn't want to acknowledge the other's presence. Then nearby was the blissfully familiar sight of Bayer, accompanied by Raede; the monitor lizard from Hadris; and next to him was Irien, the red panda Representative from Skyria whom Faria had so far met only once, before she had even last seen her father. Dyate sat on the opposite side of the Council dais, presumably to relay information to the opposite side of the delegation or to add to the theatrical nature of the summons.

"Esteemed colleagues of the Senate," Rynkath began, dragging out his words to enjoy the sound of his own voice carrying into the chamber.

Faria glared at the older fox from the north, as his insidious familiarity with the position of his peers bore him a smugness she severely wanted to wipe from his face. With her fist. At high speed.

He continued.

"I gather you here not out of pleasure but out of necessity—"

Yeah, right.

"—in order to honour the pledge we made to each other to protect and hold each other accountable for infractions upon our territories. This is one such matter, one of grievous personal proximity. Several nights ago, while conducting an investigation of espionage and diplomatic security, our sovereign, my home, was subject to a powerful and vengeful attack from Empress Faria Phiraco of Xayall."

He laid out the details – bare when they needed to be and embellished elsewhere for the same, the omissions and exaggerations mixing to a hue that would cast him only in the most honourable of lights, and her into the warning darkness of perceived criminality. The delegates listened dispassionately as he spoke; Faria felt it almost like watching blood pour over a stone, but she knew she could not be immediately combative.

She cleared her throat, and took in a deep breath. "The damage—"

"No hospitalities?" Rynkath interjected immediately, eyes fiery with the kind of glee only be experienced by someone with a lust for power and humiliation. Faria glared back, hackles rising, but with a subtle flex of her shoulders managed to swallow down her desire to melt him where he stood.

"Apologies, Representatives," she said, with as little rage as she could manage. "We have been in constant travel for many days, and are somewhat pressed in our current situation."

Rynkath cast his paw gently outward. "Seems like this 'situation' has been 'current' for many years."

Bayer swept him a fierce glare. He ignored it, mostly. "But please, *enlighten* us as to your justification."

She felt Kier shift beside her, and steeled herself once more.

"Representatives of the Senate, Members of the Council," she began, before turning rather more deliberately to the gallery where the public was watching. "And citizens of Sinédrion. I apologise that you had to be brought here today. You have all been subject to more strife than anyone should deserve to be, and it has never been my intent to add to any of it." She acknowledged Irien specifically. "Especially those of you for whom this is a long and perilous journey."

Irien gave a nervous nod to Faria. The red panda was about to open his mouth to speak when Rynkath's voice took over. "Representative Skyria arrived at Pthiris two days after you made your dramatic exit. Apparently he had been summoned by your Captain, so I explained your dramatic absence and demonstrated to him firsthand the wanton destruction of my city myself."

Faria felt the bile in her throat. "I look forward to telling the rest of the story myself," she barked.

Irien looked nervously between the two, while Jed addressed Faria with a severe, if somewhat empathetic, look, and gestured for her to continue.

"I understand none of us wants to be drawn into yet another inter-sovereign dispute, but the actions I was forced to take for my own safety, for that of my guardians, my people, even the Senate itself are something I will not apologise for. I was left with no choice, with Pthiris in continual, aggressive pursuit of an unconscious teenage raccoon in my care, and then of myself in extrajudicial malice. I witnessed corruption directly, a complete disregard for anything but fealty to power and greed, and a cowardly desire to cover their own history of subterfuge."

"Outrageous," Rynkath scoffed. "You resisted our initial investigation warrant and proceeded to be an unruly, dissatisfied guest, culminating in an act of blatant sabotage that left our city palace in ruins."

"We did not resist," she replied firmly. "We were escorted by a military fleet to Pthiris, disrupting a pre-arranged diplomatic envoy to Skryia. There was no due process."

"Absurd, you—"

Jed cast his head round to Rynkath. "Representative Pthiris, the enforcement of your warrant was crude and misrepresented the circumstances of its necessity. You overstepped your authority under Senate law and the warrant has now been rescinded."

He looked back to Faria. "We do not condone sovereigns acting as vigilantes. This is how wars begin."

That made Faria feel somewhat better about seeing Jed's signature on the decree, but the fact that he signed it at all was still a cannonball to the gut.

Rynkath held out his paws in fawning implorement. "She was supervised. It was within the remit. And it *would* have been temporary, had—"

"That was *not* the intonation upon my arrest." Her voice rose in the gallery. She was not going to let him devote any more room to his ego. "They were going to kidnap Tierenan and hold us hostage until we complied."

"A deceitful exaggeration," the older fox responded, with his own measure of firmness. "The Young Empress became immediately agitated and aggressive, clearly panicked in the face of consequences for aligning with a spy, and threatened violence from the very outset. Here we had the chance to interview a known actor in some of the worst conflicts our waking memory has ever seen. She not only refuted our Senate-granted authority, but demolished the Representative grounds upon her departure and set fire to half of the galleys in our fleet, leaving us only *more* vulnerable to her aggression, such as might come at the hand of that golden warship."

Faria's claws dug into the table. She could hear Osiris' breathing behind her.

"Is the summation of this destruction accurate?" Jed asked.

Faria swallowed back a growl. "It is. We discovered that Pthiris had been allied with Shadow's Claw, and—"

"Rubbish!" Rynkath spat. "This is fanciful nonsense—"

She slammed her fists on the pulpit, teeth bared. "You've had your words! Too many, in fact, stolen from the throats of those who need them more! I won't let you take away mine with your blades pointed at my home!" She stood, locking in him a vehement scowl. Dyate flinched slightly. "I have stared down death in my own city three times; do not dare think you have any right to intimidate me out of the truth."

Jed looked back to Rynkath. The Andarn and Tremaine Representatives gave each other wary glances. Irien wrung his paws, looking like he wanted to ask a question. Bayer simply watched, with piercing eyes, checking in case of a need to interject.

"Representative Skyria," she called, causing the red panda to jump slightly, "Tierenan is safe." She gestured behind her; the raccoon waved and Irien's expression softened. "By a miracle, he's awake. Pthiris tried to take him in for 'interrogation' for matters related to Shadow's Claw."

Irien looked cautiously to Rynkath, whose smile had

darkened somewhat. "I gathered. I already expressed my disappointment with this, both the need for confinement and the allegations. Is it true he was involved with them?"

"No!" came a voice from behind Faria. All heads turned. Tierenan stood, with Feith and the children they'd gathered, and marched down the central aisle towards the Council dais.

"Not only was Tierenan *never* involved with Shadow's Claw," she swelled, locking her counterpart with a vehement, building glare of sincere, victorious brutality, "we discovered the children who had been taken by them, across dozens of sovereigns and cities, and an underground tunnel linking Pthiris' capital palace to the very heart of the Dhrakan stronghold in which they were kept."

Rynkath's expression fell even further. Bayer smiled and gave a subtle lick of his teeth, as he heard murmurings from the gallery above.

Irien stood to greet the raccoon, an immense look of relief and elation spreading through him, making his fur puff out slightly.

"I had worried I'd never see your troublesome face again," he said kindly, voice brimming with consolation. Tierenan buzzed with excited pride.

"Not only mine," he continued. "We have *all* of the missing ones here."

Some of the children filed round, forming a barrier almost, between the Council and the gallery. Rynkath's fury was palpable as he saw Feith standing with Tierenan. The two of them together seemed to undo him far more quickly than anything Faria had hoped to do or say.

The fox shoved braced his paws forcefully against the edges of his pulpit. "Outrageous theatrics! This is a serious diplomatic crisis; we are not here to hold an audience with children!"

"Why not?" Faria demanded. "You *knew* where they were. Feith, can you elaborate?"

Tierenan's claw gently pressed to her back in quiet reassurance. Behind them, some of the children drew a little closer. One pulled their hood further down their face, looking shy, and fiddled with something under their tunic.

Feith took in a deep breath, trying to ignore the rippling chill of anxiety that washed over her fur as she addressed the Council.

"My name is Feith. For the last few years, I have been an unwilling assistant to a surgical engineer known as Talos. He is the one who not only took these children, but also conducted experiments on several creatures in order to develop advanced, weaponised prosthetics."

She gestured to Tierenan, who stepped forwards. Faria half expected him to strike a pose, but he seemed to understand the gravity of such a meeting, and instead demonstrated the viciousness of his claws.

Irien peered over. "I mean, they're definitely more elaborate than the first ones Talos gave you. But I don't see how he weap—"

With a sharp click and a hiss of released air, Tierenan's arm shot from his elbow, latching the back of Jed's chair. The claws pierced the upholstered cushion, and scraped the wood as he reeled it back, chain wire zipping back inside his arm with a high mechanical whirr. He gave Irien a serious look.

"This was not what I asked for," he said in a low voice. "Nor was I asked for it to be given."

Rynkath's dismissive sniff cut the silence. "You agreed to travel with him voluntarily, there is no way you did not anticipate what Talos would do for you."

Tierenan, Faria, Feith and Kyru all looked like they wanted

to kill him where he stood. The raccoon turned to the room. "Talos lied to me. He told me that we were heading to the Senate to gain more approval for research, and in my brief stupidity, I believed him, and let him take all of us hostage. Faria has saved me now from them, twice, and now returned every single child they stole, while *he* claims we're the villains."

Rynkath stammered a little. "That still makes you a willing accomplice of a known ally of Shadow's Claw, which means you—"

"One who was in *your* employ," Faria cut in, bold, unyielding. "We discovered Talos under the Representative mansion in Pthiris having kidnapped Tierenan, trying to bring him back as an espionage agent and assassin." She stood, pushing her shoulders back. "Do you want to explain why you were harbouring a known agent of Shadow's Claw under your own governmental palace, and what tracks ran from those catacombs directly to Dhraka?"

Rynkath scowled, muzzle pursing with cornered rage. Jed took in a long, gruff breath, and Dyate looked down and aside, her face a maze of fury and confusion.

Rynkath's mouth opened and closed for a moment. "These… are all spurious lies!" he finally spat, thrusting a claw towards the Empress. "This chaotic child has caused countless battles across Senate lands, fuelled wars and kept secrets that have been denied to the entire world! My connection to the engineer Talos was due to his defection from the Claw, which has now *disbanded*, and he had set up escape routes for our own protection in case of a siege, something which I know you are all too versed in," he said, with another vengeful look at her. "When the subject," he emphasised petulantly, vaguely indicating Tierenan with his claw, "was unable to provide information due to his catatonia, Talos was employed to extract the information from his mind physically. Had you the fortitude, patience, or integrity to understand the process, this painfully sordid affair and these unjust accusations that smear Pthiris' name would have been avoided."

Bayer stiffened and stood, drawing attention from the Representatives around him. "Talos had been active in my sovereign of Kyrryk," he boomed. "We don't take kindly to those who harbour wanted criminals for their private investigations without informing us." He gave a nod to the puma and dhole. "Both Andarn and Tremaine have him listed as an individual of interest as well. Notice how they're not blockading your ports for the same reason you did to Representative Xayall."

Rynkath was about to speak, when Bayer redoubled his verbal stride. "This to me seems a disproportionate exertion of force on an inexperienced Senate member in order to coerce self-centred outcomes," he said to the room. "I have seen how easily a sovereign can be subjugated by twisting rules and exploiting naiveté, and I am determined to prevent another tragedy such as Kyrryk's."

The Andarn and Tremaine Representatives shifted awkwardly, and the dhole cleared their throat.

Faria did not try to hide the relief or admiration in her smile, though her voice remained firm. "Thank you, Representative Kyrryk."

Rynkath flicked his muzzle in snitty disregard. "He is not a full Senate member, he doesn't have the title. Or perhaps you need further lessons in diplomatic etiquette."

"I know how not to invade other sovereigns and kidnap children, so I feel I'm on pretty solid ground," she returned scathingly, to some laughs and comments above.

Jed rumbled disapprovingly and stood, his large form

casting a shadow over table. "I have witnessed too much of this in the previous Senate. It brought us to war. We have barely licked our wounds clean of the previous battles; this is a disgrace to the memory of those who have fallen by the hands of ignorance and greed."

Faria bowed her head. "Yes, Sinédrion. That's why I had to defend myself, and uncover the truth in the process."

"We are not the criminals!" Rynkath protested.

Faria slammed her paws on the pulpit. "Who is providing Dhraka with arms and metal? Who sent soldiers into Kyrryk before the siege of the Senate?"

Some of the children started looking agitated. Feith tried to gently coax them towards the back of the room, while Tierenan and Kier advanced to the brimming argument.

Jed walked over and laid a hoof on the Pthiris fox's shoulder, about to pull him back.

Under Tierenan's arm, the hooded kit leapt onto the dais and bounded forwards. A flash of metal whipped through the air and Jed reeled back, red streaking from his arm. Before Faria knew what was happening, a sickle-like dagger was at Rynkath's throat, and the young lynx's face was contorted with a ravenous grin, now visible as the hood was thrown back. Her eyes were a strange pale, sickly, luminous green, her teeth long and glistening.

"LONG LIVE EMPRESS ARC'HANTAEL!" she roared.

In the brief second before the blade sliced into Rynkath's neck, the lynx relished the fear in his eyes. The curved blade drove into his thin skin effortlessly, slashing sideways and down in a long gash that spread crimson over the pulpit and those nearby.

The Representatives shrieked in fear. The gallery erupted in chaos. Dyate, Jed and Tierenan lunged for the lynx but all were too slow. Kier and Aeryn immediately ran for Rynkath, while Kyru and Osiris tried to block the lynx's escape. She was almost unnaturally nimble, her body seeming to flex in odd ways as she dove past their arms and blades, giving a vicious look to Faria as she clambered up the Senate hall's columns and into the gallery above, to a symphony of screams from the terrified audience. Faria pulled her staff from the bench behind her and slammed it into the seat, forming a twisting platform of creaking wood that lifted her high into the rounded balcony, before she leapt from it and gave chase.

The lynx let out a bloodthirsty cackle as she stood by the Hall's doorway, her grin wide, and fur caked in Rynkath's blood, taunting Faria with the bloodied blade.

"What have you *done*?" Faria growled.

Chapter Nineteen

The lynx's piercing laugh made Faria's ears fold back even further, and sent a chill through her fur. A haunting, familiar cold.

"I've freed you, Faria! Killed your enemy! Rid you of the burden of guilt!"

"Who… are you?"

Kier and Dyate broke through the door and shoved through the escaping crowd to flank the murderous creature she faced.

The lynx just laughed, curling the blade in their paw.

With a growl Kier gave a burst of speed to catch them, but they jumped over him effortlessly, and landed a surprisingly powerful kick to his back. Their eyes flashed that strange green again, and with a brief pause to glower at Faria with a chilling sense of familiarity, they leapt off the balcony, leaving a smear of blood on the railing.

Faria dove for the edge. She could see the odd fur and dark hood careening down the wood, scraping a claw along it like they had a supernatural grip, before they hit the floor and darted into the corridor.

She shifted her weight and moved to give chase, when a

gauntleted hand wrenched her shoulder round.

"Halt!" Dyate barked vengefully. The tip of her sword was aimed at Faria's throat.

The fox glared back at her. "Dyate, they're getting away!"

"I have you; I'll have your accomplice later!"

Faria barked back. "I don't know them! They were a child we found in Dhraka!" Below she could hear the desperate calls for assistance in trying to save Rynkath, who Faria was already sure did not survive. "They were—"

"Enough *LIES*!" Dyate roared, leaning closer, the blade tip now against Faria's fur. "This was your plan all along wasn't it? Murder him, usurp our sovereign, take over the—"

Her bile was halted by an impact to her gut. The marble folded around her, raised her up, squeezed. Faria's eyes sparked with resonance energy as the stone warped by her command.

"I've had enough of your accusations!" she roared. "Rynkath was a malicious bag of bones! If you care about your murdered despot so much then honour it by finding the *real* threat instead of coming for me!"

Leaving Dyate protesting violently against her elevated ring of stone, Faria stormed through the door and began a run to the lower level, trying to find any sign of the lynx.

Her mind raced. It had been *so quick*, their eyes so vehement and bloodthirsty. And now they were loose, in the Senate, slitting throats in her name.

She barely noticed Kier calling from behind her. She scanned every face she passed, vision darting ahead till she tore down the stairs to the next level. She didn't know if she was being hunted, or was doing the chasing herself. Her staff was a constant, on edge glow of readiness, which made her seem even more of a danger to those who believed the lynx. The temptation and fear of failing to control it as she pushed against the tide of escaping citizens, felt like it would throw her body into a violent catatonia. She was on the precipice of explosion, or falling, or *something*. So full of anger and fear and desperation that it buzzed through every inch of her and coiled around her chest like a snake, ready to squeeze her to death.

A familiar voice carried above the crush. Ahead and approaching her was Aeryn. The wolf carried a look of duty and relief in her face as she met Faria and immediately took her side, as wary and alert as the fox herself.

"I don't know where they went," Faria muttered, as the crowd finally began to thin near the approach of the hall.

"With luck she's outside," Aeryn replied darkly. "Kyru and the others are heading back to the ship. Bayer's taken the kits to Sinédrion's guard – they'll be safe. Osiris insisted we find you and bring you back."

"No, but they—"

"Faria, you'll be arrested if you don't leave; they'll ambush you if you stay. We need to go."

She growled in reply as she looked around, tail bushed and stiff.

As she went to take a step; Aeryn stopped her once more. "Faria, is that yours?"

Faria looked down to where the wolf was indicating, and saw spots of blood on the carpet. "No. But it's likely Rynkath's." Immediately she began to look for signs of more, a direction, an indication of intent and path to pursue.

Aeryn, with her keen archer senses, sighted another spot further up. They ran towards it, and found another – leading towards the large downward sloping entrance to the archives.

What was supposed to be a guarded door was still, effectively, flanked by two bodies. But that's all they were, lying crumpled at either side of the door, now unlocked and ajar.

Aeryn drew her sword and dagger, while Faria strode forwards with her staff's tip glowing in dangerous fury.

The archive was lit with glass-cupped torches in metal frames, illuminating latticed shelves reaching across the entire breadth of the building. Reams, books, scrolls, maps, cases, some artefacts and wooden placards, banners; all manner of things lay strewn over the shelves. Each red wooden rack had lists at their ends detailing where things had come from, the timelines of records; each one a cross-section of the Senate's bureaucratic legacy. Historical agreements, discoveries, disasters, requests – a library of politics and trade all stacked into organised slats.

The scent of age and information, of coated papers, varnished wood and the hinted choke of fumes from the wall-mounted torches. Faria wasn't tall enough to see over the shelves, which were also staging grounds for boxes yet to be sorted on their uppermost level. She and Aeryn stalked back-to-back, watching for movement.

To their right, a brushing scrape sliced the room's tension. They whirled round, just in time to meet the terrified face of an aardwolf, who shivered and raised their paws over their face.

"Go, get out!" Aeryn hissed. They wasted no time, scurrying away as quickly as they could.

No sooner had Aeryn turned back when something rushed past them both from behind, pushing between the two. It landed a crashing thump to Aeryn's backplate, making her stumble forwards, but she righted herself immediately and gave chase with a thunderous growl. Faria lost her initiative to keep up but sprinted behind, then lost both as they split between the shelves. She could hear the distant rattling of Aeryn's chainmail.

"Where are you?" the wolf bellowed.

Faria dimmed the light on her staff and lowered her stance, trying to mask her position.

"Little late for that," came a mocking voice from above. The lynx's form suddenly swamped her vision, slamming her against the far shelf and trying to tear the staff from her grip. The creature let out a wild yelp as Faria's immediate resistance forced a burst of energy through the haft, which disrupted the shelves around them with a rippling impact of invisible force.

The lynx spat and charged away.

From her right Aeryn approached at speed, alerted by the skirmish. As Faria righted herself, she caught the shadow darting along the shelf tops, straight towards the wolf.

"Aeryn – above!"

The wolf raised her sword just in time; it sparked as it met the sickle-like flash of the lynx's blade aimed for Aeryn's neck. The lynx spun, warped almost, deflecting a thrust from Aeryn's dagger for their side, and curled the blade towards her face. The wolf staggered back slightly and shoved the lynx away, who responded with a bloodthirsty cackle and ducked once more behind the next set of shelves.

Faria approached Aeryn, who seemed off-balanced by the sudden attack.

"Are you—?"

A torrent of blood answered her. Aeryn's dagger dropped as she covered her left eye and dropped to a knee. Faria's cry stuck in her throat, watching Aeryn's armour run red and dark with the spreading stain that blossomed through her fur. "Aeryn, come on, we'll get you out."

The wolf grimaced and shook her head. "Take them down," she growled, as she stood to her feet. "You can do this, Faria."

"Not like this. Not if you die!"

A gloating laugh sang over the archives.

"You're in a panic, Faria," they jeered. "Be careful, you make bad decisions when you panic."

The fox stood her ground, trying to keep guard of Aeryn as she scanned the shelves to find where the lynx was speaking from.

"Who are you?" she roared. "What do you want?"

"Your father was much more calculating," the lynx continued, from a voice that seemed to come from both in front and behind them. "Cold, almost. But I'm here, and he isn't. So I will put an end to cold."

There was a smash of glass, and a soft, deep *whoosh*. The dim light of the lanterns grew from one side of the archives as flames started licking along the wall.

"I thought eliminating your enemy would free you," the lynx mocked. Faria saw a shadow dart between shelves. She slammed her staff into the floor, forcing a rippling wave upwards that sandwiched the shelves together, trying to catch her in the midst of it.

But their mocking, vicious tone remained. "Perhaps I need to kill your friends instead to make you realize what was taken from us."

Her ear flicked, catching a distortion in the noise to their right. She snapped her head round and barged herself backwards, enough to prevent the lynx's blade from catching Aeryn again, yet barely missing her own stomach. She slashed her staff's glowing edge towards the lynx, whose body veered away like a yanked marionette. "Every time you tried to kill me," the feline gnarled, "I took what was around me and forged a new body, a more powerful form. Oakhe, Aidan, you: all failed, all gave me new ascensions to greater powers, and now…" She flicked her claws, which grew, sharper, wetter. Her body elongated, distorted, her arms lengthened and her face drew up and back, with eyes that flared that strange, poisonous green. The strange glow ran through her fur in tiny, hair-like veins, more on the outside of her body like a web than part of it. She laughed again, with a voice that matched the horrific distortion of her body but was now immediately recognisable to Faria. It echoed the cold, infinite pit yawing in Faria's stomach and carried the same venom that had defined her haunting presence for centuries. The burning fear in her body, an echo of the fire that ravaged her as she was connected to the crystal core lying deep beneath Nazreal.

"Raikali."

Another laugh. Scorning at first, then rising, louder, riotously, to a full howl of amusement, while her teeth glinted in the light of the rising fire.

"Didn't get your brains from him, did you? Should have inherited his paranoia. He made gleeful sport of making every problem in the world my fault."

"You're a *murderer!*" Faria seethed, as Aeryn gripped her sword as best she could, keeping her stance despite swaying dizziness and shock. Faria could feel the wolf's unsteady steps. They had to leave, get her to care, but Raikali would slay them without blinking if they turned their backs.

The fire began to spread. Smoke rolled into the ceiling.

"How did you survive Nazreal? I shattered your armour from the inside! I turned you to *dust!*" Faria demanded.

"The same way I always have," she sneered back. "And I owe you *nothing* of my power."

She lunged again, casting aside the blade this time. Faria brought up her staff and formed a domed shield of resonance energy around the two of them. Raikali's fists slammed into it, then abruptly she flinched back. Faria noticed the energy at the impact site shimmer, turn green, and begin to swell. In a panic she dropped the barrier, dispelling the strange corruption of her power. In that instant Raikali swiped at her again. This time Aeryn wrenched Faria away by the forearm and thrust out her sword, and cut deep into Raikali's stomach. The lynx's shape sloughed from it sideways and back, looking down briefly with disinterest. The crystal mesh holding her body together was still intact.

Undeterred, Raikali swung her claws again; catching Aeryn by the helmet and hooking her claws beneath its edge. Raikali twisted around and downwards, bringing the already injured wolf to her knees again.

Faria jumped forwards to intervene, but Raikali halted her with a glare.

She had the wolf's head craned back by the helmet, exposing the wolf's throat which pulsed in strained breaths. Raikali's claws flexed and pressed to Aeryn's windpipe.

"Familiar, isn't it? Watching your beloved companion fall at my command." She licked her teeth. "Do you think she'll survive? Will her partner be as forgiving as she was to you when you failed to bring him back to the Coriolis?"

The air around Faria's staff shimmered like heat over a fire. "Let her go, Raikali."

"Or what?" Raikali spat. "You have taken everything I am from me for millennia. My body burned within the wreck of the Leviathan. I destroyed myself to keep living in spite of what your father did to me. Then *you* took the rest of me in the depths of Nazreal and turned me into this crystal spectre of my former self."

Faria started to move, but froze again as Raikali's claws flashed, hesitating just enough to only draw surface blood from Aeryn's neck.

"Tell me where your father's staff is," she growled. "Tell me and I'll make her death quick, or you can hold her in your arms as she bleeds into oblivion."

"Why do you want the staff?"

"Don't spoil this with your naiveté, Faria," she replied vengefully. "Choose her execution, then yours. Because I promise both are coming. All you can control is how much you suffer until it happens."

Did she want a body? More power? A token? Faria's mind raced, but heat built in her staff even further, making the crystal's edge shimmer with gleaming white.

"Let her go and I'll give it to you."

"Don't… Faria…" Aeryn croaked through the strain of her constricted throat.

Raikali's face darkened. "A poor choice."

Her claws tensed. The flare of energy at the tip of Faria's staff burst outwards, disorientating, knocking Raikali back. Immediately Faria buried the butt of the staff into the floor a wall of stone thrust upwards between them, encircling their path to the exit.

Aeryn was on the ground. Her form shaded, blood beneath her face.

Faria stepped forwards and slid her arm under her, rolling her up. The wolf groaned and helped to push herself up the rest of the way. It had been too close. Too close.

Faria bolstered Aeryn against her and began a desperate, hauling run towards the archive doors. Though the wall separating them was thick, she knew Raikali would find a way through soon. They had to leave, they had to *run*. She picked up her pace, feeling the burn of resonance and the weight of the wolf bearing down on her. The further they got the more Aeryn began to find her own stride again; although her burst was brief it was enough to get them back into the Senate's main circular corridor again and head towards the Coriolis' berth in the canal.

Kyru and Tierenan had come back for them, and met them by the entrance. Immediately the wolf tended to his partner and Tierenan took Faria. The four continued their harried run, Aeryn trailing blood, Faria giving frantic glances over her shoulder to check for pursuit from Raikali's twisted form.

Within a brief but interminable journey they boarded the golden ship again. Thumps of crew getting into place in the hurried evacuation rumbled and bumped throughout. Two more crewmates ran to Aeryn's assistance to bring her to Maaka; Faria watched them disappear below deck before the engines rumbled and the city of Sinédrion began to shift around them, beginning to dim as they took off into the reddening sky of evening. Tierenan yanked her into the sterncastle before she could be blown off the deck by the drag of their takeoff, but until she knew there had been no pursuit, she felt the ever-clinging presence of Raikali just over her shoulder, no matter where she turned. It felt like she was within her, creeping, waiting to appear again.

Once the flight had stabilised, she all but ran to the surgery to check on Aeryn.

Her panicked rapping on the door brought Kyru straight to it from within; he whipped it open and brought her inside, followed shortly after by Tierenan and Feith, while Kier took her staff and waited outside.

"This is quite a deputation," Maaka murmured, as he ran stitches along Aeryn's cheek.

The door swung open once more, revealing the bulk of Osiris as he swept inside.

Faria edged round to see Aeryn, who cast her right eye to the clearly concerned fox.

"I'm alright," the wolf said quietly.

"I'm sorry," Faria whispered, trying not to stare but unable to ignore the slit that had been carved up the wolf's elegant face. It struck from her jowl to her forehead, and there was enough blood that it was impossible to tell if her eye had yet been spared. Maaka was doing his best, and although he was used to an audience, seemed less enthused at hosting a reunion in the middle of vital emergency surgery.

Aeryn weakly lifted a paw as if to dismiss her, but immediately it clenched as Maaka began a new stitch and the wince of pain shot through her.

"I suggest you let me work," the falcon said in gentle reprimand. "The easier it is for me to work, the more likely I can save what's needed."

Faria looked to Aeryn who, although unable to nod, closed her free eye in a manner of acknowledgement. "Go. I'll be with you as soon as I can."

The fox could barely bring herself to look at Kyru, though he followed with her as they exited the surgery and stood in the hallway just outside.

Before she could even levy an apology his way as he pulled the door shut, he gave her a half-smile. "She won't blame you, and nor do I."

"I'm…" she began, before she faltered and swayed, finding her breath suddenly not enough, a rush of panic and dizziness and resonance exertion swirling through her. She had to breathe deliberately and deeply for a few moments, prompting some movements of concern towards her, which she waved away with an outward jerk of her paws. "I've had enough of this," she managed, in a hoarse murmur. "How… how did she come back?"

Osiris cast a severe glare her way. "Do I even need to ask?"

She shook her head.

He grunted and bristled his wings. "Interminable villain."

"Not completely," Faria replied, looking to her staff, thinking about the way it had clashed with her sickly green veins. "She's changed, but she's not immortal. She… I don't know what happened to her body. I think she's… I think she's *inside* the crystal now. And around the body she's using."

Feith shuffled slightly, clearing her throat to address the hallway anxiously. "When Talos was adding her prosthetic armour, he mentioned there was little of her to work with. He said that as much of her existed in the resonance liquid used to douse her as it did the remainder of her body."

Faria frowned. "But that didn't come from her, though. So… she took it in, as she resonated with it?"

Nobody answered. She was the one who knew resonance intrinsically, instinctively. There was nobody left to teach her, not in such a way, about what it might mean. She thought about the way her first attempt to remake a staff had broken the crystal to dust, as if it had been rejected by her body. She wondered if, in the right concentration, or with the right energy, the reverse could happen, where it was taken *into* a body to absorb it. To control the crystalline decay that plagued, and eventually killed, both her parents.

The resonance energy he used became a kind of systemic carcinisation that ravaged his body. Except with Raikali now, it had become her entire body. And if she had found a way to tap into it, lock herself within it… it could, feasibly, actually make her immortal as long as there was crystal left to consume.

"She wants my father's staff," she said quietly.

Osiris frowned. "Why would that serve her?"

Faria balled a paw under her muzzle and pressed her snout into it, trying to think. Why would she want it? Why couldn't she take Faria's? "I don't know," she muttered. "I saw something when she transformed. It was like her body was held together by strings of crystal."

Osiris folded his arms in thought and apprehension. "Another form of her resonance?"

Faria shook her head in disbelief. "It has to be. But the way she contorted herself, was…"

"Not unlike Oakhe."

The others looked around in confusion, unfamiliar of the stories of Nazreal before its initial destruction; Faria waved an unfocused paw to move the conversation onwards. "But it wasn't purple, like Vionaika's powers, or blue like her own. It was green."

The gryphon's tail swished irascibly. "Elysser told me many things about what resonance could do; as did Aidan. But I fear Raikali may have created something entirely new of her own accord."

His brow furrowed still with greater concern and confusion. "But you did not even use Aidan's staff to destroy her. Why is that of specific importance, and not the crystal in your hands, or what fuels the batteries of the Coriolis?"

Her father's staff was broken. It had—

No. *She* broke it. Raikali. Did that mean… was part of her left inside it, after all this time? And would that mean the same for Nazreal, as they tore it apart in their first raging battle?

Faria raked her claws through her fur in exasperation, and then dropped her arms to her sides, in fatigue and some level of emotional defeat. "I don't know." She closed her eyes in thought, trying to reimagine the sensation of the crystals burning through her, of how she tried to obliterate Raikali in her burning panic.

It came far too easily; painfully so.

"I didn't think there would be enough of her left to even survive."

"Unless she scrounged a body from somewhere," Kier said darkly, remembering the lynx form's deathly glower.

She shrugged. "She can't have gone far without one…"

Osiris' face darkened. "There was nothing in that desert for miles," he said in a low, sombre tone. "There were only two corpses inside Nazreal, and we know Fulkore's didn't make it out."

"That's Vionaika's body?!" Tierenan grimaced.

"*Potentially* it was," Faria cautioned, holding up her paws. This was a horrifying escalation of old haunts and she was trying not to let her mind run away with them all. "She must have dragged her carcass out to regroup and plan their next move."

"Which was: build a ship." Tierenan said, with a distasteful snarl of his muzzle.

Osiris scoffed bitterly. "Both Fulkore and Sarr had long desired a power that could compete with the Coriolis."

Faria sighed, a rough, harsh breath that bore too much anger and fatigue to contain within her body any longer. She looked to Osiris.

"The staff is still safe, right?"

He nodded gravely. "I have not moved it."

Her hindpaw tapped anxiously on the floor as she looked over her shoulder towards the sterncastle.

"Let me see it."

Chapter Twenty

Osiris' room was a collection of ornate pieces of debris, weaponry, books, and artistic murals of things potentially intended as a depiction of Nazreal. All of them were old; some of them bore strange burn marks, and the books seemed to have been taken from a wide variety of places. A metal writing desk to one side attached directly to the wall and floor, with a seat that hinged out from underneath it. On top of this were two small wooden carvings of gryphons, which looked much newer and hand-made. She smiled in gentle recognition of the grey-ish one, which to her mind must have been the facsimile of Teratai. A small set of paints and brushes sat in a string-and-leather pocket attached to the wall. Despite the urgency of her need to enter, Faria always treated such a hallowed space somewhat like a museum. A testament to his survival, existence, and histories long since lost.

Just above the bed sat a rack of rapiers, exquisitely forged and detailed. Three were absent – two of which she already knew were at Osiris' side. The other must have been the explosive one sacrificed to dispatch Fulkore. They all had odd characteristics. One had a segmented blade. Another had a diamond cross-section, and the last one had a thin cable that attached to a secondary handle, with a short spike at its end.

Osiris could be inscrutable, but this felt like a defining space for him. A visualisation of his inner thoughts, avowed to duty, protection, and history, and a world that would never again be. It was all at once beautiful and heartbreaking.

The gryphon brushed gently by and reached for a panel in the wall above his nest of a bed, tucking his claws behind to unseat it. Within was a small vault-like alcove of thick, dark metal, in which were the severed remnants of Aidan's staff in three pieces, its leaf-like blades glinting in the room's light. A soft, shaking sigh rushed from Faria's nose as she saw them again, and like reaching out to touch a ghost, she picked them up.

She held them for a second. Osiris stood by the wall, while the others sat quietly in the galley behind her.

"Do you feel anything?"

"That's a… loaded question," she said, with a hint of acerbic laughter. It was a haunting familiarity she had with the tool she'd used again and again, with extreme efficiency and to great, sometimes barely controllable effects when she'd had to run from Xayall. The blades felt as sharp as ever, although she noticed now, when turning them over in the light, there was a slight undulation on their surface, almost as if they were slowly shrinking from the inside, a very faint mottling of what had once been a pristinely faceted surface. She turned them over, and saw the ends of the crystal veins where Raikali had snapped the shaft had receded away from their break point. It was not, however, in the same way that a crystal might splinter from a normal shattering impact. They were almost… shrinking. Dissolving, perhaps, from over expenditure. Or, now that their form as a closed energy circuit had been broken, perhaps it was slowly using up its own resonance simply in the atmosphere.

She watched carefully, wondering if she could try using it to see if they were still viable, but decided against it after a few twirls of it in her paw. She didn't know what would happen to the diminishing ends, whether they would simply stop the energy flow or cause it to explode outwards, or worse if Raikali was somehow still partly stored within them, and dormant until revived by energy.

"She's affected this," she said quietly.

Osiris leant in. "How so?"

She furrowed her brow as she peered into the broken ends of the staff. "Raikali's form of resonance control was distorted after she was attacked in Nazreal, right, Osiris? After that she had to atomise the crystals, turn them to dust, to restructure them."

"Correct."

She frowned, and placed them on his bed. "I think that's what she did here, and to herself."

"Can she still use her resonance?"

Faria shook her head, pounding the bed frame softly with her fist. "I don't know. She can at least change her shape. And she… was drawing energy from *my* resonance field." She paced briefly, ran her paw roughly over her muzzle and ears, and turned back. "I shattered her. I turned every bit of the crystal inside her to dust." She paused long enough to let out an angry sigh, thinking about the surge of intense energy passing from her body to Raikali's, and remembered the crystal in her paws turning to dust on the night that Shadow's Claw tried to assassinate her.

"Maybe… if she tried to resist me with her powers, between us she transformed into something new. What she may eventually have become herself if she'd never been dug from the remains of the Leviathan."

"A resonance wraith," came a gruff, familiar voice from the door.

Two bodies arrived at the threshold – one mostly supporting the other who watched Faria through a single eye, the other covered by a padded leather eye patch.

Faria immediately ran to Aeryn and cast her arms around her, hugging tightly even into the cold, hard breastplate that hurt her cheek.

"I'm so glad you're still here."

Aeryn hugged her back, and gently stroked a paw over Faria's head. "I'm tougher than that. But you got me out of there, Faria. I'm here thanks to you, more than me."

Faria's immediate response was to infer that she also wouldn't have been *hurt* if it wasn't for her, but she swallowed it down in favour of more pressing thoughts and companionship. "Did you notice anything about Raikali when we fought?" she asked the wolf.

Aeryn shrugged. "I mean, I barely even saw her the first time. She appeared after severing Xayall's Tor, then took you and left." She straightened a little, unfurling herself from Kyru's support to stand on her own. "She couldn't get through your barrier without changing it, though."

"Is that the strength of your resonance, or the crystal?" Osiris asked.

Faria could only offer another shrug. "Could be both. The older the crystal is, the more fragile it becomes. Mine were from Osiris' cache in Skyria, so much less affected by Dad's disaster, and then my near-one." She glanced back down at her father's staff. "My father warned me that resonance energy could catalyse itself. Cascade, and perpetuate. Maybe Raikali is a... different form of that process, either earlier or later, somewhere between dust and destruction, and needs more crystal to become stable in a greater form."

Osiris glowered with grave concern. "What could she do if she managed that?"

Faria's tail curled behind her. "Potentially, anything."

The gryphon growled. "Including getting back into Nazreal."

"Biggest source of ancient overpowered crystal in the world," Kier added quietly.

Faria bared her teeth. "I'm so *tired* of this."

Aeryn stepped forwards and laid a paw on her shoulder. "You're not alone, Faria. We're here to protect you," she replied. "Always."

It was a sentiment shared by Kier, Kyru and Osiris in the exchange of looks between each other and Faria.

She allowed herself a smile for Aeryn's sake, but felt the promise of 'always' was a very tenuous one for anyone else to guarantee when she knew what lay at the heart of the world.

Faria had to be the one to end it, if 'always' was ever going to happen.

Osiris bowed his head. "If you are without need of me, I will return to the helm."

She gave him a gentle, somewhat soft look. "I'm always in need of you, Osiris," she responded, a little more tongue-in-cheek than she felt like expressing, though truthfully each of them gave her great comfort in continuing to be here.

A gentle exhalation of air rushed through his nostrils, a sign that he was at least summarily content with the joke, and he made his exit, disappearing up the stairway. Feith followed quietly behind.

She was left with Tierenan, Kier, Kyru and Aeryn, and the two halves of her father's staff. There was a devastating familiarity to the shattered remnants of Aidan's tool; a kindredness in loss, almost. They felt tired. If that was proof enough of some kind of response to how they had been treated, it made sense that they too could affect someone in the same way. A sympathetic cycle of exhaustion.

Yet she already knew what could happen to her through resonance exhaustion. She had experienced it, the precipice of complete erasure, burning up from the inside.

She wondered how badly Raikali felt it.

There was a knock on the door from behind the wolves. Jala the otter, Osiris' first mate, appeared.

"Faria, one of the children managed to get back to the ship, and wanted to see you."

"What do you—?"

Sinédrion. People were running. Guards clattering. The canal lay ahead. Adorning it, the golden ship, and her prey running to board it.

She ran on all fours, breath spitting, hissing, rasping, limbs distending to increase her pace.

They reached it first, hauled the gangway up. She skirted to the side and leapt onto the engines, claws sinking into the metal as she dug her way round to the gunports.

The ship began to move. The force was incredible, almost enough to drag her off, but her warping, coiling fingers managed to keep hold.

She pried open a gunport and leapt inside.

Everything happened so quickly.

Tearing past Jala came the lynx form of Raikali shoving Tierenan aside to snatch the staff from Faria's grip. The fox grabbed the nearest thing she could to fend Raikali off, which was one of its broken ends. She slashed narrowly at her, severed haft trailing flashes of broken resonance sparks. A blinding, unwieldy lash of energy whipped from it in a slicing arc towards Raikali. The wolves and Kier dived away; artefacts and wall hangings splintered and burnt in its wake. The morphing lynx caught the swinging tip in her claw, unfazed by the slice it made in her growing, distending palm. Even as the energy charred her puppeted, stolen flesh, she kept her gaze fierce, her claw locked, and her fangs hungry.

"You're *mine* now."

With a deep crunching inside her paw, the crystal in her grasp shattered. Rather than falling, it hung in the air for a moment and began to flash and swirl in coursing black and green, before drawing into Raikali. The crystal veins expanded, covering more of the decaying body within. Raikali herself bulked, flexed, showing crystalline muscles and skeletal features that masked the body within like an empty, unwilling pilot of a possessed suit of armour.

Faria whipped away the remainder of her father's staff and reached for her own, still in Kier's grasp. Raikali dived her way, fervid to consume further. Kier was already in motion, driving Faria's stave upwards to lance it into Raikali's side. She let out a fierce roar of agony and swiped for him, but missed as he ducked his face away.

Faria took hold of her staff and sent a burst of energy through it as it lodged within Raikali's flank. The skeletal lion gave a grimacing hiss and flinched back, just as Kyru and Aeryn charged their blades forwards and pierced through her chest in a devastating cross of swords.

Raikali shook briefly. She let out a long, rasping breath, and turned her head to Faria.

She was grinning.

"Do you feel powerful?"

Something rumbled outside the ship. Jala ran to investigate.

Faria glowered at her. "I can blow you to pieces right here."

The lioness' faceted jaw split into a sneer. "You will only make me stronger. Every death you gave me has been an acceleration towards my true purpose." A jagged tongue swiped across her teeth. "Unity."

"Unity?" Faria scoffed. "By murder and war?"

Raikali ignored her. "You've felt its call, haven't you? The pull of the resonance, looking for reunion. The cold, dark, *longing* for completion."

Another boom. Louder, this time. Footfalls rattled below deck, and crewmates began to rally calls for the gunports.

Raikali craned forwards, eyes flashing with hunger. It was a terrifying desperation, a thirstful need like Faria had never seen before. "It's in every crystal, every soul who feels resonance. I couldn't see it till you tore my body to pieces. The loneliness that grows and consumes and festers, taking the entire body like it did your father, and every other resonator." Her eyes flared once more, claws reaching forwards. Kyru and Aeryn twisted their blades, hooking her back. "It keeps you awake, Faria. I *know* it does. You see it at night; the ghost that haunts you, calls you, watches us all, and craves reunion. And I know how to conquer it."

A chill ran through Faria. She knew the exhaustion, the shades of fatigue and isolation that came with resonance. The nights spent alone, awake, with nothing but the moon as a companion, with its scar a reminder of where her powers had come from.

The source of it all.

Was that… what Raikali wanted?

"You… you mean the moon?"

A sharp growl splintered through Raikali's teeth. "Now you understand. You could assist me, if you dared escape your abusive self-repression."

Faria shook her head, aghast. "You're twisted," she rasped. "Those crystals will do nothing but destroy and consume if overloaded! I won't ever let you take them!"

The lioness drew back, flexing her shoulders, and clasped her claws over the ends of the wolves' swords. "Useless fool. We are already on our way to ascension."

A volley of cannonfire exploded from the gundeck beneath them. The ship rocked, then, with a massive, tearing impact, as something slammed into the Coriolis.

The room shuddered; everything dislodged, from creatures to weapons to furniture. As the wolves lost balance and Kyru caught Aeryn, their swords slipped from the crystal Raikali's body. The lioness anchored herself on the wall and leapt for Faria, but was intercepted by Kier who, with a push of his palm, exploded a burst of force outwards, sending her cannoning back into the hallway.

He gave chase, while Faria picked herself up and ran past Kyru and Aeryn to follow behind.

The control chamber of the Dhrakan ship glowed orange; the fires of its engines mirrored in the array of glowing stones that illuminated its chambers. Sarr sat in his throne while, ahead and above him, mounted on a high platform with a very narrow, angular window, was Talos. The wolverine gripped the controls as he steered the spear-like ship, able to see Sarr with a mirror by his right shoulder. The dragon seemed to be staring elsewhere, a line of focus and vision that stretched beyond the boundaries of the long, dark room that sat above the Skypiercer's gun deck.

"Their hull should be no match for you," he rumbled.

"Carrying the weight of a second ship requires precise spearheading," Talos bit in return. "It will do neither of us good to become a fiery pit in the ground for malicious impatience."

Sarr snapped his teeth in dismissal and stood, flexing his shoulders back.

"How close are we to Nazreal?"

"The last impact altered their course; if the map is correct, we will be flying over the desert already."

Sarr grinned. "Good. Prepare to ram them at your earliest opportunity."

Osiris cursed as another rolling impact scraped along the Coriolis' hull. They had dropped to try and stave off the Dhrakan ship's fierce attacks, but the wind stream crossing the border of Xayall and Nazreal was fierce, further buffeting the ship. He braced himself against the wheel and steadied it to ride the circling, spiralling winds. Sand plastered the windows; the engines roared with the fury of their efforts. The dark form of the Dhrakan ship briefly appeared underneath, then vanished out of view. Feith, gripping the windowframe tightly, tried to scan for its location, darting around as balance allowed her. Osiris pulled the ship to starboard, trying to veer away from where Nazreal lay ahead and, eventually, breaking back out into the bright blue air to begin an ascent to escape or else round back into a charging launch of the railgun. The gryphon's ship faced an acute upwards angle; the engines rattled and the ship shook – as if something had been rammed out of place.

As Osiris brought the ship to a gradual level flight, something flashed across the windows. A shadow. Then, a shape. It swept down at incredible speed and slammed into the hull with a dull impact. Below them in the galley and gun deck, they heard cries of alarm, and thumps of combat.

More dark shapes dove in from above them, curling under the ship's deck.

Boarders.

Osiris growled once more and wrenched the ship sideways to try and avert them. The sky surrounded them on all sides.

Come on, my faithful machine, do not fail me now.

Faria tore after Raikali with Tierenan by her tail, but the second impact tossed her to the ground. The partly-shattered portion of her father's staff rolled away as she dropped it, and as she scrabbled to her feet to retrieve it, a dark shadow loomed over her.

The dragon raised their sword, aiming for the back of her neck.

In a charging thrust, Kyru shoulder-barged them to the deck, sliding off them for just long enough for Aeryn to follow behind and land her blade in their throat. She wrenched it free and turned as more dragons began swarming up from the gun deck.

Faria looked around quickly, hunting for Raikali. Through the porthole she could see the Nazreal's looming mesa.

They were too close.

And then, in a deafening impact, the landscape lurched from view.

The Coriolis shunted sideways but kept moving, its flight path now a desperate, erratic spiral that angled high and swept sideways with some incredible, unknown force. Faria again fell against the floor that rose to meet her. She felt a crack at her hip, and with a desperate grasp of her hand, felt the once more broken sections of her father's staff as the crystal shattered under her weight. She hauled herself to her feet, as did Tierenan, and ran to the porthole.

A sickening, stomach-dropping sight befell them.

The Dhrakan ship had impaled the Coriolis' hull.

Chapter Twenty-One

The Skypiercer drove further into the Coriolis, thrusting them upwards, arching its path to lift them up on its nose cone in the way a swordfish might harpoon its prey. The golden ship's hull wailed with the strain of its own distorted, broken weight and the force of the piercing ship driving through it. Its engines coughed with mechanical roars and the acrid scent of burning, twisted metal filled their nostrils.

"Infernal bastard!" Osiris bellowed, gripping the wheel tightly, trying vainly to steer the ship and resist the flight of the Dhrakan spearhead. Rage boiled in his throat.

He looked over to Feith, who clung to the table anxiously, looking between him and the helm's entrance, from which the sounds of fighting were ringing above the rushing wind and groaning, distorted hull.

"Feith!" he called sharply. "Take the helm!"

She glanced out of the window, and the uneven, undulating level of the landscape below. "I… I don't—"

"I need you, Feith," he reiterated. "Keep us steady, and try to fly us free if you can."

She quickly strode over and gripped the spokes, immediately feeling the fierce resistance of the wind shear and the weight of the Dhrakan vessel. "Where—where are you going?"

He drew his rapiers. "To destroy that ship."

He took his pommel and slammed it into one of the windows, shattering it completely in one swift blow. He folded his wings as he clambered through, and took flight to the black ship's deck.

Feith watched him leave, her hands shaking at the helm, alone, in the sterncastle.

Below, the blue-black steel hull split the decks of the Coriolis apart, buckling the floors above and below its entry wound. Its nose travelled the width of the ship, and from its front-most hatch, more dragons spilled out to assault the already besieged, stunned crew. Aeryn picked up Kyru from under an unconscious crewmate and began a violent defence of their ship, while Faria turned and thrust the buckled, disintegrating remnants of her father's staff into Tierenan's arms.

"Take them! Don't let Raikali catch you!"

He opened his mouth to protest, wanting to stay with her, but she glared emphatically to silence his refusal. "Tierenan, *please!*"

Gripping them tightly, he nodded, and ran back towards the sterncastle, slamming his free fist into a Dhrakan who emerged from behind them, sending them whirling into a displaced cannon. Faria continued on, feet pounding the deckboards through the charge of dragons.

Trapped in the gundeck's bow by the Skypiercer, Kier stood, sword brandished.

Raikali had vanished. But she wouldn't have been destroyed by the impact of his blast alone; he wasn't that lucky.

A port opened in front of him; in a flash he thrust a sonic explosion towards it – the bewildered pair of dragons trying to embark from within were immediately thrown unconscious. He leapt over their bodies and began tearing into the dragons from their other flank, till something cannoned into his side, sending him rolling across the black metal grating.

Raikali's eyes glinted in the burgeoning smoke and glimmering haze of the ship's flickering lights.

"Where's your Empress, boy?"

His lips curled in anger, revealing his fangs.

He leapt forwards, and she jumped to meet him.

Faria swept her staff in front of her as she ran, forging a metal spike from the Coriolis' ceiling down into a Dhrakan's leg, preventing him from pursuing an injured rabbit crewmate. They thanked her profusely as they ran past her to a defensive position towards the crew quarters near Maaka's surgery. Another Dhrakan approached with a grim roar; Faria cast her staff to the floor, forging a web of metal from it, trapping him immediately, constricting till all he could do was hiss muffled curses through his bound muzzle.

The whistle of air pressure sucked through the gun ports, the fervid roar of the engines scorched the air, the creak of metal tore into her ears as the Skypiercer edged further through the ship, nose already threatening to pierce the Coriolis' other side. Her ears flicked as she violent booms rumbled from within the impaling vessel. As she advanced to the hatch, she caught a flash of Kier as he did battle with the lightning-fast form of Raikali on the other side.

Faria charged forwards, ducking past the wolves and into the Dhrakan ship. It smelt of burning metal and musty, stagnant humidity.

Kier swung his sword across Raikali, who grabbed the blade in her claws and folded her body around it to usurp his guard, slashing at his chest and face. He rolled back, dropping his weapon, and aimed a sonic punch towards the agile lioness. She ducked away, and barely caught sight of what was about to hit her – a barrage of molten metal bullets. The spiralling, metal sheet from the Dhrakan hull warped at the command of Faria's energy, coiling around her staff's tip then firing outwards, trying to tear the reborn Raikali to shreds. She crouched and crawled at supernatural speed, avoiding Faria's onslaught with ease. Kier took his sword again and cut a slashing vibration through the air across Raikali's path, causing her to leap up and grab onto the ceiling.

She glared at Faria. "Your weakness precedes you."

"You won't win, Raikali!" the fox growled back.

"I don't have to win to destroy you!" Raikali laughed, shrill and manic, as she careened towards Faria and slashed at her breastplate. The claws skirted just under Faria's arm; Faria gave a heavy swing of her staff but Raikali ducked beneath and headbutted her in the chest. Faria fell back, and for a panicked moment saw Raikali's teeth aimed at her face, but a swift kick from behind from Kier threw the lioness off.

They charged at each other once more.

Osiris slammed open the door of the Dhrakan ship's upper deck and hauled himself inside. A few Dhrakan engineers jumped in fright; immediately he was upon them, showing no mercy for their complicity. As one ran, Osiris cannoned forwards and thrust his rapier through its flank, before pulling the dragon to his chest and ramming his other blade up through its jaw. It burbled and slumped to the floor, cast aside and left for its life to disappear in the dark chamber of a soulless machine.

He strode forwards, eyes ahead, till he reached a ladder to the deck above. Half-flapping, half-climbing, he launched himself through the hatch, turning swiftly around when his hindpaws hit the deck. Another dragon stood before him, but only briefly, before he too hit the ground in a flash of steel and blood. Osiris pressed forwards, his hunt spurred by the scent of Dhrakan viscera.

He barged a shoulder into the door ahead, which opened to a long, high room bathed in an infernal glow. He held his blades up, peering into the shadows.

Above was a control platform like a raised helm, at which he saw the focused, hunched form of Talos. He pointed his sword up and swept towards him; Talos caught sight of the movement in the mirror and froze.

Just before the gryphon reached him, something lurched in the darkness to his left side. He altered his course, just in time to see an axe blade tear through the air where his flight would have taken him only a moment later.

Sarr's mechanical parts hissed and jerked, his inordinate muscles now augmented even further with the cold tension of steel and cable. Another axe was resting on his shoulder, this one with its signature serrated edge, specific for cutting through feathers. He wrenched the axe forwards to brandish it, as his seams hissed with heat and pulsed with the familiar blue of resonance core liquid.

"How fitting to fight you, in the same place that forged our destined war," he laughed, a grim rumble that oozed with hunger for death. "Osiris Tallon, hero of ghosts, pathetic remnant of an arrogance long since extinct."

The gryphon flared his wings and rolled back his shoulders, rapiers gripped and aimed directly at Sarr's heart and eyes. "And yet here I stand, whole, while you suck life from others to power your corpse."

"You have never seen me as more," Sarr laughed, with a gurgling rasp. He held his arms out, his dead eye glowing yellow. "Even with Fulkore slain I persist, eternal, through my clan. You are the last of yours, and soon all memory of you shall die and be consumed by the sand."

"I am more than my body," Osiris snarled. "I am those I protect. Those I have saved. Those I have loved. I belong to the world beyond my mind and heart. If I can save them from you, then I will always be a part of this world. You speak like your son never even existed."

Sarr's face contorted with rage. "A travesty that you remain while he does not! A warrior destroyed by a being of such pathetic, disgusting sentiment."

"So long as we live, we exist in eternal conflict," Osiris replied firmly. "The cycle ends now."

Sarr grinned. "For us both."

The axe whirled and swords pierced the air as they swung for each other.

Feith had the wheel in an underarm grip, bracing as heavily as she could. The ships seemed to have reached an odd stasis; the Dhrakan piercer able to thrust against the weight of the Coriolis, and the Coriolis maintaining enough lift to not collapse or be thrown down into the sand. They were in a slow, desperate arc towards an enormous mesa. Feith watched it loom into view and begin to swamp her horizon.

Something caught her eye. Just as her vision managed to track it, a dragon folded itself through the shattered window in a spiralling dive and landed on the table, scattering the maps and equipment, spreading himself wide with twin swords bared.

He slashed down at her head; she ducked, and the blade sunk into the wheel. The dragon wrenched it free and jumped down, aiming a slash at her back that would easily have bisected her if it hit. She released the wheel and leapt away in a panic. The dragon's sword split the topmost wooden spoke and landed deep in the helm's console. He wrenched at the hilt but it stayed lodged, the blade distorted by the heft of its blow.

Quickly, Feith scrabbled for something to defend herself with.

Tierenan emerged from the sterncastle steps. "Osiris, we—"

Immediately he lunged forwards and landed a punch to the dragon; although its head reeled back with the force, it kept hold of its sword, merely pivoting around his fervid grip. As the raccoon drew close to reach for Feith, she tore the broken stave from his grip and held it up defensively, just as the dragon abandoned its trapped blade and lunged again.

She fell backwards, holding the staff upwards in frantic, blind defence, while Tierenan's resurging punch sailed over its head. The assailing reptile's sword skimmed past the end of her nose, but in his attempt to reach her he stumbled, falling straight into the upended staff. The dragon's weight pressed down; his upper chest sank over the crystal tip. She felt the sickening give of his flesh, and the heavy flow of blood on her fur. She scrambled to break out from under him while he roared and writhed, tearing himself off her. He stumbled back into the wall, gnashing his teeth. Tierenan corralled the terrified ferret behind him, but as another dragon swept into the sterncastle and a third loomed in the sky behind, they both turned to retreat to the galley.

Fighting between the spearpoint entrance of the Skypiercer and the Coriolis' gundeck, Faria avoided Raikali's lurching, distorted slashes and wild attacks, defending herself with bursts of resonance shields that made the lion shriek when she impacted them. Faria sent a wave of the energy flowing towards her; in a frantic movement Raikali threw herself into Kier, knocking him down, and used his body to springboard off and head back towards the galley. Faria leapt over Kier in pursuit.

Immediately Raikali launched at her again; Faria barely managed to block with her staff. The lioness' teeth deformed and tried to impale her fingers. A heavy kick threw her away again and almost into Kier's pommel, but it merely grazed the fur on her cheek. She glared at him with bloodthirsty fury, but a second later her eyes flared with a different kind of recognition at something further along the deck. She warped her body and careened forwards, heading directly for Feith, who still clutched the blooded mid-section of Aidan's staff before her.

Far too late the ferret realised what was happening, as the monstrous lion stole the remnant of Aidan's weapon from Feith's paw and leapt up and over her head, knocking her prone in the process. "*Yes!*"

Faria tried to send another energy wave towards her, but an interceding Dhrakan gave a deep swipe of their shield towards her back, knocking her forwards and winding her. Kier dispatched the dragon from behind, but it was a distraction enough for Raikali to clench her claws into the crystal veins and shatter the tool's remaining luminant blue completely. It shimmered and transformed from its once-lustrous colour to the same green as her eyes, which glimmered with horrifying promise.

Her shoulders cracked and jerked upwards, her maw widened; her entire form stretched and shuddered in snapping, forceful movements. Thin crystal digits tore through dead pelt and shredded fur – the last vestiges of what had been the lynx's face split apart with the lioness' wide-mawed rasp of bliss. What had once been mere crystal threads now widened and spread together, becoming wider and stronger, with a more acrid brightness. She formed a taller, angular skeleton with a lioness' face, and with a growling chuckle finally tore herself out from the remains of the lynx, which sloughed to the floor like a slaughtered animal skin.

Raikali let out a vicious, triumphant laugh.

"Nearly there…" she growled.

Feith tried to crawl away from the ethereal, cadaverous form of Raikali, but the crystal lioness quickly formed her foot into a pike which she stabbed through the ferret's leg, impaling her to the floor.

"Oh no no no, you stay!" she cackled.

"Hey!" Tierenan yelled from behind her.

As she turned, she saw the glint of the staff's final section tucked behind him.

Faria took her chance – she surged forwards and took aim at Raikali with a wide swing of her staff. An arc of blue energy sliced across Raikali – she crumpled underneath it and reformed, barely avoiding the resonance blade as it thundered into the wall behind her.

Feith was already behind Tierenan, and took the staff from him. Aeryn and Kyru were behind her at the door, having fought through the Dhrakan boarding party, while Kier and Faria flanked her other side.

"It's over, Raikali!" she snarled.

"Is it?"

For a brief moment her crystalline form rippled, then an eruption of crystal needles pierced outwards from her body, aiming at each of those surrounding her. They had no choice but to duck away or be impaled by her urchin-like stabs. She took to her feet once more, determined to reach Feith.

Tierenan guarded Feith with fists raised; before he had a chance to counter Raikali's charge, Faria managed to divert the lioness by casting a wooden cage around her. Raikali crashed into it, splintering a large enough part that she could almost clamber through, but Faria was upon her quickly. The two exchanged fast strikes: Faria's desperate, and Raikali's hungry. Each of them produced a flash of respective resonance energies that illuminated the listing deck. With Raikali's bigger form, Faria had less reach than she did before, the sparks of energy had far less effect, and the lioness was growing more relentless with each swipe. The skeleton's legs were longer in its increased mass, its ability to deform greater, the threat to Faria much deadlier. Auxiliary spines thrust out from anywhere she could try to impale them, barely impeding her ability to tear into the wood that separated her from the remaining piece of staff. Kier thrust his sword towards her, but he too was deflected by a nest of spines. Tierenan launched a punch through the split, aiming for Raikali's head. She caught his claw in hers almost lazily, flashing him a dark grin.

"Again, brat?"

A spike lanced his way; he ducked and threw an uppercut with his other fist as Feith retreated from the slowly-disappearing cage. At the same time, Faria thrust her staff into Raikali's head, and Kier leapt at her with a downward slash.

"Fools."

Raikali shrank into herself and reformed, still gripping their weapons lodged within her. She wrenched in different directions, throwing them and their guard aside.

"All this power and still you waste it," Raikali growled at Faria, her voice strangely tinny. "You'll see soon enough what your potential could have been when we unify."

"I saw enough in Nazreal!" she bit back.

Raikali grinned, an expression that split her face almost completely around her skull-like head. "Give me the staff, and you'll find out what *my* world will be."

"Never!"

Her teeth extended. "Then suffer."

She launched herself at Faria again, pushing her back, creeping the battle towards Feith, and the staff she protected.

Sarr and Osiris' blades clashed in the murk of the Skypiercer's helm, vaulting over each other's slashes, ducking past thrusts and jabs, taking glancing blows to their armour. Talos glanced into the mirror, tracking the fight as best he could, flinching if something was too loud or looked like it would get too close. His paws flexed on the controls, keeping the ship in the air, with the golden prize he craved impaled feet before him.

Osiris swept back in a wide arc after a heavy parry, and whirled his rapiers back to point at Sarr.

"Growing slow," he muttered, watching Sarr. "Your moves are not reaching as far."

The dragon's head hung slightly. His joints hissed and sputtered at greater pace, and his breathing was ragged.

Blood dripped from his teeth as his mouth split into a grin.

With a roaring, projected burst of speed he charged towards Osiris. The gryphon easily ducked below the assault, and with the combined force of his own strength and Sarr's raging charge, thrust his rapiers into the dragon's chest. They pierced deep – so far that the hilt of one snapped off in Osiris' claw. He shoved Sarr back, who staggered, and collapsed against his throne. His breathing was erratic, rasping, but he kept his fierce eye on Osiris as the gryphon strode towards him, casting aside his broken sword. Osiris stamped his foot onto Sarr's chest and grabbed the hilt of his remaining rapier to pull it free.

"Any final words, Sarr?"

"See you… in… oblivion."

Sarr's metal arm clamped tightly into a fist. A surging blue light rippled down his metal joints, and into his throne.

Talos looked round in horror. "No!"

A defiant gleam flashed in Sarr's eyes.

A massive, thunderous detonation rocked the Coriolis. The Dhrakan Skypiercer lurched forwards, deeper into the gryphon's golden ship, then buckled and began to list dramatically, wrenching the side of the Coriolis' hull downwards with it. The explosion had shaken the combatants to the floor or walls; those nearest the shockwave were blown over – Aeryn and Kyru among them, reeling towards the cannon array. Smoke started to fill the gun deck, a mix of grey haze and orange flecks of light. Feith watched the Skypiercer's spewing hatches for a moment, then kicked away Raikali's leg and sprinted for the helm as the ship began a dramatic tilt in the direction of the falling Dhrakan vessel. Tierenan pursued; Faria managed to lash metal from the ceiling around Raikali's body to try and stall her as they ran. The trapped crystal beast roared and slashed at the warped ropes of gold, carving vicious dents and sharp gouges. She began to shift and reform through the gaps to pursue them as a large, metallic groan from the entwined ships signalled a dire need to escape.

With the way to the helm now blocked by her barrier of wood and golden metal, Faria and Kier leapt through the Dhrakan ship to the Coriolis' bow. She staggered as the ship swayed, caught off-balance by the creaking, descending tilt.

Kier grabbed hold of her, already tightly gripping the stairway's railing.

Faria resisted, panic in her eyes. "Wait! Aeryn and Kyru—" He threw her a desperate look.

Feith almost toppled backwards onto them as she tried to climb the stair – the listing of the ship made the angle too acute to climb, only assailable via the handrail. Tierenan grabbed her in one arm and launched his other fist up to clamp onto a handle somewhere above, reeling them both up with an added leap. She stumbled towards the helm and half-fell onto it; he followed, and together they heaved at the wheel.

"Where's Osiris?" he yelled, as they struggled to bring the ship back to a stable trajectory.

Her jaw tightened. They were falling at a diagonal, led between the power of the Coriolis' engines and the combined weight of both ships. She shook her head.

"We can't make it."

"We have to!" he grunted through gritted teeth.

With a scowl of desperate frustration Faria burst onto the deck. The wind threatened to cast her off the ship, but she forged a rail with her staff to pull herself to the bowsprit. With Nazreal drawing nearby on their right, they were heading almost directly down to meet the dunes below.

She placed her staff against the deck.

"Sorry Osiris," she murmured. "I'll try to fix this all for you later."

As the dunes rose rapidly into view, she could hear the struggle of the Coriolis' ailerons against the weight of the Skypiercer's corpse hanging off its side. She pressed her staff to the deck and closed her eyes.

Please. Let me do this.

Her whole body tensed as she sent a deep, heavy surge of energy through the staff. She could feel the ship beneath her paws, its intricacies, its massive size, the distended skeleton, and the yawing hole in its side.

Slow. Glide.

The hull of the ship rippled and flared out, morphing into a windbreaker sail that she hoped would buffer their descent. She cast it wider, tried to strengthen it, feeling like the weight of the ship was beginning to press on her shoulders, as if she were carrying it. It wasn't enough, not yet. They were too close to the dunes…

Please…

The metal drew away from the hull at the engines, unfurling wider, shuddering in the force of the wind resistance. She felt the ship lurch; the Dhrakan vessel groaned and began to crunch rapidly backwards out of its hole. The balance point tipped, the Coriolis took a sharp, sudden turn upwards. Faria fell back, into Kier's arms. She felt a soft boom and a rush of air as the deck left her feet.

No, wait!

The air split with a deafening shear and rumbling crash. Black smoke poured into the sky as the Skypiercer hit the sand below and splintered, sending shards of twisted, dark steel across the desert.

Faria opened her eyes to see the sky above, and felt the air rushing from behind her as she fell away, wrapped in Kier's arms. She saw the Coriolis's slam into the flat of a dune. The ship crested it like a breaching whale, then arched sideways and crashed into the sand on its starboard bow. The golden ship's engines gave one last roar as it rocked and ploughed into Nazreal's desert, and then spluttered out to a dangerous, ominous silence.

Kier hit the sand holding Faria tightly; they bounced and rolled over – he released her, and suddenly her world went dark.

Chapter Twenty-Two

Faria blinked open her eyes. The hollow sound of wind rang in her ears. She lay on her front halfway down a dune, with her staff just above her paw and her fur caked with sand. Smoke painted the evening sky as plumes of acrid black against the burning orange above; she could smell the hot metal of the twisted wreckage nearby and, distantly, the roaring hiss of a damaged engine.

Her head swam with disorientation. Her shoulders and back ached from the impact, and her fur was laced with sand. Her whole body from muzzle to tail-tip swirled with burning fatigue, a resonance cry that begged her to stop, or threatened her against continuing. She groaned stiffly and pushed herself up, swinging her head round to look for Kier.

He lay some feet away further down the slope on his side, a tumbling trail of impacts in the sand above him. His sword blade had been snapped and stuck out from the dune close by. She lumbered upwards and half-fell down the dune to grab his shoulder and try to rouse him. "Kier! Kier, are you alright?"

The silver-eyed fox grunted and rolled onto his front, pushing himself to his paws and knees.

"Sorry Faria," he muttered groggily. "I had to take you—"

"Shush, don't—don't apologise," she interrupted, adrenaline beginning to rise and clear her focus. "We have to find the others."

She pulled him to his feet, and then climbed the dune in a growing urgency. He shook his head for a moment, then was able to properly keep pace with her.

Faria crested the desert rise and a breath fell from her at the sight of the crash. In the ship's wake and crater crew members were pulling each other free, clambering from holes and helping each other across the deck. Maaka was alive, and somehow still in possession of his glasses, though one of his wings was held back at an angle that looked like flight would be out of the question. With a swell of relief she saw Kyru and Aeryn appear at the sterncastle windows. They clambered out, slid down the hull and dropped the last few feet to the sand. Aeryn landed, but Kyru impacted the sand and crumpled to his knees with a growl. As she helped him up and scanned the wreckage quickly, she sighted the two foxes.

"Thank the damn stars," she sighed, as Kyru hauled himself up.

Faria was already running down to meet them, with Kier close behind. Faria threw her arms around Aeryn, then Kyru, in grateful relief, but the moment she broke away she was already looking around to tally the others. Not only did she need her kindred companions, but to find any sign of Raikali in the wreckage or skirting outside it. They would all be too lucky if Raikali were shattered already.

"Did you see Tierenan and Feith?" she pressed.

The wolves shook their heads.

"Try and find them, please," she urged, as she ran towards the Coriolis.

With her powers she bent the metal hull so make a hurried

set of steps and climbed to the gun deck. She crouched to peer into the section she'd escaped from, and had tried to restrain Raikali to.

The ship was in ruins. Cannons were strewn around, gunpowder barrels had burst, the floor was twisted and splitting, loose cannonballs had made large dents in the walls and had caused wooden chests to splinter.

But, more concerning – Raikali's cage was both broken and empty.

Faria tore through the metal strands with her staff and searched further within the shattered Coriolis.

"Tierenan? Feith?"

Nothing.

She navigated her way up the steps and back outside along the Coriolis' twisted, sloping outer deck and survey the Dhrakan craft nearby. Both broken hulls creaked in the sun, each one producing eerie noises of further breaking as they began to sink under the weight of their crumpled structures.

She held her staff in front of her as she made her way down to the crook of the Coriolis and Skypiercer, a haunting nest of blast and debris that lay between them. Burnt metal and blasted pipes littered the sand, along with soot, droplets of formerly-molten metal, shrapnel, and scorch marks. She trod carefully, waiting for an ambush.

A clash rang out behind her from Sarr's craft. She jumped as the steel plate that had fallen rocked back and forth on its warped curve for a moment, while over it she stared into a dark void that had been blasted open in the storm vessel's fuselage.

Something shifted within. She sent a pulse of energy through her staff as she approached, and entered, casting a soft light into the chamber. Darkness clung to every surface, remnants of blast and fire. What used to be a high platform with a window to the sky was now little more than a molten, twisted remnant of an iron frame.

In the centre of the room lay a mass. A glint of gold and red armour.

Shattered, torn.

White feathers, painted with fire.

"Osiris!"

She wedged her staff under the metal plating that crushed him and hefted her weight against the shaft. With a strained cry she managed to lever one away, and used her staff to fold out the other. No amount of resonance burn could surmount the anguish of seeing the strongest creature she'd ever known so destroyed.

His armour was badly scorched and dashed with shrapnel. He was on his side, head hanging, with his left wing slumped over his body. The other… was gone. Where the gryphon's golden right wing had once been now only remained a blooded, burnt stump. She let out a wavering gasp as she hauled him onto his back, barely able to roll him for his bulk.

"Maaka!" she screamed. "Maaka, help!"

She shook the gryphon, trying to rouse him, her voice cracking with desperation. "Osiris. Osiris, wake up. It's Faria. I'm here, Osiris."

His eye flickered open. She had never seen him so weak before, wearing a paleness in his face that was viscerally harrowing.

"Faria…" he whispered. "Glad… to see you… safe."

She nodded, letting out a soft whimper as she swallowed down her emotions. "For… for a time, yes." She looked around at the blasted chamber, and then dragged her eyes away from something she didn't want to pay close attention to. "What happened?"

He groaned softly. "Sarr was ready. He blew up his own ship… to try and kill us all."

His body rocked with heavy coughs. He couldn't move his right arm to try and cover himself, and winced deeply.

"And you?" she asked quietly. "Are you… can you make it?"

A hint of a wry smile curled at the edge of his beak. "I have not… yet decided," he said, with a slight laugh. "But I fear the choice…" he croaked, "…will not be mine."

His eyes fluttered as another wave of pain shot through him and he tensed against the floor. She could feel him falling weaker, his breaths becoming more laboured.

"Maaka, please!" she called again, desperately.

His left claw rested faintly on her armour. "Do not… worry, Faria. I have had… too much time in this life."

She took his claw in her paws and shook her head. "There's no such thing as too much time in a life, Osiris," she whispered. "Please. Don't leave yet. Please."

He smiled again. His eyes were becoming unfocused. "You… you have always had… what you needed. Just like… your father."

She shook her head again. "That was you, Osiris. *You* were what we needed. You gave us—" she fought to choke back the sadness and fear in her throat "—you gave us protection, and knowledge, and kindness… Osiris, please…"

His eyes drifted closed. "Osiris?"

He took in a long, rattling breath. "You changed me again… Faria," he breathed, barely a whisper. "Greatest… greatest gift I ever… had, from… from you both. Thank… you…"

She gripped his claw tightly with trembling paws, the bubble of emotion in her throat bursting forth. She sobbed into it, holding it to her muzzle, curling forwards with the wracking devastation of her cries.

Maaka, Aeryn and Kyru appeared at the rift behind her, and all three froze immediately. After a second to collect herself, Aeryn ran to Faria and hugged around her shoulders. The fox fell into her, shaking, and gripped her tightly. Kyru and Maaka solemnly moved to Osiris' body. Both of them breathed with deep control, trying to push back their own shock and anguish, as they began to find a way to move him.

Faria picked herself up, pulled out from Aeryn's arms, and tremulously took her staff from the floor, stumbling towards the hole in the ship.

"Faria?" Aeryn called softly.

The fox glared back with tearful eyes. "Where are Tierenan and Feith?"

She and Aeryn marched outside. Faria wiped her nose and threw the tears from her eyes with a claw, surveying the sands as acutely as possible for signs of the raccoon and ferret. As she strode around the Coriolis, to the side that was tilted up to the sun, she saw two shapes mounting a dune in the distance.

One was waving.

She broke into an emotional, fast run.

Tierenan waved with his one good hand, clutching his loose other arm in it. Its cable had unravelled completely, leaving him stuck having to wind the spare cable around his wrist or step over it. Next to him, Feith clutched the remaining section of staff.

Faria ran faster, desperation, relief, and uncertainty taking her over.

Something else appeared over the dune.

A skeletal figure, behind them.

It raised its piercing claw-like arms, shimmering green in

the light.

"NO!" Faria screamed.

Tierenan turned just in time to see the green spike pierce his left shoulder. He tumbled backwards as Raikali tore it back out, while Feith froze in fear as Raikali's other blade aimed directly for her chest.

Faria plunged her staff into the ground, sending a searing blade of sand directly towards Raikali. It sliced its way across the dune but the wake of its travel obscured the impact.

Feith's body had fallen back. Faria sprinted to them, paws pounding the sand as Aeryn appeared at her side. The wolf grabbed Tierenan and quickly pressed a paw to his shoulder to stem the bleeding. He grimaced, but tried to pull himself upright.

"Feith!" he called.

Faria skidded over to the ferret. She was curled in a ball, clutching her chest. The fox dragged her over with fearful anticipation.

Bloodless. Safe.

Feith shook and withdrew.

"It's okay," Faria called urgently. "It's me – are you alright?"

Feith chanced a touch to her chest, then opened her hands and looked down to check herself for injury. "I… yes."

Faria's fur pricked with alarm. "Where's the staff?"

Snap.

As she stood, the other side of the dune came into view. Below, she saw Raikali's form distend further as she consumed the remaining crystal from Aidan's staff. Her skeletal form grew a strengthened, fuller body, filled out her face, making her reminiscent of the angular, armoured, augmented lioness that Faria fought in the depths of Nazreal.

Raikali took in a deep breath, then exhaled.

Within a second, the sand burst under Raikali's paws as she closed the distance between her and Faria in a single bound and latched her crystalline claw around the fox's neck. The lioness' strength was monstrous. Faria slashed her staff across Raikali's stomach, creating an arc of resonance against her green, armour-like body. The lioness drew back, but otherwise all she did was laugh, and advance again. No scars, no pain.

Her fangs were the colour of bile under the evening sky.

"Are you ready, Faria? To witness what your insipid coward of a father denied me?"

Faria cast her staff across the sand; the grains rolled over Raikali like a wave and began to harden, creaking, condensing. She held the form as tightly as she could, staff quaking in her grip.

"You won't—"

A fist exploded through the sandstone, sending fragments flying. One bounced off Faria's breastplate and up against her cheek, leaving a growing trail of red in its wake. Raikali hooked her claws over the edges of the rocky shell and hauled outwards, crushing, the hole around her with her grip alone.

"I won't what, *Empress?*" she purred, stalking towards her. Faria swung more blades of sand towards her, which she deflected each time with a simple raising of her forearms. "I have made Nazreal quake under my powers *twice*. Shaped it to my will in the heat of battle."

She lunged forwards again, travelling even faster. Her claws pierced Faria's breastplate as she took her on a driving sprint towards Nazreal. The fox stabbed at Raikali with the butt of her staff, but the lioness didn't relent.

"Did you think that after two thousand years of darkness I would simply crumble at the first sign of your power? You're nothing! Worthless!"

Faria could feel the claws digging against her chest. She rammed her staff harder into Raikali's body. The staff's tip began to glow and send a desperate, high whine from its crystal tip.

Raikali continued her spitting tirade, claws clenching deeper. "I have spent a hundred of your lifetimes basking in the crystal's radiance, examining its power, and then taking it as my own! You can never match me!"

"I killed you once, I can do it again!" Faria yelled, thrusting her staff heavily against Raikali's chest. The whine at the crystal's tip ballooned into a piercing glassy shriek, and released a huge eruption of blue crystal energy. Raikali's claws slipped from the holes in Faria's breastplate – she dropped to the sand and fell backwards down another dune, while above her the air rippled with the distorted wave of blue energy.

She watched fearfully as it dissipated.

Raikali still stood, looking down at her with a deadly sneer.

"It's time, Faria," she said, voice reverberating in the crystal cavity of her chest. "I'm taking what's mine, and I will no longer let the world be hindered by your fearful secrets. And I'll give you the courtesy your father did not: I'll let you watch the end of this world."

Before Faria could move, Raikali turned and tore across the sands at blistering speed. She took a long, flying leap into Nazreal's mesa. Faria's staff crackled with the energy of her fearful, horrified rage as Raikali's distant form flickered in the light for a moment, then vanished.

There was a distant boom.

For a moment the sands shook and spread.

Then, the grains slowed. The winds fell, and the sands' drift ebbed, leaving a terrifying, deadly silence in the desert.

Faria's paws spasmed as they held the staff, as if the crystal itself were trying to pull free and escape. Then with the sensation of an incredible, invisible storm, something deep, distant, and horrifying, tugged at her chest.

Her ears folded back. A rumble shook the sand. The air split as a vibration punched through it and grew louder, harder.

Back at the Coriolis, the crew backed away from the unsteady wreck, as beyond it, Nazreal's mesa began to crack and shake.

The rock started to rise.

The sheer cliffs lifted from the sand, growing, ascending, drawing up from the ground beneath it. The rock on the outermost edges crumbled away, sending clouds of sand into the air beneath the climbing megalith. The pillar continued to grow and shed, till finally from underneath the huge column of crystal beneath Nazreal's heart could be seen, glowing fiercely. Its hue wasn't the blue that Faria expected – not entirely. It rippled with veins of green that slowly began to creep through and overtake it, transforming its colour.

Then, with one final colossal snap, the rock beneath Nazreal splintered, and the section enclosing the city began to rise by itself, listing slightly at first, and then as the veins of green began to sharpen and grow thicker, moving in a steady, whining rise towards the moon.

Faria watched the mesa climb higher into the sky, with wide, terrified eyes, as the others caught up to her side.

"What… what is that?" Aeryn stammered.

Faria growled. Every hair on her body stood on end. "She's… she's taking Nazreal. She's transforming it."

"What do we do?"

She shook her head, fear and rage choking her, freezing her to the spot. The Coriolis was destroyed. Osiris was gone. All she had was her staff.

"I don't know."

Chapter Twenty-Three

The mesa hung in the air, rising rapidly with its sickly, harrowing green glow, while the moon watched with its distant, cold indifference beyond the sky.

Kyru ran to Aeryn and Tierenan, who waved him away and pulled himself to stand.

"Can we get up there?" the raccoon asked through his teeth, clutching his shoulder.

Faria wrung her paws along her staff, twisting it tightly in her grip. She could create a burst of wind perhaps, but only so far. Sand was difficult to control for its granularity and lacked continual strength; far moreso when affected by buffeting winds. Kier would destroy himself trying to climb that high with his sonic tread.

She shook her head.

"What about Osiris?" Tierenan asked.

She closed her eyes and tightened her jaw.

"He's... he's gone, Tierenan."

He looked at her in shock. "What do you mean?"

She turned away and began walking back to the Coriolis, unable to answer him.

"F-Faria, what do you mean?" he cried after her, as Kyru

put an arm around his shoulder.

She could hear him as she walked. She tried to put his soulful, heartbroken voice out of her mind and ignore the tears on her cheeks as she marched back to the ship.

There had to be *something*. This couldn't be the end of it. She wouldn't be a bystander at the final cataclysm.

She made her way up the stairs she'd created in the Coriolis' side and walked inside, feeling its emptiness acutely – not just the absence of power or crew, but the lost heart of Osiris now casting it into an ever colder dormancy. She gave a cursory nudge to the wheel. It spun listlessly, with a broken, mechanical squeak.

It would never fly again.

"Osiris, I'm so sorry…" she whispered.

She rubbed her muzzle as she leant against the navigation table and looked at the bowsprit, pointing forlornly over the sand. This ship had meant so much. Carried them from danger to safety, from safety to danger and back, time and again, with weapons and grace unlike anything she had ever seen, or would likely see again. Much like Osiris.

She gripped the wheel, digging her claws into it, as part of the bowsprit's casing glinted in the sun. Even that, a part of a ship that seemed so innocuous in itself, was…

The railgun.

She spun immediately, and yelped as a figure stood before her. The slight Feith leapt back with a mirrored cry of surprise – so lost in thought Faria had been that she didn't hear the unassuming ferret enter the ship behind her.

"Feith!" she sighed heavily, with a little frustration. "You…" she paused and checked her temper. "You're really good at that."

The ferret gave a half-smile in return. "I had a lot of places

I was told I shouldn't be heard."

Faria patted her shoulder reassuringly. "Well, I want to hear you anytime. And actually, I need your help."

Feith tilted her head.

Faria pointed to the bowsprit. "That is a cannon. A very powerful, accurate one. Can you help me power it?"

The ferret chewed her lip slightly. "I… if there's a cell remaining, yes. We need to find out. But—" She grabbed Faria's arm as the fox already started to move towards the ladder. "Faria, I'm s-sorry for—"

Faria put her paw on Feith's. "We'll deal with that later. None of this, if you're about to apologise for it, is your fault. We're all in this fight together, with our choices, and now…" She looked out of the window, spotting the other four running along the sand to join them. "…is a time more important than any before to fight and survive."

The two of them traversed the sloping ship down to the bottom most deck, their path lit by Faria's staff. The keel had buckled with the force of its impact against the dune. Much of the machinery was displaced, and the finely-tuned mechanics that once whirred and thrummed with incredible ancient technology were now bent and lifeless, as much a shell for old memories and lost promises as Nazreal had been.

Faria tried not to involve herself too much in dark thoughts as they squeezed through the narrowed, listing deck, and crept cautiously towards a gentle blue glow closer to the ship's middle. The rest of the lower deck was taken up by the engine array and the parts that aided in its energy transmission, but before that was the battery. Thankfully, the two resonance cores remained, although their power had been deeply exhausted by the intense amount of flying the ship had had to do without refuelling. Now, without Nazreal, there was no chance to recharge them.

Faria's stomach tightened.

They had *one* shot.

"What do you need?" she asked Feith, as the ferret made sure the cores were still seated in their mounts, and studied the battery block and connecting cables.

"Looks like it's mostly the engine mechanics that are damaged. The core shuts off when there's a descent speed past a certain threshold, so it should be a case of opening the safety regulators back up again."

Faria blinked. "Did Osiris teach you that much?"

She shook her head. "I read the journals Talos stole. When he was away I didn't have much to do. They were all I had, so… over and over I just read them. That was how I knew which areas of the ship to target to throw you off course, too."

Faria smiled softly. "I'm sorry you went through what you did, but I'm glad you're here, and that you know what you do."

Feith's cheek fur bristled bashfully and she pulled a little at her fingers. "I'm ready for us to have some quiet." She turned immediately around and ran her paws over the console by the core battery, and pulled down a lever to the right, while pushing two others forwards. "This eliminates the engines from the circuit, but should bring power back to the rest of it, if things aren't disrupted too much."

A large switch remained in the middle of the panel. Feith looked to Faria expectantly.

She nodded.

Feith put both her paws on it and pulled downwards. A soft, electronic hum rang out. A gentle ambience of light from the crystal filaments around the upper edges of the room bloomed gently. Faria felt a wave of relief wash over her as the systems remained on. She clambered her way back outside and slid down the deck, carefully dropping down to the sand to stride around the front of the ship.

"Alright, you big golden bird," she said with reverent solemnity to the Coriolis. "Lift your head up for me one last time."

The sand swirled around the base of her staff. It coalesced and drew from the ground around her, sweeping past her and pushing the bow of the ship upwards, collecting underneath it in a building mound that angled the Coriolis towards the sky, and gently swept it sideways to face the slowly diminishing mesa as it continued its ascent, a trail of sand still trickling from it.

Once Faria had settled the Coriolis, she let out a soft breath of focus, and trod back to the side of the ship where several of the crew stood around, along with Aeryn and Kyru, who still had his arm around Tierenan's shoulder. The raccoon's eyes were wet still, but he straightened at the sight of Faria, and gently removed Kyru from him as he held his unreeled right arm.

She cleared her throat and took in a deep breath to address them all.

"Anyone who's able, help Feith get the railgun ready. The rest, make sure the injured are safe. Take whatever resources you can from either ship and gather them together. Someone needs to send word to Henryk in Xayall – anyone who can. We may be here for some time."

The crew began their work. Kyru, Tierenan and Aeryn immediately entered the ship. Faria climbed back inside and helped Feith adjust and connect what she could, while the crew began preparations for the railgun's firing. The two halves of the bowsprit slowly shuddered open, enough for a projectile to pass through its aperture. As the crew were beginning to load one of the long metal rails into it, Faria held up her paw.

"Don't load it."

Jala furrowed his brow in confusion. "So, what are we firin—?"

"Me."

The otter glanced around; concerned looks and mutters of dubiosity were exchanged among the crew, especially Faria's closest friends.

Tierenan's eyes went wide with fear, one of the few times she had seen him genuinely share such an emotion.

"Can you survive that?" he asked quietly, stepping forwards.

She looked down the delivery chute and along the rails, to the sky beyond. "I have to."

Kier clenched his paw. "If… when you travel that fast, all of the blood will go to your feet very quickly. Try to increase the pressure around them to force the blood back up into your body so you don't pass out, or die."

She nodded. "I'll do my best. Um… can you show me what you do?"

He took her aside and explained as quickly as he could how he used his sonic abilities to create vibrations that compressed his feet, to allow him to travel faster.

"It's not foolproof. I have issues controlling it in bursts depending how fast I'm trying to go and what direction I'm heading in. If you're creating constant pressure it may be easier for you."

She nodded. She upended the staff and placed it by her paws, setting off a subtle vibration that Kier seemed to be able to see and hear, as his ears flicked uncomfortably.

"Sounds about right. How does it feel?"

She winced. "Not pleasant."

"Never is," he said, with a soft laugh. "You'll want to protect your eyes, too. And don't open your mouth."

She leant back a little from him. "You've done this a lot."

He laughed again, looking a little sheepish. "Bayer and I… did a lot of potentially stupid things when we were off duty."

"I'll have to ask you about that when I'm back," she replied, with a sly smile and softly narrowing eyes. She returned to Feith at the railgun's delivery chute. It looked just about wide enough for her to fit into.

"This won't fry me, will it?"

She shrugged. "Might be an idea to have some kind of sheathing over you, but that'll also get hot, so try to cool it from within, if you can."

It was definitely not wide enough for that, she observed. With a gentle touch of her crystal to the barrel, she widened its aperture along its length, being careful to retain the connections between each side and not disrupt the travel needed for the outer rails to buffer the force of the projectile. Feith watched with a little alarm as to how it might affect the structure, but if one shot was all they had… it wouldn't really matter if it exploded, as long as the crew were safe, and Faria was airborne in the right direction.

Faria walked along the Coriolis and looked for metals she thought would be strong enough to withstand the shot. As she picked her way through the messy deck, she stubbed her paw on a cannon. She let out a grumbling yelp and whirled round.

"Alright, bastard. You just volunteered."

She jabbed her staff to it to send through an angry pulse of energy; the cannon unlaced in metal ribbons from where her staff was pointing and reforged into a longer, wider tube with spiralling wings that ran down its casing, and an aperture for her to squeeze into. It toppled from its carriage and onto the floor, see-sawing in place for a few moments.

She looked at it with trepidation.

This was it. A sabot to carry her as the sole body to stand in the way of Raikali's ascent. If she failed, it would become the world's fastest coffin.

She waved to some of the crew and indicated the shell; they quickly climbed over and hefted it up, carrying it to the newly-reforged railgun barrel, ready to load it. Faria followed, feeling an intense pit of anticipation open in her stomach.

She stood in silence, wringing her hands around the haft of her crystal stave as the fog of apprehension and hesitation roiled within her.

But she knew this was all they had.

"I... we're running out of time," she said quietly, more to convince herself than anyone else. "I have to go."

Tierenan swallowed hard and threw his good arm around her while he let the other drop to the floor. He buried his face in her shoulder and held her tightly.

"Please... please come back," he pleaded in a whisper.

She hugged him. "I'll do everything I can. I promise."

She felt more bodies add to the hug as Kyru and Aeryn enveloped her, and Kier rested a paw to her back.

Aeryn pulled back slightly and gave her a stern but admiring look. "I know there's nothing we can do, but... we love you, Faria."

Faria smiled, and rested her head against the wolf. "I love you too. Thank you, all of you, for everything you've done for me."

"There'll be more yet," Kyru said gruffly, with a little clear of his throat. "We'll be watching for you."

Reluctantly Faria pulled away, and slid herself into the metal projectile. After manoeuvring her staff inside with her, the tip pointed downward toward her feet, the crew lifted the missile into place. She felt the coldness of its inner surface around her as she drew its casing closed, and began increasing the pressure around her hindpaws.

She didn't know how long the missile's flight would be. How to cushion her landing. What to do if she never actually made it. There was so much that relied on her alone now. She had to find a way to succeed, to protect them all. This was her only, final try.

She tapped the casing, trying not to panic in the very, very tight and reverberating space around her.

The delivery chute slammed shut.

Aeryn took her place at the targeting periscope, peering through it with her remaining eye to sight the ascendant mesa.

"Up six degrees," she commanded. Kyru wound the wheel attached to the bowsprit mount. The railgun barrel rumbled and squeaked, and gently tilted upwards.

"Alright," she sighed, gripping the trigger lever tightly. "All hands, prepare to fire!"

The crew backed away; Tierenan held his hand at his chest, and Kyru ducked his head.

"Good luck, Faria," he whispered.

"Firing!"

Aeryn pulled the trigger.

The railgun let out a thunderous boom. The whole ship rocked back with the force of the impact, dislodging it from its place in the sand. The rails exploded outwards, splintering and flipping over the dunes.

Aeryn peeled herself from the side of the deck, ears ringing. She gave them a shake and tore onto the lop-sided deck, holding her paw above her eye to track the path of Faria's projectile.

The sand cleared. An airborne spark arced through the sky towards the flying, crumbling mesa.

"Come on, Faria…"

Chapter Twenty-Four

Faria felt the impact blast through her. Almost immediately she felt faint, but gripped her staff tightly and increased the pressure on her legs, forcing her head to equalise a little. It was an awful, crushing sensation, like being pressed back down into the base of the projectile by an invisible weight on her head. She closed her eyes tightly as she felt the pressure build in them, and tried to remember how far away Nazreal was. The terror of the fast-approaching pillar of rock filled her mind. She had seconds left to make a decision.

All or nothing.

She jabbed the staff into the metal casing once more. The wings folded open in a spiral, giving a halting jolt to her travel. The unfurled casing left her standing on a small circle of iron just about big enough for her paws, connected to the wings by a pole that ran up her right side. As the light burst into the seams and opened her up to the sky, she saw the ground, far, *far* below her. It was dizzying, made her stomach lurch. She gripped the pole and her staff tightly as she felt the wings decelerate her, and chanced a look upwards. The void of sky was another piercing shot of vertigo. She clamped her jaws tightly, and looked desperately for Nazreal in the rocking, unsteady sky.

Her answer came quickly as a large shadow loomed overhead. She thought she was still ascending, but saw it start to fall upwards as her flower of wings began to topple back down. Immediately she hit the casing with her staff again. Two of the wings deformed into metal-chained spears that folded around each other and launched upwards to harpoon the city's rocky underside. It fell taut; her emergency high-speed birdcage swung violently beneath the edge of the gigantic floating rock. The chain hook embedded in its outer crust was her only anchor. She looked up, keeping her focus on the city to avoid passing out, throwing up, falling off, or some humiliating combination of all three. She turned her staff carefully towards the chain, and tapped the crystal to the metal to begin reeling it in; morphing the rescinding links into the body of the ex-cannon shell once more. She almost smiled to imagine what Tierenan might say when she told him how he'd inspired her aerial anchor-shot.

It seemed to take an eternity. She meticulously drew the metal down and spiralled it around her in a cage, giving her more security against falling and to finally relieve her shaking paw that had gripped the pole with vital desperation. Still the cage swung in uneven arcs, made even more acute by an impact from a falling rock on its upper edge that threw Faria to its floor as it caused a wild pendulum swing. Despite this, she willed the cage to keep absorbing the chain. The mesa loomed closer and closer, till finally it stopped and the remaining metal butted up against the plateau's rocky, sheer edge. She reformed it into a platform that embedded itself deep into the mesa, and allowed herself a breath she didn't know she'd been holding in. She had to hold herself for a moment to curtail the rush of dizziness, the strange distortion of internal energies playing on her chest and equilibrium more acutely now.

She didn't know if her intrusion would alert Raikali. Using her powers could be a risk, but with luck, there'd be so much interference from the transforming rock that she might get seen as an anomaly, if she was detected at all.

She was sure it wouldn't take long to find out.

She closed the rock behind her, sealing away the deafening rush of the sky. Her staff was the only thing lighting her path into the familiar, yet now unknown space of the stolen Nazreal. Everything was muffled except for her own breaths, which she felt were ripping into her ears with such volume that there was no way she wouldn't be discovered. So far, each step she took was a timid one to ensure her safety. She could hear rock splitting through the mesa's shell around her, and the constant fear that her section might plummet away if she wasn't fast enough rose only higher with every stride she took into the rock. Until something glowed as she passed over it.

A blue resonance crystal, isolated in the rock. Untouched so far by Raikali's corruptive reconstruction. Faria plucked it from the stone. It glowed in what felt like a kind of lonely sympathy. She tucked it quickly away under her breastplate, and kept stepping upwards. A tiny hope. A palmful of resistance.

Without warning, the resistance of the rock she had been pushing through vanished. An undulating green pulsed from the slit beyond her staff. Carefully, she split the gap further open and peered through in horror.

The city that she had briefly known in her previous frantic attempt to escape Raikali, was a strange spectral visage of what she remembered. The buildings remained, but their crystal-imbued dust and outcrops of blue surged with rhythmic pulses of green energy. The large crystal dendrites that sprouted from the floor had branching green veins within them that pulsed and shone, imbuing them with the corrosive light. If she looked closely enough, she could see the tendrils creeping further, spreading fractally to complete recombination. She dared not touch one, unsure what it might do to her body, or her resonance.

A splitting crack made her jump. A tower to her right crumbled; the crystal that had formerly been supporting it in the darkness eroded away, splintering to dust that swept towards the centre of the city.

A light caught her eye. At the apex of the mesa's disintegrating shell was a hole, just above the Tor and its twin spires. She could see the sky through it, becoming clearer and darkening as Nazreal continued its upward flight. Between the spires she could see a shape, something grossly distended, growing, pulsing.

Raikali.

She crept forwards, keeping as far away from any crystals as she could. The stone itself was bare and didn't thrum with the stifling, creeping energy of the crystals around her. It was like the breath of an enormous creature. It oozed into her fur, stuck to her skin, and dried her mouth. It felt like electricity was jumping between her fangs and stabbing at her nose, tasting sharp and acidic. This was the eminence of Raikali: her hate and the poisonous bile that consumed her, now embodied in totality. As Faria crept round a corner, a crystal suffused entirely with the green veins shattered, showering her with dust. It swirled round her for a moment, then drifted, much like the previous one, over to the mass at the Tor. Her body forbade her from moving as she frantically studied whether she'd been detected. With a glance down she saw her own pawprints left in the dust behind her, a faint shimmer of blue in them at their deepest points, quickly swallowed by green.

Her head snapped back up to the Tor.

The mass had gone.

With a breath held in her chest she kept her staff in front of her defensively, eyes wide and sharp as her gaze quickly tracked her surroundings.

"Where are you?" she whispered.

"Me?" came a sudden, piercing voice. Faria whirled round to its source – a clawed arm whipped out from a growth of crystal, trying to grab for her. She slashed her staff upwards, bringing a blade of stone from the floor that severed the crystal limb and sent it crashing to the slabs. The limb thrashed towards her once again; she planted the base of her staff against it and wrenched outwards, flinging it away, before she pelted down the distorted, glowing street.

"Faria Arc'hantael. Daughter of chaos," the voice dripped in pursuit from every resonant crystal around her. "Child of naivety and weakness. You intrude on my triumph."

"I won't let you do this!" she yelled to the darkness, coming to a halt at a crossroads between four half-broken, trapezium-shaped buildings.

A gloating laugh seeped into her ears.

Another claw struck out at her – bigger this time, from a growth beneath the stone. Faria caught it against her staff's handle and swiped hard, aiming an obliterating burst of her own crystal energy towards it. It crumbled away, though the swirling green remnants began their trail back into the shadows.

"Insipid petulance," Raikali spat, from everywhere at once. "Your family held the ability to change the world for millennia and all you did was sit on your paws, while I screamed into darkness at the hand of you and your father."

The ground surged beneath Faria. She leapt aside as the paving split and a huge arm rose up, trying to grasp her in its thick, bladed claws. She formed a vortex of wind beneath her feet and blustered up and away, then a second to blast herself back to the roof of a nearby tower. The claw snaked round and thundered up towards her, drawing from the crystals around it. The whole mesa groaned and the stars outside shifted their angle; almost in response the claw seemed to slow just for a moment. It was brief, but enough. With a spiralling flick of her staff Faria pulled up the tower's wall into a spiked shield that the hand crashed into. The limb split and spread its digits around the edge, half extending, half crawling, aiming to catch her or pierce her. Faria reeled back, almost toppling over the edge, but a desperate plunge of her staff into the stone first formed, then fell onto a platform that she immediately reformed into a slope that carried her into the street below, and onto her paws to escape as fast as she could.

Another laugh rippled under the mesa. "Is that all you can do? Run?"

A splitting crack beside her turned her ears. Faria dove past a falling facade as it ruptured, revealing an elongated, almost snakelike visage of Raikali's lion head crashing from it, maw wide, fangs gleaming and lengthening as it pursued her. She turned, planted her staff, and sent a roaring wave of energy through it, keeping all of her focus on trying to send Raikali away. A large orb of blue light surged at the crystal tip and fired towards the advancing monster. It seared through the crystal face and down a portion of its body; a metallic, echoing rasp signalled its injury.

The mesa veered once more. A brief look of disgust and pain echoed on the Raikali-serpent's face, before her laugh swelled once more in the fabric of Nazreal. It halted its path as Faria stood before her defiantly with gritted teeth and a burning ache through her body.

"You *do* have fight in you," Raikali mused, while the crystal creaked and twitched with sharp snaps of transformation behind and around her. The mesa stabilised again. "There is the vicious self-preservation I came to respect."

"This world deserves more than this, Raikali!" Faria yelled, surging another build-up of energy through her weapon, making her fur blowing in the duel of pulsing energies. "I'll destroy Nazreal if I have to!"

"Spoken like your father!" Raikali roared, her body rippling backwards before launching into another charge. Faria honed the orb into a large resonance blade that she cast forwards in a wide slash, splitting Raikali in two. The head half crashed aside and thrashed, while the other began to form a new head that took hold of the first in its proto-mouth to merge with it. She spun on her paw and broke into run towards the Tor, deflecting an opportunistic blow from the snakelion as she hurtled past.

"I should thank you," Raikali echoed after her, in sickening facetiousness. "With my new form, I am insurmountable."

"Nothing is," Faria spat under her haggard breath as her paws pounded the streets, leaving a trail of blue prints behind her.

"Oh, but you believe *you* are," the lioness purred. Faria could hear stone creaking around her, beginning to close in from all sides. "The way you preach. The lies you tell yourself. The fear you cloak yourself in. You believe in the immortality of hope."

The buildings around her contorted and split as a wave of jagged claws came crashing through, a cascade of spines and angled spikes descending towards her.

"You will never last!" Raikali bellowed. "This city is my body, and soon it shall become the world."

Her serpentine head rose above the closing storm of claws. "I will bring the glory of resonance to all of Eeres!"

Faria butted her staff against the stone under her paws. A column of brick shot directly upwards, carrying her out of the spiralling maw, which quickly severed the pillar beneath her. She felt it tilt and topple; another jab of her staff punched the rock into her side and threw her away from Raikali's swarming reach; in a fluster she summoned another wind that just barely carried her back to the ground, though she slid and rolled a few feet before dizzily finding her paws again and stumbling to a mad sprint to somewhere, *anywhere*.

Through one of the crumbling gaps in the mesa's ceiling she saw Eeres' moon.

Like a pole vault she pushed her staff against the ground again and used it to deliver her to a rooftop, causing a cloud of dust to billow from her paws as she landed.

"You'll destroy Eeres!" she warned adamantly, her staff glowing with her growing fury. She had to force her right eye open, as a surging headache threatened to trap her in place if she didn't resist it. "You could stop this now, and give us all a chance to live peacefully with what we have."

"Liar!" Came the erupting reply. Something thundered under the street towards her, flinging slabs of stone away from its trail. With a running leap she jumped out towards the other building, firing a gust of wind at her back to carry her crashing onto its dusty platform. The roof she formerly stood on was sundered to pebbles by the surging form of Raikali's body erupting through it. She was almost like a centaur now, with her own lioness torso attached to a larger, muscular mass behind her drawn from the city's crystal roots. The mesa wavered and shifted, sending some of the rocks above crashing down into the streets as the ancient rocky tomb failed to withstand her shifting focus and control.

Raikali wrenched her head round to Faria, who had already shaped the building's wall as a slope to slide down, and tore across the pavement towards the central tower again.

"We are done negotiating," the lioness seethed.

Faria whipped around a corner and thrust a stony platform over herself to cover her tracks. She watched Raikali's glowing form steam past, then she ripped herself to her feet and began running again. The tower loomed into view above her and the moon leered through the gap, its surface becoming brighter as the mesa ascended.

If she could reach the resonance chamber below the Tor, perhaps destroy enough of it or restore the crystal spire to its former state, or even somehow separate it from her, it might be enough to stop Raikali from reforming over and over or gaining further mass and control. She might even be able to match her.

In Faria's frantic sprint, she heard a rumble from her left. She plunged her staff into the ground, opening a tunnel directly beneath her feet. She plummeted down and hit the twisting slope of it just as one of Raikali's deadly claws swiped the air above her ears. She rolled and skidded down the opening channel of stone, till she was met with a wall of crystal ahead of her. She blasted it away with her staff, and before her opened up the resonance chamber.

Already most of the abundant crystal had been augmented, corrupted by Raikali, the last vestiges of blue shimmering away at the tips of the prismatic clusters. The whole chamber thrummed with buzzing, deafening energy that seemed to increase the longer she was in the room. She could feel it beginning to wake with alarm, though perhaps Raikali's conscious was too focused on the hunt above and her continuing ascent to have felt her intrusion yet.

Faria's heart leapt.

At the centre of the chamber remained a small circle of diminishing blue.

Faria used the rock behind her to leap over the green spires and land at the centre of the blue crystal, feeling a soothing familiarity in their energetic reciprocation. It glowed appreciatively at her presence.

She pressed her staff tip to it, and in a soft, almost willing morphing of its shape, it split from the floor beneath her and swept around her body, attaching to her backplate as a pair of crystal wings.

The surge of the green crystal was so intense down here, almost dizzying. It felt so close, and strong, but so different – like a familiar song with a new voice and tune, or played with another instrument. If she could find a single moment away from Raikali's pursuit, she might be able to harness it.

Just as Faria reached a paw out to it, heavy impacts above quaked through the room. The ceiling buckled, then exploded downwards as Raikali's ravenous, ferocious form punched through the rock.

Faria blasted open the tunnel she'd entered through and took to the air with a beat of her wings, sweeping above the city. Raikali writhed and her form distended again with a volley of crystalline cracks, bringing down two more buildings with her swelling size. Her body lengthened, drawing in more crystal from the city around her, leaving the outer areas dark and empty.

The air was getting thin and biting cold against Faria's snout as she twisted in the air to try and get a shot at Raikali. With a spiralling circuit of the lioness' head Faria unleashed crackling bolts of resonance energy that lashed across the glowering facets of her structure. They sparked small blue explosions where they landed, leaving craters in Raikali's body, now grown to about a third the size of the Tor. She growled in ire and whipped her claw towards Faria again. Her mass was beginning to slow her, as the resonance-winged fox managed to roll away and land another searing volley at her. She could feel the tide turning, if she could just persist.

Raikali lunged forwards to snap at the flying fox with her maw and missed; as Faria spun to take aim at her a third time, another claw spiralling from Raikali's chest immediately ahead caused her to bring her wings in and dive, uncontrollably, towards the cobblestones. Instinctively she brought the wings around her, then felt them shatter against the ground. Her back hit the stone; the wind was knocked from her and her head spun with the force of the blow. While the world spiralled around her she picked herself up to her knees and reached for the shards of her wings, but two large, green spears impaled the ground at their impact points, releasing a spidering whip of fractal veins that immediately sucked the fragments into Raikali's form.

The lioness' towering face loomed grimly in the darkness.

"Hope is meaningless. What you want must be taken. From other cities, from your father, and now from you."

"And look where that led you!" Faria roared back, voice hoarse with the thin, cold air. "Neither you nor the Dhrakans had to be our enemies. Was it really that hard to help instead of conquer?"

Her staff glowed; she held herself up with it as a pillar of stone formed beneath her and drew her up towards the immense, sneering face of Raikali, the lioness' head alone about three times her full size. She glowered defiantly as she felt Raikali's growl rumble in the walls. "It did not have to be this way, and it still doesn't."

They stared each other down. For a moment, Faria swore she saw the lioness' expression soften.

A flash of green shot from Raikali's chest. Faria flinched. Something cold, burning, pierced her stomach. Shuddering paralysis took over as she felt it push all the way through and begin to spread within her. Her staff fell from her grip. She looked down, eyes wide, breath punched from her body. The crystal spike drove deeper and further into her stomach. She clamped her paws around it, claws scraping at the smooth and bloodied facets.

Raikali grinned hungrily. "All of your heroism comes to this. Very noble. And ultimately, useless."

She straightened, raising Faria up with her. The fox scrabbled desperately at the crystal, trying to push her paws inside it to stop herself from slipping further down. The smooth, piercing spike did not resist her weight as she shifted along it; she felt it creeping within her, pushing against her chest and abdomen, bending her spine. She let out a faltering, breathless cry, eyes wide with terror and pain.

The crystal monster's mocking laugh echoed in Faria's ears. "Maybe now, in your final moments, you will appreciate my point of view."

Raikali raised her head, looking towards the moon through the rift in the mesa's ceiling.

"Your body is mine now. Join me, as we transform our world."

Faria's paws shook at the spike still sinking through her abdomen. She fixed Raikali in a desperate, defiant stare.

No.

Please.

Her claws dug into its surface.

I can't let this happen.

I can't...

Her eyes flickered. She struggled to keep them open. She felt warmth trickling over her paws.

Please... let me find... a way...

Her claws stopped shaking as they scratched the crystal, and her eyes closed. Her tail fell limp. Her breathing drew shallow, faint, and then... stopped.

Raikali's eyes flared with green as she saw Faria's form hanging before her.

"Finally... beautiful silence."

She turned her face back to the moon, licking her lips, staring at the celestial body that she would soon merge with, and bring down to Eeres. She watched it, bold, glowing, and *hers*.

Her eyes flicked with confusion.

It wasn't moving.

The wind had stopped.

At the distant edge of the city, something crumbled.

Another crack. Part of the mesa's wall split open, falling away to dust. Through the gap, she could see Eeres' horizon.

They were no longer ascending. The split at the city's edge widened, the stone around it spreading, dissolving. She let out a confused growl and looked back to Faria.

The fox grinned through her blooded fangs. Her claws were deeply embedded in the crystal, blue sparks shimmering at her pawpads within it. She opened her eyes triumphantly, glowing with the same lustre as Raikali's crystal.

"Time to fall, Raikali."

"NO!"

Raikali's defiant scream shook the mesa. More rock shattered away. She threw a claw towards Faria, but with a flash of the fox's eyes the limb stopped dead, hanging in the air. Its tips began to grey and dissolve into dust. Raikali let out a horrified cry.

"What are you doing?"

"*Ending it!*" Faria roared. "I won't see you destroy the world for your fearful hatred!"

More of the mesa crumbled, opening them up to the sky beyond. Raikali saw the moon begin to drift upwards, and the horizon start to tilt beyond the mesa's edge. Buildings that had not seen the sky in millennia were illuminated by the high moonlight, for the briefest of moments, before they broke apart and fell into the beyond as Nazreal started its downward plummet towards Eeres.

Far below, on the splintered deck of the Coriolis, Kier jolted, gripping the railing.

Tierenan stepped to him, looking up. "What is it?"

"It's…" Kier whispered. "Nazreal's breaking."

The mesa that had encased Nazreal fractured and dissolved, casting the entire glowing city in the light of the sun. Faria gripped the spire at her midriff tightly, staring down Raikali, who kept trying to stab at her, but each time her slashes ended in dust that swept up into the sky.

"How dare you!" she shrieked.

A whole section of the city behind her split, drifting behind them as it disintegrated. The city's diminishing edges began to creep in, and the world fell into view more and more. It began to rock and spin, its stability no longer held in place by Raikali's power. She growled and thrust herself into the spear on Faria's chest, surging her body out through the other side of her, to try and explode her from within. Faria screamed in pain but kept her grip, forcing Raikali through the spike, preventing the lion from tearing her in half.

"You… you're afraid, aren't you?" Faria growled through her teeth. "You always have been."

"No!" Raikali screamed, bringing her fists down towards Faria. They exploded into dust inches from the fox's head. "I fear *nothing!*"

"I can feel you, Raikali! Your history, your memories, all of it woven inside the resonance!"

"*NO!*"

At her words, a chasm opened up on one side of the city, forcing the city into two spiralling halves that plunged rapidly towards the sand.

Kier gasped as his resonance-augmented vision spotted something glint at the now-exposed heart of the city, and leapt forwards with a sonic *boom*. Ripples of sound shook under his feet as he began a desperate running climb into the air towards it.

Tierenan leapt over the deck, followed by Aeryn and Kyru, and sprinted after him.

Faria clamped her eyes shut as the wind roared in her face. The acidic burn of Raikali's crystal flooded her body, and further – she could feel it in the furthest reaches of the quickly deteriorating Nazreal beneath her even as the crystal crumbled to dust. Raikali raged and spat, surging her body to either side of Faria in an attempt to wound her. Faria kept her focus, channelling her determination into the crystal spike, remembering everything they had lost, every moment of hurt, every ounce of joy worth protecting. She opened her eyes, and the world spiralled around them. Raikali was not much bigger than her now, her face a mix of horror and fury. She kept thrusting her claws towards Faria, trying to explode the crystal within her chest and shred her. Faria felt its pulse, as Raikali's ability to take hold of a smaller crystal became much more concentrated.

She glared at the lion defiantly as the world fell towards her.

"I'll show you, Raikali, what we have always tried to show you. Hope isn't weak."

Raikali spiralled into Faria again, reforming behind her as a set of four angular wings, their feathertips slowly dissolving. The buffeting wind altered their fall, sweeping them up, among the falling rocks and billowing dust of Nazreal's demise.

"Lies!" she cried. "You know nothing! I'll tear you to shreds!"

Faria clenched her paws; the spike exploded backwards from her stomach and two of the wings shattered. Raikali let out a screech of pain from her crystalline voice.

"This world... deserves better... than fear!" Faria cried, shaking with the burning, painful efforts of her resistance against Raikali's shifting form and desperate persistence. Her whole body trembled with the scorching fury of Raikali's rage. She let out another cry of pain, feeling like her own body was dissolving along with the city, such were the two now so entwined as they plummeted.

Kier's steps thundered as he climbed higher, leapt faster, trying to meet Faria's freefall before she hit the ground. He felt a massive, bursting pain in one of his feet, then the other. He ignored them both, the explosive steps of his sonic charge driving him closer in desperate flares. Every movement was a new explosion in his legs, a powerful rupture that thrust him forwards but ate at him a little more each time.

He was so close.

Kyru sprinted ahead of Tierenan, seeing Faria in the distance. All three of them pounded the sand with their fervid run to catch her.

Faria felt herself growing weak. Raikali clawed at her back, crying feverishly.

"Stop! You'll kill us both! Faria, *stop this*!"

She smiled, teeth tight.

"Never, Raikali."

Just as her eyes closed, a flash of sand passed by her as she fell below the dune top.

Boom.

Epilogue

A young maned wolf sat on a marble bench inside Xayall's Tor, against the wall of the ground-floor foyer. She bounced her long legs and cracked her knuckles in anticipation, and kept adjusting the large round glasses on her muzzle. The spectacle hooks that hung around her head were not enough to keep them in place while her tall, wide ears swivelled continuously with the overstimulating sounds and sights of the eminent building's impressive entrance chamber. Creatures in magnificent dress strode in and out, important dignitaries and overloaded scholars bustled this way or that, and climbed the grand, wide staircase that led to what she could only imagine were wondrous libraries and even more ornate, intimate meeting halls. Her cerulean eyes darted around with great interest, feasting on everything there was to take in.

The door on her left bumped loudly open. She froze, her wide ears perking. Her tail flicked with anticipation. She chanced a furtive look, and the first thing she saw was a set of immaculately articulated metal feet. She couldn't help but trail her eyes up to the owner of them. A red fox with a gentle smile and silver eyes looked back at her.

"Oh, I'm sorry," he said quietly. "I had intended to meet

everyone in the forum. Did nobody direct you?"

The maned wolf stood immediately, thwapping her tail against the bench, and bowed deeply from her waist. Her long-tailed leather swished behind her, and the heels of her boots squeaked slightly on the polished floor.

"Oh, yes! I mean n-no, it's not you! Or anyone!" she blurted. "I uh—" She paused and straightened herself, tugging at her waistcoat. "It's an honour to meet you," she said, quickly but grandly, with a nervous heightening to her voice. "My name is Ardor Elara."

She straightened her back and hung her hands nervously on the strap of her satchel, clutching it tightly enough that it was almost about to braid itself into a cord.

"Kier Lugos, Representative of Xayall. It's a pleasure to have you," he replied with a smile, before gesturing gently towards the stairway with his paw. "I hope it'll be a fortuitous time here as you train, and study."

She smiled with wistful excitement as she looked around. "I'm sure it will be! I heard the stories of what the former Empress achieved, and I'd love to be able to do even some of the things she did. Most of the time in Al-Mayena I'd just play with the water, turn it into foxes and dragons and make them dance around each other."

"Sounds familiar," Kier laughed. He stopped and turned as he noticed Ardor had nervously halted her pace.

"Is everything alright?"

"I, um… you mentioned in your letter that you wanted everyone to visit her before we started, but um… I was supposed to arrive yesterday so I didn't get to and then I wasn't sure where to go, so…" Ardor wrung her paws and took in a deep breath, while Kier waited patiently. "I just get nervous in front of too many people and haven't been here before, I…"

she gestured vaguely with her hands. "…know this is important, so I want to do this right."

He nodded. "Yeah, I can take you to her."

He led her outside of the Tor, into the wider grounds, winding the pathways through the grounds of the Imperial Palace. His metal feet clinked softly on the ground as they walked. Her ears flicked slightly at each touch of the slab. She kept glancing down at them, despite herself.

"Um…"

He looked at her expectantly.

"I'm sorry, is it okay to ask? I've never seen such fine construction before."

He gave another soft laugh as they continued. "It's okay. Prosthetics are one of the many things we want to build for people, so I'm not trying to hide anything by wearing mine."

She clutched her strap tightly again. "Was it an accident?"

He shook his head. "No. I used too much power trying to save someone. That's one of the downsides of resonance, as I'm sure you've experienced at least some of, and another thing we want to research further. It can be very easy to harm yourself if you push too far too fast."

She nodded in quiet reverence, massaging her fingers into her paw pads. "Does it always hurt? Mine mostly tingles, at least so far."

"Not always. Sometimes it's a buzz that passes quickly. The more you do, then… yeah, the greater the chance of doing damage." His brow furrowed briefly, quizzically. "Sorry, how old are you again?"

"Seventeen," she said brightly. "Just about the same age as the Empress was when everything unfolded."

He scratched behind his ears. "Wow, that's uncanny. She fought a lot of battles that hopefully you'll never ever have to.

That's… another thing we're trying to work on." A dark grimace flashed across his face for a second. "Even after three years the memories are hard to escape."

Ardor looked ahead to the building they were approaching, with apprehension creeping through her fur. "Is she… at peace now, at least?"

Kier took in a long, soft sigh as the Imperial Mausoleum filled their view.

"Mostly."

He stopped at the base of the stairs, and clenched his paw softly. He took a step, paused, then continued. Ardor waited at the bottom for a few seconds, till he turned and gently curled his paw up.

"It's okay," he said quietly. "Come on up. It's just a… place with a lot of feelings."

She nodded. Her tail curled around her legs and held her bag closer to her front as if trying to use it as a sort of security pillow.

As they climbed the steps, sarcophagi came into view; each one carved with reliefs of various eminent figures in Xayall's history – mostly the old Imperial family.

"We're here," he breathed.

Ardor looked along the walls, her eyes drawn along the lines of the carvings, till they reached the end of the small alcove ahead of them.

Kneeling between the tombs, with her paws held at her midriff, was another fox. Her black ears tilted slightly. Just in front of her, Ardor saw the wall pulsing with a very soft green glow that gradually faded, like a diminishing heartbeat. The fox at the end opened her palm, and poured a tiny handful of dust into a small stone jar, and closed the lid. She sat there for a moment, her head back slightly.

"It's done," Faria said, with a somewhat sad serenity. "She's gone."

Kier trod gently forwards. She looked up at him and wiped her eye. She was wearing robes of silver, brown and green, with an open section at her midriff where lay a large, spider-web like scar.

"Do you think she changed?" he asked.

She shrugged softly. "We all change, some way or another. She hadn't spoken much lately." She looked at the small jar, very unassuming in its clay construction. "But even though it took so long… I think she knew it was time to leave. I'd like to think she saw some kind of resolution from what we've done, how we've survived, and the world we're trying to build but…" she shook her head and looked up to the windows that brought light into the array of tombs. "…even if she refused to change, at least we were able to change for her."

Kier nodded, looking at the tombs in front of them that he recognised well. Aidan, Kaya, Elysser, Teratai; and the fifth, the newest one, which bore the image of a gryphon with his wings spread wide, a ship to one side of him, and a towering city on the other.

Osiris.

Faria rose to her feet and picked up the urn, giving a somewhat cold look to where it had been amongst the graves of her kindred. It would be a cold joke to all of them to entertain putting Raikali to rest in the same place.

"I'll take her to be buried in the land she was from. Or where it would have been," she said, with soft resolution. She closed her eyes again and let out a shaky breath.

"Are you alright, Faria?"

She nodded, and reached for the staff by the wall. Its spiralling wings were set around a prism of bright blue, and dangling from its tip on a golden chain inside a small filigree cage was the crystal she'd found within Nazreal's stone. "It's just… been a long time since it was just me inside here."

She jumped slightly at the other presence in the mausoleum.

"Oh, hi," she murmured, swiping the dust from her knees, prompting an immensely fast and nervous bow from Ardor.

"I'm sorry, your Emp—er, Miss Arc'hantael! Or is it Phiraco? Um, I'm Ardor. I'm due to study here."

Faria smiled warmly and held out her hand. "Faria is fine. I'm not an Empress anymore. It's wonderful to meet you, Ardor. I'm sorry to have kept you waiting – I know we start soon. Today was… important, though." She smiled, and gave a soft flick of her claw towards the maned wolf's eyes.

"I recognise the colour," she said, fixing her with a sly gaze.

Ardor beamed, showing her fangs. "Oh, yes!" She flipped open the buckle to her satchel and drove her paw inside, picking out a long-cuffed glove with the fingers cut free. Mounted into the back of the glove, running down the fingers and over the wrist, was an array of crystals the same lustre as her eyes, the deep cerulean blue of Faria's.

"That's beautiful," Faria marvelled.

Ardor grinned, and pulled the glove on. The crystals flashed slightly. She waved a paw palm-down over the floor; the dust that had gathered in the corners of the mausoleum swirled and coalesced, till below her palm sat a small dust dragon, looking around and roaring silently.

A warm, bright laugh rolled from Faria's muzzle. "That is… incredible."

Ardor blushed, still grinning from ear to ear. "Th-thank you, Faria. I want to learn to do even more."

"I don't doubt you'll make fantastic use of such a wonderful, powerful gift." She looked at the wolf with distinct pointedness. "More than what you can do with your powers, though, is what you can do with your heart. Let that guide you first and foremost, and the rest will follow after."

She nodded reverently, and together they began to walk outside. Faria leant heavily on her staff, moving slowly, and the other two kept pace with her. She seemed quiet but resolute to Ardor, who kept glancing shyly over to her.

They trod their path back around the Tor, and then finally up the grand entrance stairway, along an ornate, clean corridor to a set of large, arched double doors. Faria and Kier each took a side as Ardor stood between them.

"Is… shall I?"

They nodded, with kind encouragement in their smiles.

Ardor took a breath, and pushed the door open. Light flooded the corridor for a second; she blinked rapidly until it became clearer moments later. A tiered semi-circular room, with each level being a long arc of desks with padded benches, at which already sat a good number of creatures. Some looked like dignitaries, and some looked far more normal, aside from the colour of their eyes, which Ardor was immediately drawn to in each. The sun shone brightly through a large window that bordered one top edge of the room, lighting the moderate-yet-grand lecture hall in a soft, rich light. Kier stepped inside and down towards the front, waiting patiently for the two. A few heads turned back towards Faria and Ardor; the maned wolf tugged at her bag strap, making the bulk of it shift up her back.

"I hope you don't mind the extra guests in here." She leaned gently across to Ardor as she spoke, having seen the maned wolf's tail press towards her legs. "They're all friends, I promise."

The young canine looked around in bewilderment, blinking behind her glasses. "Who… are they?"

"Some are resonators like yourself, as we invited. Others are scribes and Representatives from other sovereigns; those who have promised to support us, and that we promised to remain open to. Some are those who… have been invested in this potential for co-operation for a long time," she said with a smile that was both wistful and proud, as her eyes were drawn to a pair of dragons in the middle-left section. "And some," she sighed, smile brightening a little as her gaze passed to the block of assorted creatures at the very front corner, some of whom had metal augmentations, "are my family."

Faria gestured for Ardor to enter fully. The wolf paused a moment, nodded to herself, then took her first timid steps into the room. Kier gestured to the front, where many of the distinctly-coloured eyed attendees were sitting. Faria followed down, but split across to the group of her long-time friends and guardians.

Tierenan bounced from his padded chair launched his arms around her in a deep, squeezing hug. "Proud of you," he half-sang.

"You too," she replied, with a little constriction to her voice at the enthusiasm of his embrace.

"Me?" he drew back, looking faux-aghast. "I haven't just exorcised the lingering spirit of a resonance despot who tried to kill every single one of us whether we knew it or not, some of us *twice*, all before addressing the first public gathering of allied resonators since Nazreal."

"Three times for you," added Feith.

"Oh yeah…"

Faria rolled her eyes, unable to help the smile from warming her voice. "Well, if you put it *that* way…"

"I do!" he said firmly, with his hands on his hips, just as Feith gave him a soft slap in the stomach.

"Don't bully her, she's tired."

"I am the anti-tired," he chirruped.

Kyru leant in from the chair behind and pulled at Tierenan's ear to bend him backwards, almost meeting nose-to-nose. "You are possibly the most exhausting thing in this room – more than the rest of us combined."

"Then you should sleep well," Tierenan retorted, unfazed. "But obviously you haven't had enough of me because you still got bags under your eyes."

Their exchange of bickering rose, leaving Aeryn to sigh and turn to the pangolin Alaris on her other side, who looked a little worried about the level of interaction between the two.

"This is normal," she muttered.

"Ah."

Kier, after checking on the young resonators in the front row, slipped into his seat between Bayer and Raede, who both took the fox in a deep, close hug. Kier smiled, and snuck a brief kiss to the ocelot's cheek.

Around the arc of the front row Ardor saw other animals around her age. A dhole, a hyena, a rabbit, a bat, a frilled lizard – each of them with vividly coloured eyes, all different to hers. Alongside them was a wolf, Seanathan, whose sword hung proudly at his waist as he half-leant on the far edge with a smile of greeting. She smiled back, and raised her paw in a soft wave.

As everyone settled, Faria quietly stepped onto the stage at the foot of the semicircular forum. She studied the wall briefly, most of it blank, save for a shelf to one side, on which rested three thick and ancient journals, rebound in shining gold. Before her was the lectern; carved over its vertical surfaces were wooden reliefs of a flying ship, shining prisms, and the cities of Nazreal and Xayall.

She moved behind the platform and rested her staff in a special hook on the side, taking a moment to ensure it wouldn't twist out or fall over mid-address. Her notes were in front of her, but her attention wavered. A gentle anticipation grew in her stomach. Her fingers drummed on the varnished wooden surface for a moment, while her eyes carried her thoughts across the room as she passed her gaze over everyone present, stopping at the friends who had protected her since she had first escaped Xayall.

She smiled.

It had been a long journey.

Now, a new one began.

She cleared her throat, a final signal that drew the room into attention. Ardor shifted forwards little, eyes bright, leaning her muzzle on her paws in avid expectation.

"My name is Faria, former Empress of Xayall," the fox began. "It's an honour to meet you all. Thank you all for attending what is, for many reasons, a rather momentous day."

She gestured to the section where Bayer, Raede, Cove and Riemu sat. "To begin, it's the anniversary of two of our partner nations becoming full-fledged sovereigns in the Senate – Kyrryk and Draik. And, more personally, it's also the day I renounced my title as Empress, to focus on teaching resonance to those who still have it, and opened our libraries and vaults for the world to study." She pulsed her fingers at the edges of the lectern. "Without Nazreal, there may be fewer of us as time goes on, but nonetheless, knowing your potential, seizing it, growing to your fullest sense of self, is vital for us all."

She gave a nod to Seanathan. "As is, of course, our protection. And protection begins with communication. So we have decided to end the vows of secrecy that kept a world fearful and divided, and come together, and hope to build something greater between us."

Faria let out a soft laugh, and scratched behind her ear. "Despite being here before you all I'm still learning things, some of which are about myself. But… what I *can* begin with is that anything done with kindness as its first step, is the best way for any endeavour to continue. The path may change, but in vigilance, in duty, in practice, in self – always step with kindness. With that in mind, the first thing I should tell you is about the crystals you have an affinity for, and where they came from."

She looked over the room, to her friends, and new students, and smiled.

"This is a story of our deepest past; one that will carry on to our furthest future. I have played most of my part in this story already, and now, the time is yours."

She looked to the maned wolf.

"I'm sure you will use it well."

Ardor smiled eagerly, as Faria began her story.

Dear Reader

Thank you for reading *Edge of Ascension*. If you enjoyed this book (or even if you didn't) please consider leaving a star rating or review online Your feedback is important, and will help other readers to find the book and decide whether to read it, too.

Acknowledgements

I'm sat here staring at this blank page (which is now finally not blank, yay) wondering how to summarise about twenty years of having these characters and stories in my head. It's massive. And despite spending so many days forming words to describe things into existence the feelings I try to capture are so big that my net of words just doesn't reach that far.

And I'm okay with that. Some things can just be felt, or watched, or read, like a passing sky of stars.

Now that Eeres' story has escaped open paws and taken flight to become a world of its own, it's humbling and exciting to think about what's next. I've never finished anything this big before, though still I find myself remembering things I had forgotten to write about somewhere along the way. I like that, though, that the sky can still come to visit so you can paint a few more stars in it.

It's been a wild and weird few years since Ruin's Dawn appeared, at the apex of lockdown in 2020. I hadn't intended for the gap between each book to be as long as this but for this one I'm kind of glad it's had extra time to sit... and that *I've* had extra time to sit and find out about the world, else I think the story would have turned out differently, and less authentically. It's very easy when you write fantasy to forget the practicalities of trying to govern a world when you can, effectively, say 'this works because it works', and ignore that fantasy isn't only an escape, but for many a means of finding camaraderie and motivation to conquer things that are very real. Chronic tiredness and brain fog. Isolation. Gaslighting.

Fear. Oppression. Things that a character can be written out of very easily where we can't. But seeing them able to do so helps to give us hope that we can at least persevere till things are brighter, or make them brighter ourselves.

Words have saved me over these years. Words and kindness. Writing, reading, talking, listening—all of these exchanges have helped build me up again whether in anger or indignation or hope or joy or heartbreak.

Every one of you has given me words to save me.

Mads, for listening and venting and supporting and being there for me and the household creatures every day.

Aaron, even though you keep thanking us for letting you be weird, thank you for letting *us* be weird and for giving us adventures we would never have taken on ourselves.

Brittney and Shani, for being just THE BEST PEOPLE EVER; seriously, you are like mythical creatures with how incredibly good you are and I KNOW you will try to deny it but as a certified creator of mythical creatures with magical powers I can tell you they're all pointing at you in friendly accusation and going 'yes, you are'.

To Sav, for involving me in one of the most affirming, satisfying and massive writing projects I have ever undertaken, for finding me a creative place in a world I had long quietly abandoned and helping me forge a home there.

To Solace, for being a wonderful companion, a very patient observer and avid reader of our massive creative hyperfixations even without context.

To Kiara, Crypt and Jonie, for being incredible collaborators and wonderful people who have helped build this world and home to a greater size and bigger heart than I ever thought possible.

To all of the writers of the Korps for your incredible and

righteous villainy, and to Karen King especially for giving us the place to play and explore and find ourselves. May the Overlord protect you always.

With special mention among the Korps writers to Mabel, who inspired me in the first place, and who has been unstoppably supportive and kind to all who take shelter under her smoky wings.

To Cyrus, the wonderful cryptid who found the foundation for my fursona's lore and gave her a chance to grow, an effect that has permanently grounded me. It is something I will ever be grateful to you for.

To Fyger, whose generosity, creativity, and devious fae mischief have long been mainstays of my days and happiness. May your soul always find itself in the same heights and the Cloudskimmer (and I have legitimately forgotten if that's the correct name now whoops).

To Morgan for the colourful and wonderful worlds of our fantasy creatures and gritty cyberpunk worlds that helped me write more and find passion in genres I hadn't tried before. It has meant so very much.

To Lyra, for the incredible, indelible, fantastical sword lesbians within your sprawling fantasy world. Never has completing a circle been more dramatic or satisfying.

To Skye and Ruby, for your wonderful kindness and invigorating creativity. I would have had very little of this had you not taken a chance on me, and there is no way I will be able to give enough thanks for what that has meant to me.

To Ceru, who has brought me life with incredible memes of the Resonance series and my own Korps fics. They, and you, are hilarious, and both your art and stories are wonderful.

To all of the wonderful amazing creatures in my Discord server—each of you is a cherished creature to me and I am forever grateful for your time and support.

The remaining four people I have to thank are deeply special to the Resonance Tetralogy.

Blu, for your wonderful kindness, your incredible energy, and heartfelt and passionate remembrance of someone so dear. I have not stopped thinking about how much Alexxi means to you, and that he was a fan of the story; I hope I have been able to capture some of his light through Seanathan that will continue and inspire others in his memory. Thank you for allowing me the chance to pay tribute to him.

Sara-Jayne, for your unending patience and gentle but enthusiastic encouragement in getting these not only to print, but wading through all of the publishing rigmarole before, during, and after. For being one of the most important influences on my writing and how to analyse it, making it better with every question or gentle comment about the world I've created. Thank you, endlessly, for this partnership. It has changed me forever for the better in ways I could never have anticipated.

Eskiworks, aka Katie: whose resilience, skill, patience, and beautiful creative spirit have brought the books to life in each and every one of their covers. There isn't a single day that goes by that I don't think about the work you've done and how vital it has been to me as well as the books. To see my fantasy creatures brought to life in the way you do will always be one of the best and most fantastic things ever to have been part of my life. Sincerely, and deeply, thank you, for everything you do.

Finally this word of thanks goes to someone who probably has no idea they're about to get called out in such a way, but I'm going to do it anyway.

Quill.

I can't remember exactly when it was we started talking but

I was elated that you enjoyed my books. It meant a great deal to me that you reached out, and obviously from talking and following you I started to think more specifically about the work you do and how important it is. And that, in turn, affected how I wanted to shape Faria's story. There is an absolute ton I wouldn't have been able to know if it weren't for you just being you. I hadn't met a teacher before, and it quite quickly dawned on me that for a fantasy world to be truly meaningful, to know that Eeres is left in the best possible kind of care and future as I would want any kind of 'happily ever after' story to end, I wanted to change Faria's future.

It's very easy in fantasy to get roped into the convenient idea of a tacitly (or explicitly) divine power, that the right or wrong person in the right place can basically shade the world as ontologically good or bad, without any of the repair work needed to depose or sustain it. Especially with the way things have been the last… geez, eight years (and more, for people who should have been paid attention to far earlier), writing a system that healed itself by simple virtue of Bad Lioness Dead didn't feel sincere anymore.

So I made Faria a teacher.

Because two of the most vital things you can do ever, at any time, are love and learn. If every heart was led by those two driving forces, this would be such a brilliant place.

So thank you, Quill, for being you. You do amazing things.

Thank you, finally, to each and every one of you who has read and followed and supported anything of mine, whether these (although considering you're reading this right now that's very much a wonderful and humbling given) or my Korps stories or Love and Quota, or my streams or other weird projects I've been involved with. From the deepest centre of my soul, thank you.

About the Author

Hugo is a British-born author living in North Carolina. They began life as a starry-eyed creature with a fascination for fantastical adventures, heroes, and animals, and invested as much time in their own imagination as they did on animations, video games, and music.

In their spare time, Hugo is heavily involved with the furry fandom, standing as an advocate for LGBT+ rights, mental health awareness, inclusion, and artist/author visibility and fair treatment. They talk about many of these things on their intermittently-updated blog, and occasionally produce their own videos.

Find the author via their social media:
@PangolinFox

More From This Author

The Resonance Tetralogy

Book 1: Legacy

Her power is unmeasured. Her abilities untested. Her destiny inescapable.

Faria Phiraco is a resonator, a manipulator of the elements via rare crystals. It is an extraordinary and secret power which she and her father, the Emperor of Xayall, guard with their lives. The Dhraka, malicious red-scaled dragons, have discovered an ancient artefact; a mysterious relic from the mythical, aeons-lost city of Nazreal.

When her father goes missing, Faria has to rely on her own strength to brave the world that attacks her at every turn. Friends and guardians rally by her to help save her father and reveal the mysteries of the ruined city. She soon realises that this is not the beginning, nor anywhere near the end. A titanic war spanning thousands of years unfolds around her, one that could yet cost the lives of everyone on Eeres.

Book 2: Fracture

The shadows are coming…

Months after the tremors that shook the world, repercussions of battle still lie in Xayall's broken streets. Among the debris stands Bayer, former bodyguard to Faria, Empress of the city state. His position redundant, and his injuries still healing, he struggles to find new purpose.

Unrest between nations is already stirring. A Councillor from Andarn has been murdered, and only a handful realise that sinister machinations are blackening the root of the whole continent. Questioning his duties, Bayer finds himself escorting Captain Alaris on a mission from which neither may return, although their failure may spark a brutal and catastrophic war.

As blades rise, threats both new and old emerge from the darkness and bare their teeth at the world.

Book 3: Ruin's Dawn

"I want to hear everything, Osiris. All that you can tell me."

In the desert town of Mahrae, a young fox is about to discover his power.

A single bolt of crystal energy begins Aidan's journey, one that will test him to his furthest limits and deepest loyalties. The gryphon Osiris takes Aidan under his wing and together they battle shadows and suspicion to bring warring nations to the pinnacle of invention and prosperity – the new city Nazreal.

But not every creature strives for a bright and industrious future.

Conflict is an unsteady foundation for the burgeoning metropolis. The launch of a thousand incredible dreams plants the seed for an immeasurable disaster that even Aidan and his friends do not have the power to prevent.

This is the story of Nazreal's ascension… and the end of the world.

Remnant's Hope: Tales of Resonance

An evening. A limb. A country. A world.

As each shatter, lives are forever altered and the consequences ripple beyond imagination: legacies of the past, and the catalyst for an uncertain, fractured future.

These are the stories of what is left behind. Between the ruins of the past and the dawn of new beginnings, discover tales of renewal, transformation, relentless struggles, kindred souls, and the enduring ache of loss.

Remnant's Hope collects tales from across the Resonance Tetralogy timeline, revealing previously untold dramatic, emotional, and heartfelt histories of both well-loved characters and newfound heroes.

Amidst these fragments, a beacon sparks to life—a glimmer of something both fleeting and timeless.

Hope.